Praise for Lois Richer
and her novels

"*Mother's Day Miracle* by Lois Richer is quite possibly her finest book!…The only problem with this heartwarming story about blossoming love is that it ends too soon."
—*Romantic Times BOOKreviews*

"*Blessed Baby,* another keeper by Lois Richer, will bless you."
—*Romantic Times BOOKreviews*

"Lois Richer's *His Answered Prayer* is another winner and will please readers who love traditional story lines with new twists and terrific characters."
—*Romantic Times BOOKreviews*

"*Baby on the Way* by Lois Richer is a delightful gem that sparkles with tender poignancy.… The interaction between the characters and the emotional appeal of this story make it a must-read for romance fans."
—*Romantic Times BOOKreviews*

LOIS RICHER
Mother's Day Miracle

Blessed Baby

Steeple
Hill®

Published by Steeple Hill Books™

STEEPLE HILL BOOKS

Steeple
Hill®

Recycling programs
for this product may
not exist in your area.

ISBN-13: 978-0-373-65127-6
ISBN-10:   0-373-65127-9

MOTHER'S DAY MIRACLE AND BLESSED BABY

MOTHER'S DAY MIRACLE
Copyright © 2000 by Lois Richer

BLESSED BABY
Copyright © 2001 by Lois Richer

www.SteepleHill.com

Printed in U.S.A.

CONTENTS

Books by Lois Richer

Love Inspired

A Will and a Wedding	*Inner Harbor*
*Faithfully Yours	†*Blessings*
*A Hopeful Heart	†*Heaven's Kiss*
*Sweet Charity	†*A Time to Remember*
A Home, a Heart, a Husband	*Past Secrets, Present Love*
This Child of Mine	‡‡*His Winter Rose*
**Baby on the Way	‡‡*Apple Blossom Bride*
**Daddy on the Way	‡‡*Spring Flowers, Summer Love*
**Wedding on the Way	§*Healing Tides*
‡*Mother's Day Miracle*	§*Heart's Haven*
‡*His Answered Prayer*	§*A Cowboy's Honor*
‡*Blessed Baby*	§§*Rocky Mountain Legacy*
Tucker's Bride	§§*Twice Upon a Time*

Love Inspired Suspense

A Time to Protect	*Faith, Hope & Charity
††*Secrets of the Rose*	**Brides of the Seasons
††*Silent Enemy*	‡If Wishes Were Weddings
††*Identity: Undercover*	†Blessings in Disguise
	††Finders Inc.
	‡‡Serenity Bay
	§Pennies from Heaven
	§§Weddings by Woodwards

LOIS RICHER

likes variety. From her time in human resources management to entrepreneurship, life has held plenty of surprises.

She says: "Having given up on fairy tales, I was happily involved in building a restaurant when a handsome prince walked into my life and upset all my career plans with a wedding ring. Motherhood quickly followed. I guess the seeds of my storytelling took root because of two small boys who kept demanding, 'Then what, Mom?'"

The miracle of God's love for His children, the blessing of true love, the joy of sharing Him with others—that is a story that can be told a thousand ways and yet still be brand-new. Lois Richer intends to go right on telling it.

MOTHER'S DAY MIRACLE

For I am convinced that neither death, nor life, nor angels, nor principalities, nor things present, nor things to come, nor powers, nor height, nor depth, nor any other created thing shall be able to separate us from the love of God.

—Romans 8:38–39

To my friend and fellow writer Lyn Cote, who is ever and always willing to help out, coerce, cajole, push, encourage and generally mother or bully me, as the situation requires, into getting the job done. From one rebel to another, thanks, chum.

Chapter One

"Dear God, I wish You'd send me a husband—"

Clarissa Cartwright chewed on her lower lip as the words echoed around the empty library. The patrons were gone now, trickling away one by one, hurrying toward family and home. She could imagine them gathered around the dinner table, laughing as they shared the day's events with their dear ones, making plans to sample the sweet-scented spring evening with that one special person who made your heart thump in anticipation.

Clarissa sat alone, her heart longing to be included, to be part of something. To be needed.

She tried to formulate the petition in her mind, to choose just the right words so God would understand how deeply the ache went. It wasn't hard to say it out loud. She'd been turning the words around in her heart in a silent prayer for ages, even more frequently since her cousin's Hawaiian wedding two weeks ago.

But here in the Waseka, Missouri, town library, alone

among the books she'd cared for these past ten years, Clarissa felt strangely comfortable about voicing her request to the One who'd promised to answer.

"I didn't want to be a burden, Lord, as I was growing up. But I'm an adult now, and I'd really like to be a wife." She hesitated, then breathed out the rest of it. "I want to be a mother."

It sounded like such a big request, so demanding. She hurried on to quantify it, make it easier for God to fulfil. "He doesn't have to be rich. Or even handsome."

That sounded desperate. And she wasn't. Just lonely.

"But not just any husband," she modified, staring at the stained and peeling plaster ceiling as she spoke. "A man I can love with all my heart. A man who doesn't care that I'm not young and gorgeous with lots of money, or smart, and upwardly mobile. What I really want is a man who wants to settle down and have a family. I'm so tired of being alone."

Was that everything?

Clarissa tried to get her mind off chubby babies with rosy cheeks and fisted hands. It wasn't easy. Lately she dreamed of babies all the time. She thrust the bundles of joy out of her mind. But her replacement vision of glistening white tulle over satin and lace didn't help matters in the least. Clarissa twisted her homemade flowered cotton skirt between her fingers, scrunching her eyes up as tightly as she dared.

"Could You please send a man who will love me?" she whispered, whooshing the words out on a wish and a prayer.

"Excuse me?"

Clarissa opened her eyes so fast she saw stars. A man stood at her counter. A big man. He had the kind of straight black glossy hair that hung over his collar as if he hadn't had time to get it cut. His eyes burned a deep rich chocolate in a face full of angles and planes. His lashes were—

"Excuse me, miss?" He cleared his throat and frowned at her. "Can you help me?"

Could God answer this fast? Clarissa dismissed the question almost as quickly as it entered her brain. Of course He could. He was God!

She swallowed down her surprise and nodded. "Uh-huh."

"Oh." He looked as if he wasn't sure she was telling the truth. But when a quick glance around assured him there was no one else lurking nearby he shrugged. "I'm looking for some books on birds. They're for my ne—son."

He had a son. He was married. Her hopes dashed to the worn marble floor. It was all a mistake. A silly, childish mistake. This man wasn't for her.

"Miss?"

"Yes. Yes, I heard you. I'm just thinking." She pretended she needed time to recall that section eight held most of her books on bird-watching. "What kind of birds?"

His eyebrows rose. "What kind? I don't know." His brow furrowed, then he shrugged defensively. "The kind that fly, I guess. Just birds, that's all."

Clarissa smiled, rose from her perch behind the big oak desk and clambered awkwardly down stairs that normally gave her no problem whatsoever. "I'll show you," she offered and led the way.

The nature section was only two rows over. Clarissa stopped in front of it, considered the contents, then pulled out several of the largest picture books.

"Depending on how old he is, he might like these. They have wonderful illustrations." She opened it to show him the gorgeous colors of a parrot, and then flushed with embarrassment as the hardcover tumbled to the floor.

It was a good thing the kindergarten class wasn't here to see this. Her cast-iron rule about respecting books would be open to criticism by those curious five-year-olds.

"I'm sorry," she murmured when he handed it back.

"It's okay. Actually, I should have been clearer. I'm looking for something that would show some birds native to the area. Pierce is doing a project for school."

He tossed back his hair, raking through it with one hand. Clarissa caught the fresh clean scent of soap and smiled. She liked a man who didn't pour overpowering cologne all over himself.

You have no business liking this one, her conscience reminded. He's married. With a son.

"Feel free to look through any of these then. Maybe you'll find something you like."

She stepped back, indicating the shelf. When he bent to peer at the titles without answering her, Clarissa decided his actions spoke louder than words. He hadn't even noticed her. And why would he? Nobody noticed Clarissa. She'd become a fixture around here.

Why, I doubt anyone even noticed I've been gone, she told herself sternly. It wasn't as if she had a tan to show for her vacation in Hawaii. Her skin was too fair to do anything but burn an ugly beet red that peeled in the most unbecoming way, and she'd prevented that with liberal amounts of sunblock.

Turning with a sigh, she walked slowly back up to her desk and began tallying the column titled "Lent for the Day."

"I'll take these. If you don't mind, that is. I don't have a card." He held out four of the biggest books hesitantly. "Is that too many?"

"Certainly not. And I can make a card up for you right now. Name please?" She smiled and pulled an application form over, her pen poised to record the necessary statistics.

"Wade Featherhawk. Box 692. Telephone…"

He listed the information rapidly. Clarissa had to write quickly to get it all down.

"Good." She picked up the card and leaflet and handed them over. "The books are due in two weeks. The library hours are posted inside the leaflet, but you can always slip the books through the slot if it's after hours. By the way, I'm Clarissa Cartwright." She held out her hand.

Stark, utter silence greeted her announcement. The brown-black eyes that twinkled mere moments ago now frosted over. His hand, halfway up, dropped back down by his side.

"Oh." He took the books from her carefully, making sure that their fingers had no contact. "I, uh, I should probably tell you right off that I'm not interested."

"I beg your pardon?" Clarissa frowned, glancing at the clock. She was two minutes late closing. Hm, according to Hawaii time, that was…

"I'm not looking for a wife." The blunt-edged words came from lips stretched in a thin line of animosity. "I can handle the kids myself. I don't need somebody tagging around after me, nagging me to do this or that. I can manage my life just fine."

Clarissa froze. Surely he hadn't heard her praying? Her face heated at the worried look in his eye. She licked her lips and stuttered out a response.

"I—I d-don't know what you mean. I have never—"

"Look, I probably shouldn't have said anything. It's just that Norman Paisley told me about you being single and all. Then Mrs. Nettles expounded on your assets as the perfect wife. After that a lady I've never met before told me how great you are at caring for people. In fact, that's all I've heard for the past week."

He didn't sound exactly thrilled with what he learned either, Clarissa decided grimly.

She shook with the sheer humiliation of it. They were trying to marry her off again! And to the first available man who stepped into town. The heat of embarrassment clawed up her neck and flooded her face. Desperately she searched for composure while praying that he hadn't heard her prayer.

"I'm so sorry!" She flushed again at his disparaging look and searched for the shortest possible explanation. "I was orphaned when I was young. My parents worked overseas, and I was too much of a burden. My Gran raised me. Along with half the town. They feel responsible, sort of a community of adopted parents. They're kind of…well, rather like a big, nosy family." Clarissa gulped, knowing she was babbling, but unable to stop.

"I've been away, you see. On vacation. I didn't realize…"

She made herself stop at the less than spellbound look on his face. It was obvious he couldn't care less. He shifted from one foot to the other in patent disinterest, politely waiting for her to stop speaking.

"Well, I just wanted to warn you that I'm not in the market." His lips pinched tight as he glared at her. It was obvious that he hated having to spell it out.

Only when she peered into his eyes did Clarissa catch a hint of the suspicion in his eyes. Wariness. As if he were waiting. But for what? Clarissa mustered her composure, straightened her spine and smiled cooly.

"I'm sorry you felt you had to defend yourself, Mr. Featherhawk. I've lived here all of my life, and the people here tend to think of me as their responsibility. Rest assured, I have no intention of chasing you. In spite of what they told you, I don't need a husband that badly."

"Sorry. My mistake." He frowned as if he didn't quite believe her, but was prepared to accept it just the same. "No problem."

The odd look he cast over her made her wonder if he hadn't heard every word of her desperately uttered prayer, but Clarissa refused to speculate. It was done. She couldn't change anything. Far better to keep her pride intact and pretend nothing untoward had happened here this afternoon. There would be time enough to cry over spilled milk later, at home, alone.

"The library will be closing in just a few minutes. Is there anything else I can help you with?" She kept her friendly smile in place through sheer perversity, merely nodding when he shook his head. "Fine. Have a good day."

"You, too," he mumbled before striding across the room and out the door.

As the heavy oak banged shut behind him, Clarissa heaved a sigh of relief mingled with regret. He was so handsome!

"Okay, God. I get the message. You're in control. You'll decide when and if I should get married, let alone be a mother." She closed and locked the fine drawer, which never held more than three dollars anyway, placed her pen in the holder and pushed her chair neatly behind the big desk.

"It's in Your hands," she acquiesced with a sigh. "But I'm not getting any younger. I hope You keep in mind that I'm no spring chicken, and I would like to enjoy my kids while I'm still young enough to keep up with them. If I get kids, that is."

Since there was no audible reply, or any other sign from above, Clarissa picked up the sweater she'd worn this morning, grabbed her handbag and her empty lunch sack and walked out of the musty building. It took only a second to lock the solid worn door.

Clarissa trod down the steps carefully, grateful for the fresh late-afternoon breeze that still blew. She needed a little air after her first day back at work.

A busy little town that drew on the agricultural industry surrounding it, Waseka hummed with early springtime activity. The place was so small that everybody knew everybody else, and their business. Which was part of Clarissa's problem, but also part of the reason she loved it here.

It meant that they all knew how Harrison Harder had abandoned her the day before her wedding, to marry that city upstart who'd only been back in town for three weeks and claimed to be Clarissa's best friend. Today the reminder of his defection only made her smile.

Harrison Harder! The same man who'd trailed after her since seventh grade, defended her from Tommy Cummings when she hadn't needed his help, and vowed that he'd never love anyone else.

Clarissa had smiled her way through those awful days, too. The nights she spent weeping for a precious dream that had died. It was then that she'd realized that Harrison had only been the means to an end. Now she wasn't sure she'd ever *really* loved him, not the way a wife needed to love her husband. He'd been her way of getting the family she craved, of avoiding having to move in with one of the great-aunts just for company.

Her minister had tried to counsel her, to tell her that sometimes God sent roadblocks so people could see they were going down the wrong path. He was staunch in his belief that God had something much better in store for her. Clarissa tried to accept that, but with every day that passed, all she felt was more empty, more alone, more of an outsider in a town where everyone had someone.

That solitary feeling magnified when Gran died three years ago and Clarissa was left with a big, old house, and a hole in her heart. Who would she love now? Would she never have the family she'd longed for ever since her parents had died?

But all that was years ago. Clarissa didn't have any tears left for Harrison. Instead, she stubbornly clung to her dream. A family, a big, happy family where she showered all the devotion she wanted on people who would reciprocate with enough to fill her needy heart.

She ached for her own circle of love, especially now, after that wedding in Hawaii where honeymoon couples abounded. In fact, the surfeit of amorous couples found at those weddings was a perfectly good reason for avoiding the next one!

"Hi, Clarissa. Noticed you met our newest resident." Millie Perkins giggled, her broad face wreathed in smiles. "Now there's a fine specimen of a man. He'd make a good husband for you. And is he handsome!"

"You mean Wade Featherhawk? Yes, I met him." Clarissa blushed, recalling that prayer. "I don't think he's interested in me, Millie." Belatedly she remembered he was married.

"Nonsense! Of course he's interested. Just doesn't want to seem too eager is all. A man in his condition needs a good woman." Millie thumped her purse as if that settled the matter.

In his condition? Clarissa's radar went on high alert. She didn't want to fix anyone else's problems. She'd had enough of that with Billy Stuart and Lester Short, two men she'd once agreed to date. She still regretted those hastily made encounters.

"He said he was looking for a book for his son." Clarissa half-whispered it, wondering how long it would take the older woman to spill the beans she was obviously so anxious to share.

The day had been long. Clarissa was tired and hungry and she wanted to go home. She wouldn't tell a soul that what she really wanted was to spend some time thinking about that tall, dark man she'd met this afternoon. Instead, she prepared to hear the local's lowdown on one Wade Featherhawk.

"You've been away so I'll fill you in. Came to town the day after you left. Seems Jerry Crane is a friend of his, and Wade put a bid in on that country club Jerry's building." Millie stopped just long enough to gulp for air. "Jerry announced the winners last week, and first thing you know we have a new resident." She nodded smugly, as if she'd done her share of arranging that.

"So he's a carpenter. That's nice." Clarissa pushed away the thought of those big, rough hands.

"Apparently a good one, too. Or so Jerry says." Millie huffed once more and continued. "He didn't come alone. No, sir. He's got a passel of kids. Not his, though. And no wife. Myrna Mahoney over at Sally's Café told me that. The bunch of 'em were living at the motel for a while. Must have been terrible expensive. Heard they moved. She couldn't find out where. He doesn't talk much. The strong, silent type."

Millie hitched up her purse, adjusted the snug skirt surrounding her burgeoning hips and shoved her hat farther down on her freshly permed hair. "I've gotta go, hon. Burt doesn't like for me to be away too long when they're seeding."

"Yes, of course. Bye, Millie." Clarissa, embarrassed to find herself so interested in a perfect stranger, waved politely and started toward home once more, quickly jaywalking across to the fire hall to avoid Betty Fields, whom she saw waiting on the next corner.

She opened the white picket gate that led to her yard and stepped inside, appreciating the lovely old house as she went.

"It needs a coat of paint and some work on the roof, but it's still a great house," she assured herself. "A perfect house for a family. With a little work."

Dinner didn't take long. She'd set out her pork chop to thaw that morning. As she waited for her potato to boil, she wished again for a microwave. Better yet, a family to cook for! Making food for one was so boring. Baking one potato in the oven meant heating up the whole house, and it seemed foolish to do that with electricity so high. As she pulled a bottle of blue cheese dressing out of the fridge, she caught sight of the chocolate Valentine she'd given herself.

"Should have thrown that out." Instead, she closed the door on it, just as she'd shut down her hopes and dreams. There was no point wishing for something that was never going to happen.

Since it was still light outside after her meal and the silence inside the house was somehow depressing, Clarissa decided to finish working her flower bed. She'd always been one of the first to have pansies and petunias blooming. This year wouldn't be any different.

It is a silly dream, she lectured herself, kneeling to insert the delicate bedding plants. *Lots of people would say I'm too old to keep daydreaming about kids. Even if I had a husband who wanted them. Which I don't.*

She sighed at the hopelessness of it all and transplanted another flat of flowers.

"Can I see your birds?" A little boy with freckles on his nose and a spot of dirt on his cheek, peered through the pickets of her backyard fence. "They're goldfinches, aren't they?"

Clarissa thrust the dream of cherubic babies out of her mind and stared at the chubby little boy who stood impatiently waiting to enter her yard.

"No one ever uses that gate," she murmured, frowning. "I keep it oiled, of course. But still, it's very difficult to open."

"I can climb over." In a matter of seconds the little boy hiked himself over the fence. He stood before her, panting as he studied her birds. One bit of his jeans still clung to the top of the fence, but he ignored that. "How many do you got?"

"What? Oh, the birds. I'm not sure. Eight, I think. I don't keep them caged, but they always come here for the seeds."

"That's 'cause they like livin' in the woods over there." The child inclined his head to the wild growth of trees and shrubs that occupied the land next to hers. "Finches prefer to build their nests in low bushes or trees."

"I expect so." She studied him. He was a curious blend. A child, yes, but with intelligent eyes and an obvious thirst for knowledge. She remembered the man at the library. "Do you like birds?" she asked curiously.

"Oh, yes!" His face was a delight to watch, eyes shining, mouth stretched wide in a smile of pure bliss. "I collect pictures of them." He flopped down on the grass beside her and opened the pad he carried. Inside he'd detailed a carefully organized listing of birds he'd seen, with the odd picture taped here and there. "What's your name?"

"Clarissa Cartwright," she told him smiling. "And yours?"

"Pete. Do you have any cookies?" His look beseeched her to say yes. "I sure am hungry."

He couldn't have known that was the path straight to her heart, Clarissa decided. He couldn't possibly know how much she longed to share her special double fudge nut chip cookies with a child who would appreciate the thick chocolate chunks.

"As a matter of fact, I do have cookies. Would you like some?"

He nodded vehemently. "I'm starved! I didn't eat nothin' for supper."

"Why ever not?" She frowned. Children needed good nourishing food. His parents should be more careful. She wondered who they were.

"Supper didn't taste so good. Tildy made it an' she burns a lot of stuff." He glanced behind quickly, then lowered his voice. "But I'm not s'posed to say nothin' so's I don't hurt her feelings."

"That's very kind of you." Clarissa got to her feet, happy to leave the planting if it meant sharing her cookies. "I'll bring some milk out too, shall I?"

He trailed along behind her, up the stairs and in through the back door, with nary a hint of indecision.

"Do you live here all by yourself?" he asked, his face filled with curiosity as he looked around.

"Mm-hm. It was my grandmother's house. She left it for me to live in when she died." Clarissa set six cookies on a plate, poured two large glasses of milk, then checked to be sure Tabby the cat had some milk in her bowl. "My parents died when I was a little girl. My grandma looked after me."

"I don't gots no mother, neither." Pete took the plate and obediently carried it out onto her veranda behind her. "She died. My dad, too. Me an' my brother and my dopey sisters are the only ones left." He took a huge bite of cookie. "I'm getting 'dopted."

"That's nice." Clarissa smiled to hide the shaft of pain she felt at the sad story. "I'm sure your new parents must love you very much." She set the milk down and pulled out a chair.

"Enough to confine him to his room for a week if he doesn't learn to stay in his own yard," a husky voice informed her sardonically. "There's something wrong with your back gate."

Clarissa gasped at the familiar timbre of those low tones. She whirled around, her face draining of color as she met the dark forbidding gaze of the man who'd been in her library that very afternoon.

"What are you doing here?" she demanded, noticing that he'd left the front gate open. She hurried to close it. "I don't allow cats in my yard," she told him soberly. "They bother the birds."

"But you got a cat in your house. I seen it." Pete's shrill voice burst into the conversation.

"You 'saw' it. And Tabby doesn't go outside." Clarissa

stood where she was, her hands buried in the voluminous pockets of her long skirt. "Are you Pete's father?"

"His name is Pierce and you know very well that I'm his uncle. I'm sure the entire town has informed you of my existence by now. I have to tell you that I do not appreciate having to scour the neighborhood to find my nephew, Miss Cartwright."

"Hey, I didn't steal him!" Clarissa burst out, affronted by the implication in that low voice. "He came to look at the birds." Another thought occurred and she whirled to face Pete, who was now enjoying his fifth cookie. "Is Pierce your real name?"

"Yeah." Pierce looked shamefaced, his soft melting eyes begged forgiveness. "But I like people to call me Pete. It's not so...weird." He pocketed the last cookie, then stared up at the big man who stood towering over them both. "I'll go home now, Uncle Wade. I'm sorry I disobeyed."

Clarissa hadn't thought it possible, but the stern craggy face softened, just a little.

"It's all right this time, son. But please stay in the yard. That's why I rented the place, so there would be room for all of you to run and jump and play without getting into trouble." His uncle eyed the torn jeans with a rueful smile. "Another pair? How do you manage to do this, Pierce?"

"I dunno. It just happens." Pierce shuffled down the steps, then raced around to the back of the house for his book. "See ya later," he called to Clarissa, then vaulted over the fence with a huge leap.

"You're his *uncle?*" Somehow the knowledge just

now made its way to her brain. "But this afternoon you said you were looking for a book for your son. And Pete, I mean Pierce, said he was adopted." She frowned, trying to fit it all together.

As the worst possible scenario flew into her mind, she gasped. She'd seen those milk-carton pictures for years, children who'd been stolen from one parent by another.

"You can forget whatever you're thinking. I *am* their legal guardian." His rumbly voice openly mocked her.

"They?" She pounced on the information, struggling to assimilate it all. "Who are they?"

His face twisted into a wry smile. "One of the meddlers around here really must have slipped up."

When Clarissa only frowned in perplexity, he sighed, rolled his eyes, then thrust out one hand.

"I suppose we didn't get off to a very good start. You already know my name. And yes, before you ask, I'm part Cree. On my mother's side. She kept her name." His dark fuming eyes dared her to make something of that. "My sister and her husband died and left their kids for me to look after. Tildy and Lacey are twins. They're twelve. Jared is ten and Pierce is seven. We moved here for the work. I would have thought the gossips would have imparted at least that much."

Clarissa took his hand and shook it, feeling the zap of his touch shiver all the way up her arm.

"I don't listen to gossip," she assured him in a daze. *Four children? This man was raising four children? Alone?* "Welcome to Waseka." She managed to get the words out despite the shock that held her jaw tense.

"In case you didn't understand earlier, I think I

should make one thing perfectly clear," he muttered, yanking his hand away and shoving it into the pocket of his worn but very well fitted jeans. "I'm not looking for a wife. Despite what people think, men are as capable of parenting as women. Nobody's going to go hungry or get abandoned or forgotten about. I promised my sister I'd care for them, and I'll keep my word. I'll do my duty. Me. By myself." His lips tightened. "In spite of the locals' opinion, I've been doing just fine for several months now. And I intend to keep it that way."

She wondered why he sounded so torn about it. Then the impact of his words hit home.

"Now, just a minute here." Clarissa felt the flush push up from her neck, right to the roots of her string-straight hair.

"No, you wait. I know what small towns are like. Nosy bunch of old fools! Everybody's been hinting about you since the day I walked into this one-horse place. 'Clarissa's a wonderful cook. Clarissa's so good with kids. Clarissa would make you the perfect wife. She just loves to care for people.' Yak, yak, yak." He snorted derisively, eyeing the plate that now held only a few crumbs. "I can see you've already been practicing your motherly wiles on my nephew."

"Wiles? I wasn't—"

"I've heard it all before, you know. Too many times. The sweet praise for a man who can care for four children. The innocent suggestion that I might need help. The generous offer to cook us a healthy meal. Out of friendship, of course! Matchmakers!" One corner of his unsmiling mouth tipped down.

"Forget about whatever you're planning, Miss Cartwright. We're not in the market. I don't need the aggravation." Wade Featherhawk turned and stomped down the walk, his face grim and forbidding.

Clarissa followed him down, her brain working furiously. "But, wait a minute. I didn't even—"

He whirled around faster than she expected, bumping into her. One tanned hand grabbed her arm, waited until she was steady, then fell away as if it had been burned.

"No, you wait. Maybe I didn't make it clear enough. I'm not interested in whatever you're offering. My family is doing just fine. I don't need your interference." His snapping black eyes told her just how little she interested him. When Clarissa didn't back off, he smiled darkly.

"I don't go for blondes, and even if I did, I'd pick someone strong enough to handle four kids, not a woman who looks like she'd blow away in the first storm that came along." His eyes glinted black as ebony. "You want to mother someone, *Miss* Cartwright? Find your own kids."

Clarissa cringed away from him, but she refused to allow him to get away with saying such things to her. Whatever was behind his glowering countenance, it couldn't cover this deplorable lack of good manners.

"Believe me, Mr. Featherhawk, I wouldn't bother to give you the time of day! But I feel sorry for those children. If you're this cranky all the time, they must really bask in your company. A veritable joy to live with!"

Clarissa had never been so furious in her life. She stomped up the stairs, picked up Pierce's empty glass and plate, and stormed into the house, slamming the door behind her. As usual, the door immediately flopped open, and waved back and forth on its hinges with the annoying creak it always made when ill-treated.

A burst of laughter from outside made her flush even hotter. She slapped the dishes down and whirled back to the door to face his supercilious look.

"While you're looking for someone to share your life with, I'd make sure he knows how to build. This mausoleum is going to fall down around your ears if you don't do something soon, Miss Cartwright. Not that I'm volunteering." He frowned, took a step backward and shook his head. "No way! I'm not into masochism. Good night."

Clarissa seethed with indignation. Of all the arrogant, rude, obnoxious men, Wade Featherhawk had to take the cake. She closed the door firmly on his snide words and then wondered if he'd been referring only to the house.

The phone pealed a summons and Clarissa picked it up reluctantly. *Please Lord, not another busybody.*

"Hi, Prissy! How was Hawaii?" Her college buddy, Blair Delayney's bright voice echoed from the far reaches of the Rocky Mountains. "Meet any gorgeous men?"

"Nope, not a one. I'm still part of the group. How about you and Briony?" She wouldn't say a thing about the one who'd just left her front yard.

It was an old joke. In college, all three women had planned to be married and then lost their grooms one way or another before the ceremony. Down but not out, they'd banded together, calling themselves the Three Spinsters, vowing never to go looking for love again.

The only problem was, none of them could seem to accept in their hearts that love wouldn't find them. Someday.

"Oh, we're both still old maids. How was the wedding?" Blair always demanded details.

"It was lovely. On the beach, at sunset. That exclusive club was something else, though I felt out of place. I didn't know anyone except Great-Aunt Martha and she's deaf." Clarissa described the elegant dresses of the guests as best she could.

"I told you to take along a friend. Hawaii's a hard place to be alone." Blair's voice softened in commiseration.

"Tell me about it." Clarissa rested her cheek against the coolness of the wall. "Everywhere I went there were couples. Old ones, young ones, but always couples. Even some with kids."

"I'm sorry, Priss." Blair and Bri were the only two who knew how much she wanted to be a mother.

The old nickname came from her college days when she was constantly chiding them about cleaning up the apartment. It was somehow comforting to Clarissa. "Don't be. I managed all right once the aunt left and I got to look around on my own. There's this museum, Blair. You wouldn't believe the stuff!"

She launched into a description of the Bishop Museum that left little time for her to recount the lonely evenings spent walking along the silver-lined sand by herself, longing for someone to share all that beauty with. By the time Blair rang off, she was hooting with laughter. Which was exactly what Clarissa wanted. No one feeling sorry for her.

She rinsed off the dishes and stacked them in the cavernous dishwasher, empty except for her dinner plate and cutlery. She considered Wade's stinging assessment as she worked. Her lips pinched tight in anger as she remembered Pierce's yearning look at the pie she'd made for Mr. Harper.

"We'll see who has the last laugh, Mr. Wade Featherhawk. We'll just see. I wouldn't offer to help you if you begged me on bended knee!"

The mental picture this brought to mind made her burst out laughing. Wade Featherhawk, on his knees, to her?

"In your dreams, woman." She giggled out loud. She'd often dreamed of being proposed to, but it wasn't going to happen this time either, prayer notwithstanding. "Just forget about him."

If only it was that easy.

Chapter Two

Two weeks later Wade glanced around the old-fashioned church and grimaced as he caught sight of Clarissa Cartwright's willowy figure two pews ahead. Her dainty blue-and-white-flowered dress accentuated her gorgeous blond hair and the narrowness of her waist, along with other assets he forbade himself to notice. She was tiny. As he studied her clear profile and smooth white skin, his body tensed, his hands clenched and his jaw tightened. Wade told himself it was anger.

Everywhere he went these days, *she* seemed to be there, waiting in the wings, a silent reminder that he wasn't a very good father, that he didn't know diddly about parenting. That duty and obligation were no substitute for the mother's love that the kids needed.

She never said a word, of course, but he knew she was inaudibly pointing out the fact that he didn't have a clue as to what he was doing when it came to raising kids, especially girls.

Just his luck that Tildy and Lacey had Clarissa for a

Sunday school teacher, Jared drew her as his special pal in Boys' Club, and Pierce couldn't stop singing the praises of her dim, moldy old library. Some luck, Wade decided grimly.

No sooner was Wade's back turned than Clarissa invited one or the other of them over to that mausoleum. For a snack, to plan an outing, to practice a new recipe. Blah, blah, blah.

Wade was fed up to the teeth hearing about Miss Clarissa Cartwright and her wonderful life! All it did was make him look incompetent and lacking. Which he was! But he didn't need it rubbed in.

"Good to see you here." A man whose name Wade couldn't remember pumped his hand up and down, his face beaming. "Glad to have you in Waseka."

"Uh, thanks." Wade felt vaguely ashamed of his churlish behavior. Not everyone was all bad.

"You ever bowl? We're one short on our team and I sure wouldn't mind getting someone who can roll a few strikes. Call me up if you're interested. Ed Mason's the name."

"Thanks. I don't have a lot of free time, but I'll think about it." Wade watched the other man saunter away, then turned to gather his brood. Instead, he found himself virtually alone inside the building. Now what?

He sauntered down the aisle and out the door. They were there on the lawn, all four of them, clustered around *her,* laughing and giggling. Probably at some remark she'd made about him. Wade felt his jaw tighten in annoyance and struggled to suppress it. Why did she get under his skin like this?

"Really? A picnic? What would we have?" That was Jared, consumed with the condition of his perpetually empty stomach.

"Mm, fried chicken, maybe? With potato salad. And watermelon scones." Clarissa brushed a hand over Tildy's riot of inexpertly permed curls. "Maybe some chocolate layer cake for dessert. Or strawberry short-cake. How does that sound?"

"Like I died and went to heaven." Jared groaned, patting his ribs. "When can we go?"

"You can't." Wade walked up behind them, frowning in reproof at Clarissa. "Miss Cartwright has other things to do. And we can manage meals perfectly well on our own."

"But Clarissa was going to teach me how to make fried chicken for my home ec class," Tildy protested. "And Lacey wants to get some help with that biology paper."

"I'll help her. And we can buy fried chicken in town. Or make it at home. Let's go." He herded them toward the sidewalk. "Tildy, you, Lacey and the boys go ahead and get lunch started. I just have to stop and talk to someone for a minute. I'll be right there."

"Yes, Uncle Wade." Tildy didn't even look at him, but he could tell from the pout on her pretty face that she wasn't happy with his edict. Her heels hit the pavement with hard, knee-jarring thumps.

Wade winced at the girl's anger while his own temper inched up another degree. It was all *her* fault! All this meddling from their nosy neighbor had made the kids rebellious. He turned back toward the church with ven-geance fogging his brain.

"Miss Cartwright, I asked you to leave us alone. Why can't you respect my wishes?"

She stared at him, her eyes big pools of innocence in her long thin face.

"I didn't encourage them. Really! It was just that Pierce mentioned it was a lovely day for bird-watching. Then Jared suggested a picnic, and I joined in his game of pretend. I wasn't hinting anything."

Her face, open and oh, so innocent, peered back at him.

"Yeah, right." He led her out of the way of the crowd and off to one side. Then he stood in front of her, daring her to try to wiggle out of this one. "I'm asking you for the last time to leave my kids alone. We don't need your help. It was nice of you to do what you've done, and I do appreciate it, but we're settled in now and we're doing just fine by ourselves."

She looked a little surprised and confused by his words. That blank, credulous look made him say something he shouldn't have.

"Please, lady, just leave us alone. I know you want to help but you can't. No one can. I've got to do this on my own, no matter how much I might want somebody there to share the load. We've got to learn how to be a family together. Alone."

"I'm sorry! I didn't mean to offend you," she whispered, her face ashen. The twinkle of happiness he'd glimpsed earlier disappeared. "I just thought I could help out. I didn't think you'd find out about the jeans or the ironing."

Wade felt his face freeze. He allowed his gaze to slip

just a little lower, to the pressed cotton of his shirt. He should have known Lacey hadn't done it!

"They're so busy doing chores all day, they don't have time to play. Everything is so serious for them. I was just trying to lend a hand." Her earnest voice pleaded with him to understand, dropped almost to a whisper. "I know what it's like to feel as if you have to earn your keep."

Wade felt the pain in those softly spoken words and wondered what had caused it. Clarissa Cartwright hardly looked like a little Cinderella. In spite of that, he couldn't stem the tide of chagrin that rose in a wave of gall. How dare she go to his house, check out his family and how he provided for them? How dare she snoop through his home on the pretext of mending their worn clothes? He knew they weren't the best, but at least they were clean and paid for. Well, most of the time they were clean.

"Look, maybe we don't live the kind of dream life you want. I know the kids have to pitch in. But it won't hurt them. They'll learn accountability. Raising them *is* up to me, not you." He felt a tide of red rise in his cheeks as he noticed the tiny mending stitches on the knee of his jeans.

Even in the best of all possible worlds, his nieces couldn't sew like that, and he should have known it, would have known it if he'd paid more attention to them.

"I love those kids as if they were my very own. They're not going to get mixed up in drugs or booze or any of that stuff as long as I'm around." He took a deep breath and continued. "But they're not going to have a mother, either. Not even a pretend one. And they have to face that." He took a deep breath and went on the attack.

"So I wish you'd stop trying to weasel your way into

our lives just so you can prove to everyone how much better off you'd treat them. In two words, Miss Cartwright—butt out!"

Wade turned and found several pairs of eyes on him. He knew then that the congregation had heard every word he'd said. Before the noon siren screamed across the town, they'd spread it far and wide. A surge of remorse washed over him, but he thrust it away, his mind boiling with frustration.

Maybe now these people would stop shoving Clarissa Cartwright's single status in his face!

Wade made himself spend time talking with Pastor Mike, chatting to Jerry about the walk-in cedar closet he wanted in his house. By the time he strode down the sidewalk, hands clenched inside his pockets, most of the folks had dispersed. And that included Clarissa. He'd known the exact moment she'd scurried away, head downcast, shoulders slumped.

He forced his mind away off her and took a detour on the way home in order to concentrate on the list of jobs he'd garnered around town. With a little luck, maybe he could make enough to put some money in the bank for that rainy day that kept happening when work ran out. He was going to need a little extra cash. Especially now, with the country club project delayed.

It wasn't five minutes before he got caught up in studying the Victorian architecture of the row of houses on Primrose Lane. He kept walking, trying to remember the details he'd planted deep in his brain last year in order to gain acceptance to the college of architecture.

As he studied gables and turrets, Wade let his mind

turn over the problem of life in Waseka. He'd tried to keep to himself, tried to avoid the inevitable match-making. He'd been through it enough times. And every time the kids got their hopes up, he had to dash them because the woman in question always wanted some-thing he couldn't give. She sure wasn't looking to take on a ready-made family that belonged to someone else. At least, that's what he told himself. The truth was, he didn't want the responsibility of yet another person clut-tering up his life.

Wade trudged down the street with the sun beating on his head, lost in his thoughts of providing a future for four needy children who were totally dependent on him. His shoulders bowed under all that being their parent demanded, the knowledge that he was no good at responsibility nagging in the back of his brain.

He flinched in surprise when small, sharp-nailed fingers closed around his arm, pinching tight in their effort to penetrate and thus slow him down. Wade flung the hand away, then whirled around to see who was attacking him.

She stood there, sea foam eyes turbulent with temper. Clarissa might have to look up to meet his gaze, but she certainly didn't seem intimidated. She looked more like a wasp about to sting.

"How dare you embarrass me like that? I didn't help them out because of you! I wouldn't do anything for you. You're too stubborn and far too arrogant to want to help, Mr. Featherhawk." Her words were so sharp, they could have torn a strip off him.

He waited, mentally flinching at the fury in her face, but keeping his own countenance impassive.

"Did I mention self-absorbed?" She crossed both arms across her chest and glared. "Or conceited? I did it for them, you know. Because they deserve some decent food, some time to play, a clean house and a shoulder to cry on once in a while. They've had to grow up awfully fast since their parents' deaths. Can't you let them be children for even one afternoon without lording it over them and forcing them to wallow in the drudgery?"

Oh, brother! Over the past two weeks they must have poured out the whole ugly story. As if he wanted to deprive them of anything when they'd already lost both parents. Wade sighed, his whole body sagging with tiredness as she continued her diatribe. As he waited, she slapped her hands on her hips and laughed, a harsh discordant sound that didn't match her delicate looks.

"You're so worried about getting trapped—who would want to marry you anyway?" She sniffed, her snubbed nose tipped upward in haughty reproof. "It's not as if you're the least bit *pleasant* to be around. I feel sorry for those kids, living with a bear like you, Wade Featherhawk. You carry a chip big enough for the whole Cree nation."

Clarissa gave him one last huff, then turned and stomped away, her heels tap-tapping on the sidewalk. Openmouthed, Wade watched her until she closed her white picket gate, climbed the steps to her rickety old house and firmly closed the door on him. He shook his head to clear it, wondering why he'd chosen this street anyway.

Then he turned the corner toward home, his shoulders hunching forward as he thought over what she'd said.

"Way to go, bud! You've already got so many friends in this place, you can really afford to slap down the one person who was willing to help out, no questions asked. Smart, very smart."

He shut his mind on that mocking inner voice and kept walking toward the park. He needed to think....

Wade wasn't sure how much time passed before he wandered out of the park and down the street. He scanned the sky, but that didn't help. Heritage or not, he couldn't tell time by the sun. His eyes narrowed as he focused on the plume of smoke coming from down the street. From his house! Wade broke into a sprint that carried him through the front door and into the kitchen in less than a minute.

"Tildy? Something's burning." He grabbed a pot mitt and lifted the smoke-belching pan from the stove, searching for a place to set it down.

Since the counter was covered with dirty dishes and the table still held the remains of breakfast, he carried the pot outside and across the backyard to dump its charred remains into the garbage barrel.

Clarissa Cartwright stood across the alley, in her own yard, fork poised over a barbeque. She raised one eyebrow quizzically.

"Problem?" she enquired softly, glancing down at the pot.

"Not at all," he lied.

"Oh, good. Well, if the children want to accept my invitation, I have extra steaks in the fridge and lots of potatoes right here, ready to roast. There's apple pie for dessert and I made fresh lemonade. *They're* more than welcome."

Meaning he wasn't? Wade sighed. No question about it. He'd burned his bridges there. She'd probably cross the street to avoid him from now on. But that was what he'd wanted, wasn't it?

She turned the item on her barbeque and Wade felt his mouth water, his tongue prickle, his stomach rumble. A T-bone steak! What he wouldn't give for a nice juicy steak on the rare side with a fluffy baked potato heaping with sour cream. And a slice of apple pie.

He closed his eyes and gulped, swallowing the gall that rose in his throat as he humbly ate crow. You didn't take someone up on an invitation like that after you'd embarrassed them in front of half the town.

"Th-thanks anyway. But we've got our dinner ready." He wished he could chuck the pot into the garbage can, too. It would take forever to clean.

"Yes, I can see that." She gave him one last questioning look, then turned her back and lifted a sizzling steak from the grill, watching as the juices dripped onto the coals. "A little too rare, I think." She laid it back down.

Wade swallowed again, scraped what he could out of his pot and returned to his messy, smoke-filled home with legs like cement.

As he gathered the kids around the table to munch on tasteless, white buttered bread spread with gobs of oily peanut butter, he faced the condemning looks in their eyes.

"To think we could have been eating real food. Steak," Jared grumbled, glaring at the sandwich. "And pie. I heard her from my window. Pie!"

"Know what my Sunday school lesson was about today, Uncle Wade?" Lacey's pretty face darkened like a thundercloud about to dump its contents all over him.

"I can't imagine." He chewed slowly, almost gagging when he tried to swallow the sticky concoction.

"Pride," Lacey informed him sagely. "Silly, stupid pride. It always comes before a fall."

"Oh. That's nice, dear."

A resounding silence greeted his words. Then, one by one, the kids left the table, their sandwiches torn apart, but mostly uneaten.

Wade took a gulp of water, then folded his napkin over the rest of his sandwich. He couldn't eat another bite either.

Grimly he wondered how much damage it would do to his image to admit defeat and take them all out to the fast-food place for supper. He'd almost decided to do it when he saw Pierce sneak across the backyard and vault over *her* fence.

Not two minutes later the boy was sprawled on the grass, happily munching on something, his freckled face the picture of bliss as he gazed lovingly at Wade's nemesis.

As he worked on cleaning up the kitchen, Wade had lots of time to notice that it wasn't long before Jared, followed by Tildy and Lacey, decided to go for a walk. And when Clarissa and Pierce disappeared from her backyard, he knew exactly where all three had gone.

"Bribing them," he muttered, viciously scraping last night's burnt hamburger out of the frying pan. "That's all she's doing."

His stomach rumbled agreement, and he threw down the pot scrubber in defeat.

"Sally's Café is open this afternoon. I believe I'll stop by for coffee with the boys."

Wade pulled open the door, his toe thudding against the box that sat leaning against the closet door. Why had he hung on to his drafting table anyway? It wasn't as if he'd ever realize that ambition. It was better to get rid of all the evidence of his aspirations to become an architect. Supporting four kids took every dime he made and more moments than he had in a day. Finding time to study would be impossible.

Wade picked up the box, opened the closet and stuffed it against the back wall, standing the rolls of vellum filled with his carefully sketched ideas behind the winter coats. He had only himself to blame—his sister, Kendra, would be living somewhere with her children if he hadn't insisted she give her husband another chance, try to make their marriage work. That's what had killed her and ended his dream, his insistence on avoiding his duty to her.

Wouldn't it have been better to let Kendra move out on Roy, come and live with him, instead of asking her to work things out? He'd laid it on heavy, reminded her how much the boys needed their dad. Not because he thought Roy was any role model, but because Wade didn't want the responsibility, didn't want to put his own plans on hold. That had always been his problem— trying to get out of what other people expected of him.

Well, it was far too late to change it all now. All he could do was fulfill her last wish and care for them the best he knew how.

Wade sighed, closed the front door and strolled

down the street toward the local café. When a light breeze ruffled the apple blossoms overhead and fluttered their petals to the ground, Wade thought he heard sweet, joyful laughter from the librarian's house across the back alley. He ignored it and kept walking. If he didn't get something to eat soon, his stomach was going to devour his backbone. Too bad it wouldn't be steak.

Three weeks later Clarissa picked up the basket holding a pot pie made from her grandmother's famous recipe. In the other hand she snuggled a basket of homemade biscuits and the carrier that protected her triple chocolate fudge cake—the one that had won a blue ribbon at the state fair.

"I don't care what he says," she told herself firmly as she forced open the back gate. "I promised those kids a decent meal tonight, and I am going to deliver. He can rant and rave for another two weeks if he wants. It's no skin off my nose."

But she hated the acrimony. She knew how hard it was for him to manage everything. The kids had told her enough for Clarissa to get the picture. Wade Featherhawk had not had an easy life and by the sounds of it, he wasn't scheduled for a reprieve anytime soon.

Apparently life on the reservation he'd grown up on, had not been a picnic. According to the kids, there was little work and lots of bad memories. Once he'd packed the kids up and left, he'd had to fight for every opportunity to prove he did quality work. Not that he deserved a second chance, her brain piped up. He's too cranky.

But she wouldn't dream of slighting someone's work ethic just because he was in a bad humor.

Clarissa had heard the talk in town, of course. Awful bigoted talk about his heritage. There had even been rumors. Not that she paid them any heed. She encouraged those who had hired him to speak openly about Wade's good solid work ethic, and the able way he completed the jobs he contracted to do. She'd asked to keep one of the extremely good sketches he'd drawn for a renovation, and showed it to several ladies she knew wanted work done on their homes.

Gradually, people in Waseka were coming to accept the little family as a permanent fixture. Or they would do if they could only stop talking about how needy the children always looked. As a hint on her behalf, Clarissa felt it was blatantly overdone.

She'd done what she could, of course. But it wasn't easy with Wade's orders to stay away ringing in her ears. Last night Pierce's grumble had torn a sympathetic hole in her heart, and she was determined to repair it one way or another.

Clarissa stepped out her back door and peered across the lane, checking to make sure *he* wasn't around. It was too early for him, of course. And he couldn't know that she always took Wednesday afternoons off, or that his kids' sitter, Mrs. Anders, had to cancel out for this afternoon.

Feeling like a burglar, she crept across her backyard, managed to yank the gate open and carry her booty across the way without dropping a thing. Jared let her into his yard with a wide smile, his lanky height towering over her.

"Hey, something smells excellent, Clarissa."

"Why, thank you!" She felt the heat rise in her cheeks. "I hope you enjoy it." She watched him peering in the bushes. "What are you doing?"

"Trying to find my football. I have practice tonight, and I need it."

"Oh." Clarissa nodded at the basket. "If you'll carry these inside, I'll help you look."

Ten minutes later, her shoes muddy from traipsing through the garden, Clarissa found the missing ball behind the shed.

"Wow, thanks, Clarissa!" As he took the ball, Jared glanced up and frowned, his eyes on the kitchen window. "Uh-oh. Tildy's in the kitchen again."

"That's because I said I'd help her with her home ec project. Jared, do you think you could mow the grass? It's awfully long." Clarissa wasn't sure grass this long could be mowed, but it was either try to cut it now or declare the yard a part of the rain forest.

"It's bad, I know." Jared's thin cheeks went a faint pink. "I'm supposed to do it every week, but our mower is broken. Uncle Wade just hasn't had time to fix it."

"Go across the alley and get mine, then. Okay?" She waited for his nod, then went inside, confident that he knew what he was doing. After all, she'd been paying him to do her yard work for two weeks now.

Tildy stood in the kitchen, peering into the oven.

"What are you doing, honey?"

"It's not getting brown," the young girl told her. "Our home ec teacher said the crust should be golden brown."

Clarissa smiled as she closed the oven door. "The

crust will get brown, just give it time. It's supposed to bake for at least an hour at a low temperature. Now, what's the project for tonight?"

"Coleslaw. I got the cabbage, but I don't know what else to do with it."

She looked so forlorn Clarissa couldn't help but smile.

"Okay, coleslaw it is. But we'll need some room. Let's do a little cleaning first." Tildy frowned, but Clarissa wasn't giving up. Opportunity didn't knock that often. "If you load the cutlery into the sink, it can soak for a few minutes while we wipe down the counter. Put the glasses in, too."

She showed the young girl how to organize everything efficiently so that a minimum amount of time was needed to clean.

"See, it doesn't take that long," she murmured, half an hour later, surveying the sparkling room with satisfaction. "Just don't let it get so far next time. Remember the first rule?"

Tildy nodded. "Clean up as you go," she repeated.

"Good. Now, where's the cabbage?"

Clarissa managed to show Tildy how to mix the dressing and got her started on slicing the cabbage into tiny strips before Lacey burst into the room, her face a mass of frustration.

"I'll never ace this dumb old biology," she muttered. "I don't even know where to get a frog."

"By the creek. There are always lots of them in the spring." Clarissa offered to help her catch one later that evening. "Hi, Pierce," she greeted as the young boy looked in through the screen door. "What's the matter?"

"There's a bird out here that I can't name. And I have to. It's important for my collection."

"Okay, well I've got a book—"

The doorbell cut across her response.

"Isn't anyone going to answer that?"

"I can't stop now. I'm just getting good at this." Tildy chewed her bottom lip as she concentrated on the thin strips of cabbage.

"Fine, I'll get it." Clarissa walked through the living room and opened the door. She almost groaned aloud. "Rita," she greeted, calmly enough. "Can I help you?"

"I doubt it. I'm here in response to the petition to adopt these children. I have to check out their home conditions." Social worker Rita Rotheby surged inside with all the pomp and ceremony of a battleship bound for duty as she tried to sidestep Clarissa. "Excuse me."

"Uh, Wade isn't here right now, Rita. Maybe it would be better if you waited until he came home." Clarissa could picture his face if he walked in right now and found *her* there.

"Nonsense! Part of the information gathering has to be done when he's absent. To see how the children are managing."

Okay, then. It was up to her, Clarissa decided. She'd have to make sure this inspection went well.

"The children are fine. Jared is cutting the lawn."

"Unsupervised?" Rita scribbled something down.

"I'm here," Clarissa reminded her and had the satisfaction of seeing the woman erase the words. "Tildy is making coleslaw for her home ec project. Lacey is doing her biology and Pierce is cataloging birds." She trailed behind the other woman, but stopped short when Rita dragged a finger over the kitchen counter. Surely she hadn't missed a spot?

"You have dinner already made?" the woman asked Tildy in disbelief.

"Yes, and she's got all the major food groups covered, too. Isn't it great?" Clarissa smiled at Tildy, willing her to smile back. "As you can see, Rita, Wade is doing a fine job with these children."

"Hm. Things do seem to have changed. For the better." Rita inspected the laundry room and found the machines purring.

Clarissa breathed a thank you that she'd thought to start a couple of loads earlier. She followed Rita back through the house. With all the finesse of a person who has a right to be in someone else's home, she opened the front door and smiled her best hostess smile. "Everything's fine, Rita."

"Well, it does seem to be. I'll file this and send a copy of it to Mr. Featherhawk. I don't like to do anything behind anyone's back." Rita surged through the door, then stopped. "Oh, there you are. I must tell you, sir, that I found a vast improvement this time. Keep up the good work." Having given her blessing, Rita bustled down the sidewalk to her car.

Clarissa gulped, gaping at the frowning face of Wade Featherhawk. He glanced at Rita's disappearing back, then at Clarissa, then at the house.

"It's nice someone in this town is honest about their intentions." His voice chewed her out for her insolence. "I thought I asked you to leave us alone."

Clarissa carefully shut the door behind him, checked to make sure no children were around, then faced him.

"Yes, you did. And I tried to respect your wishes. But I was asked over here to help out. And I was glad to do it." She held her head up, daring him to question her further. "Now that you're here, I'll be on my way." She turned her back and walked toward the kitchen.

"There's a load of jeans in the washer and a bunch of your shirts in the dryer. You might want to take those out before they wrinkle. Tildy, you've done very well with that cabbage, although I think you've cut a bit more than you need. Just follow the recipe I left there and you'll be fine. Bye for now." And gathering up her purse, Clarissa headed for the back door.

She'd hoped to get away without another lecture, but it was obvious that Wade wasn't prepared to let this go.

"I'll walk you out." His fingers wrapped around her elbow determinedly.

Clarissa marched out the back door, down the steps and across the newly mown yard. Jared was now working at the side of the house.

"He must have fixed it," Wade muttered, staring at the shorn lawn. He shook his head and focused on her. "I don't know how many times I have to say this, Miss Cartwright."

"Don't bother! I already know what you're going to say. You've told me enough times."

She kept on walking. Or she would have if he'd let go of her arm.

"Then why—"

"Why do I keep coming back here?" She rounded on

him angrily. "Because *they* asked me to, that's why. And I can't say no." She gulped down her frustration. "I know you don't want me here, but the children need my help. And so do you."

"No, I don't." He enunciated each word with frustrated precision.

"Well, you need something. Rita is the head honcho around here, and Judge Prendergast will do whatever she recommends. If you don't get her on your side, you're going to lose those kids to the state welfare agency. Is that what you want?"

"No, of course not!" Wade raked a hand through his hair, his face weary. "But I can't be here all the time. I can't do everything."

"I know," Clarissa told him calmly. "That's why it makes sense for them to come to me. I'd love to help and I don't mind in the least. I like them. I think they're smart kids."

"But I don't want them to become dependent on you. They shouldn't have to lose someone again. That's not fair to them."

Clarissa shrugged. "Is it fair that you lock a *friend* out of their lives, won't even let me help a little by providing a meal now and again? Is it fair that Lacey and Pierce and Jared and Tildy all come to me for help and I have to send them away because you're too stubborn to accept a little assistance once in a while?" She said the words that had begged release for days now.

"Is it fair that I can't mother them a little?"

"Probably not," he agreed grimly. "I don't think it's fair that their mother died, either. Or that I—" He stopped, clenched his jaw, then shrugged. "It's just the way life has to be."

Clarissa saw red. The hidden words poured out of her mouth with no regard for the consternation spreading across his glowering face.

"No, it doesn't! Can't you see that I only want to help these kids? I'm not asking you to be involved," she added scornfully. "And I'm not after your money or your house or anything like that."

"No, you're after my kids." His eyes glinted belligerently.

"All right! Yes, I am. I'm asking you to consider them and what it must be like to grow up like this. They can't have friends over because there's no one here to supervise."

"I hired someone." His chin jutted out as if to say "so there."

"I know." Clarissa nodded. "Mrs. Anders. She couldn't come this afternoon so she asked me to stop in once they were home from school. But it's not the same." She continued. "They haven't any spare time to go out with chums because there are so many chores." She waved a hand at the house behind them.

"You talk about my house being run-down, but at least it has more than one bathroom and lots of bedrooms. This place is too small!"

As she searched his face for a hint of acquiescence, Clarissa let her heart's desire pour out. "Why would it be so wrong to let me coddle them a little bit? I promise I'm not after you. I know I'm not wife material—I'm not beautiful or desirable or any of those things men want in a wife, but that doesn't matter, does it? I can still be a friend to them, and a darn good one! I can love these kids and be there for them. Why won't you let me? They'll still love you, Wade. I would never do anything to change that."

Wade stared at her, his mouth hanging open. He reached out and lifted a strand of her hair and tucked it back behind her ear, his fingers brushing against her cheek. When he finally spoke, his voice was quiet, sober. Clarissa steeled herself for the rebuff she knew would come.

"There's nothing wrong with your looks, Miss Cartwright. You have a soft-spoken kind of beauty that any man in his right mind would find attractive. But I'm not that man. I have nothing to give. It's all I can do to provide for four children. I don't need a wife to look after, too."

"Actually, I was in no way suggesting that. But those children are exactly why you do need a wife," she countered, then stopped as the grim line returned to his mouth. "I'm not proposing, Wade. Really, I'm not! But will you at least let me help out once in a while? Will you come over for a meal now and then? Will you let me help Pierce with his birds and Lacey with her biology? Just until you've got things more settled?"

Wade studied her for a long time, but when he spoke there was a hint of amusement in his low tones. "Frankly, I'd be ecstatic if you'd take over Lacey's biology. It's a subject I detest, especially the dissecting. And you know very well that Pierce has never stopped questioning you about his collection, in spite of my protests."

It was an admission, but Clarissa wanted more.

"And you'll come for dinner? Tomorrow? No, Friday. You'll let me help Tildy with her school cooking stuff?" She waited, her breath held till it hurt her chest.

"We'll come for dinner on Saturday," he finally agreed. "And I suppose it won't hurt for Tildy to get some help, once in a while. But that's all. Nothing more. You won't drop over and clean the house or mend clothes or do the laundry." His eyes narrowed suspiciously. "Do you promise you won't pretend there's something more going on when the busybodies start talking?"

"Of course not!" Clarissa was scandalized by the very idea. "I'm just a friend, and I'd like to help you out."

"Fine. Then I'll help out, too." He sniffed. "Whatever's cooking in that oven didn't come from Tildy's hands. In repayment for your assistance, I'll fix your roof."

"Oh, but it's just a chicken pie!" She frowned, trying to imagine how much fixing her roof would cost him. "I didn't expect you to—"

"Take it or leave it," he warned, but there was a glint in his eye that warmed her heart. "If you help us, we help you. Friends."

Her decision was unfairly influenced by the drop of rain on her nose. "I'll take it. I've got to get going."

"To put pails out, no doubt. You should have had it fixed months ago." Wade shook his head as he surveyed the sorry condition of her weathered gables and red-rimmed turrets. "I'll come over tomorrow and take a look."

"You don't have to—"

His look silenced her.

"All right. Thank you very much. I'll be at the library till eight. We stay open late on Thursday."

"I know. Believe me, I think I've been told everything about you." He didn't make it sound like a compliment.

"Really?" Clarissa frowned. "Like what?"

"You have this," one finger trailed across her jaw where it curved up to meet her ear, touching the hairline scar, "because, at age six, you helped get Johnny McCabe out of a tumble-down barn. You broke this arm when Petey Somebody dared you to jump off a granary, and Sarah Kingsley stopped being your best friend when she stole all your doll babies in grade two."

Clarissa gaped at him, nodding her head as he spoke.

"Mercy, they must be serious," she whispered. "The townsfolk haven't told anyone that stuff since Harrison."

He frowned. "Harrison? Harrison was the man you were engaged to. He dumped you when your old friend came back to town. He married her instead of you." Wade's voice held a hint of sympathy. "What a jerk!"

"Harrison wasn't a jerk," she murmured, staring into Wade's knowing gaze. "He was just confused. I wasn't what he wanted, but Grace was. She was very beautiful, just like a model. I couldn't compete with that."

"He was a fool. Beauty goes a lot deeper than the skin." Wade's hand dropped away from her face as he took a deep breath. His eyes hardened. "But don't get any ideas, Miss Cartwright. I'm not in the market for a wife. And I am *not* Harrison's replacement. Not in a million years."

The pain he inflicted with those words bit deep and it was all she could do not to burst into tears. She didn't want someone to replace Harrison! She wanted someone better than him, a man who would think she was as wonderful as Harrison found Grace; she wanted a storybook kind of love.

Clarissa walked out of his yard, crossed the alley and yanked her own gate open. She stopped, turned and stared at him, only then realizing that he'd followed her.

"No, you're not him," she agreed quietly. "I don't think anyone could ever replace Harrison in my life." Then she closed the gate, walked across the yard and into her big empty house.

"Harrison was a sign," she whispered as she stared out the window at the falling rain. "A sign that I'm supposed to be alone. And you, Wade Featherhawk, just confirmed it."

She forgot all about the pails as tears, hot and bitter, coursed down her cheeks. How it hurt, to have those children there and not to be able to love them as she wanted, to mother them.

"It doesn't matter," she sobbed to the Lord, determination setting her jaw. "I'll be their mother in my heart. He can't stop me from loving them. No one can."

But as the tears dried and her heart calmed, Clarissa couldn't help remembering the look on Wade's face. He'd *wanted* to let her help, wanted to let her in. She'd seen that.

So why didn't he? Why was he so afraid to trust, let her into his world?

Chapter Three

Eight weeks to the day after he'd moved to Waseka, Wade pulled up to the curb in front of his house at five minutes to six, and parked, grinding the gears as he hadn't done since he was thirteen. He forced himself to open the truck door, even though every muscle in his body begged him to just sit there and vegetate.

Man, he was tired. He couldn't ever remember being this bone weary before. His eyes were bleary and unfocused and his hand wasn't steady. Maybe if he put his head down, just for a moment, maybe then he could get his second wind. Or third.

"Wade?"

Oh, no, not *her* again! Wade huffed out a great puff of air, his brain groaning. What now?

"Wade, I think you'd better open your eyes and listen to me."

Clarissa's soft voice sounded deadly serious. He blinked his eyes open. Her face was white. Of course, it was always pale, but now it had lost all color. Her eyes were red and her hands blackened, as if she'd been playing in the dirt. There were the smudges all over her long floaty skirt.

How many times had he dreamed of that skirt?

"Wade? There was a fire."

He jerked awake, his brain revving into high gear. "The kids?"

"They're fine. They're at my place." She took a deep breath. "That's not all."

Not all? Wasn't that enough? What else could there be? He tried to focus on what she was saying. "Huh?"

"Rita was here today, doing another inspection. She's, um, pretty steamed."

"Why?" He eased himself out of the truck, knowing he had to move but wincing at every budge of his smarting muscles. "What happened?"

"You'd better look for yourself."

Her delicate hands helped him stumble to the sidewalk and up the path. She pushed open the front door and guided him inside.

The living room was littered with stuff, as usual. Smoky, water-soaked stuff, he noticed. Dishes cluttered the kitchen counter and food sat on the table as flies buzzed over it. A huge black spot covered the ceiling, most of the stove and a section of the floor.

He shuddered, immediately alert to the fact that he could hear no children's voices. "What happened?"

"Tildy was frying. The oil caught on fire."

That woke him up. He gulped at the idea of his lovely young niece covered in burns.

"She was trying to help Pierce and forgot to pay attention. Jared saw it start and thought he could put it out with a dish towel. That caught on fire too." She pointed to the corner. "The oil set the cloth alight and when he tossed it to the floor, it caught onto the laundry Lacey was going to wash. I saw smoke and came over. By the time I got here, Pierce had finally found a fire extinguisher and put it out, but by then Rita had already arrived."

"But where was Mrs. Anders?"

"Apparently the hospital called to say her husband had a heart attack. She told the kids to call me when she couldn't reach you, but they didn't want to be a bother. I think Tildy was afraid I'd make her wait to fry. She's desperate to get an A in that class."

It was clear to Wade by the glint in her eyes that Clarissa felt the children were reciting his precise words. He clenched his fists, drew a breath and summoned all his courage.

"And? You might as well spit out the rest of it." His heart dropped to his boots as he surveyed the damage and considered how much worse off they could have been.

"Rita told me to take the kids. I wanted to call you but no one knew where you were." There was a hint of censure in her voice. "I tried to stall her, but she'd already made her decision by then."

Wade saw her swallow, heard her voice drop, and knew the worst had happened.

"I think she's going to recommend foster care, Wade."

"She can't!" He couldn't bear the thought of it, his sister's kids split apart, separated, living with people who wouldn't understand them. His own life, empty and barren of the joy they brought, the small glimpses of his sister he caught in each child. Worst of all, the promise would be broken.

He shook his head, refusing to accept it. "She can't."

"Yes, Wade. She can. I just wanted to warn you." Clarissa didn't meet his glance, but stood staring at her feet, her head bowed in sadness.

Wade stared at the mess he'd made of things. "I should have been here, should have been nearby. Why did I have to pick this afternoon to run to the city for supplies?"

"It doesn't matter now." Her head lifted as if she'd come to some decision. She studied his face for a long moment, then tugged at his arm. "Come on, Wade."

"It does matter." He felt the responsibility and almost bowed under it. "It's my fault. It's *all* my fault. They could have died. I should have managed better. No matter how hard I try, I never seem to get it right. I messed up here. Again." He couldn't look her in the eye, knew he'd see condemnation.

Clarissa's fingers tightened on his arm. "I'm sure you've done the best you could. No one was hurt. And it's not anyone's fault. Accidents happen." She pushed against his chest. "Come with me. I've already called the insurance agency. It's the only one in town, remember. Your renter's policy covers most of the damage, they think. But you can't stay here. Not till they've assessed the damage."

He stared at her, his mind numb with the realization that his little family was now homeless. His brain wouldn't move on from that. He felt the tug on his arm as if through a fog. "Oh. No, I suppose not. Thank you."

"You're welcome. Can you get up?"

Dimly Wade realized that sometime during their conversation he'd flopped down onto one of the kitchen chairs. His eyes noted the places where fire had singed the flooring, and he shivered at the thought of what might have happened.

"Wade?"

"What?" He blinked and refocused on her, forcing his mind to function. "Oh. Get up? Why?"

"You need a shower and something to eat, for one thing. You can have that at my place. The water heater's turned off here. The firemen said it was better that way. Come on."

He managed to get up and stumble to the back door, grateful for her calm even voice and the gentle hand under his arm. His brain couldn't take it all in. It was like a bad dream.

A pile of charred bits of fabric lay outside the back door. Wade stopped in his tracks and stared. He couldn't seem to move his eyes away, couldn't stop imagining the scars...

"Wade, listen to me." Clarissa turned his face toward her, her palms cool again his cheeks.

She felt good, he decided. Soothing. He didn't even try to free himself. Her flower-soft fragrance tickled his nose. Roses, he thought. Or lavender maybe. Something like his mother would have worn.

Her eyes were clear and calm. "You have to get out of here now, Wade. Everybody is fine. They're okay. Come on, let's keep going."

He moved on only because he knew she would nag him until he did. He walked across the grass, and into her yard with its pretty flowers and trim grass, marveling at the contrast between the two houses. His fingers curled around her small soft hand. Such a tiny hand to be so competent.

"I'm fine," he mumbled when her other hand slid under his arm. He forced his rubber legs to move one foot in front of the other.

"Of course you are. Three steps up now." There was a hint of amused mockery in her quiet tones.

"I'm just worried about the kids. My boots—"

"Are fine." She urged him inside. "Sit down here and drink this."

He took the cup from her fingers and sipped the dark steaming brew. "I don't take sugar."

"Today you do. Drink it." There was no room for argument in that prim order.

Wade drank, his mind picturing that awful scene again.

"They're fine, Wade. See, there's Pierce working on his birds in the front yard. And Tildy's sitting out there, too. With Ryan Adams. Lacey's over in the park. You can just see her red shirt through the trees." She pointed.

Wade followed the direction and caught sight of Lacey's favorite blouse. "Jared?" he choked, his heart swelling with relief.

"I'm right here. I'm trying to fix this stupid—uh, broken cupboard." Jared came to stand before his uncle. He frowned. "You don't look too good, Uncle Wade."

"That's funny. I feel fine. Just fine." Wade noticed his sister's distinct features in the tall boy and felt the guilt wash over him again. He was growing up so fast. "Are you all right, son?"

"Of course. We all are. Clarissa's taking care of things. That's okay, isn't it, Uncle Wade?" Jared's face contorted with worry. "You're not mad that we got her? Tildy didn't mean to do it, you know. It was an accident."

"I know. No. It's perfect. Okay, I mean." Wade glanced around with bleary eyes, noting the sparkling kitchen, the yeasty fragrance of fresh baked bread, the utter hominess of it all. No matter what he did, his kitchen had never looked like this. He noticed Jared's frown and refocused.

"It's just fine," he repeated, then stopped when his stomach began a low but very audible rumbling.

"Jared, will you show your uncle where the shower is? And here are some fresh towels. As soon as he's ready, we'll have dinner." Clarissa smiled, her eyes meeting Wade's. "Go ahead. Everything is all right. I'll watch them for you. We'll talk later."

Wade followed Jared up the stairs, easing up on the balustrade when he felt it give under his weight.

"Another thing to be fixed," he muttered, trying to smother a yawn. "This house sure needs a lot of catch-up work."

"You should have let me help you finish Mac-Gregor's roof last night," Jared told him, frowning. "I can do stuff. Besides, you can't work morning, noon and night, Uncle Wade. Nobody can. You'll burn out. I heard the teachers talking about it."

"I'll do whatever it takes to make a home for you kids. I promised your mom, and I'm not breaking that promise." Wade let himself be led into the bathroom. He accepted the armload of towels and listened as Jared explained the old-fashioned shower.

"Make sure you keep that curtain in the tub or

Clarissa's place will be flooded," the boy ordered, frowning up at him as if he wasn't sure Wade understood.

"Uh-huh. Curtain inside. Got it." Wade repeated the words mindlessly, unable to hang onto any thought other than that the kids were all right.

After a long searching look at his uncle, Jared left the bathroom, apparently satisfied that Wade could manage on his own. Wade grinned at such consideration, but decided it was rather endearing coming from the boy.

He stripped off his clothes, fully conscious of how much dust he was leaving in the pretty lavender-and-white bathroom. He'd spent the sunrise hours of this morning replacing hundred-year-old attic shavings with insulation so that the owners could move in right away. Most of the dust had settled somewhere on him.

As he felt the warm sting of the water trickle over his aching body, Wade closed his eyes and searched for an answer.

Please God, what should I do now? I can't give up Kendra's kids. I just can't. I promised her.

Sometime later, Wade didn't know how long, the water grew cool, then the chill of it finally penetrated to his brain. He turned the taps off and grabbed a towel, rubbing himself fiercely to warm up.

Someone, Jared maybe, had set some clean clothes on the toilet seat. He pulled them on automatically, barely noting the newly replaced buttons and carefully stitched tears.

Then he sat down to think.

He had to do something. Figure out something. He wasn't going to lose Kendra's kids. Not now. He'd promised and, no matter what it cost, this time he was keeping his promise. He wasn't going to mess up again, social worker or no.

His eye caught sight of the silk lavender bathrobe hanging on the back of the door. Clarissa was a lavender kind of woman. Her pale skin and silver-streaked hair would look perfect in the color. A pair of slippers lay on the floor, and he imagined her padding around this old house in the morning.

He'd seen her several times when he'd risen early. She always put out birdseed first thing. Then he'd catch the hint of fresh brewed coffee and pretty soon she'd be sitting at the table by the bay window, sipping it as she watched the birds peck at their meal. It took her a long time to wake up, but eventually she'd move, and Wade would catch the aroma of frying bacon or grilling sausages.

Now that the weather was warmer, she'd begun eating outside, sharing her breakfast with whatever came along. Then she'd pull up a few weeds, water her garden, finish her coffee and undo her hair.

Wade always liked watching her brush out her hair, though he felt a bit embarrassed, like a Peeping Tom or something. But once she undid that knot on top, he couldn't tear his eyes away. He would never have believed her hair was so long, not when she wound it up on the top of her head like that. Free and cascading down her back, it flowed well past her waist in a river of sparkling silver.

A shrill childish laugh penetrated his musing and Wade got up to look out the small bathroom window. Pierce was pointing at a tree and ordering everyone to look. Seconds later Clarissa came outside, a big book in her hands. She and Pierce sat together on the grass and searched through the pages until they found what they wanted. Wade watched as Pierce leaned his head on Clarissa's shoulder, his voice barely audible on the late afternoon air.

"Am I a nerd, Clarissa?"

"Of course not! I don't know many children who could identify as many birds as you can, Pierce. Why would you think such a thing?" She sounded truly amazed by his question.

"That's what the kids call me. They say it's stupid to spend so much time on birds." Pierce shrugged. "Maybe they're right. I don't play their games very well."

As Wade watched, Clarissa hugged the little boy closer.

"Listen, sweetheart. Everybody has different interests. You like birds, and there's not one thing wrong with that. There's nothing wrong with games, either. The problem comes when we make fun of other people for their choices."

"But I don't fit in! I don't even know how to catch a ball."

Pierce's rueful tones told Wade that catching a ball was very important, and Wade chewed himself out for not spending more time with the boy.

"Then we'll have to practice. That's not such a hard thing to learn. Not like a baby bird learning to fly, for goodness sake." Clarissa's beautiful smile coaxed him to join in and a minute later Pierce called his big brother to help him practice.

"She's good," Wade muttered to himself in admiration. "She's very, very good with them."

"I got the frog, but I lost the guy." That was Lacey, glum with disappointment as she flopped down on the lawn beside Clarissa. "What is it with this biology stuff?"

"Oh? Didn't Kevin want to study with you?" Clarissa sounded amused. "He certainly rushed over here quickly when he heard about the fire."

Wade frowned. Who the dickens was Kevin? And what did the kid want with *his* niece?

"Kevin had to go home for supper." Lacey sprawled on the grass, bare feet nestling into Clarissa's skirt. "Honestly, he's so smart, I feel like a dud."

"He's not smart about everything." Clarissa fiddled with her skirt, but Wade caught the glimmer of a smile twitching at the corners of her mouth. "I happen to know that he's only recently taken to studying biology. You might ask him for help with your own work."

"You mean like spend a date dissecting a frog?" Lacey made a face. "Ugh!"

"Well, why not? You'd get to spend time together. Anyway, you're too young to date."

Wade watched as Clarissa rose lithely to her feet, her hand gently smoothing the other girl's hair.

"Think about it," she murmured. "I've got to check the kitchen. I think Tildy's forgotten something."

Wade adjusted his position and spotted the tiny funnel cloud of smoke coming out the back screen door. He groaned. "How many times is it going to take for that girl?"

When no one answered him, he realized he was talking to himself. Gathering up his dirty clothes, he headed downstairs to face the reality of his messed-up life.

"Tildy, honey, you have to set the timer. Then things won't burn, even if you do forget. The timer will remind you."

"How many cakes is that?" Tildy's tearful voice warned Wade that she'd been at it for a while. So did the acrid odor of smoldering sugar.

"It's only a bit of flour and sugar, Tildy. It doesn't matter. We'll just try again after supper. Okay?"

A huge sigh. "Okay. Thanks a lot, Clarissa. I really appreciate it."

"You're welcome, sweetie."

Wade walked in just as Clarissa hugged his niece. He stood there, studying their obvious camaraderie for a long time. It was only when she touched his arm, that he realized Clarissa had been speaking to him. He jerked to attention, pushing his thoughts away. "Sorry. What did you say?"

"I'll take the clothes and put them in the washer. You sit down. We're all ready." In a matter of seconds she had the others gathered around her worn oak table. "I'll just say grace."

Wade automatically bowed his head, listening to her few soft words of thanks.

"Now, if you could slice this roast, we'll be all ready." She handed him the carving knife and a platter with a piece of succulent beef sitting in the middle of it, juices dark and tantalizingly pooled around it.

Wade watched as she set out a heaping dish of mashed potatoes, peas, gravy, fresh rolls and a salad. His mouth watered. His stomach rumbled again, more loudly this time. The kids burst out laughing.

And suddenly, with piercing clarity, he knew exactly what he had to do. Wade set down the carving knife beside his plate, focusing his entire attention on Clarissa's face.

"I need to say something before we start."

"Yes?" Clarissa looked up from pouring Pierce a glass of milk. There was mild interest in her eyes, but nothing more. It was obvious that she had no idea of his intentions.

"Clarissa, uh…" He stopped, looked around and realized that everyone was staring at him. He couldn't do this now, not here, in front of the kids!

"Yes?" Clarissa set the milk jug down on the counter, seated herself and carefully spread her napkin in her lap. "Pass the potatoes around, please, Jared."

Wade frowned. He really should do this properly, in private, where she'd pay full attention to him, listen to all his arguments. Yeah, later.

He glanced around the table. The kids were gawking at him, their mouths hanging open in amazement as he ladled yet another spoonful of peas onto his plate.

"I didn't know you liked peas so much, Uncle Wade." Tildy almost hid the laugh that tilted up the side of her pretty mouth.

"What? Oh. Sorry. Here, Pierce, take some of these." He pushed half the plateful onto the boy's plate, opened one of the golden rolls and watched the butter he spread on it melt into a puddle of soft creamy yellow.

Yes, marriage was the only way to go now. He didn't have a choice, not if he intended to keep his promise. His wants, needs, had to come second to what was best for the kids. With Clarissa as their stepmother, no court could deny the children her tender caring. He could only hope she still wanted a family.

"Clarissa, I—" He stopped again, searching for the right way to ask her for a date. Sort of. Not a real date, of course.

"Go ahead, Wade. I'm listening." She smiled that gentle, Mona-Lisa-like smile that made his palms sweat, but her attention wasn't on him. "Use your fork please, Pierce. Tildy, would you open the window a bit more? It's quite hot in here. What did you want to say, Wade?"

When no answer was forthcoming after several minutes, Clarissa looked up. She stopped spooning out potatoes for just one moment, stared at him inquisitively, then glanced around the table at the curious faces that watched him so closely. Finally, she broke the silence, her eyes darker as they studied him.

"Go ahead, children. Eat your dinner. We've some homework to do later. Your uncle is tired. Let him relax."

Everyone else seemed to follow her lead as one by one, the kids took up the signal, dishing up her food like locusts on a field of tender green shoots. Soon the conversation was going a mile a minute. Wade decided to go with the flow. He picked up the salad and filled his bowl.

"Clarissa's house is a great place, Uncle Wade. Do you know she's got a screen porch back there? I'm gonna sit out there tonight and watch the fireflies. Some people around here call them lightning bugs. Isn't that a silly name?"

Pierce chatted away a mile a minute, and Wade let

him, content to eat while he examined Clarissa's ability to get his whole family involved in the conversation.

How did she do that? The most he got some nights was a grunt or a heap of complaints. Of course, it wasn't while they were eating food like this!

Jared looked pleased by his reasoning.

"Yeah! And we can live in this house, right, Uncle Wade? For a little while anyway." He grinned happily. "I love this old house. It's kinda like staying with an old friend. It's got some problems, but it's homey."

The words stabbed Wade with the wealth of longing he could hear beneath those words. He had no idea the boy felt that way. When had they ever hung around anywhere long enough to make old friends? Of course, he'd lost a lot. Kendra had a knack for making her house a home, probably because she'd loved her kids so much.

"I think it's a romantic house with all these crocheted curtains, and especially those frilly things over Clarissa's bed."

Lacey sighed and hugged herself in a melodramatic way that Wade knew meant she'd been reading sappy love stories again. Oh well, she'd run into reality soon enough. Why spoil the illusion of happy ever after?

"If we lived here all the time, I could take all kinds of pictures of the birds. Clarissa's got way better birds than we have, plus she's got the woods right out there. We've just got that dumb old playground, and the noise scares them away. Can I have some more meat? Please?"

The topic of the conversation said nothing, merely smiling at the children as they talked and munching on the minuscule amounts of food she placed on her own plate.

Though Wade spent a long time studying her, Clarissa did not return his look. She waited, hands folded in her lap, until everyone was finished, then gathered up the plates.

"Would anyone like some peach cobbler?" She lifted a golden delicacy from the oven. "I have some ice cream to go with it."

Wade closed his eyes and breathed. Heaven help him! Peach cobbler was his favorite dessert. And no one had ever made it better than his sister. The words brought back fond memories of their times together on the reservation when they'd had to depend on each other for companionship. They'd picked peaches one year and earned enough money to buy bikes. They'd also taken home cases and cases of the ripened peaches, until his mother had begged them to stop.

How had Clarissa found out?

Wade jerked up his head to study her, his eyes narrowed as he tried to search out some hint that she'd known about his past. But Clarissa simply stared at him with that bland smile, holding out a dish, ice cream melting on top, as she waited patiently for his response.

"Oh, I'm sorry," she murmured when he didn't take it. "Perhaps you'd rather have something else? I know some people don't care for peaches."

"I'll try it," Wade managed to say and took the dish from her hand. "Thank you."

"You're quite welcome. Coffee?"

Wade *tried* three helpings of the dessert, and by then he knew that he'd done the right thing in deciding to propose to her. A man didn't find a woman like Clarissa

Cartwright every day, not one who made peach cobbler that melted in your mouth, or one who could dissect a frog without wincing. There sure weren't many women who'd calmly take in five people, feed, shelter and care for them as if it weren't a stitch out of the usual routine.

He'd better hang on to her before somebody else beat him to the punch. After all, hadn't she been praying to get married the day he'd met her? Wade was pretty sure he wasn't an answer to prayer, but she would get her family. That ought to make a difference.

"We'll do the dishes, Clarissa. You and Uncle Wade go have coffee on the veranda," Tildy ordered. "I'm sure you have things to talk about."

Wade noticed a sparkle in her eye that hadn't been there before. Had his niece figured out what he was going to do? If she had, Wade dearly hoped she'd shut up about it until he got everything arranged.

Would Clarissa agree to his preposterous scheme?

He helped the thin, silent woman into the big woven willow chair, handed her a cup of well-creamed coffee, then took his own seat. He set down his mug and faced her.

"Clarissa?"

"Yes?" She calmly sipped her drink, her eyes on the blooming apple tree in the garden outside.

Wade felt his temperature begin to rise at her obvious disinterest in what he was saying. For the kids, he reminded himself as he licked a crumb of peach cobbler off the edge of his lip. He was doing this for the kids.

"Would you marry me?"

"Oh, I don't think so." She said it so matter-of-factly, he wasn't sure he'd heard right.

"What? Why not?" he demanded.

"Because you only want someone to look after the kids until you can get things straight with Rita. We can do that without getting married." She avoided his eyes, peering up into the sky instead. "You don't have to marry me to get my help. I've already offered a number of times. Remember?"

Wade flushed. He'd been rude with his refusal, and he'd hurt her feelings. Besides, what woman wanted to be proposed to like that? He could at least make this part of it special. He opened his mouth and then clamped it shut as she spoke.

"Don't worry about it, Wade. It will all work out. Everything will be fine. You'll see. You just have to trust God to handle these things."

He took a deep breath, hating the idea of spilling his guts, but knowing he was going to have to open up a little, let her inside. He hated that, hated feeling exposed and vulnerable to anyone. It only made it easier to see how many mistakes he'd made.

So why did he have this strange feeling that he could count on *this* woman?

"I do trust God, but I am also worried, Clarissa. I made a pact with my sister. Before she died, I promised I would take care of her kids, that I'd keep them together, raise them as my own. I vowed that I wouldn't let them get into the trouble I've had." He gulped. "So far, I'm doing a lousy job."

"I think you're doing very well." Clarissa motioned toward his house. "That was just an accident. I'm sure Rita will come to understand that. In time."

"It's an accident that shouldn't have happened. I should have done better for them. They need someone to help them through the tough parts. I wasn't thinking properly, you see. I thought giving them a home and food and a sense of security was what they needed most."

Clarissa smiled, her face thoughtful. "It's a good deal to ask of anyone," she murmured. "The children have done very well under your care."

He flushed with pleasure. "Maybe. But I have a hunch they'd do even better with you as their step-mother." He said it deliberately, wanting to shake her out of this Mona Lisa stupor she'd sunken into. When that didn't work, Wade kept talking.

"I'm not very good at listening to what they're not saying, to finding out what's bothering them. And I can't be there all the time, even though I'd like to be. But I really do want the best for them."

Clarissa nodded. "You don't have to convince me. I know that anybody who got to love those children would be very happy." She said it mildly, her fingers busy fiddling with her skirt again. It was the only sign that she was in the least bit nervous, but Wade took courage from that.

"So, will you marry me?"

She shook her head. "No. I don't think so."

Wade huffed out a sigh, half anger, half frustration. "I don't get it. You love kids, you want to be married, you're not involved with anyone else. Are you?" He frowned, then relaxed when she shook her head.

"No."

"So why not? I'm not an ogre. I do an honest job. I'm

fair with my employers and with the kids. I'm certainly not rich, but we're managing. What else is there?"

"Love."

The whispered word made him frown. "Clarissa, I've told you I like you. I think you're a very special person." He couldn't say more than that, couldn't tell her that he thought she had grit and gumption and an inner strength that he admired. It wasn't, well, romantic.

Clarissa shook her head as she smiled, her eyes avoiding his. "I'm not talking about special. *Special* is a mean-anything word." It was clear that she held little stock in the term. "I'm talking about love, Wade. The real thing that holds marriages together long after the children have left and the attraction has gone. The deep abiding commitment that two people make to each other until death does them part."

"But that's what I'm offering. At least…" Wade was beginning to wish he'd never opened his big mouth. A man shouldn't have to work this hard to convince someone to marry him!

"Uh-uh." She shook her head again and a few curling tendrils tumbled loose of her topknot. "You see me as this sad spinster woman who's shriveling up inside, don't you? And maybe I am. But I believe in the power of love to change people, to change lives." She finally met his stare, her eyes intent. "Do you?"

He nodded slowly, visualizing the kids in ten years. "I believe your love could transform those children into even better adults. And you do love them, don't you, Clarissa?" He waited, hoping she wouldn't deny what was so obviously the truth.

"Of course." She didn't even bother to pretend.

"So do I. And that's what this is all about. You and I are adults. We know the score, we know how many marriages fail even *with* love. We also know that lots of people have happy marriages without love." He took a deep breath and continued, praying for guidance through this minefield.

"I'm offering a commitment to you. I won't walk out on you or them, Clarissa. I will never walk away. I like you. I respect and admire you. And I want you to marry me."

"For the children?"

He nodded. "I won't lie. For the children. To keep them together, to give them the kind of home they won't have if they go into foster care. Because I think you care enough about them to help me keep them together."

She sat back in her chair, her eyes closed, head tilted back against the soft cushion as if she were praying. Wade sat there, studying her. Even with only her grandmother, Wade knew she'd enjoyed all the things he'd missed out on in his childhood, all the things he wanted for the kids.

"It would be good for you, too. You want a family, somebody to eat all that wonderful cooking, to share this place. Someone to laugh with and enjoy life. I know you'd be taking on an awful lot, but I believe you're the kind of woman who can do that and enjoy it." Hadn't he seen that for himself? Wade let a tiny bit of his heart unfold to her.

"This way, you'd get to mother the kids the way you would your own. You wouldn't have to work if you didn't want to. I'd provide a home for us, either here or in a new place altogether, if that's what you want."

She was watching him now, her eyes shadowed, hiding her thoughts. Wade couldn't tell if she was buying into the dream or not, so he played the only card he had left.

"Love could happen, Clarissa. Maybe someday. You're a very beautiful woman, you know. When you relax and forget to be so prim and prissy, your natural beauty shines through. That's why the kids latched on to you so quick. They're good judges of character."

If Wade was sure of one thing in his life it was that Clarissa Cartwright was decent, caring, loyal and true. She wouldn't run away or back out of a deal because of something in his past. So there was no need to tell her.

Was there?

Her huffy voice broke into his thoughts. "I am not in the least prim!"

"Yes, you are. But in the nicest way." He grinned. He was getting to her, he could tell.

Silence.

Then she spoke again.

"All right, Wade." Her voice carried to him softly, barely audible above the crickets. "I will marry you. For the children."

A wave of relief swelled, then cascaded all over him. Wade sighed his relief, stood and drew her up to stand beside him. In the dim light from the living room he could barely see into her eyes. She looked soft, vulnerable in the wash of twilight that made her round, solemn eyes seem lonely. He wanted to reassure her that she wasn't making the biggest mistake in her life taking him on.

"No, that isn't quite right." He shook his head, suddenly wanting their relationship to be more than that. "Not just for the children. For us, too. We'll make something good of this marriage, Clarissa. I promise you that."

As he tilted her chin and leaned down to touch her lips with his in a promise, Wade shoved thoughts of the past out of his mind and concentrated on the shy, timid, butterfly-woman in his arms. Her lips were soft, untried, and he touched them reverently, asking a question.

When her arms lifted to encircle his neck and her mouth molded to his, he thought he had his answer. The tiny fire of hope flickering inside his heart told him they would make this work.

Only later, when he was checking into the motel, did it dawn on him that he was doing the one thing he'd promised himself he would never do. Wade would be starting his married life with a lie. He would never allow love to blossom in his heart.

But for now, there wasn't any other way. He needed Clarissa.

Chapter Four

"Oh, I'm so glad you're here, Blair. And you, too, Briony. You've made it the perfect day." Two weeks later Clarissa hugged her dearest friends in turn, paying careful attention not to crush her wedding dress. "It's been so long since we were all together. The three musketeers—Blair Delayney, Briony Green and Clarissa Cartwright. I miss college sometimes. We could just flop on each other's bed and chat nonstop."

"Of course we're here! We wouldn't miss this for anything! If you remember, *this*—" Blair waved a hand around the bride's room at the church "—is what we chatted about." She dabbed at her tears. "You've waited a long time, honey, and Wade is a wonderful man. I know you'll both be very happy."

"You will be happy, Prissy. I can feel it right here." Briony tapped her chest, giggling as Clarissa rolled her eyes at her indignation of that old nickname. "I only get that feeling at special times and this is one of them."

"I think you get that feeling when you eat as much

pepperoni as you did last night. Try some antacids." Blair winked at Clarissa, reminding her of the impromptu shower the two college friends had held in her bedroom.

They'd given her frilly nighties made of the silkiest fabric. She'd never had anything so lovely. She hadn't wanted to tell them she was getting married because of Wade's kids. Neither had he. In fact, they hadn't told anyone the truth, not even the kids.

"It's a private matter between us," Wade had insisted. "Let them think whatever they want. I want the kids to believe we're going to be a normal family, that their world is as secure as every other kid's in this town."

She'd agreed because it made things so much easier. The problem was, even on her wedding day, Clarissa still wasn't sure what "normal" was in their case. He'd said she was pretty a lot of times. And lately his arm had taken a liking to her waist, especially if she left her hair down.

It made her breath catch when his fingers trickled through the strands and he compared it to silver in that muted growly voice. She'd learned a little about his family, too. His mother had been a silversmith. At least, she wanted to be, until her husband deserted her and she had to waitress to make ends meet.

Clarissa pushed the reminders of romantic dreams away as she felt heat rise in her face. If he hadn't said it, lately Wade's kisses had shown he found her attractive. But what did that *mean?*

This was still a marriage for the children's sake. No matter how much she wanted to pretend, Clarissa knew that romantic love had very little to do with it.

Mrs. McLeigh poked her head around the door, her

round face beaming. "Come along now, dearie. The music's just starting. You follow your friends down the aisle, and then Bertie Manslow is going to sing something or other. I forget the name of it. Then the reverend will get busy and marry you two lovebirds. All right?"

Clarissa felt a surge of panic and held out a hand. "No! Wait."

"Prissy? Honey, is anything wrong?" Briony's soft fingers covered hers.

Clarissa dredged up a smile as nerves twitched her stomach around like a little boat on gigantic waves. "No, I just need a moment to compose myself. You know, pinch myself to make sure it's real. Can I do that?" she asked Mrs. McLeigh, who'd designated herself wedding coordinator and organized the entire community into sponsoring what seemed to be the wedding of the year.

"Oh, of course you can, you sweetheart! Out you go now, ladies. Into the powder room. Let's give the bride a few moments. It won't hurt her groom to cool his heels."

Blair stayed where she was frowning, but Clarissa patted her hand reassuringly. "I just want to pray a minute," she told her, smiling away her fears. "I'm fine."

Blair's face cleared. "I'll pray too," she whispered back. "But I think God's already done His best work putting you two together."

"Thanks." But as she sat alone in that room, listening to the organ music, Clarissa closed her eyes and prayed desperately for reassurance. Was this the right thing to do? Was she making an awful mistake? She'd tried so hard to build bridges between herself and Wade, even asked his uncle to be part of the ceremony.

"Ah, there you are." Carston Featherhawk slipped inside the room after one quick knock, his mouth slashed wide in a grin. "Time to walk the beautiful bride down the aisle. Wade's a lucky man to have you take him on. 'Specially with all his trouble. I just hope he's learned his lesson. Not like last time."

"Last time?" A niggle of fear grew by leaps and bounds. Clarissa stuffed it down. "What do you mean?"

"Never talks about himself much, does he?" Carston nodded. "Can't say as I blame him. Had a pretty tough life with his dad leaving like that. Like to killed my sister to find out he'd just dumped her and the kids and walked away. But she stuck to it, got herself a job and devoted herself to Kendra and Wade. Wasn't her fault her man couldn't handle his duty to the family. Ran away, he did. Just when Mary, my sister, needed him most."

His mouth tightened, his eyes grew cold. "She killed herself caring for that boy, and what did he do? Just like his dad. Up and left her to face the music on her own when she got sick." Carston stopped, then frowned as if he'd only just realized to whom he was speaking.

"It's all right. We're going to be married. I should know this, I think." Clarissa wasn't sure that was altogether true, but it was too late to back out now. She wanted to know all about Wade, but she'd never been able to coax any of his past out of him. Was this why?

"I suppose, being as you two are about to be wed, you should know the worst." Carston nodded, scratched his chin again and then plunged into the past. "Wade was always a wild one. Hated it when the other kids made fun of him, his clothes, his race, his drawing. Learned to fight young. He'd get a rebellious streak in him and nothing could stop him from fighting. Once he busted up a house and then ran away. Mary cried herself to sleep for days, aching for him to come home. When he did, he acted as if he'd never done a thing wrong. Don't suppose he ever paid her back, either."

"Wade ran away?" Clarissa wanted to get this clear.

"Sure, lots of times. Made it a habit, you might say. Always wanted his own way, did Wade, even if it cost somebody else. He's the one who got Kendra killed, you know." He tsk-tsked at her white face. "Oh, not directly, of course. But it was his fault, all the same. He's to blame and that's the truth."

Clarissa's heart dropped to her shoes. Wade had never spoken to her of Kendra except to say that she was his sister, the kids' mother and that she was dead. Was this why? Because he felt guilty? But for what?

His uncle was saying Wade ran away from trouble. Was that what he would do at the first sign of problems in their marriage? Clarissa didn't kid herself that there wouldn't be any. All marriages had problems. Especially ones based on a lie, and she had lied when he'd asked her if she thought their friendship would carry them through.

She didn't, because she was counting on building more than a friendship with Wade Featherhawk. That's what she'd prayed for every night for the past two weeks.

"I'm just gonna get me a drink of water," Carston muttered, licking his lips. "Then we'll get this shindig on the road. I think you'll be real good for Wade. He needs a strong dependable woman to keep him on course, make him face up to reality."

After Carston left, Clarissa closed her eyes and groaned. Was that what she was? Some kind of a rudder! It was not what she wanted from her marriage.

Here I am, on what should be the happiest day of my life, and all I can think of are questions.

What if things got hard, very hard, and Wade ran away from his responsibility—her and the children? What would she do then?

"Pray," Clarissa reminded herself, wishing Carston had delved into this before today.

What should she do now? The whole town had gotten into the spirit of their wedding, donating flowers, decorating the church, sponsoring a shower and a reception, even arranging for a short honeymoon at a nearby campground.

If she didn't go through with it, she'd be a laughingstock. Again. Not only that, Wade's business would suffer. She wouldn't be able to tell them why she opted out, of course. How could she say she had doubts? They thought she was deliriously in love with him because that's what she'd wanted them to think so they wouldn't pity her! If she dumped him on their wedding day, the whole town would speculate and the awful rumors about him would surface once more. Could she do that to him? To the kids?

I've got to start this marriage with trust. I don't know what happened back then, but I know Wade now. I've seen his love and devotion to those kids. And I know he's committed to our marriage. He won't let me down.

Clarissa gathered up her bouquet, straightened her dress and pushed her shoulders back in determination. She'd wished and prayed for a husband and a family.

The answer had come. Now it was up to her to fulfill her part of the deal.

I won't be a burden, she promised silently. *Not like with Gran. I won't ever make him feel that I can't carry my own weight in this family. I'll make him see he doesn't need to feel responsible for me, to give up anything for me.*

The door burst open and Carston stood on the threshold grinning. "Ready?"

Clarissa took a deep breath, whispered one more prayer for peace, then nodded. "I'm ready," she murmured.

"Good! 'Cause those kids are like to popping their buttons outside, waiting to parade down that aisle. I don't think I've ever seen so many attendants in a wedding." He folded her arm in his and led her into the vestibule, his voice soft with pride. "Wade's a lucky fellow. Getting a second chance doesn't happen for everyone."

Clarissa ignored the shiver of worry his words ignited. She chose instead to concentrate on Tildy with Jared, then Lacey and Pierce, gliding down the aisle in the measured step Blair had shown them. Next came her closest friends, Briony and Blair, wearing their soft pink gowns.

Finally it was her turn. She glanced toward the front just once and caught sight of Wade, standing beside the pastor in a black suit that fitted him to a *T*. She saw his eyes widen in wonder at his first glance of her in her grandmother's wedding dress. It was a Ginger Rogers style gown with layers and layers of sheer white silk falling away from the tiny pearl-studded bodice. It was the one thing Gran had left behind that Clarissa didn't harbor the least bit of guilt in accepting.

Clarissa felt elegant, beautiful, desirable for the first time in her life. And it was all because of the very tall, very handsome groom who stood waiting for her with that crooked smile and that glittery look on his face. Was he as nervous as she?

Clarissa met Wade's uncertain smile with one of her own, then nodded at Carston. "I'm ready," she whispered and stepped out.

This was right. This was good.

This marriage would last. She just had to do her part.

"It was a nice wedding. They must think highly of you to have gone to so much work." Wade tugged his bow tie off and tossed it into the back seat of her car. "I intended to change before we left, but somehow I never got time."

She knew what he meant. All those last minute instructions for the kids had taken eons. But Bertie Manslow had insisted that the bride change into her going-away outfit and then toss the bouquet. Clarissa still wasn't sure how it came about that Blair caught the huge sheaf of purple-blue spring iris. Could she have been thinking about her own cancelled wedding and about the fatherless little boy who waited at home for her?

"That's quite an outfit, by the way. It's very…" he thought for a moment. "Elegant," he finally said.

"It is a little overdone, isn't it?" Clarissa fingered the red shantung jacket with its neckline of frills. "But since it was a gift and I'll only ever wear it this once, I suppose it doesn't matter."

"Oh." Wade drove on, obviously unsure of how to

continue the conversation. "Are you hungry? You didn't eat much of the mountains of food they laid out."

"I was too busy talking to everyone, I guess. It was kind of them to arrange it all." Clarissa sighed, slipping her feet out of the stiletto heels that pinched, to rub them in the soft carpet.

"I can't understand why anyone would ever *want* to go through that again." Wade shook his head in disgust, his voice telling her he certainly hadn't enjoyed it.

Clarissa felt the prick of tears and ordered herself to be sensible. "I'm sorry you didn't like our wedding," she said in a small voice.

"No! I didn't mean…aw, shucks! I've spoiled it again, haven't I." He huffed out a sigh that told her reams about his state of mind, and in particular, his opinion of this wedding. "I can't seem to say anything right today. I just meant that it was so busy. All those people, all those gifts to open! It seemed, well, overdone. Too busy. More like a public spectacle."

"I'm so sorry. *If* you wanted a more private wedding, you should have said so. They've waited a long time to see me married. I guess they wanted to do it right. Especially after Harrison." She was about to explain more about Harrison, but Wade cut her off.

"I do not want to hear another word about your first fiancé. I got an earful of him already." His voice didn't encourage her to continue. Neither did his face. It might have been chiseled from granite.

Her heart sank. Here they were, only hours married, and already they were arguing. She swallowed hard.

Don't be a burden on him, don't weigh him down with
your problems or he'll hate you for it.

"I'm sorry, Clarissa." The gruff apology barely
carried over the boisterous voice of the radio deejay.

Without asking, Clarissa reached over and shut off
the annoying sound. "It doesn't matter," she muttered,
surreptitiously brushing away a tear.

She turned her head and stared out the window, wondering how and when this day would end. Her nerves
were stretched so tight, she wanted to scream, but
grabbed a handful of red shantung instead. "It really
doesn't matter."

With a muttered epithet, Wade pulled over to the
side, out of traffic, and brought the car to an abrupt halt.

"Yes, it does matter." He shut off the engine, then
reached out a hand to press her shoulder so she would
turn around. "The only way we're going to make it
through this is to be truthful with each other. We can't
hide our feelings. Agreed?"

She nodded, but kept her eyes downcast.

"I liked the wedding. I especially liked your dress. You
looked beautiful." His right hand brushed across her hair,
fingers rubbing it between them as if it were a fine silk.

She heard the funny catch in his voice and wondered
why it was there. "It was my grandmother's wedding
dress. She always said she'd wanted my mother to wear
it, but my parents eloped. I don't think she would have
minded." Her own voice came out in a breathy whisper,
but Clarissa ignored that because her heart had just
speeded up to double time.

The fingers on his left hand closed over hers in a

squeeze, then opened and threaded through hers so their hands were interlocked. She could feel his plain gold wedding band pressing against her knuckle and automatically rubbed at her own.

"It was gorgeous...*you* were gorgeous." A tiny laugh came from low in his throat. "I guess I'm a little nervous. I've never been married before."

"Neither have I." She risked a glance up at him, and found him gazing down at her with a quizzical stare. "It was pretty rushed, wasn't it?"

He shook his head slowly, his eyes burning into her with a steady flare glowing in their depths. "No. Actually it was perfect. All of it. You did a wonderful job."

There was something in his voice, something she didn't understand. But she couldn't look away from him.

"Actually, I didn't do any of it," she babbled in a rush. "It was mostly Mrs. McLeigh...." Her voice died away, the words stuck in her throat. Nothing would come out when he kept looking at her like that.

"Clarissa?" His voice dropped to almost a whisper.

"Yes?"

"I'm going to kiss you."

Clarissa blinked. How did she answer that? "Oh."

"Do you mind?" His mouth moved nearer, his lips very close to hers, his breath, sweetly scented with the chocolate from their wedding cake mixing with the tang of the punch they'd toasted each other with.

Clarissa took a deep breath. "No," she whispered. "I don't mind." She held her breath and closed her eyes as his mouth came down and grazed across hers. "Not at all."

"Good." There was the sound of laughter in his voice. "Then would you please kiss me back?"

She looked up at that, her eyes widening as she saw the caring in his face. He wanted this day to be special for her! That knowledge eased her fears and she slid her hands around his neck, nodding as she did.

"I'll try. Though I'm not very good at kissing." Yet, she amended silently. "But I can learn."

Then Clarissa kissed him with all the pent-up emotion she'd kept so carefully in check during the many times their lips had met during the reception. This time there were no observers, and she tried to put her feelings for him into actions rather than words. If she was a little confused about exactly what those feelings were, well, he didn't need to know that.

When the kiss ended, Wade's hands dropped away from her with obvious regret.

"Is something wrong?" she whispered, aghast at her own nerve in kissing this man.

"Yes," he nodded. "Something is definitely wrong with my brain."

"P-pardon?" She straightened her jacket and pushed her hair back, conscious of the fact that he'd loosened the entire mass so badly that she couldn't possibly get it back in order without a mirror and her brush.

"I must be nuts to be sitting here on the side of the road, kissing you with the whole world watching us."

He jerked a hand toward the window and only then did Clarissa see the interested spectators craning their necks for a better look. Wade rolled his eyes, shook his head and then grinned at her ruefully.

"Shall we, Mrs. Featherhawk?" he asked, almost playfully.

"We shall." She joined in without a second thought. "Drive on, Mr. Featherhawk."

After that it was simple to stop for dinner at a small wayside restaurant, to find the campground where a cabin had been rented in their name, to drive through the overhanging boughs of spruce and cedar to a small log building nestled between two massive pines.

"It's really lovely, isn't it?" Clarissa stood on the porch and looked around at the beauty of God's world shown to best advantage in the clear moonlight and a few strategically placed lights. "How kind of them to do this for us."

She gasped when his hands caught her up against his chest, barely managing to stifle the shriek that would have alerted the other campers, wherever they were, to their presence.

"What are you doing?" she whispered loudly as he struggled to reach the doorknob. She leaned down and unlatched it with her free hand. The other one refused to move from its anchoring position against his neck.

"Carrying you over the threshold. Isn't that what you were waiting for?"

"No!" Clarissa gasped as he lowered her to her feet, her face burning with color. "I never even thought of such a thing."

"Well, I want to keep up with tradition," he mumbled, his face darkening. "Isn't that what all the hoopla was about earlier?" Then he turned and went back out the door.

Clarissa blinked and tried to pretend that she didn't wonder if he was coming back. But her sigh of relief when he staggered in the door with their cases gave her away, if he'd been paying attention.

Which he wasn't. In fact, as he closed the door on the cabin and surveyed the rustic interior, Wade tried to convince himself that he hadn't noticed anything about his new wife at all. That project was not a success.

The gold band on her finger gleamed as if she'd spent the ride here polishing it. Her hair, loose and flowing down her back, just begged to be brushed until it once more resembled the sheet of burnished silver-gold that he'd glimpsed so many mornings. And that suit of hers—that blazing red drew attention like a fire engine.

Wade didn't like what he was feeling. None of it. He wasn't a family kind of guy. Deep down the stark truth was that Wade didn't believe in families. He sure as shootin' didn't believe in his ability to manage one. He'd only done it out of necessity.

Maybe he should have told her that? Yeah, right. Before or after he kissed her?

"Is anything wrong, Wade?" Clarissa studied him with a tiny frown that pleated the porcelain skin between her elegant brows. "Is something the matter?"

"No. Yes. Uh…" Wade shook his head in disgust, trying to come up with a way to tell her. "That is, maybe you'd better sit down, Clarissa. There's something we need to discuss."

"All right." Her voice was quiet, almost frightened. As if she expected the worst and needed to steel herself for it. She sat down across from him in the overstuffed recliner that almost swallowed her delicate body whole. Her hands settled primly in her lap, her chin tilted upward to receive the blow. "Go ahead."

"It's not anything bad," he muttered, mentally kicking himself for spoiling the ambience. She deserved better. He forged on. "It's just that I wanted us to understand one another right off."

"You don't have to tell me, you know. I am quite aware that this is what is called a marriage of convenience. And I'm quite willing to take the sofa." She forced a timid smile to her lips, obviously striving to pretend that the little quaver in her voice wasn't there.

"It's not just that." He flopped onto that sofa, squeezed his eyes closed and desperately searched for the right words. They weren't there. "I'm not a family man, Clarissa. I'm too selfish, I guess. I spent a lot of time watching my parents' marriage fail, and while it did I was responsible for my sister. I didn't want her to see the ugliness when they were fighting, to hear the awful words."

Clarissa nodded as she listened. "That's perfectly natural," she murmured, her head tilted to one side. "As a big brother, you must have been a wonderful friend."

He shook his head. "Not really. I made her play the games I wanted to. She had to fall in with my wishes, because I was in charge. But that's not it." He chewed his lip in frustration. Why was this so hard to say? Wade thought for a moment, then started again.

"I hated the responsibility of it, you see. I wanted *them* to look after her, to make sure she was okay. There were so many things I wanted to do and she got in the way." He shook his head. "I messed up so many times. Once I made her eat some berries and she was sick for a week." One hand raked through his hair as he remembered her thin body shaking with the fever. "Anyway, my dad left. Uncle Carston probably told you that?"

She nodded.

"It was pretty rough then. I was the man of the house, but I did a lousy job of looking after my mom and Kendra. I couldn't wait to dump them onto somebody else so I could go after my own dreams." He stopped abruptly when he realized where this was going. No way was he digging into that now. He straightened his shoulders, drew in another breath and continued.

"Let's just say it wasn't any paradise. After Kendra got married, I finally felt free. I made up my mind then and there that I would never be tied down to anyone again. I never wanted the responsibility of someone else's happiness." He tried to read her. "Do you understand what I'm saying?"

"Yes, of course." Clarissa nodded, her eyes clear and calm. "You don't want to be accountable for my problems. You took the children on because you promised your sister, and you've done the best you could with them because you figured it was your duty. But it's not the life you would have chosen for yourself. Close enough?"

She didn't get it, not all of it anyway. But she was pretty close. Wade nodded slowly, rephrasing his thoughts. "Well, yes, but…"

She held up a hand. "Oh, I'm not finished yet. I'm not stupid, you know. I understand exactly what you're saying, Wade Featherhawk. You think I'll add to your responsibilities, that I'll be even more of a burden on you. And you're scared stiff. Is that about right?"

Wade gulped. Meek and mild little Clarissa Cartwright, no Featherhawk, had a lot more on the ball than he'd given her credit for. Now she'd made him feel like a jerk, which he probably was, for wanting to live his life without thinking about anyone else.

"Not scared, no." He couldn't let that go. "It's just an awful lot for me to handle at one time, Clarissa. Four kids! Nobody has *four* kids in this two-point-five-family world. If they do, they get them one at a time!" He groaned at the selfish words that poured out of his own mouth.

I sound like a wimp. Wade shoved his head into his hands and dragged at the roots, trying to realign his topsy-turvy world.

"I love them, Clarissa. I do! But it's hard to go from being independent to being a father of four, and then a husband. It's gonna take me some time to adjust, that's all I'm saying." That sounded better, didn't it? As if he just had a few issues to work through and then life would be rosy.

If it wasn't the way he felt, she didn't need to know that. After all, Clarissa was taking them all on and she wasn't even related! She was going to have to adjust far more than he.

"What I'm trying to say is, don't get too upset if I'm not very good at this. I'll probably need a lot of practice before I come anywhere near being the kind of husband you deserve."

She laughed at him! Wade could hardly believe that

light, tinkling sound that shattered the tension in the room like a high note splintering a crystal goblet. He stared, frowning at the smile curling her lips.

"It goes both ways, Wade. I've never been a mother or a wife and now I've got to get used to all of you at once. At least you had months to train." She got up and walked over to sit beside him. Her hand patted his. "I promise I won't expect too much of you," she said quietly. "We'll learn as we go along. But please, don't feel you have to be responsible for me. I'm an adult. I can look after myself. I can look after you and the kids too, if you'll let me."

Relief, pure, unadulterated relief washed over him. He didn't have to be some kind of Superman or Romeo for her. She knew and understood. God had worked a miracle in this woman.

Wade leaned down and brushed his lips across her cheek. "Thank you," he whispered with heartfelt emotion. "Thanks for understanding."

She nodded, then got up and moved toward the other rooms. "Let's have a look around, shall we? Then I wouldn't mind going for a walk. I need to breathe fresh air."

Wade managed to maintain her light-hearted approach to life for the rest of the evening. He made fishing jokes, teased her about leeches in the lake, insisted she take the bedroom and he the couch.

But late that night as he lay staring through the patio doors at the big moon outside, he wondered if he should have told her all of it. Maybe he should have made sure she knew that he would never love her.

Maybe Clarissa should know he couldn't afford to love anyone. Not anymore. Everyone he loved died because he was too selfish to care for them when they needed him. Their pain was always his fault. It was also his secret.

Chapter Five

On her very first morning of being Mrs. Clarissa Featherhawk, the bride decided to set the tone of her marriage as she meant to carry it on.

She wanted to know Wade better, certainly. She craved the personal details that all couples learned after months of courtship. But she didn't have that basis of information to rely on because Wade seemed to think he had to protect himself. Or perhaps he wanted to protect her. She wasn't sure. Her only hope lay in calming his fears, showing him that she intended to be an equal partner, that she had no intention of dragging him down.

Which was why, tired as she was from the busy day before, she managed to drag herself out of bed as the first threads of sunlight drifted across the sky. By the time she noticed Wade stirring from his uncomfortable position on the sofa, Clarissa had cinnamon buns ready to emerge from the oven and coffee, freshly brewed in a big mug on the table beside his makeshift bed.

"It can't be morning yet," he grumbled, his tousled

head emerging just above the back of the sofa. "I've only had my eyes closed for ten minutes."

"Rough night?" she murmured, turning away to hide a smile when she saw him force his eyes apart. "There's a cup of coffee by your elbow. Maybe that will help."

"Maybe," Wade muttered doubtfully, but he downed a mouthful just the same. "What are you doing?"

She turned to find him frowning at her, one eyebrow quirked upward in a question. Her cheeks grew warm under his steady regard.

"I was just making some buns, before the day got too warm. This year has been a strange one, hasn't it? You never know if you're going to fry or freeze." He was still staring at her. "Anyway, I thought it would be a good idea to do this before the cabin heated up too much. I've got our dinner started in that Crock-Pot."

"Dinner?" He blinked twice, took a gulp of coffee, then winced as it burned down his throat. "I didn't realize you were so industrious."

Clarissa wanted to pinch herself. How stupid of her! Of course. He wanted to sleep in and she'd disturbed him.

"I'm sorry," she muttered, transferring one of the buns to a small plate. She kept her eyes averted. "I'll just pour myself some coffee and go outside. I didn't mean to disturb your rest. Go back to sleep if you want. I'll sit in the sun and read."

He muttered something in that low husky rumble of his, but Clarissa didn't hang around and listen to what it was. She scurried out the door like a frightened mouse and carried her breakfast to the edge of the lake where earlier that morning she'd set out two of the chairs from the veranda.

"So much for romantic dreams," she scolded herself. "Just get on with your life and quit expecting it to change. It's a marriage of convenience, girl. Not a love match."

She'd known that, of course. But still the foolish dreams had filled her mind last night. Those teasing "maybe" dreams. Maybe one day, maybe if they got to know each other, maybe somehow she could be a real wife, a real mother.

The sun rose slowly, its warmth spreading like fingers across the tree strewn landscape, rippling over the lake on butterfly wings. Birds drenched the air with their song. The put-put of a motorboat echoed the presence of a fisherman out early to cast a line.

Clarissa closed her eyes, tipping her head up to let the sunshine chase away the doubts. "Lord, I thank You for this wonderful creation. And for Wade. I know Your hand was in this marriage. 'All things work together for good.'" She stopped a moment to wonder what life would be like in another five years. The murmuring sounds of other campers drew her back to the present, and she hurried on with her prayer.

"I want to do my part, to be all that You want me to be. But I don't know what to expect, what Wade expects. Please give me patience and strength to wait on You." She opened her eyes, her attention riveted on the man who'd just stepped outside their cabin door. She'd have to hurry.

"And God, if You could make him care about me, just a little bit, it would make this marriage so much easier." She breathed a sigh of relief. "Thank you, God. Amen."

Wade flopped down in the chair beside hers, his bare arm brushing against her hand where it held her coffee mug out of harm's way. "This place is like an isolated piece of solitude in a messed-up world," he told her, his eyes on the trees sparkling in the bright sunlight, their reflection shimmering in the smooth lake water. "In a way, I guess it reminds me of the reservation, though there wasn't much solitude there. In fact, when I lived there, I felt as if nobody else knew I existed."

Clarissa saw through the undertones to the pain he tried to mask. "Abandoned, you mean?" she murmured softly, keeping her gaze on the water. "I know what that's like. When my parents died and I went to Gran's, it was as if the life I'd known died. Gran was wonderful, of course," she rushed to assure him. "But she was older, and she'd just lost her only child. I didn't want to impose."

She could feel Wade's eyes on her. "It must have been tough."

Clarissa nodded. "It was. Maybe that's why I can empathize with your kids. In one split second, everything you've ever known is changed and you can't ever go back." She took a deep breath, crossed her fingers, then plunged in to something she had no business questioning. If she was going to learn more about Wade, this was the time.

"You must have felt that way when Kendra died and you had to take over for her. Your plans, dreams, hopes for the future. They all had to be put on hold, didn't they?" She hoped he'd tell her what those hopes and dreams were. She hadn't expected his mocking chuckle.

"Snooping, Clarissa?" He caught her chin and forced her to meet his glinting stare.

Clarissa knew he could see the round spots of embarrassed color that burned in her cheeks but she didn't back down.

"Yes, maybe just a little. I'm hoping I can learn to understand you and the kids a little better, get to know what your lives were like then." She refused to look away. "Is that wrong?"

He stared at her for a long time before his hand fell away from her jaw and he sighed, a deep huff that told her he would give just so far and no further.

"No, it isn't wrong. It's normal, I suppose. What do you want to know?"

Clarissa groaned inwardly. This wasn't what she wanted. She wanted him to open up of his own accord, to share a piece of himself because he could trust her. Maybe it was too early for that.

Please help me, Lord.

"I want to know anything you want to tell me," she murmured, wishing she could smooth away the lines of tension around his eyes. "What were you like as a little boy?"

Clarissa settled back in the chair and drew her knees up to her chest, smoothing her skirt over her legs to hide from the prickles the sun was already making against her skin. Thank goodness she'd thought to tug on the old straw hat she'd found. That along with her long-sleeved shirt should give some protection. She didn't want to go home looking like a boiled lobster!

She turned to nod at Wade. "I'm listening."

He shook his head wryly. "Don't give up easily, do you?" His eyes darkened, then glassed over as if he'd gone far away, to a place where she couldn't go. "What was I like? I was a brat, Clarissa. Disobedient, willful, argumentative. All the things you were probably instructed not to do—" he raised one eyebrow, then continued when she nodded her understanding "—I did them. All of them. There wasn't a younger kid I didn't terrorize, a teacher I didn't sass back, a rule I didn't break."

"Problem child," she murmured, more to herself than to him. But he heard it and nodded, his face drawn.

"Worse." He summed it up succinctly. "I'm sure you can't possibly understand."

Her lips smiled, but inside her heart ached. "Can't I?" She remembered the times she'd cried herself to sleep, begging God to bring her parents back so they could be a family again, promising anything if He'd just stop punishing her.

Wade frowned as he watched her, his eyes inquisitive. "You couldn't. You've had the perfect life."

"Have I?" She pleated the fabric between her fingers, noting the glossy pink polish that Bri had applied just yesterday morning was now chipped. Sort of like her dream of blissful married life. Clarissa decided it was too ironic to dwell on. "Don't get sidetracked so easily by what you see, Wade. Truth is sometimes hard to find."

He inclined his head. "I guess. Anyway, it got worse when the fighting got worse. My parents couldn't agree on what side to butter the bread. They sure couldn't compromise on raising Kendra and me. Dad got fed up and pretty soon I figured out that if you were out of sight, you were out of mind. I made it a point to be out of his sight as much as possible."

The wealth of understatement in those words drew tears to Clarissa's eyes. She wanted to say so many things, to comfort Wade, tell him she understood. But more than anything, she wanted him to continue talking. She made herself be satisfied with touching his arm as she whispered, "I'm sorry."

He didn't turn her way, but his head jerked in acknowledgment.

"My mother, bless her, never gave up on me even though I disappointed her so many times. She wanted me to have all the things she'd missed and to her, that meant living on the reservation, learning about my heritage." He grimaced. "All I could see was that being an Indian and loving a white man had made her life a misery. She didn't fit into his world, and he sure didn't fit into hers. I fit into neither. I was determined to get as far away from there as I could, to find something better."

"So that's when you ran away?" Clarissa laid her head on the back of her chair, her fingers light on the bunch of muscles that clenched and unclenched as he spoke.

"Yes, I ran *away,* but I thought I was running *to* something. I just couldn't figure out how to find it. When I was seventeen, I finally ran far enough that I ran into someone who showed me there was more to life, if I was willing to take it. His name was Ralph Peterson and he was an artist, a good one. He picked me up when I was hitchhiking, took me in and kind of adopted me for the two weeks I was gone. He showed me the places he'd sketched, real and dreams, places he could draw on a piece of paper. Places so wonderful they took your mind off your problems. He had a house full of pictures—buildings and places around the world. I was hooked on those cathedrals, castles, temples."

"So you decided to become an artist?"

"Not really. I just got more and more curious about the process of how you got a building from a picture. When the police brought me home, I spent every spare moment I could find at the library. I read about Frank Lloyd Wright, I studied the styles and I started to sketch." He made a face. "You can imagine how that went over—a macho male sitting around drawing! I got into a few fights over it."

"I'd like to see your drawings sometime," she whispered, aching for the almost-man who'd searched so hard to find himself. "You have a real talent with building things, so I'm sure that's where it came from."

"Thank you." He paused a moment as if reflecting, then his face hardened. "I was awful to Kendra. I was so focused on what I wanted, what I had to have, that I couldn't see that she was upset by the parents, too. She needed someone to talk to, but I wasn't there for her."

"Wade, your parents had that responsibility. Not you. You were a child. You should have had the freedom to dream."

He shook his head, his mouth tightening into a bitter line. "She was my sister and I was so selfish I wouldn't even let her use my stuff." He puffed out a scornful half laugh. "I'd decided, you see, that I was going to make myself into somebody the world had to notice, that people were going to sit up and pay attention to Wade Featherhawk. I was too good for the reservation, too smart for my mother's plans and too old to bother with

Kendra. As soon as I could, I took off and got a job, con-
struction. I learned as I went how to do a good job.
Kendra and Mom seemed okay then and I'd work away
summers. Then Mom died."

Clarissa nodded. She knew this part. "And you had
Kendra."

"Yeah, I had Kendra. There wasn't anybody else.
My dad had disappeared and the folks who wanted her
were bad news. It was up to me, and I hated being the
one dumped on." He swallowed, his voice choked but
insistent. "You had to know Kendra to understand how
loving she was. It tears at me even now when the kids
look at me in a special way and I see her. She didn't care
if I was rich or famous or not. She loved me. All the
time. No matter what."

"I guess that's what sisters do." Clarissa let the
silence stretch between them as he remembered his
sister's joy.

"She was such a happy kid. Always chattering a mile
a minute. I loved her so much. But I didn't dare take her
with me to the sites. We lived in bunkhouses a lot of the
time. She was young and gorgeous, and the men I
worked with weren't the type for her to be around."

Clarissa could tell from the hard chiseled lines his face
had fallen into just what kind of men he'd worked with
and was fiercely proud of the way he'd protected his sister.

"I tried to take care of her as best I could, but I had
to leave and find work whenever we ran out of money.
She'd stay with some friends." His voice dropped to a
whisper. "She'd throw her arms around me when I got
back and hug so hard my ribs ached."

"She loved you." Clarissa felt the sting of tears for that young girl burn in her chest.

Wade looked up. "Actually, you remind me of her sometimes. She wouldn't take no for an answer, either. She was soft but so stubborn." His eyes glinted reproof.

Clarissa grinned. "You have to stand up for something or you'll fall for anything," she teased.

He nodded slowly. "She should have stood up to me," he muttered.

Clarissa wanted to ask why but he began speaking again.

"The building industry went into a slump right after I finished high school, and I couldn't find work. I didn't know what to do. I only had sixty-five dollars when I came home. I was scared stiff to tell her I'd have to leave again so soon. And I was fed up with grubbing along, just barely managing." His fingers fisted until the knuckles grew white.

As Clarissa watched, he slowly straightened each finger, his jaw hard with the discipline of stifling his frustration. "She was so young and so innocent, I couldn't imagine her leaving the reservation, getting a job. Then I had a better idea. Why didn't she marry Roy? He'd been chasing her for years, she'd be eighteen in a couple of weeks. Everything would be wonderful." He smiled but there was no joy in his face. "Or that's what I thought."

"It wasn't?" Clarissa couldn't stop herself from reaching out and feathering a hand through his hair, brushing it back, her fingers soothing against his scalp. "It sounds reasonable."

Wade shook his head, leaning back so her hand fell away. *It's as if he can't bear to accept kindness,* she decided. *As if he has to lash himself over and over with his faults.*

"It was grasping at straws and I latched on to that one for all I was worth, eager to get rid of my burden. That's what I thought of her. My own sister was a burden I had to get rid of."

The recrimination and self-loathing she saw in his eyes tugged at Clarissa's soft heart.

"I could hardly wait to be free of my own sister. Isn't that sick? I had all these dreams of what I was going to do if I could just be on my own. I'd begun to earn my high school credits. I knew the college I wanted. Big man on campus, that's who I wanted to be!"

"There's nothing wrong with that, Wade. You were just trying to plan ahead."

"Yeah. That's what I told myself, too. I had to dump her on the first guy she liked for her own best interests. Because I couldn't be bothered hanging around that reservation. *I* had to be free to find my dreams."

There was nothing she could say. Nothing that would obliterate the sorrow he carried inside. All she could do was help him understand that God still loved him, as He loved them all in spite of their shortcomings. She whispered a prayer for guidance, then concentrated on Wade's next words.

"I should have checked him out more, come home more often, paid attention to her letters. When she finally got hold of me in California, her life was a mess. Her marriage was on the rocks and her husband was dumping her and the kids, just like good old Dad." He shoved his head into his hands, his fingers tugging on the glossy strands of black.

"But did I get her out of there, even then? No! All I could see were my selfish plans going down the tubes, my life getting put on hold, my dreams unfulfilled." He kept his head bowed, his face averted. "I hurried home to talk her into trying to make it work, just a little longer. Just until I got what I wanted. That way, I could avoid my responsibility to take care of my sister. It was the one thing my mother made me promise I'd do and I failed her. Again."

Wade's face was carved into hard lines when he finally shifted in his chair, his bitter gaze pinning Clarissa where she sat.

"Kendra died in that car accident because I sent her there. She didn't want to go with Roy, he'd been drinking. But I persuaded her that she could make it work if she just persisted. It's my fault those kids have no father or mother." His eyes shone like polished iron, his mouth tight.

"So you tell me, Clarissa. Am I the kind of person you want to be married to, the kind of man you want making decisions about your future?"

He lunged to his feet, his eyes blazing. "Don't bother to answer. I know you only wanted to help the kids. So do I. You probably think they'd be better off without me messing up time and time again. You probably wish I'd take off for good and leave them in your capable hands."

His voice dropped to a whisper as he turned away.

"And I would. God knows I'd leave in a minute if I

could. But I promised her I'd raise them. It's the last promise I ever made to her and I can't break it. I just can't."

Clarissa sat stunned and immobilized by the heart-rending grief that shredded his voice. She wanted to reach out, to assure him that he was doing the right thing.

But was he? Were they?

She watched him walk around the lake, a lonely solitary figure lost in a brooding silence that clearly stated *Keep out*. When he disappeared into a stand of towering blue spruce, Clarissa let the tears roll down her cheeks.

"Oh, God," she whispered, "what have I done? How can I help this hurting family?"

Though she sat there for an hour, the answer evaded her. Eventually she got up, picked up her and Wade's empty mugs and returned to the cabin. She cleaned it, made some sandwiches for lunch and set a fresh jug of iced tea in the fridge. But Wade did not return.

As she lay at the side of the lake later that afternoon, Clarissa forced away the thought that Wade had run away, left her behind. Not this time, she told herself. He's committed this time. And I intend to see that he doesn't feel chained down. I'll go on with my life as usual and he'll realize that I've accepted him for exactly who and what he is. He won't have to fulfill my expectations because I won't have any.

She pulled off her cover-up and stretched out on the towel, allowing the hot sun to touch her sun-screened skin.

"'They that wait upon the Lord,'" she reminded herself. "Your timing is best."

* * *

"You're going to burn if you stay out here much longer." Wade's soft voice broke through her dream, the words tentative. "Maybe you should cover up?"

"I think I'll try the water first." Clarissa sat up, surprised to see him clad in his swimsuit, a towel looped over one arm. "Are you going in?"

He nodded. "I love swimming. The colder the better. We used to have an old swimming hole…." His voice trailed away. "Never mind."

Clarissa let it go. "Well, I'll try," she mumbled doubtfully, accepting his outstretched hand as she got to her feet. "But if it's cold, I'm outta here."

He tilted up one arrogant eyebrow. "I never thought I'd see the day when Clarissa Cartwright would back down from a challenge," he teased.

"Featherhawk," she reminded him. "And I'm not backing down. I'll go in. And then I'll get out."

He rolled his eyes when she tentatively toe-touched the clear water lapping against the white of the beach. "Uh-huh. Chicken. That's what I said."

Clarissa could feel the tension in him, knew he was trying to lighten things between them. Very well. She would help him. She untied her beach jacket and tossed it to the sand, then dashed into the water.

"Last one in is the biggest chicken," she bellowed, then gurgled as she stepped off a ledge and the icy water closed around her sun-heated body and filled her gasping mouth. "Oh!"

"You live on the edge, don't you?" Wade's big hand wrapped itself around her arm and tugged her toward shore. "You don't have to prove to me that you're brave, Clarissa. I'm the guy you married, the fellow whose four crazy kids you took on. Remember?"

"I remember." She hugged herself tightly, arms wrapped around her middle to conserve what little warmth still pulsed through her body. "Since you already know how brave I am and that I'm not a chicken, c-c-can I get out n-now?"

Wade threw back his head as he roared with amusement at her chattering teeth and shaking lips. Gently he led her out of the water, wrapped her beach coat around her and wrapped his own towel around her dripping head.

"You don't back down, do you, lady?" he said, admiration lacing his voice.

Clarissa gathered her stuff into her bag and headed toward the cabin, fully aware that Wade was right beside her. "Feel the fear and do it anyway," she mumbled. "That's my motto."

They walked toward the cabin and up the steps. At the top, Wade reached out a hand and stopped her. His eyes held a quizzical look that she couldn't quite decipher.

"Sometimes fear is a good thing, Clarissa. It makes us stay away from situations where we can get badly hurt." His dark eyes bored into hers.

She held his gaze. "And sometimes hurt teaches us things we wouldn't have learned if we hadn't stepped out in faith, believing that God is always in control. 'If God is for us, who can be against us?'" she quoted softly.

His hand dropped away, his face a study in conflicting emotions.

"I'm going to change," she told him finally.

He nodded, wet hair drooping into his eyes. He slicked it back, his eyes on her. "In that bag of tricks, have you hidden the ability to cut hair?"

She winked. "I can cut it." She shrugged. "It might end up a little shorter than you like, but I can cut it."

He nodded. "That's what it's all about, isn't it? Trying." He opened the door. "After you, Mrs. Featherhawk."

She curtsied. "Thank you, Mr. Featherhawk."

As beginnings went, it was a start. A good start.

Chapter Six

As honeymoons went, Clarissa didn't think it ranked among the most romantic, but she'd enjoyed it more than she'd believed possible three days ago. They spent their time hiking around the lake, sunbathing, dipping their toes in the frigid water and talking.

She knew he liked beef, didn't like three-piece suits and was a master at both sketching quirky little pictures and avoiding talking about himself. She told him about her grandmother's dutiful raising of her, the freedom she'd found at college with Briony and Blair, and her friendship with half the town.

They'd figured out an accounting system for household needs. Wade argued that the children were left enough money for their needs, though he admitted that he'd tried to hoard it for the college educations their mother had wanted.

Wade refused to allow Clarissa to chip in more than a minuscule amount to the budget, insisting that he would cover the improvements they made to her house.

He was her husband, he would also be her provider. She didn't like that, but he ignored her argument and she'd eventually given in to prevent further debate. Which didn't mean she wasn't going to let him pay for everything. After all, she had some pride!

He held her hand when they sat by the campfire at night, even kissed her again. And she kissed him back. But those occasions were few and far between. On the whole, they'd spent their time as good friends might, which was rather a nice way to begin.

In fact, by the time they were sharing the return drive to Waseka, Clarissa felt quite comfortable in this new relationship. Sure, she wished for more. Who didn't? But every night she reminded herself that God had given her far more than she'd ever dreamed of. It was up to her to be happy with that.

"Have you got anything special lined up for this week?" he asked, turning off the highway onto the narrower road that led into town.

"No. I thought it would be enough to get used to everyone for the first little while. Anyway, the kids will be finished school soon and there will be all kinds of outings before that." She had a list of them in her purse. Picnics, trips to the local forestry farm, the usual end-of-year school field trips.

"I thought it might be nice for them to go to summer camp, even if it's only for a few nights. What do you think?" She waited, anticipating his negative response.

"Summer camp?" He frowned. "Isn't that kind of expensive?"

"Not the church camp, no. They have scholarships if

you need them. Or the kids can earn a deduction on their fees if they bring someone." She whispered a little prayer for help before listing the benefits. "I thought going might get them to interact with other kids a bit. It's kind of the norm around here and they need to start settling in, feeling secure in their place here."

He shrugged, lips pinched tight. "I guess. I was sort of hoping to take them camping myself. I promised them a long time ago that I would, but I've never done it. Kendra probably could have used the break."

She heard the self-condemnation in his tone and ignored it.

"Family camping! What a good idea. We could go back to the lake." She fell into a daydream of the six of them splashing in the water, building a campfire at night, forming the bonds that made a family secure. And one day, maybe, just maybe...

"We're home. Oh, boy!"

Clarissa jerked back to reality at the amusement in his voice. She stared at the huge banner that decorated the front gate. *Welcome home Mr. and Mrs. Featherhawk.*

"I'm afraid that's probably due to Blair," she told him with a sigh. "She always loved plastering signs all over our room at college."

"I wonder what else she's encouraged. It was nice of her to stay with them, though." Wade helped her out of the car, then followed behind her with their suitcases, his voice filled with amusement. "She really steps in and takes over, doesn't she?" He motioned toward the newly enlarged flower bed.

I've got to make sure he doesn't feel overwhelmed by

all of this. Clarissa made a mental note to have supper on the table when he came home at night. The house would be spotless, the children organized. Wade would only see the benefits of having married her. She would make sure he didn't feel hemmed in or burdened with his wife. Far from being a responsibility, she intended to become an asset he couldn't lose.

"They're here!" The shriek of joy came from Pierce. Seconds later the door flew open and all four of the children bounded outside and down the stairs. "Welcome home."

"My, what a welcoming committee! You all look like you've grown six inches." Clarissa hugged each of them in turn, marveling at this family she'd been gifted with. "You've done wonders, Blair! You'll probably need a month-long rest."

"No way! I know all about the demands of motherhood. Remember?" Blair winked, reminding Clarissa of her young son who'd stayed at home. She hugged her close, then leaned back to survey her friend of ten years. "Is that a tan you've started, Prissy?"

Clarissa blushed. "If it isn't, it's not for want of trying."

"Well, good for you. You look great. Marriage agrees with you. Both of you." She made no bones about hugging Wade, too, then ushered everyone inside. "Come on, supper's ready. And then I've got a flight to catch. Daniel wants his mommy back."

They giggled and laughed all through the meal. It wasn't until Wade left to drive Blair to the airport that disaster struck unannounced.

"Come and see, Clarissa. We've fixed your room up."

She smiled and followed them up the stairs, only to stop, aghast, at the entrance to her bedroom. The room was the same, yet it was totally different. Her little vanity desk still sat there, but next to it, the chiffonier had been cleared of its photos and a host of male paraphernalia lay on its polished surface. Her closet had been altered to accommodate Wade's jeans, chambray shirts and one good suit. In the adjoining bathroom, his electric razor lay beside the collection of perfume bottles she'd assembled from her grandmother's stash.

"He's going to need that razor." Jared chuckled from his position on the edge of her canopy bed. "He didn't shave the whole time, did he?"

"No." Clarissa didn't know what else to say. It was obvious that they expected her and Wade to inhabit this room together. And why not? Didn't most couples sleep in the same bed, in the same room? How could she tell them otherwise without opening a new can of worms?

Better to let Wade deal with it when he returned.

"What is that heavenly fragrance? Don't tell me the lilacs finally opened?" She whirled around searching, then stopped as she spotted her grandmother's crystal vase filled to capacity with a mass of the tiny deep-purple blooms. "Thank you, children! This is just lovely."

She hugged each of them again, taking care not to muss Tildy's new, rather precarious hairdo. Only Blair could have sprayed that much goop on it and left someone else to get it out.

"We thought we could watch a video together. You know, kind of our first night together?" A flicker of doubt washed through Lacey's young eyes. "Or maybe you'd rather not."

Clarissa instantly changed her mind about shooing everyone off to bed. Sure, they needed an early start for church in the morning. But they needed time with her and Wade more. They needed time to assimilate the new family that they were now part of.

So did she. Lots of time before she climbed these stairs and shared her most personal space with the man she'd married such a short time before. She grabbed on to the diversion like a lifeline. "That's a lovely idea! What's the movie?"

They trooped down together, each child vying for the important part of telling her some tidbit about the show. Clarissa laughed.

"Sounds to me like you've already seen this. Why do you want to see it again? And why don't we wait for Wade?"

They fell over each other trying to explain how long he'd be and how great it was and, rather than crush their joy, she joined in with the fun.

"All right, all right! We'll watch it. How about some popcorn to go with those sodas?"

By the time Wade returned, they were settled in and Clarissa had tears rolling down her cheeks at the plight of the little boy on the screen.

At the kids' urging, her husband flopped down on the sofa beside her, flicking away a tear from her sad face. "Really enjoying this, are you?" he teased.

She nodded, smiling at him through the mist. "It's a wonderful show," she sobbed.

"Shh!" The kids' eyes were riveted to the screen.

Wade shook his head, took the can of soda she held out, and grabbed a handful of popcorn. "I'd hate to see it when you *really* like a movie." He winked, then focused on the movie.

Caught up in the plot, Clarissa thrust the bedroom issue to the back of her mind. She'd tell him about it later, she decided. After the movie. When the kids had gone to bed.

They were all weeping by the time the credits rolled.

"Man, it's good to be home. Nothing but happy faces to greet me." Wade surveyed the mass of soggy tissues Lacey clutched in each hand and sniffed in sympathy.

But Clarissa knew he wasn't unaffected by the trauma the family had suffered, or by the happy ending when everyone had been reunited.

"Oh, stuff it!" She pretended to tap him on the shoulder, then turned to the kids. "It's pretty late. I think you'd better get to bed."

They put up no arguments, merely bid her and Wade good-night, kissed each of them and trundled up to the rooms they'd taken over after the fire. There was some good-natured squabbling, of course, but nothing serious.

Clarissa had just breathed a sigh of relief that they'd left her in private to explain the bedroom situation when Pierce came rushing back downstairs.

"I hope you like the room, Uncle Wade." A huge grin split his face. "Evan North told me you're supposed to put cornflakes in the bed after people get married but I didn't do it. There wouldn't have been enough for breakfast."

Wade's lower jaw was approaching his chest, so

Clarissa stepped in. "That was very kind of you, Pierce. It would be pretty hard to start a morning without corn-flakes, wouldn't it?" She smiled and patted his back, knowing how much the boy treasured his favorite cereal. "If you don't mind, I think I'd like to show Wade your handiwork. Is that all right?"

"Sure. 'Cause you're married now, right?" His big eyes moved from one to the other of them with something like satisfaction glowing in their depths.

"That's right. Good night." She ruffled his hair, hugged him again, and gave him a little push toward the steps.

"Yeah. Okay. Night." He stopped for one last look, grinned, then raced up the stairs.

"Bedroom?" Wade peered down at her curiously. "What's that all about?"

She pulled him into the kitchen and let the door swing closed. After checking to be sure no one had come back down the stairs, Clarissa cleared her throat and launched into an explanation.

"They thought it was the thing to do, I guess. And actually," she hesitated, then blurted out, "they were right. I don't have another empty bedroom. Not since you made one into an office anyway."

He stared at her for a long time, his eyes dark. She knew he was trying to come up with an excuse, a way out. She knew because she'd tried the same thing. There wasn't one. Not unless he wanted to tell the children the truth.

"I thought I'd let you decide what to do," she murmured.

"Oh, thanks! I should tell them we got married, not because we love each other, but because of them. That we thought they needed a stable home, that we had to get married or they would end up in foster care?" He shook his head determinedly. "I don't think so, Clarissa. It's not even an option."

"So, what will we do?"

"I don't know." He poured out another cup of coffee, tasted it, then dumped the entire pot down the sink.

"It's been there since supper. Shall I make you a fresh cup?" She fluttered around, tidying up the kitchen. "Wade?"

"What? No. Thanks." He shoved his hands in his pockets. "I think I'll sit outside for a bit. Maybe something will come to me."

"Good idea." She followed him out, sank into the chair opposite his and tried to pretend she wasn't staring at him. "Blair got off all right?"

"Fine. On time. Said she'll call you tomorrow. I was supposed to give you some kind of message." He frowned, rubbing his temples as he tried to remember. "You owe her? I think that was it. For when it's her turn, I think she said. Her turn for what?"

"Her turn to get married." Clarissa explained about their college pact, formed after they'd been dumped at the altar, or rather, just before it. "We decided that if one of us eventually did get married, there must be hope for the others. Wade—" she peered at him through the gloom "—we perpetuated the myth that we were in love with each other and Blair bought it. Just like the kids."

"Yeah, just like the kids." He huffed out a sigh, then leaned back in his chair and studied her. "I know it's an imposition. It was supposed to be for public, not for private. But if you think you can handle having me sharing your room, I'll try not to get in the way."

She saw his eyes jerk away from hers and study the floor. And then Clarissa knew just how much he hated having to ask.

"I don't know what else to do. I want the kids to feel secure and I'm afraid that if word got out why we were married, Rita would renew her campaign. As it is, we still have to be approved to adopt them." His eyes narrowed, dark and intense. "Is it too much to ask that we share? Just for a while. I promise I'll try to respect your privacy as much as I possibly can."

Clarissa gulped. He was going to share her room? He was going to be there, every morning she would wake up and see him. Every night she'd go to sleep knowing that he was right there. Even someone as naive as she was knew it was asking for problems!

But what else could they do? She'd promised to help him however she could. She'd also promised not to be a burden. This was one way of making his life a little easier.

And satisfying this silly craving to be near him that you have. She stifled that mocking voice and summoned a smile.

"Of course we can make it work. And I'll respect your privacy, too. I'll do the very best I can, Wade. I promise."

"Thanks." He sighed, his shoulders sagging.

Suddenly Clarissa knew how worried he'd been. And she felt a thrill of pleasure that she'd been able to do this for him. She cared about Wade. And about the children, of course. After all, God had sent them to her. She was sure of that. So it was her duty to make the best of this awkward situation.

"I think I'll go up to bed, if you don't mind locking up?" She tried to think of how she could make it easier for him to fit in. After all, it was already her home. She wanted him to feel as if it were his, too. "Come whenever you're ready."

"I'll just sit here for a bit. You go ahead." He didn't bother with the customary peck on the cheek she'd received for the past three nights. Instead he stared off into the darkness as if it held the remedy for the frown that marred his handsome good looks. "Good night, Clarissa."

She couldn't think of anything else to say, so, finally, she turned away, went inside and slowly climbed up the stairs. She unpacked quickly, then prepared for bed by having a shower, shampooing her hair and drying it with the blow dryer, brushing her teeth until her gums bled, and applying the moisturizer she'd bought in Hawaii and never touched again. And as she did, she listened for his footstep.

But when she came back into the bedroom, Wade still was not there. Clarissa lifted off the white satin wedding ring quilt her grandmother had made to match the canopy, folded it and laid it on top of her grandfather's army trunk. She turned the lights off so that only a small lamp burned on the nightstand on Wade's side of the bed.

He wasn't coming.

The knowledge stabbed deep into her heart. She was so homely that he couldn't stand the thought of sharing her room, let alone this huge bed with his own wife. But then, she wasn't really his wife, was she? She was just going to be the mother of his adopted children.

Clarissa snapped out the light and curled up in the bed. She said her prayers, then huddled up into a little ball, as close to the edge of the queen-size mattress as she could get while hot tears trickled down to soak her pillow.

"This isn't what I wanted, Lord," she prayed. "But You know best. I just have to wait on You."

It seemed as if it was only minutes later that the bedroom door flew open and a chorus of four happy voices chanted "Happy Mother's Day!"

Clarissa blinked through the curtain of hair that covered her face, trying to convince herself that it really was morning. Ow! Something sharp—an elbow poked into her ribs. Why would an— Wade! She sat up with a jerk, fully awake now as she dragged her hair off her face and swallowed.

"Uh, thank you," she managed, edging as far away from him as possible. It was a little embarrassing to have to tug her arm out from under his and his foot was on the corner of her long flannelette nightgown.

Lacey was the first to speak, her voice hinging on tears, her eyes bright. "We know you're not really our mom. She died with our dad in the car accident. But we thought, since you married Wade, and he's looking after us, well…"

"She means that we'd really like to have you for our stepmom. Or aunt." Pierce frowned, scuffing one toe against the carpet. "How does that work, anyhow?"

"It works however you want it to." Clarissa risked a sideways glance at Wade, who'd managed to draw himself up against the headboard. By the look of him, he hadn't slept any better than she. "We just want to be here for you whenever you need us. Right, Wade?" She looked at him full on, waiting.

"Yeah. Right. Of course." He finally came to enough to comment. "What's on that tray?"

"It's for Clarissa. For Mother's Day. From all of us." Tildy carried the tray forward and carefully set it on Clarissa's lap. "I hope you enjoy it."

Clarissa lifted the soup bowl that covered the plate and made herself smile at the runny concoction that oozed out all over the plate. "Scrambled eggs! And look, Wade. There's bacon, too."

"And toast. I made that." Jared preened a little bit. "It's your day so we wanted to make it special."

"You've made it very special," Clarissa told him, feeling teary at the effort and thought they'd obviously put into this. "Thank you for the kind welcome to the family. I really appreciate it, guys."

They stood there, four children who'd lost the most important people in their lives, and grinned at her as if she were the best thing to happen since sliced bread. Clarissa felt proud all the way to her heart. These were her kids now. Hers and Wade's. And she owed them her very best effort at mothering.

"Hey, not bad!" Wade had reached out and was now sampling one of the blackened strips of shriveled-up bacon. He licked off his fingertips and tilted his head. "Where's mine?"

"Uh-uh. You get to come and help us clean up the kitchen," Jared told him. "This is Mother's Day. Not Father's Day."

"Oh. Right. I can hardly wait." He waved a hand

toward the door. "Out you go and let Clarissa sample her breakfast in peace."

"But we hafta see if she likes it!" Pierce frowned at his uncle. "It's important."

"It's delicious. I don't know when I've tasted better." Clarissa gulped the forkful of egg down, ordering herself not to gag as it slipped and slithered down her throat.

"It's nice not to always eat your own cooking, isn't it?" Tildy laid her hand on Pierce's shoulder. "Come on. If you'll help me clean up, I might even make you pancakes." In mere seconds she had them out the door, pulling it closed behind her.

"I think I'd better go supervise. I'd hate to think what she could do to pancakes." Wade shuffled out of bed and toward the bathroom. He stopped and turned around suddenly, his eyes glinting with wicked humor. "Do you want me to dump that before they get back or are you going to play the martyr and make yourself sick eating it?"

Clarissa held up the tray. "I love those kids, but I'm afraid I can't bear this sight any longer. Please, do the honors."

He walked back, picked up the tray and popped the bacon into his mouth as he headed for the bathroom. "Actually, this isn't bad. If you like your bacon crisp. Really, really crisp."

Clarissa straightened her gown while he was out of the room and pulled her hair back into some kind of order. "I did drink the juice," she called out in self-defense. "And I sampled the toast."

He plodded back into the room and set the tray on

the night table. "Which one was the toast? That black cardboard stuff with the lines on it?" He grinned at her. "I thought maybe they were coasters or something. And where's the coffee? Nobody has breakfast without coffee."

"Don't suggest it. Please? I shudder to think what might happen to my delicious mountain-grown blend."

He sniffed, eyes winging up to the canopy. He frowned, his eyes busily studying the frills and flounces. "It's all mountain grown, Clarissa. There isn't any other kind of coffee."

"Oh." She yawned and laid back down, tugging the covers up to her chin. "You can have the bathroom. I'm going back to sleep."

"How can you dare?" he demanded. "Don't you realize they're down there, running rampant all over this house? Life as you know it may never be the same again."

"Oh, it's not that bad," she mumbled, closing her eyes as she snuggled against the pillow. "They're good kids."

"Yeah, they are." He stood there staring down at her. "Clarissa, about that canopy—"

She hid her smile. It hadn't taken him long. She stretched her neck and peered upward at the ornate, totally feminine concoction her grandmother had insisted was perfect for a young girl. "What about it?"

"Well, no offense, but it's not me." He scratched his forehead, then fingered the quilt on the chest. "Nor is this. Feels like satin or something."

"It is."

He jerked his hand back as if it had been burned, his eyes huge. "I can't be around satin."

"Why? Are you allergic?" Clarissa shifted into a sitting position. She wasn't going to get back to sleep now.

"Allergic? I guess you could say that. I'll wreck it, Clarissa. Look at that, I've snagged it already." He balled his hands into fists. "I work around sawdust and stuff. I'll get everything dirty. My hands are rough. I'm not used to all this frippery."

She giggled. "If it makes you that uncomfortable, I'll replace it. But you haven't ruined it, Wade. It's just a thing. A nice thing, true. A gift from my grand-mother. But it only has meaning because it came from her. We can always get another bedspread, if that's what you want."

She wouldn't tell him that she'd really wanted a bedroom with flowers, blue flowers. And a bedspread that didn't show every bit of dust. It seemed ungrateful when Gran deserved all her gratitude for the sacrifices she had made.

"You don't mind?" He sighed his relief, then jerked a thumb upward, crossing his pajama clad legs. "What about that? Can we change it, too?"

Clarissa faked perplexity. "Change the canopy? Why?"

"It's a girl bed, Clarissa." Wade looked pained by the words.

She pretended to scratch her neck so she could hide a smile. "Of course it's a girl bed. I'm a girl!"

"I know *that*." He sounded strange, as if he were being tortured. "It's just…oh, never mind. I think I'll go have a shower."

"Okay. I'm going to sleep a little longer. Wasn't it nice of them to think of making this a Mother's Day for me?" She snuggled down. "They're wonderful kids, Wade." She was almost in dreamland when his softly mocking voice penetrated her brain, his breath brushing against her temple as he whispered against her ear.

"Yeah, they are. Wonderful little dears. So why do I have this mental picture of your house in ruins?"

"Oh, boy!" In a flash she was up, had her robe wrapped around her and was flying down the stairs. Sure enough, the bottom floor of the house was filling rapidly with smoke. In fact, the smoke alarm began to whine. "Tildy? What are you doing?" she called, opening windows as she went.

"Don't come in here!"

The words stopped Clarissa outside the kitchen door. "But there's smoke all over. I have to come in."

"No, you don't. Anyway, there's no fire now. I put it out."

Clarissa's closed her eyes. "Oh, Lord, please help me," she whispered.

"Uh, Clarissa?" Tildy's voice came through the thick wood.

"Yes?"

"Do you think you could get Uncle Wade and send him in here? It's, uh, kind of important." There was a certain urgency in Tildy's voice that transmitted through the swinging door.

Clarissa wheeled around and raced back up the stairs. She pounded on the bathroom door, and when there was no answer, shoved it open and stuck her head inside. Steam filled the room.

Wasn't that great? Smoke all over the bottom floor. Steam all over the top. Or there would be soon if he didn't shut off the hot water. And what was that awful caterwauling noise?

Clarissa shoved it all to the back of her mind and bellowed for all she was worth. "Wade?"

He stopped midnote, pulled back a tiny corner of the shower curtain and peered out. "Is something wrong?"

"Yes. There's smoke all over downstairs, and Tildy won't let me in the kitchen. She says you're to come right away."

She heard the water shut off, winced as something fell to the floor, then blinked at the yelp of pain. "What's wrong?"

"Somebody keeps turning on the hot water, that's what's wrong. I'm almost frozen, the parts that didn't get scalded the last time, that is!" He sounded very grumpy indeed. "You need a temperature regulator."

Clarissa frowned. "Do I?" She had no idea what a regulator was. "Are they expensive?"

There was a long drawn out sigh. "Look, Clarissa, I'll explain it all to you later, okay. Right now, would you mind leaving this bathroom?"

From the top of her head to the souls of her feet, Clarissa felt herself burn with the mortification of it. It spread through her body like a poison ivy rash. How could she have stood here, yakking like that!

Married four days and she was acting as if she had every right to be standing in the bathroom while Wade took a shower. What must he have thought of her? She gulped. No time to think about that while the house burned.

"Yes. Yes of course. Naturally. Right." She backed

out of the bathroom as fast as she could, and jerked the door closed just a touch too forcefully. It didn't stay closed, of course. It never did when you banged it like that.

But without a backward look, she scurried out of the room, down the stairs and found the farthest corner of the sofa in the living room to crunch down in.

What was wrong with her? She'd actually enjoyed the camaraderie of it! Before she'd realized what she was doing, of course. For the first time in years, aside from the odd occasions when Blair and Bri had come to visit, she'd woken up feeling safe and no longer lonely in that huge bed.

"Oh, no!" She squeezed her eyes closed as the idea birthed inside her brain. "It isn't possible. It's silly, stupid, schoolgirlish. I'm too old for it." But it wouldn't go away.

"How could I possibly be falling in love?" she whispered. "It was supposed to be an arrangement that benefitted everyone." She tested the idea out loud. "Do I love Wade?"

It didn't sound bad at all. In fact, there, cuddled up inside her heart, it felt snug and secure, like a little pilot light that burned steadily and wouldn't go out. It didn't matter that she'd only known him a short while. The problems, the kids, the differences in their backgrounds and expectations, none of that mattered a whit.

She was falling for her husband!

Clarissa grinned and hugged herself with the sheer joy of it. She'd known it would come, had known she'd find it one day. It was just as Gran had said, love came when you least expected it. It kind of sneaked up on you, grew inside until it was ready to bloom.

She sat there and reveled in it without paying the least attention to the strange noises from the kitchen. Who cared about kitchens? She loved her husband.

Clarissa fell to dreaming about all the wonders that awaited her in this marriage. There were so many changes she wanted to make, in herself and the house, but also for the children and Wade. She wanted this to be the perfect family, the perfect marriage. And it would be if she worked at it.

But out from under all that joy, a nasty little voice poked its head up and reminded her of the facts. They were hard to acknowledge and they rubbed the glow off her discovery. Wade didn't love *her.* In fact, he'd already told her that love was out for him.

He didn't believe in families and the forever kind of love that she'd waited for for so long. To Wade, this marriage was just a necessary step in the care and feeding of his nieces and nephews. He'd made a promise, he'd stick by it. He sure didn't want or need Clarissa fawning over him, uttering protestations of love.

She bowed her head as a tear worked its way out of her eye and plopped onto her folded hands.

"Father, did You give me this family, these wonderful children, and Wade, just to take it away again? How am I to be a wife to him if he won't let me past that barrier he keeps up? If he won't let me in, how can I love him? How can he learn to love me when he won't talk about what's wrong?"

Silence.

And then the piercing truth dawned. She'd asked God for a husband and a family to love. Hadn't He sent both? So what if Wade wasn't exactly the kind of husband she wanted, the children weren't either her biological children, or the fluttering little cupids she'd imagined?

She'd married Wade knowing the facts. He'd made it abundantly clear on their wedding night that he never intended to fall in love. She'd agreed to take on the kids because they were wonderful children and they deserved a chance to grow up happily with their siblings around them.

But how can it possibly work when I love him so much? Wade doesn't want responsibility, he doesn't want to be tied down to someone like me. He just wants a mother for the kids, a friend and companion. He doesn't need another encumbrance.

In a split second the decision was made.

She would never tell him of her love. She would play her part, do what he needed done, but she'd love him secretly. And if the folks in the community saw the truth, they wouldn't be surprised since they'd assumed she'd married for love.

"I've got to do it, don't I, God? I've got to go on with what I started, keep my promise." Some of the chill that surrounded her dissipated a little and a remnant of warmth snuggled around her heart. "Okay, maybe I didn't get all of my dream, but I got the best part and I'll love all of them the very best I can."

What if he leaves you like he left them?

No sooner had that thought crossed her mind than she

remembered Paul's letter to the Philippian church when he'd told them to be full of the joy of the Lord.

"Don't worry about anything; instead pray about everything; tell God your needs and don't forget to thank Him for your answers."

"I won't worry about it. I'll leave the answers up to Him. He is *God,* after all. He can do anything." Saying the words out loud made them more real, more official somehow.

Clarissa closed her eyes and poured out her heart to her heavenly Father, telling Him her heart's desires. By the time Wade came to find her, she had brushed away the tears.

"Are you okay?" he asked carefully.

"I'm fine. Why?"

He shrugged. "Just wondered. She didn't wreck anything this time. Just dumped the entire bowl of pancake batter on top of the stove. I cleaned it up, but—"

"—it's going to take a while to get it back to normal," Clarissa finished for him. She burst out laughing. "Who cares? As long as everyone is all right, that's what matters." She felt the joy she'd prayed for bubble up inside. "Kids will be kids."

He tilted his head to one side, his eyes bright. "You're a wonder, Clarissa Cart—Featherhawk. I wonder if I'll ever understand how your brain works."

She got to her feet, brushed a kiss across his cheek, then walked to the door.

"You will if you practice, Mr. Featherhawk. It'll probably take about, oh, forty or fifty years of marriage before that happens, but you can do it."

He blinked. "That long? What goes on underneath all that hair anyway?"

She giggled and raced up the stairs to get ready for church.

"You'll find out," she promised as the shower hissed over her. "You certainly will find out."

Chapter Seven

"I'd love to give him the message, Mr. Chapman, but he hasn't come home yet this evening. Mm-hm." Clarissa shifted from one foot to the other uncomfortably. It was so hot, and she was so tired. Why had Tildy picked today to bake?

"They're trying to finish up the golf club, so every moment counts. I'm sure he'll get to your garage door as soon as he can. But if you can't wait, I know Wade will understand if you have to hire someone else. Actually, it would be easier on him, too. His list is so long." She listened to the protest with a tiny smile curving the corner of her lips, then rang off thoughtfully.

Over the past six weeks, the remarks about Wade's heritage had died down until almost everyone in Waseka wanted him for one odd job or another. His workmanship was top-notch, though Clarissa felt his prices were a little low. She intended to speak to him about it, if he ever showed up before she was asleep and stayed until she was awake. The only way she knew he'd been there was the stack of laundry and the wet towels he left behind.

"I don't think it's a good idea to tell them it's all right to go elsewhere, Clara. I need those jobs to pay the bills."

She jumped at the sound of his low voice, then whirled around. "I wish you wouldn't sneak around like that. I almost dropped the teapot." She inspected his dear face and winced at the lines of tiredness around his eyes. "Are you going to finish in time for the grand opening on Saturday?"

"Of course." There was nothing but exhaustion in the words.

"You don't have to push yourself so hard, Wade. The people here know you do a good job. You've got them lined up until Christmas, according to my list." She held out the sheet on which she'd compiled the incoming calls. "I only gave approximate dates because I didn't know how long each project would take. You'd better look it over while I get you something to eat. Is a salad platter okay? I fixed fruit salad for dessert. The kids are upstairs. Asleep, I hope."

He flopped into a chair and began unlacing his boots. "I don't need anything. I'm too tired to eat anyway."

She ignored that and began pulling things out of the fridge. "Nonsense. You have to eat. You're working yourself to the edge as it is." Clarissa smacked the plate on the table in front of him, poured out some of her freshly made iced tea and added six ice cubes.

Wade ignored the food, long enough to take a huge gulp of the tea. "I'm fine, Clara. Don't fuss."

"Fuss?" she sputtered. "I haven't begun to…why do

you call me that? Clara?" The indignation died away to curiosity. "That's the second time you've said it."

"Well, it's better than Prissy, which is what I heard Blair call you." His eyes dared her to deny it. "Anyway, that's how I think of you. Kind of like an old-fashioned character in one of those musty books you're always reading. Heidi maybe, only older and without pigtails." He began eating automatically. "You know the kind I mean. They look stern on the outside, but you know very well that deep down they're made of mush. The kind that need protecting."

Clarissa stared. She hadn't known he thought anything about her, let alone what she was like underneath, in her soul.

"I don't need protecting," she said after a long moment, intent on making him understand. She sank down into a chair across from him. "I am exactly what I seem. Tough. Durable. Able to handle any knocks life dishes out."

He chuckled, his eyes dancing as he surveyed her scrunched-up body, folded like a pretzel into the chair. "You have got to be kidding! Look at you, sitting there in that white sunsuit thing, as elegant as if you stepped out of one of those magazines Lacey likes. You haven't got a hair out of place."

She huffed. "That's because I just had a shower, silly. I was in the garden after work and I got filthy. Then Jared needed me to help him with the mower, and we had to take some stuff apart. I wasted a huge amount of water trying to get the grease out from under my fingernails, you know."

"You tackled the lawn mower?" Wade picked up her left hand and studied the perfect ovals, now tinted a pale-pink shade. "Yes, this delicate little hand is definitely that of a laborer," he grinned. Then his face sobered. "It's far too hot for you to be working outside. Leave the gardening to Joe Franklin. He said he'd do it for you."

She yanked her hand away, frustration mounting. "You're not listening to me, Wade. I'm *not* some delicate flower. I *like* gardening and I *want* to do it myself. I have been for years. Besides, I know more about that motor than Joe ever will." After prevaricating for a minute, she finally decided to get out all the frustration that had mounted during the past weeks.

"This is supposed to be a partnership, remember? I have a job, I want to contribute to this family, too. I'm not some anemic little hothouse flower you have to take care of. We're partners. If you'd just tell me a little bit about how you do things, I could handle some of the book work, too. I'm good with numbers."

He shoved the half-eaten plate away, red-rimmed eyes suddenly blazing. "Along with managing a house full of four demanding kids, sewing the girls special outfits for camp, mending Pierce's terminally torn jeans and working full-time, I suppose?" He shook his head in disgust. "You should have let me get someone to stay with them during the day, instead of having them come to you at the library."

"Wade, they *help out* at the library. And they get paid for it, courtesy of the town, not me. It's good for Jared and Pierce to be able to earn their own money. Tildy has that job helping Mrs. Simmons with the baby every morning, and Lacey is busy with vacation Bible school at the church. We're doing just fine!"

He jumped up so quickly, his chair upset with a crash. Wade ignored it, stomping around the table to circle her wrist with his thumb and fingers.

"Fine? Look at you—you're skin and bones! You haven't had a moment to call your own in weeks and you keep taking on more. Why can't you let me be the breadwinner in this house?"

In a flash, Clarissa's frustration hit white-hot. She jerked her wrist out of his hold and jumped to her feet. "You *are* the breadwinner! You're gone night and day, working yourself into an early grave so that you can prove you're doing your duty by the family." Temper took over her brain and she forgot to pick her words carefully.

"Do you think having a few extra dollars in the bank means anything to Pierce when you missed his first Little League game? Or to Tildy when she won that home ec award at school last month? They just want you to share their successes. Way down deep they don't care if you buy them a better bike or brand-name shoes."

His hands came up to fasten onto her shoulders in a steely grip. "I can't just walk off the job whenever there's something they want to show off," he growled. "I'm the only one they have left. I have to make sure they're taken care of."

I'm the only one they have. Clarissa wrenched her body out of his grasp. White-hot indignation rose inside, and a shaft of pain pierced her heart.

"Well, silly me! I thought I was in their lives, I thought we were together in taking on this responsibility. Sorry for being concerned. And I am *not* a bag of bones! I can't help it if I'm just naturally thin."

Clarissa saw the frown roll across his face like a thundercloud and knew she'd blown it. She turned and flew up the stairs to her bedroom, hot angry tears flooding down her cheeks as she carefully closed the door so the children wouldn't wake up.

Ohh! She could spit she was so angry. After all this time, he was still keeping her out, refusing to share his life with her. Why did he keep doing that, insisting that he would take care of everything, as if he alone were responsible for how the children grew up? Didn't their marriage mean anything to him?

"Clarissa? Can I come in?" He stood in the doorway, his shoulders slumped with exhaustion as he waited for permission to enter their bedroom.

The utter weariness on his face touched a chord deep in her heart, but Clarissa couldn't forget his earlier words. She wanted to share and he wouldn't.

"Why not?" she mumbled at last. "It's supposed to be your room, too. Even though you're never here."

She sat in front of the mirror and pretended to ignore him, though she knew the exact moment he stepped through the door, closed it and advanced toward her. To hide her nervousness, she reached up and pulled out the pins securing her French knot, letting her hair fall down around her shoulders.

"Stop that, Clarissa, and listen to me!"

His voice barked out harshly, and she let her hands drop away, frowning as she turned around to study him.

"I'm sorry. I didn't mean to yell at you, but I need

you to pay attention to what I have to say." He crouched down in front of her, took her hands in his, and held them. His voice was soft but a thread of tension wove through it. "I don't want to argue with you. God knows I've had my fill of arguments and I don't intend to do that in my marriage."

"Arguments aren't always bad, Wade," she murmured, enjoying the feel of his work-roughened hands on hers. She leaned forward to look directly into his eyes. "Sometimes they get the truth out so people can deal with it instead of a lot of silly pretense."

"You think that's what I'm doing? Pretending?" He frowned. "About what?"

She decided to be candid. "About this marriage, about this family, about my role in it and yours." Clarissa drew a deep breath and plunged in. "About what would happen to this family if you slowed down and took a look, a good look at who we really are."

"Who you are?" He dropped her hands as if they burnt him, then backed away to perch on the edge of the trunk, his mouth drawn in a line of bitterness. "I know exactly who you are. You're the person I drew into this mess. You're the person who is stuck caring for four kids that are my responsibility, one which I've dumped on you. I don't blame you for being angry."

"I am not *stuck*," she blurted out furiously. "I love those kids. And I am not angry. Well, maybe a little."

He continued on as if he hadn't heard. "But I promise that I won't take off and leave you with them, Clara. I know that's what you've been afraid of ever since my uncle blabbed about the past." His eyes met hers steadily. "I'll do whatever it takes to make sure we don't drain you of every penny you earn. Put your own money somewhere safe, somewhere you can draw on when you want to retire."

"My own money? I thought it was ours." Clarissa stood, defeat dragging at her now, when she'd felt so much anticipation just an hour ago.

"You're not listening," she told him sadly. "You won't hear what I'm saying. I married you because I wanted to help you and those kids find a way to stay together. And I wanted to be a part of it. I thought I could make a difference in your lives, that I could be part of something wonderful."

Wade stayed where he was, staring at his toes. Clarissa decided they had to start somewhere and she might as well be the first. She took a deep breath and dove in.

"I never had a family, Wade. Never had a sister to chum around with, or nieces and nephews to play with. I only ever had Gran. She was a wonderful woman, but she wasn't what you'd call warm or loving. She had a strict sense of her duty and she intended to do that duty by me, come what may." She swallowed the lump in her throat and continued.

"You have no idea how much it hurts to be the person someone else is responsible for. You lose your freedom to be spontaneous, because you're afraid it will cost them something else. You're afraid to say what you really think because maybe they'll feel they gave up more than you deserved. You're afraid to get mad because maybe they'll hate you and then where will you go? You live your life in a tight little box of restrictions, knowing always that your indebtedness can never be paid off."

Wade said nothing, merely stood there frowning at her.

"I won't live like that anymore, Wade. I won't let you make me live like that. I am a part of this family because I care about the people in it, and because I have something I can and *want* to give." She walked across the room, took his chin in her hand and forced his eyes to meet hers.

"When I've given too much, I'll let you know. Until then, don't try to smother me with your false sense of duty. And don't protect them so much they can't fly."

"I—I—" He stopped and shrugged. "Go on. Finish what you have to say."

"I'm an adult, Wade. I am responsible for myself. And with you, I'm responsible to raise those children. I'll let you know if I need your protection, but I'm telling you right now that they need you around. You can't make their lives perfect, you can't make sure nothing bad ever happens again by killing yourself with work. You can't make up for the past."

Tears came then, but she brushed them away. She stepped forward and wrapped her arms around his waist. She laid her head on his chest and said the words she'd waited so many nights to say.

"I'm sorry Kendra's gone. I know you felt responsible for her, for the kids losing their mother. I'm sorry you hurt. But you can't bring her back with guilt. They need to talk about her with you, to remember the past, good times and bad. They're strong. They can deal with it. Can you?"

* * *

Wade's hands automatically moved to wrap around his wife. He couldn't have stopped them. He wanted to hold her, to squeeze her so tightly, to bind her to him in a way that would prevent her from ever leaving.

Yet, what she was saying hurt so much.

"What do you know about Kendra's death?" he muttered, his chest tight with the stabbing pain of bringing it all into the open again.

"Nothing. Only what you've told me and what I've seen on your face. I hoped you'd tell me about it. The children won't speak of it because they think it hurts you too much. Pierce keeps a little book under his pillow and every time he remembers something happy about his mother, he writes it down, so he won't forget her." Her eyes begged him to understand what she was saying.

"Tildy treasures certain little bits of clothing. She won't wear them because they're so special, the only memory of her mother that she has."

Her words stabbed at him piercing him with condemnation. Had he done that to them? To all of them? Made them afraid to remember the girl who dashed out and met life head-on, regardless of how much it hurt? Wade bent his head so his face was buried in Clarissa's hair and tried to think through what she'd said.

"I've got pictures and stuff." His nose twitched at her soft lavender fragrance. "In storage. I thought having them around would make them sad, so I packed them away. I—I can't talk about her death. But it was my mistake that caused it."

"I don't believe that, Wade." She lifted her head away

and leaned back to peer up at him. "But never mind. Maybe some day you'll tell me about it. For now, focus on the kids. You wanted them to forget because you want to forget the hurt." She nodded. "I know. But they can't forget all of it. They need to remember that she loved them, they need to believe that she would be proud of what they're becoming."

He thought it over. She was right. Kendra *would* be so blown away by her kids' maturity. They'd struggled through so much and yet none of them had ended up as bitter and frustrated as he'd been at their age.

Clarissa's intelligent eyes were studying him again, assessing him. He didn't like it. They saw things he wasn't ready to talk about. He pulled her back into his arms, and held her the way he'd wanted to for days now.

"What made you so smart?" he teased, unable to cover the gruffness that shielded his feelings.

She sniffed, but her eyes clouded over with sadness as she pulled away to glare at him. "Time. A whole lifetime of wanting a family of my own." Her voice was little, scared like a kid's. "I know it sounds dumb, but I always envied the other children their cousins and aunts and uncles. I never had that."

Her disarming honesty touched him deeply. "It doesn't sound stupid. It sounds normal. I never was normal, I guess. I only ever wanted to get away from my family. To be free."

"To do what?" Her breath brushed warmly past his chin.

Wade shrugged. "I dunno. To do all the things kids want to do, I guess. Eat what I wanted, when I wanted, sleep all day, sky dive. Anything that I wouldn't have to answer for." He laughed at himself bitterly. "Stupid."

"It's not stupid. It's perfectly normal. You were sick of being the responsible one, the one to blame. You shouldn't have had to be. Your parents took on that job and then dumped it on you. That was wrong." Her voice came softly through the stillness of the evening.

The windows were open, but the evening was as silent as if they alone inhabited the planet. Wade knew he couldn't stay like this much longer. It was asking for trouble. Clarissa got to him like no woman ever had, made him ask himself questions that he didn't have answers for.

She made him wonder if he deserved her, if that soft spot she'd made in his chest would ever grow into something stronger, and what he would do if it did.

He set her gently away with a rueful smile. "I was wrong earlier." He studied her in the faint pink glow of her bedroom lamp. "Your skin is perfect for those bones. You look lovely."

She blushed, but didn't look away. "It's all right," she whispered. "I know I'm no Venus."

Almost of its own volition, his hand lifted, one finger tracing the stubborn tilt to her chin, grazing over the porcelain skin. "Venus was untouchable," he muttered, marveling at the softness of her cheek as his rough thumb scraped against the fragility of her smooth forehead.

Clarissa stood there, silent. At one point, when his finger moved to touch her lashes, she closed her eyes, silent and trusting under his touch. In some far-off part of him, Wade knew he shouldn't be touching her. And yet he had to. It connected him to her, somehow. He felt as if he could see her as a child, solemn, dutiful, but never yelling like a banshee as she tore across the unmown grass, or plunged beneath the icy water of a spring river just for the sheer pleasure of feeling it on her skin. He'd done all that and more.

Her voice broke into his memories. "Wade?"

"Uh-huh."

"Could you kiss me? Please?"

It was evident from her tone that she didn't expect him to do it. And he knew why. Clarissa had this idea that she was some kind of plain Jane. That was partly his fault. Somehow he always got the words out wrong when he wanted to tell her she was too fragile to manage all that he'd handed her.

Maybe this was one way to restore her self-confidence.

His brain mocked him. He wanted to kiss her, and it had nothing to do with her self-confidence or his.

"I'm sorry. I shouldn't have put you on the spot."

She tried to step away from him, but he held her fast with one arm while his other hand caught her chin and tipped her face up toward his. Then he bent his head and touched her lips with all the reverence and thankfulness he felt whenever he thought of all she'd done for them.

As his mouth covered hers and found a response, Wade forgot all about thankfulness. For a minute he let himself believe that she really was his wife, that they were happily married and it was his right to kiss her like this.

Right! He didn't have any rights where Clarissa was concerned. Certainly not the right to pretend something he knew wasn't real.

Wade gently pulled back, dropping his hands to his sides so she could step away. "Good night, Clarissa. I'm going to work downstairs for a while."

She never said a word, but her big eyes blinked as if to stem tears as she watched him leave. Wade trod quietly down the stairs, brewed a pot of coffee and took it into the little study.

Life was confusing. Sure he cared about Clarissa. She'd gone out of her way for him and he didn't want to see her hurt because of it. But that didn't mean anything. He'd do the same for anyone.

So, what about those feelings? The ones that made him dream of a future together?

He gulped some coffee and winced as it burned all the way down. That's all it was—a dream. He hurt the people he loved. He always had. They expected stuff from him and he could never fulfill those expectations, no matter how hard he tried.

It was the same with Clarissa, he told himself, as he pulled forward a pad of paper and the calculator. She would expect him to be that dream husband she'd been waiting for, one who was always there for her, spending time with the family, pandering to her every whim. But he wasn't like that. He needed his space, time to organize his thoughts. He was a private person.

Wade got up to open the window and, as he did, he glanced around the little room. Okay, so she'd let him have his space. Here he was, alone.

So, why did his thoughts keep going to the small, gentle woman upstairs with hair like beaten silver and a heart as big as all outdoors?

Chapter Eight

"I've never gone camping before. What do you do?"
Pierce stood at the edge of the table almost a week later,
watching as Clarissa lifted one after another of the
cookies off the sheet and into a plastic container.

"Well, we'll go swimming, of course. And we'll have
campfires each night. If you like, you can sleep on the
porch. The cabin is quite comfortable." Mentally she
checked off cookies on her list and moved to fill the
cooler that stood waiting. "Then of course, there are the
fireworks."

"They have Fourth of July fireworks at the lake?"
Pierce look amazed. "Can I get my own sparkler?"

"We'll see. Did you pack a bag and put in all the
things I told you?" She waited for his nod. "Well?"

"I don't need to take a jacket, Clarissa. It's boiling
outside!" He glared at the stove. "In here, too."

"Pierce, it cools off at night. How can you sit around
the campfire if you're shivering?"

"But Clarissa—"

"Pierce!" Wade's voice was sharp with reproof. "You will obey Clarissa. Go and get a jacket now."

Pierce glared at his uncle, but he did as he was told, leaving Clarissa alone with Wade in the kitchen while the other children bustled around getting ready for the promised trip.

Clarissa turned away, clamping her lips together to prevent the words from escaping. She wanted this to be a happy time, a time to relax and enjoy each other.

"Wow! There's enough food here for two weeks, even with this mob to devour it." Wade poked a finger into the icing bowl that sat nearby and ran it around the edge. "Keep the cake for me. I love chocolate." He closed his eyes, obviously savoring the dark richness.

"I'm sure you'll get your share." She forced her attention back on the cooler, trying to ignore the shiver of excitement that wiggled up her spine. "I deliberately packed a lot of food because I don't want to have to run to the store. Everything is so expensive in these resort villages."

His hand on her arm stopped her from continuing. "Clarissa, we're not going to starve. You don't have to scrimp all the time."

"Waste not, want not," she muttered, reminding herself of her vow to try to cut corners so he wouldn't have to work so long and so hard.

"I've always hated that saying." He stuck out his tongue at her as if he were Pierce.

"I want to talk to you about something, Wade."

He waggled a finger at her, shaking his head. His fingers on her arm prevented her from moving away from him. "Uh-uh, you're trying to change the subject.

Tell the truth, Clarissa. When was the last time you actually bought something for yourself? I notice the girls have new sandals and there's a box with a dinghy in the front porch that I assume is for the boys. What's your gift?"

"I don't need anything. My clothes wear for years, and I have new sandals that I bought for my vacation in Hawaii." With her eyes, she challenged him to argue. "I did pick up two new shirts for you, though. I can't mend those blue ones anymore. Do you have a partiality for blue? You have six blue shirts."

He shook his head, but his eyes were troubled. "Kendra bought them. It was her favorite color."

"Oh." She didn't know what else to say. The fun and gaiety had drained away.

"What did you want to ask me?"

"What?" She jerked out of her daydream about families at lakes and stared at him. "Pardon?"

He sighed, picked up the pitcher of lemonade and poured himself a glass. "You said you had something to discuss. What is it?" While he waited, he swallowed half the drink. "Well? Am I supposed to guess?"

"No. Uh, sit down, Wade." She tried to think of the right way to approach this.

"Why?" His suspicious glance warned her he was wary. "Is it bad news? Are we overdrawn or something?"

"Of course not. Though we will be if that golf club job isn't soon paid for." She fiddled with a stack of pop cans. "No, it's something else. Something I've been thinking of for a while now."

"Okay." He sat, his eyes darker than usual. "Shoot."

"You know how much trouble I've had with my car? It spends more time in the garage than the mechanics." She let out a squeak of laughter that sounded as false as it felt.

Wade obviously agreed because he frowned at her as if he thought she was sick. "Just say it, Clarissa. You want to stay here, is that it? You don't want to come on the camping trip. Can't say I blame you. It must be driving you nuts having us underfoot all the time."

"No! That isn't it." She took a deep breath and said, "I want to buy a van. A minivan. I've got one all picked out, too."

He blinked. "So that's what he meant?"

"Who?"

"The pastor. He was at the game last night and said something about my life changing for the better. When I asked him what he meant, he said he figured hauling the kids around would be a lot easier for you if you didn't have to worry about reliability. That's all he would say."

"It's his brother's van. They don't want it now that their kids are away from home. It's three years old, has every feature we could possibly want." It came out in a tumbling rush of words and Clarissa stopped, breathless.

"It is a good idea," Wade nodded, sipping his lemonade. "But he'll want his money up front and there's no way I can swing buying a van now. No matter how much he wants."

She told him the price, steeling herself for the next bombshell. "You don't have to. I want to buy it myself."

"No. I'm not going to have my wife going to the bank to take out a loan so we can buy a van." A muscle in his jaw flicked as he clenched it, his eyes on the floor. "I know they wouldn't give me one because I'm self-employed and I haven't got the kind of credit rating they want. But you're not putting your job up as collateral. I won't let you."

"You won't *let* me, Wade?" she repeated archly. "Just now you called me your wife. Well, if that's what I am, then let me be a wife. I have some money put away. It was a gift from my grandmother when she thought I was marrying Harrison. I never touched it because it always brought back some bad memories."

"Now you want to drive a van around to remind you of him?" There was bitterness and yes, maybe even envy in his voice.

She laughed, enjoying the very idea of it. "Hardly! Believe me, I was only too happy to forget him. No, I just meant that there's no reason not to use it now. How can we go to the lake with all this stuff and four kids piled in one compact car, Wade? It doesn't make sense."

"I'll take the truck," he insisted stubbornly.

"Drive two vehicles, spend two tanks of gas? Come on. That's silly." She sat down opposite him, prepared to duke it out, if necessary. She had no intention of letting him refuse her this time. "Why don't you want me to be a part of this family, Wade? Why won't you let me inside that little circle? If I'm your wife, start treating me like one."

"I haven't stopped you from being part of this family." His eyes burned her with their fury.

"Haven't you, Wade?"

She got up and left the room, left the house, too. She

couldn't stay there anymore. Not right now. Instead, she walked into the park next door, found a secluded spot in the shade, and poured out her hurt feelings and aching heart to the Father.

Wade watched her go, hands clenched at his sides. Why did she insist on doing this? Burying him further and further in her debt? Who knew how long it would take him to pay her for a van, let alone the other things she'd splurged on with money he knew hadn't come from the checking account he deposited into.

"You hurt her feelings." Jared stood behind him. "She was so excited about that van, she thought it was such a good idea. And you spoiled it for her. Why did you do that, Uncle Wade? Why did you hurt her? Clarissa wouldn't do anything to hurt you."

"You don't understand, Jared." Wade bit down his frustration in order to reason with the boy. "I can't afford a van right now."

"She wasn't asking you to afford anything. She was asking you to accept a gift that she wants to give." Jared walked over and flopped into the chair Clarissa had sat in. His face was sad. "She tries so hard to do things for us. Last night I got up to get a drink of water and she was down here making a batch of cinnamon buns because you liked them."

"She shouldn't go to all that trouble," Wade muttered, his voice gruff. "She wears herself out because of us and I don't want that."

"But she loves to do it! That's what makes her happy. Yesterday was her day off and she took us shopping at the mall. I didn't really want to go. You know how I hate trying on clothes?" He waited for Wade's nod. "But I went anyway because she was so excited about it. She had it all figured out. We got the girls those sandal things, Pierce another pair of pants and your shirts. Then we went to the theater. She said she'd always wanted to go there when it was really hot outside, just to cool off, but she never had anyone to go with."

Wade refused to let the poignant words get to him. "A van is a little more expensive than some theater tickets, Jared."

The boy nodded, his long narrow face thoughtful. "I know. But it's her money. And this is what she wants. Why do you have anything to say about it?" he asked, without bothering to mince his words. "Why is it so wrong to make her happy? She does things for us all the time."

"Buying that van will make her broke."

"How do you know? Maybe she'll feel really rich, driving around all over town in it. Maybe she'll feel like a real mother. That's what she wants most."

Wade stared. "She wants to be a mother? How do you know this?"

Jared's freckled skin flushed a deep, embarrassing red.

"Well?" Wade didn't relent in his scrutiny.

"I heard her praying one day."

"Jared!" Wade's temper rose like mercury in the desert. "How dare you!"

"I didn't mean to. I was shelving books one day, and she was supposed to be having a coffee break. I went to ask her something but she was praying so I just waited a minute. She was thanking God that He'd given her the chance to have a family, even if it was borrowed. She prayed for all of us, individually. It was kind of nice. Reminded me of Mom." He slapped a hand over his mouth, obviously only just realizing what he'd said.

Wade sighed. So Clarissa had been right there, too. The kids wanted to talk about Kendra but were afraid to around him. Was she right about other things, too? Things like him deliberately shutting her out?

"Your mom prayed for you a lot. She always said you guys were God's gifts to her and could never thank Him enough." Wade swallowed down the hurt and continued. He should have done this months ago. "She had so many plans for you. She used to sit out on the haystack and dream of what you would each be when you were grown up."

Jared's face tightened up, but that didn't stop him from speaking his mind. "Did you love my mother?"

Wade nodded. "I sure did. She was a pain in the butt sometimes, but she was my kid sister. I couldn't help but love her from the first time she flashed those big brown eyes. When she got bigger, I teased her about her lisp." He shook his head, remembering how mean he'd been. "Kendra didn't care what I said, she just had to tag along wherever I went. She'd get mad if I made her stay behind and her lisp would get worse until no one could understand what she was saying. Boy, that girl had a temper!"

"So did Dad." Jared rubbed the back of his hand across his eyes. "I hated it when they were fighting. They tried to keep it down so we didn't hear, but I always listened. It hurt, Uncle Wade."

Wade reached out and clapped a hand on his shoulder. "I know."

"Why did they get married, Uncle Wade? Did they start out in love and then it died, or something? Is that what's gonna happen with you and Clarissa? Do you think she'll get tired of trying to be in our family?"

Wade could have burst out bawling. Or he could have smashed his fist onto the table. Anything to relieve the pent-up emotion that roiled inside at the problems he'd caused with his blind selfishness. But he did neither. Instead he focused on the boy and tried to reassure him.

"Do you think that after waiting all this time for a family, Clarissa is going to just give up? That doesn't sound much like her." He waited for Jared's nod of agreement. "I think Clarissa is going to do everything she can to be the best stand-in mom you guys could have."

"But it isn't going to work if she isn't happy, Uncle Wade." Jared's forehead rippled with worry. "We've got to do things to help her feel like she's part of us, that we want her to stay." He watched Wade anxiously.

Wade sighed. The kid was right. If he expected Clarissa to be the kind of mother the kids needed, he was going to have to open up to her. The secrets he kept stuffed down inside, that's what was standing between them. He couldn't tell her, couldn't tell anybody, about his part in Kendra's misery, and yet that was at the bottom of all their problems. He was guilty and not worth all her time and attention.

"Uncle Wade?"

"I'll try, kid. I promise I'll really try."

"And you'll go and find her and at least look at the

minivan? It's kind of a good idea, Uncle Wade. Her car is pretty cramped, and that van has lots of room. Plus headphones for the ones in back." Jared stopped, obviously wondering if he should have given away this tidbit of information.

Wade burst out laughing. "Well, that clinches it! Headphones are a must." He ruffled the boy's hair, then hugged him close. "Thanks for the pep talk, kiddo."

Jared blushed. "It wasn't really a pep talk. I just wanted to explain. Clarissa's kind of like me. She keeps things inside, where nobody can see them, so that when her feelings get hurt, nobody will know. She doesn't want anybody to think she expects stuff from them."

"You're pretty smart. Know that?" Wade grinned at his perceptive nephew. "For a kid."

"I'm pretty smart, period. But I won't let it go to my head." Jared grinned, high-fived him, then grabbed a cookie and rushed out the back door. "I gotta go check with Evan North about a snorkeling set. See ya!"

"See ya," Wade mumbled, knowing what he had to do and yet dreading it. "Maybe if I just agree to the van, we won't have to get into the past," he mumbled as he set out for the park. He was almost there before the reality of what he was contemplating hit him. Expose his deepest thoughts to Clarissa's probing honesty? "Why do women always have to dig around in the past?"

"Because men won't." Clarissa voice startled him. She stood at the edge of the trees, hands thrust down into the pockets of her flowing cotton skirt. "What's wrong now?"

"Nothing." He studied her, standing there in her sleeveless white eyelet blouse, her hair tumbling wildly from its topknot. "Do you want to comb your hair before we go check out this van or what?"

Her eyes came alive, flashing and glinting with a joy that shook him to the core. Why did she never smile like that for him?

"You'll let me pay for it?" she demanded, then didn't wait for an answer. "Oh, thank you, Wade. Thank you, thank you, thank you."

She threw herself into his arms, wrapping her hands around his neck as she lifted her feet free of the ground. Wade grabbed her around the waist to keep from being knocked over, and swung her around with a laugh that couldn't be suppressed. After all, that's what Clarissa did, made him laugh when he didn't deserve to.

"If that's what will make you happy, who am I to stand in the way?" he murmured, enjoying the feel of her in his arms, the warm scent of her lavender perfume tickling his nose. "How can I deny you such happiness?"

"You can't!" She giggled with pure delight, pressed tiny kisses all over his face, then pushed away from him to do a little jig in the grass.

"Do you know how long I've wanted to be rid of that horrible car?" she laughed, her hair trailing out behind her in a curtain of waves, the topknot completely destroyed. "Years!"

"Why didn't you, then?" he asked curiously, folding her hand in his as he walked back to the house with her.

"I never had a good enough reason," she told him solemnly. "You see, Gran taught me that one doesn't just do things on the spur of the moment. You need to think things through, plan your action, be sure of your next step, then carry it out, and all that. She was very big on waste not, want not."

"Did you plan this out carefully?" he demanded, holding open the screen door for her. "Are you sure about blowing your money on this van?"

"Positive." She grinned impishly, showing off her beautiful smile.

"Okay then, let's go look at the thing." He handed her the car keys and her purse. "If you're absolutely certain this isn't going to ruin your life?" He thought of the pension fund she could be subsidizing for her future, but repressed the words when she pinched his arm.

"Ruin it? I have the best life I've ever had! Come on, Wade. Turtles move faster than you." She bustled out the door and was in his truck before he had a chance to open the door.

Her happiness was infectious and Wade found himself discussing the van's assets on the way over to the seller's house. He had more qualms about her decision when he watched her write the check on their account, but he stuffed them down. He'd pushed his own way too many times. It was time to sit back and see how this worked out.

Besides, it was her life and she was old enough to decide how she wanted to spend it. He just prayed she'd spend a little more of it with him.

"This was the best idea we've had yet," Clarissa whispered to him on the Fourth of July, her shoulder pressed against his on the rough bench they shared with a host of other campers anxious to see every detail of the fireworks. "Look at them, laughing and giggling like regular kids."

He grimaced. "Well, they're as dirty as the others anyway."

"Oh, don't be such an old poop," she chided, her face inches away from his in the dusky evening. "You've had a good time, too. Admit it, why don't you?"

"I've had a wonderful time," he agreed, studying her face. "Searching the bottom of a frigid lake for a paddle that won't stay attached to the dinghy *you* bought."

"Hey, I got a good deal on it at a yard sale! You can't expect mint condition." She wiggled on the bench. "So there were one or two pieces missing."

"Oar holders are a necessary feature of that dinghy," he muttered, his blood pressure rising as her hauntingly beautiful face glowed in the light from the fireworks. Her eyes were starry bright, like a little kid waiting for Santa. "I also had a wonderful time trying to put out that forest—er, campfire you built. We're lucky it rained!"

She blushed adorably, and Wade longed to wrap his arm around her and hug her close. Which was an absolutely stupid idea. This was a marriage of convenience, for Pete's sake! She sure didn't want him fawning over her.

"I didn't realize the boys had put on that lighter fluid. It's lucky no one was hurt." She perched her elbows on her knees and stared off into the night. "Not like the popcorn."

He groaned. "You had to remind me." Wade opened his palm and grimaced at the two blisters that lay white and stark against the darkness of his skin. "Throw that relic out! Nobody pops popcorn over an open fire anymore. They have hot air poppers or microwaves, or even skillets."

"I'm an old-fashioned kind of girl." She turned her head to peer up at him through the gloom. "I like old stuff like that popper. They remind me of the past and how much fun somebody else had before video games and television."

"Yeah, like when the popcorn filled up the basket and had nowhere to go except by pushing the lid off and falling into the fire, thereby sending the whole batch into oblivion." He shook his head, remembering the kernels that had flown out every which way, pinging anyone within twenty feet, but most especially him. "If it's so much fun, how come you didn't take that poker-hot thing from me?"

"Ah, poor baby." She lifted his hand, opened his fingers and placed her lips on each of the burns. "There, does that make it better?"

Wade's blood pressure hit the danger zone. He shook his head slowly, his eyes riveted to her laughing face. "No, that doesn't help one single bit," he muttered huskily, watching her eyes widen.

She stared at him for a long time. Wade had just decided to go ahead and kiss her when a sonic boom broke the mood and she looked away.

"Oh, look, Wade!" In her excitement she grabbed his injured hand and squeezed it tight.

Not for anything would Wade have pulled away. In fact, with her fingers wrapped around his like that, he barely felt the pain of his burn. Nor did he let her delicate little hand go. It might well be that he was acting juvenile, callow and that he was taking advantage, but he didn't give a fig. For just a few minutes he belonged here beside her, no expectations, no duty, just the two of them enjoying some time together.

While Clarissa watched the fireworks, Wade watched her. She was so cute in her long fluttery flowered skirt and ordinary cotton T-shirt, pink-tipped toes peeking out from her sandals. There was nothing unusual about her, she looked like a zillion other women at this fairground.

And yet, there was something extraordinarily unique about this woman. With just one look from those swirling eyes, she could make him forget about two-by-fours and floor joists. This weekend, he was supposed to be planning a renovation for the widow Saltzburg, his richest client so far and the most challenging job he'd landed.

But all he could do was watch Clarissa teach Pierce to swim, play water polo with her and Jared and provide the sunscreen while the girls tanned. Whenever she looked at the kids, there was love, bright and true, shining in her eyes. A touch, a smile, a softly spoken word. In so many ways Wade could see how much she cared for them.

Why didn't she ever look like that at him? Didn't she want a normal marriage?

Yet still Clarissa treated him as if he were…what? The boss? No, not exactly. The kids' guardian? Yeah, but it was more than that. She treated him as if he were her good friend, almost like a brother.

As Wade studied her pale profile in the light of the rocket bursts, he knew he wanted more than friendship from her. He'd detested that canopy bed of hers for weeks now because it reminded him of her innocence and his lack of it.

But sleeping at the cabin was infinitely worse. Every night she crawled into her own sleeping bag, leaving him wishing he had the right to hold her close, to kiss her more than a peck on the cheek.

It was ridiculous, really. He was the one who wanted to be free, unencumbered, a loner. He'd always wanted to go his own way, forge his own path. Yet now, he craved Clarissa's touch, her gentle smile, her soft encouraging words.

Worst of all, he had no right to think about a future, a real marriage with Clarissa. Not until he told her the truth. Then she'd probably decide that she didn't want a deserter in her life and it would serve him right.

"Oh, wasn't that a beauty?" She dropped her head on his shoulder, content to watch the waterfall of cascading fireworks as they died away into the last embers.

Wade slipped his arm around her waist and held her, a swell of something bursting inside as he supported her head, his fingers tangling in the silken stream of hair that flowed down her back. Why couldn't he just tell her that he wanted more from this relationship? That he wanted to get rid of the wall he'd kept up and finally share a part of himself with someone else, someone who really mattered, to form a bond that would last no matter what. How could he want this closeness—crave it? Would she ever agree to it?

As the crowds in the stands stood and began to leave, he came back to reality with a thud.

No, Wade shook his head mentally. It would never work out. She was a homebody, a nester. He was a rolling stone.

But just for a moment Wade let himself imagine what it could have been like. If only he didn't always have to be the responsible one.

Chapter Nine

⌒

"What a dreary job on such a lovely day."

Two weeks later Clarissa dusted off the library's encyclopedias for the third time, her mind busy with thoughts of the lake. It had been a wonderful three-day vacation, everything she'd hoped for. They'd laughed and giggled and had fun. Even Wade had forgotten that taciturn manner and had unbent enough to join in the water fight.

She blushed remembering their walks in the woods after the kids had gone to bed when he'd kissed her as if she were a rare and precious object, the times around the fire when his hand had caught hers and held it fast, the way he sneaked up behind her and kissed her on the neck when nobody was looking.

Wade had changed. She felt that he'd loosened up a little, though there was nothing specific in his demeanor that she could put her finger on. He whistled a lot these past few weeks and teased the kids into a good mood when their plans were rained out. He hadn't said even a word of protest when she bought a microwave with the money that was left from the van.

He was also more affectionate. Which was nice, but Clarissa wanted more than affection. She didn't want to go to sleep alone. Maybe that's why she liked mornings so much. Wade wasn't a morning person. The alarm clock buzzed for a long time before it penetrated his blurry brain.

For Clarissa it was a golden opportunity to lie there and watch him sleep. Sometimes she reached out and touched his hair. It was as glossy and black as a raven's wing and lately had grown quite long. She never mentioned it, though. She liked it that way, liked to see its blue-blackness caught in a morning sunbeam.

Some mornings she leaned over and kissed his cheek, just the way she would if they were really husband and wife. Sometimes she just stared at him and begged God to make him love her.

But the second the alarm issued its annoying beep, she whipped into the bathroom to have her shower so she wouldn't hold him up. By the time he came down, breakfast was ready, she was neat and tidy and the house had been straightened. He might never love her, but Clarissa was determined that he would never find her a burden, either. She would do her part no matter what.

"Clarissa, what is wrong with you? I've asked three times for that book on zinnias." Mrs. Rothschild tapped her cane on the floor abruptly. "I don't hold with day-dreaming, you know. Focus on the present. It gets more things done."

"Yes, Mrs. Rothschild." Clarissa moved to behind the

counter, found and stamped the book and handed it to her. "I hope you enjoy it. It's not due for a month, so take your time."

"Won't need it that long. I read very fast."

Mrs. Rothschild disapproved of taking her time over anything, and Clarissa knew it from the other woman's fraternization with her grandmother years ago.

Mrs. Retter peered over the desk, her eyes darting here and there through her tiny round spectacles. "My turn, dear. My book on asparagus?"

"I've saved it for you. Right here. It looks very interesting." Clarissa handed it over, then turned away from the two ladies who were busy discussing an upcoming rummage sale. "Jared, could you run these letters to the post office? Take Pierce with you and stop for an ice cream on the way back. That's an order."

"Yes, ma'am!" Jared saluted smartly, grinned as he pocketed the letters, then hurried off to find his brother. Clarissa turned back to her work with a smile.

"She says the work was inferior."

The voice was Mrs. Rothschild's. She must be standing behind the magazine stacks, for Clarissa couldn't see her. She shrugged, ignoring the whispered discussion until Wade's name pricked her ears.

"It's no wonder, is it now? The man is working far too many hours. How can he do a good job when he rushes from one job to another?"

Mrs. Retter tut-tutted. "I don't think that's what she said, dear. I think she was implying that he used poor material. That's why she fell. You know how it is nowadays. Knotty this and second grade that."

Mrs. Rothschild sniffed in a way Clarissa knew only too well.

"If you hire that sort, you must expect that they take shortcuts. If you talk to Hilda again, tell her I shall stop by tomorrow, whether she likes it or not. At eighty-six, she can't afford to keep playing this hermit's game. She should be in a nursing home."

"She hates the home. Says it takes away her independence. Why, do you know she eats breakfast at eleven-thirty in the morning? I might try that."

The whispering got fainter and fainter as the two moved toward the door, then through it. Clarissa frowned. Hilda had to be the widow Saltzburg, especially since they'd called her a hermit. The widow seldom, if ever, came to town. That's why Clarissa often had to send someone up to the mansion with her order of books.

Wade's next job was there, wasn't it? Clarissa remembered how happy he'd been to land the contract. She'd tried to warn him about the grumpy, perfectionistic harridan, but he'd brushed off her concern.

"I've built my reputation around here on good, solid work. She can't argue with that, now can she?"

"It was probably nothing," she told herself. "Quit worrying and think about what you're going to make for dinner."

By the time she got home, Tildy had arrived and scrubbed down the kitchen floor, so Clarissa decided to take a shower while she waited for it to dry. Dressed once more in a tank top and shorts, she felt much cooler.

"Hi, guys!" The kids, three of them anyway, sat

grouped around the table. "What do you want to eat tonight?"

"Ice water," Lacey muttered, swiping her hand across her head.

"Anything that doesn't take an oven." That was Tildy, fanning herself with the phone book.

Clarissa was about to open the fridge when the phone rang. "I'll get it. Hello?"

A tirade of anger poured over the lines in the aggrieved tones of one widow Saltzburg. "That young man should be barred from going into other people's homes and creating havoc. It's his fault I've hurt myself. He's careless. Yes, and sloppy, too. Imagine using such poor quality materials that I fell through them."

Clarissa started to speak, but it was quite clear that the widow had not finished. She ranted and raved for a good five minutes more.

"Those kind of people should be forced to go to school and learn the proper way to do things. How could you marry that kind of man, my dear? You're not a stupid girl, not since you got rid of that silly Harrison, anyway." The widow cackled nastily. "He was a taker. And I fear this one is the same. He's no good, you know. Wasn't raised right. He's certainly not our kind."

Clarissa unclenched her fingers one by one until she held the phone loosely in her hand. She took a deep breath and cut right through the spurious remarks about Wade's character.

"Mrs. Saltzburg, I will thank you to stop spouting such defamatory remarks about the man I've married. I assure you that I know him quite well, and he is by no means unskilled or untrained. In fact, his work is in demand all over town. He works night and day, and I happen to know that he put several other people on hold because you demanded that he do your work right away!" She stopped for a breath.

"Well, miss, perhaps he did." The old lady harrumphed in disgust. "That doesn't change the facts. He's ruined my place, just simply ruined it. That man is bad news, young lady."

Clarissa sniffed. She hadn't been called that since she was ten, but it no longer intimidated her.

"I wasn't finished speaking, Mrs. Saltzburg," she said quietly. "'That man' voluntarily took over the care and feeding of his four nieces and nephews so that they would have a good stable home, food on the table and a built-in support system. He didn't have to, but he did it to prevent their family being broken up."

"Probably to get at their money." The snide comment whispered over the line.

Clarissa saw red. "Oh, yes, of course, that's the reason. That's why we live in such luxury. Listen to me, Mrs. Saltzburg." Clarissa ignored the noise behind her, figuring the kids were up to something. That would have to wait. But this maligning of Wade's work and his character wouldn't.

"My husband leaves for work in the morning before any of the children are up. He works the entire day, often not returning home until long after they've gone to bed. He missed seeing them in the school play, misses chatting with them, misses many of their special moments, just so he can make sure they have what they need. And he does this, not because he's trying to steal from them, but because he wants to make sure they never have to go without, as he did."

"All very praiseworthy, I'm sure." The snideness again came through loud and clear.

Clarissa ignored that. "Yes, it is praiseworthy. Even more so is the fact that, despite your changing the plans several times since he bid on your project, Wade has never had one miserable word to say about you, or about anyone else in this town. For that matter, he doesn't complain at all. He just goes about doing the best work he can. Which in your case, I might add, is being done for far less than anyone else would charge."

"It's faulty work," the querulous old woman insisted. "I don't pay for faulty work."

"Is it really?" Clarissa squeezed her eyes shut and counted to ten, praying for heavenly direction. "Well then, Mrs. Saltzburg, I'll have Wade and his lawyer out there first thing tomorrow morning. They'll take pictures, assess the problem. If the work is without fault, as I know it will be, I'm afraid Wade will be advised to seek some compensation. He won't want to, of course. But his lawyer will insist that he not allow your spurious remarks about his character or his work." She waited a moment, then dropped the bombshell. "I'm afraid all work on your house will have to cease until this is sorted out."

Wade stood where he was, directly behind Clarissa, his mouth cracking into a smile as he heard the widow squawking something into the receiver. He couldn't believe his ears. Prim, perfect, calm and quiet Clarissa had defended *him*. And so staunchly, too. He couldn't help smiling at the words she'd used. First-class, top-notch, superior. She liked his work!

"Perhaps you didn't mean to suggest such a thing, but that *is* what I heard, Mrs. Saltzburg. Talk like that is dangerous, not to mention hurtful."

Wade couldn't hear what the cranky widow was saying, so he reached around Clarissa and stabbed the speaker phone button. His wife whirled around, eyes wide with surprise. He caught her in his arms, his finger on her lips to stop her from interrupting the apology that flowed from the telephone.

"I'm sure I never meant to imply anything negative about the man, Clarissa. It's just that one hears talk and I did want to warn you about what was being said."

"You don't need to warn me about Wade Featherhawk, Mrs. Saltzburg. I know everything I need to know about him." Clarissa held his eyes with her steady gaze, her voice firm and unrelenting. "There's nothing you or anyone else could say that would alter my opinion of him."

"Yes, of course. And you would know him best, dear. Please accept my humblest apologies. I certainly didn't mean to upset anyone. There's no need at all for lawyers or any of that nonsense. Now that I think about it, I'm sure I stumbled because of that carpet runner. Beacock is always leaving it too loose." They heard her bellow something then she came back on the line.

"There's no need at all to bother the man with my little fall, dear. I'll expect him tomorrow, as usual. I'm anxious to see how he finishes the summer house."

She prattled on for a few minutes more, alternately apologizing and seeking reassurance that Wade wouldn't know of her call. She hadn't meant a word of it, she insisted.

"Tell her goodbye," Wade whispered in her ear.

"I'm sorry, Mrs. Saltzburg, but I have to get dinner for the children. Goodbye." She hung up the phone and clicked the speaker button off, trying to ease out of his embrace as she did.

Wade knew she was thinking of the kids, but he'd shooed them all out as soon as he figured out who was calling and why. Now he kept his hands firmly in place on her waist and tipped up her chin with one finger.

"She apologized. I can't believe it! After all the miserable things she's said today, I was ready to quit." He shook his head in disbelief. "What on earth did you say to change her mind?"

Clarissa's face grew pink. Her eyes flew away from his curious stare, her hands fiddled with the button on his shirt. "I just told her the truth."

"You defended me. I heard it—part of it, anyway." He couldn't quite believe it even now. No one had ever defended him before. Clarissa had said she knew everything she needed to know about him and yet, Wade knew she didn't. He'd kept the worst of his past a deep, dark secret. "Why did you do it, Clarissa? I could have stood up for myself."

"I know. You don't need me to stand up for you. You don't *need* my help or my concern." She tried to swallow the wobble in her voice. "But that's what I do, Wade. I defend people I care about."

She was furious, he could see it in her face so he held his tongue and let her vent.

"She said horrible things, and hinted even worse. I wasn't going to let her get away with that." Her whole body was rigid with anger. "No way."

"But why?" He kept at it, trying to figure it out. Why wouldn't she let the widow get away with it? "What does it matter to you?"

Clarissa glared at him so fiercely, he expected to see steam come shooting out of her ears.

"What does it matter to me? Let me tell you, Wade Featherhawk, I have backbone, and I won't stand for lies. I don't let anyone malign the people I love, especially when they've done nothing wrong. That's why it matters, Wade Featherhawk. Just because your heritage isn't the same as hers is no reason for her nasty little innuendos that hint at some kind of character flaw. I wasn't going to let her get away with that."

For a moment Clarissa looked smugly satisfied with her defense. Then she clapped a hand over her mouth, her eyes riveted on him. "Oh."

"Yes, oh." He grinned, refusing to set her free, though she wiggled like an eel. "You love me, Clarissa?"

She glared at him, then to his utter amazement, strong, defiant Clarissa, champion defender, burst into tears. "Oh, why did you have to come in? Why couldn't you have waited?" She sobbed the words out, her fingernails tapping on his chest in reproof.

Wade took that dainty little hand in his and held on for dear life. He couldn't believe it. She loved him!

"I'm sorry! I didn't mean to tell you. I was trying to keep it a secret."

Wade tenderly mopped her face. "It's all right,

Clara," he murmured, snuggling her head into his neck. "It's okay. It was a wonderful thing you did for me. I can't tell you what it felt like to come in and hear you defending me. It was—a new experience."

"Nobody defended you before?" she gasped, her sobs still near the surface. She pulled back to peer at him through the tumble of her hair.

He puffed out a harsh laugh as he brushed the glossy curtain behind her ears. "Usually the opposite. Most of the time, what they said was true." He stared into her dear face and marveled at how easily she'd wound herself into their lives. "I tried to live up to their expectations and ended up doing some pretty awful things, Clara. Nasty things. When I couldn't face up to them, I ran away." He cracked a smile. "But there wasn't anywhere to run and the cops always brought me back home to face the music." He fell into thoughts of those sad days.

"Wade?"

"Yeah?" He stared at her, startled by the compassion he could hear in her quiet voice.

"If you need to get away, be by yourself for a while, I can handle things here. You don't have to stick with us all the time. Why don't you go golfing or something?"

He wanted to cry. It was a ridiculous thing for a grown man to admit, but the sweet tenderness of her words made his eyes ache with unshed tears. She gave so much, poured herself out for them. And asked nothing in return. Instead she offered even more.

He leaned forward until his forehead was touching hers. "I don't want to go away, Clara," he murmured.

"What do you want to do?" she whispered, a frown

wrinkling a furrow of barely tanned skin between her eyebrows.

"This." He dipped his mouth down and covered hers, telling her without words how grateful he was for her concern, her care, her love. At first he hadn't wanted it. Now, he didn't know what to do with it, but he was grateful for it all the same.

Through a fog of enchantment that kissing Clarissa engendered, Wade heard a discreet cough. He frowned, finished kissing Clarissa the way he'd wanted to for weeks now, and turned his head to chew out the interloper.

Four sets of eyes stared at the spectacle of the two of them entwined in each other's arms. Four mouths grinned in smug satisfaction. Only one shocked voice demanded an answer.

"Do you *like* all that mushy stuff, Clarissa?" Pierce apparently couldn't believe such a thing.

Wade took pity on Clarissa and set her free, but not before he hugged her once more. "Thank you," he whispered for her ears alone. "I'm going to have a shower. Please don't turn the water on."

She nodded, but Wade wasn't sure she heard a word. He did hear Tildy ask to get a pizza and go to the park. As he showered, he couldn't help thinking it was a very good idea. This house was far too hot. He supposed he'd have to think about central air for the old barn.

Wade had to admit, he was getting fond of the place, even thought of it as home. That should have bothered him, but it didn't. And Wade had no intention of asking himself why.

* * *

It was late by the time they got back from the park. Clarissa straightened up the kitchen while the kids, tired from their impromptu game of volleyball and mad dashes through the sprinklers, tumbled up the stairs and through the shower with scarcely a word of protest.

She avoided Wade as best she could by scurrying through the house to open all the windows and check screens, hoping that the night breeze would cool the place off. By the time she'd finished, the kids were ready to be kissed. Then she took her glass of iced tea, her Bible and hurried out to the veranda, hoping God would send some clear directions on where she should go next.

She was well into Corinthians by the time Wade came out, but the answers still eluded her.

"Why don't you read it out loud? I like to listen to you reading. Your voice is very expressive." He flopped down in the big wicker armchair, his fingers snagging her glass for a quick swallow. "Go ahead. I'm listening."

Clarissa glanced down and gulped. The "love" chapter? She was supposed to read that out loud to him? *All right, God.* She took a breath, then plunged in, reciting I Corinthians as best she could with her eyes closed.

"'If I speak with the tongues of men and of angels, but do not have love, I'm like a noisy gong or a clanging cymbal. If I have all faith, so as to remove mountains, but do not have love, I am nothing. And if I give all my possessions to feed the poor, but do not have love, it profits me nothing.'" She opened her eyes.

"Interesting, isn't it? He seems to be saying that

nothing matters much without love." Wade fiddled with his glass. "Finish it, please."

Clarissa took a deep breath and continued.

"'Love is patient, love is kind, and is not jealous; love does not brag; it is not provoked, does not rejoice in unrighteousness, but rejoices with truth. Love bears all things, believes all things, hopes all things, endures all things. Love never fails.'"

"'Love never fails,'" he quoted in a soft whisper.

The night sounds echoed in the background. Crickets nattered away in a constant rhythm, the wind breathed its way through a screen that kept out the high-pitched whine of mosquitoes itching to snack on humans. In the garden, the sprinkler clicked a pattern over, around and back again.

Wade heard it all through the questions that rose in his mind. "Love believes all things." He'd never believed in Clarissa, not even when she married him. He'd always assumed she had some secret agenda of her own, something she wanted from him. And he'd always assumed that he didn't have it in him to give it to her.

But now Wade wondered about that. Why was he so positive that both he and the kids could depend on Clarissa? What made her any different from the women who'd hounded him in the past? Why was it so easy to go to work and let her handle their problems? It wasn't just that he didn't want to deal with them. He did, but she did a far better job with less fuss and faster results than he'd ever managed. Why did she do that?

The answer lingered deep inside and it took a minute to hear his brain answer. What Clarissa did, she did because she loved them. She was independent enough to stand on her own two feet. She had it all together, she wasn't always searching for something. She didn't *need* him, but he sure needed her.

Oh, sure, she claimed she was in love with him, but if he disappeared today, she'd manage just fine. He could count on her to see things through. Then why did he want to be an integral part of her life, to be the person she depended on, ran to for answers, talked things over with? He wasn't a family man, he'd told her that. Did he want to change now?

Wade studied her as she sat there, head bowed as she perused the words on that fragile onionskin paper. Had she been in love with him before he'd suggested marriage? Had he trampled on her delicate feelings, hurt her with his blunt refusal to do anything but take from her? No responsibilities, he'd told her. No strings.

His face burned as he thought over the words. "Love bears all things, believes all things, hopes all things, endures all things," she'd read. Surely that was a picture of the woman sitting across from him, silently studying her big black Bible. Whatever else she was, Clarissa Cartwright was a gift from God. She didn't play games, didn't try to hide anything. Her clear trusting face gave away her thoughts. With a certainty, Wade knew he could depend on her, count on her to give him a chance.

Why me, he wondered. Why send her my way? I've done nothing but hurt her.

Pictures from their short past tumbled through his brain. Clarissa, lips pinched tight as she forced herself to unhook the fish she'd caught. Clarissa, skirt billowing out behind her as she raced him around the lake. Her head a silver halo in the clear moonlight as she'd sung about moonlight and roses when she thought she was alone. Clarissa, cheeks burning with embarrassment as she insisted that she defended him because she loved him.

He didn't deserve anything she'd given him. He'd taken it all like a greedy kid, without a thought to what she wanted or felt or needed. It had even taken Jared's insight to make him see how much she wanted to buy that van.

He watched as she closed her Bible, got to her feet and wished him good-night. He answered automatically, staring as she left the porch. She moved with a light-footed grace that intrigued him. Why did she always tiptoe around, as if she were afraid she'd disturb him?

She had a skirt on again and it swirled and swayed around her ankles, drawing his attention to her elegant bare feet, slim, pink-tipped toes. Clarissa made no attempt to draw attention to herself and yet, he couldn't stop watching her, couldn't stop his brain from noticing when she bit her lip in concentration, pushed her hands behind her back as if they were in the way, paused before she spoke, giving him time to say what was on his mind.

The clawing in his midsection crawled to his brain. Why did she care? This love she claimed to have—it was an enigma that he wanted to understand. He craved it, desperately wanted to bask in the love she felt for him, to let it flow over and around him, to let it wash away the hard bitter places, ease the hurting that the widow's ugly accusations had resurrected. Was that so wrong?

With a sigh, Wade got up from his chair, locked the house up and climbed the stairs praying for help to understand these strange new feelings that whirled inside like a maelstrom that would not be silent. He coveted the freedom to tell her things, things he'd never told anyone before. He yearned to share a piece of his heart with her, let her see the misery he carried inside. Maybe she could help him get rid of it, cleanse him of this awful guilt for so many failures.

He pushed open their bedroom door, thinking she'd be asleep. The sight of his wife wrapped in what he privately thought of as her rosebud robe, and seated before her little vanity had him rooted to the spot, mesmerized by her long pianist's fingers as they combed through the braids, loosening the strands. When she reached for the brush, he moved forward wordlessly, sliding it from her hands to sweep it through the silver-gilt threads, carefully smoothing them into a cloak of gossamer moonlight.

"Clarissa," he murmured, his fingers lacing through the silken cascade. "I want to make this marriage work."

She sat where she was, head bowed, a dainty figure in a wash of white cotton moonlight. "So do I," she whispered.

"But I don't know how. I look at you and I can't understand why you would love me. There's nothing I could ever do to deserve someone like you. There's no plausible reason why you should care about a guy like me." He kept up the rhythmic strokes, puzzling it out without success. "I'm not the guy you need. I hurt people who care about me, Clarissa. I don't want to, but I always end up hurting them, disappointing them."

In one graceful motion she slipped to her feet and

stood in front of him, her hair a glowing static halo cloud around her calm, smiling face.

"I love you, Wade. You can't deserve it, or make me not feel it. You can't change it. All you can do is accept it." Her fingers cupped his cheek, her eyes soft and welcoming as his hands slid to her tiny waist. "I don't expect anything from you. I don't want you to say or do anything. I just want to be your wife."

She stood on her tiptoes, pink toenails softly glowing in the light as they scrunched into the carpet. Wade tipped his head up and watched her mouth move to within millimeters of his.

"Is that okay with you?"

No matter how much he tried, Wade couldn't deny himself this wonderful gift. He felt guilty accepting it, he wanted to explain things, tell her how bad it was inside him where nobody saw, explain that this was all too new—that he didn't know what to do with love like hers.

But maybe that could come later. Right now, it was getting awfully difficult to resist those full pink lips.

"Very okay," he murmured, drawing her close.

Her hands slid around his neck, her fingers tangling in the length of hair that still needed cutting. "Me, too," she whispered before her mouth touched his sweetly.

He kissed her back, then drew away to search her eyes. "You're sure?" His heart dropped when she moved away.

Clarissa pushed the door closed, then laced her fingers in his. "Positive."

A long time later, Wade touched the silver swath of hair that lay against her flushed cheek. She was beautiful inside and out, like the fairy princess his mother had read of so long ago. As she sighed and shifted in her dreams, one blue-veined hand moved to cover his heart. Having Clarissa as his for-real wife was the most wondrous thing imaginable.

Wade reached out to take her hand, to kiss her awake and tell her how much he cared for her. But he stopped midreach, thought again, let his hand fall away. After all, what could he say?

That he wasn't worthy of her love? She already knew that. That he wanted to love her but was afraid that once he said the words, she'd end up depending on him for things he couldn't give? That he was scared spitless at the thought of living his life without the rigid control he'd always had over his emotions? A control he knew he would willingly relinquish if ever she asked. That he'd never wanted to be a husband, to be responsible for someone else's happiness?

No, he couldn't do it.

"It doesn't mean I don't care about you, Clarissa," he whispered. The words sounded hollow, empty. And Wade knew such a paltry admission wasn't enough. In fact, compared to her heartfelt gift of trust in a man she knew so little about, it was woefully inadequate.

But for now, it would have to do, because Wade had no intention of telling her how unworthy he was to have anyone love him. He wasn't going to explain that caring about him meant you got hurt. He was just going to make sure that this woman didn't suffer for his faults.

"Love never fails."

They'd just have to wait and see how true that was.

Chapter Ten

Monday, August 24, rolled around, two weeks into the heat wave of the century that threatened to scorch everything in Waseka and the surrounding area.

Clarissa huffed a sigh of relief as she waved a tearful goodbye at the children who waved frantically from the bus now leaving the church parking lot. Off to camp for the last week of summer before school started! Maybe now she could get done some of those jobs around the house that had waited far too long. Working would numb the ache around her heart. She hoped. She loved Wade. She was his wife. Would he never say the words she wanted to hear? Was she fooling herself?

"I missed them, I guess?" Wade took her hand, helped her up over the curb and opened the van door. "I tried to get here in time, but I had a flat. Sorry, Clarissa. I didn't mean to make you handle this all alone."

She climbed into her seat, and wiped a hand across her forehead. "It doesn't matter. They were so excited, I doubt they noticed I was here. What are you doing today?"

"Nothing! You scheduled those jobs so far apart that I'm free as a lark until the Martins get back from vacation next week. I might even take today off." He grinned like a little boy who'd skipped school. "Wanna help me play hookey?"

She'd specifically taken this week of holidays so she could get caught up on her housework. But when would she next get a chance to spend some free time with her husband, a man she was only now just beginning to really understand? At least, she thought she did.

Clarissa made up her mind in an instant. "Sure. What did you have in mind?"

He grinned, then winked, a devilish glint in those mischievous dark eyes. "Meet you at home."

For the first time in ages, Clarissa didn't consider her food budget. She stopped at the grocery store and stocked up on deli meats, rolls, salads, some ice cream, a dozen lemons and a basket of fresh strawberries.

Those strawberries made her blush. She'd seen movies where the hero had dipped one in chocolate and fed it to the heroine, then kissed her hand, her arm, her neck…well, kissed her!

She wasn't expecting Wade to do that, of course. He didn't need strawberries or anything else to be romantic, or to make her heart thud so hard it hurt. It was just that she craved a melding of their spirits….

Clarissa forced the thought away and wheeled her cart into the nearest checkout. *God is in control,* she reminded herself. *He wouldn't forsake them. Somehow, it would all work out.*

* * *

"I'm home," she called, lugging the bag through the front door as the heat dragged at her. Wade was standing in the kitchen, an odd look on his face. He moved forward to take the bag from her, his eyes roiling with some dark emotion. "I stopped to get some— Oh, hi, Rita."

She swallowed her disappointment at seeing the social worker lounging at the kitchen table, chewing on one of the brownies Tildy had insisted on mixing last night.

"I wouldn't eat too many of those, if I were you," Clarissa warned, unpacking everything and storing them in the fridge.

"They do have an odd taste," Rita agreed, sampling another. "But the icing is delicious."

"She tripled the baking powder, hoping to get them to rise. It has a rather, um, odd effect." Clarissa shrugged as Rita helped herself to a third bar. "Or maybe it's just me," she murmured, winking at Wade.

"Some people do have weak stomachs," the other woman agreed. "I was just telling your hubby here that in adoption cases, I like to get the messy stuff dealt with out front, before it causes problems." Her beady eyes fixed on him with a stern look. "You might have told me about your past."

"I didn't realize it was important." Wade shrugged, then leaned against the cupboard, a coffee cup in one hand.

But Clarissa wasn't fooled. He was anything but relaxed.

"Running away from your home, willful destruction,

terrorizing the neighbors—that's not important?" Rita wiped her fingers on a napkin and shook her head.

He shook his head, his eyes averted from Clarissa's. "No, it isn't. It was over a long time ago. I was twelve."

"It doesn't exactly qualify you for parent of the year, though. All of this stuff came up in the background check, Mr. Featherhawk."

Clarissa wanted to ask about this "stuff" that Wade never spoke of, but she held her tongue. If God was in control, it was time to let Him handle things.

"How can my childhood interfere with my caring for and adopting my nieces and nephews?" Wade's face darkened, anger evident in the clenched jaw and ticking muscle at the side of his neck.

"It's not just your childhood. You were practically an adult when you stole your uncle's car and ran away from home. You left your sister at home, alone, with no one to watch out for her. Your mother had no idea where you'd gone. It was only sheer chance that the highway patrol officer noticed the trail off into the woods and followed it."

"Kendra wasn't a baby. Besides, I had to get away, to think about my life. It was getting pretty hot at home and I needed a cooling-off time." Wade's low voice oozed with bitterness.

"Children who feel uncomfortable in their home situations often do need a cooling-off period, Rita. That's not a bad thing for a boy to recognize." Clarissa felt compelled to point that out as she watched the misery of the past creep across Wade's glowering face. "It doesn't mean he isn't a good father."

"Sometimes it does." Rita's scrutiny was unrelenting. "Sometimes the past gives us a clue to what the future holds." She straightened, her voice growing harsher as her eyes riveted on Wade.

"I have a responsibility to make sure these kids will not be abandoned just because the going gets rough. Four kids create a lot of heat, Wade. You can't opt to take off and 'think things over,' even if Clarissa is here and the kids are getting older. You've got to commit to a lifetime of being there, of fulfilling their needs first, before your own. I'm concerned that your commitment is going to dwindle down to the point that regret for what you've sacrificed takes its toll on this entire family."

Wade's cup hit the counter with a force that shattered it. He ignored the pieces, his face twisted with anger and something else, something Clarissa could see glinting at the back of his tortured eyes.

"Look, I've said I'll do it, and I will. I know how important this is, Miss Rotheby. I know exactly how much those kids have lost." He stopped, obviously changing what he was about to say. "I give you my vow that I will not leave them, I will not run away from my promise to my sister. I owe her that much."

Clarissa stood, moved over to stand beside Wade, her hand stroking his arm. "We both will, Rita. The kids are doing very well. They've settled in here, Wade is working day and night. We're managing. It's not easy, but we will get through. I promise you that."

Rita glanced from one to the other of them, her eyes speculative. "I'm not worried about you, Clarissa. You've always been bedrock solid, dependable as the sun. It's his predilection for avoiding obligations in the past that has me worried."

"Well, don't be afraid any longer, Miss Rotheby." Wade jerked his arm away from Clarissa, his face dark with fury. "Believe me, I've finished running away. I'm well aware of how my hurry to avoid my duty led to my sister's death. I also know that there is nothing I can do to atone for that, except to look after her children for as long as they need me."

Wade leaned over, brushed a caressing hand through Clarissa's hair, then let it drop away as he straightened. "I'm going out for a while," he told her, his lids hiding the turmoil in his eyes. "I won't be long."

"I'll be here," she promised, ignoring Rita's interested stare. "I'll be right here."

He nodded, his lips pinched tight. "I know. Good old conscientious Clarissa. Backbone of the community."

Clarissa backed away, hurt by the tone in his voice. He closed his eyes and shook his head, raking his fingers through the black length in a gesture that signaled his hurting heart.

"I'm sorry, Clarissa. I didn't mean that the way it sounded. I'm sorry for everything." He left without a backward glance, the screen door slamming shut behind him.

"He's a powder keg, just waiting to blow." Rita dug in her copious bag for a pad and pencil.

Clarissa reached out and touched her fingers, willing her to listen.

"No, Rita. He's worn out and grieving and doing his

best to be strong and invincible. Every time he looks at the kids, I think he sees Kendra. He's in a lot of pain."

Rita nodded thoughtfully. "And some of it has to do with his sister's death," she muttered. "I'm a little concerned about that. What did he mean by 'avoiding his duty'?" She peered up at Clarissa, waiting for an answer.

But Clarissa couldn't answer, because he hadn't told her, hadn't explained the one detail of his past that still held the power to tear him apart. He didn't trust her enough.

"You'll have to ask Wade," she murmured, sadness creeping through her tired body. "I can't answer for him. But I will assure you of this. He isn't going to run out on me or them. He's committed to this marriage. He's committed to this family."

Rita huffed to her feet. "If anybody can bring him around, Clarissa, you can. You're strong enough for the both of you." She said thank you for the brownies, picked up her bulging briefcase and waddled out the door.

Tears welled in Clarissa's eyes. "I'm not strong at all," she muttered. "I'm just too afraid to ask him outright what happened in the past. I'm afraid, Lord."

She spent a few moments asking for heavenly direction, then, since Wade hadn't returned, decided to stick to the original plan and get to work on the basement. The youth group needed a cool place to meet for their Bible study. If she could fix up an area down there, it would be perfect.

The boxes from Wade and the children's move were stacked helter-skelter all over, some with their contents tumbling out.

"Jared, I might have known you'd dump your schoolbooks down here." She pushed the stack of looseleaf into an empty box and set it aside for a fire she'd have later. There were winter clothes, photo albums, pots, pans, curtains and a host of other things that she sorted into two piles, give-away and storage.

As she carted the last of the storage cartons to a place under the stairway, Clarissa stumbled over a small brown box that must have fallen out of one of the others. She flipped it open, wondering which stack it belonged in.

The name of a prominent university leapt out at her from a letter addressed to Wade. She recognized the envelope as one that had arrived only last week. Her eyes scanned the words, as the ache inside grew.

"He wanted to go to school," she whispered, recognizing the date for classes to begin as only weeks away. "An architect. He was going to train as an architect."

She lifted the letter and read about the funding in place for mature students. Because his preliminary marks were so high and his renderings so technically correct, one of the professors had recommended a very generous tuition scholarship.

"This is a one-time only offer," the letter stated. "We reserve the right to withdraw it if you do not appear on September 15."

He gave it up. He gave it all up to raise Kendra's kids. The knowledge caused a surge of tenderness to rise inside Clarissa. How long had it taken to acquire the credits necessary for entrance to the faculty? She remembered him once telling the kids that he'd never finished his senior year.

As her fingers loosed on the box, it tumbled to the floor and papers scattered everywhere. Columns, turrets, gable roofs and transom windows, precise in every perspective, lay scattered across the floor.

"Clarissa?" Wade's voice broke through her study of the sketches.

"I'm down here," she replied, forcibly restraining herself from hiding the evidence of her meddling.

He got halfway down before his eyes flew to the white papers littering the cement. He didn't say a word, merely looked at her.

"I was straightening up these boxes," she whispered. "You know, so the youth group could meet here. These fell out."

He stalked down the rest of the stairs and toward her, stopping along the way to pick up his drawings.

"I didn't mean to pry, Wade. Truly, I didn't."

He ignored her words. "Doesn't matter. I should have thrown them away. It's past."

The utter void of any expression of feeling in those words made her want to weep.

"It doesn't have to be," she murmured, resting one hand on his arm. "You could still attend classes. I could get a job…."

Her voice trailed away as he turned on her, his lips stretched in a mocking grin. "Oh, sure. You could find a job that would support six people while I whiled away the hours at school? Come on, Clarissa. Be realistic. It isn't going to happen."

"Perhaps if we—"

"Just let it die! It was a stupid idea. I'd probably

make a lousy architect, anyhow. I hate being cooped up in an office."

Wade pulled the papers out of her hands and tossed everything into the big cardboard box that lay open under the stairs. "My priorities have changed, Clarissa. Why waste time on the past?"

She wanted to say something. Anything. She wanted to tell him that she had money enough to fulfill his dream, but that would be a lie. Belatedly she remembered the van. Why had she insisted on that van? If only she'd known about this!

Wade quickly heaved the rest of the boxes out of the way, lugged the give-away ones upstairs and helped her shift around some old leftover furniture so that they eventually created a kind of informal den. He said nothing while he did it, offered no words to explain, nothing that would help her understand or allow any commiseration.

"I think that should do it. It'll be all right for the kids, don't you think?" She looked to him for confirmation.

"It's fine. They can crash down here in comfort. These old cement basements never seem to get very warm, even on the hottest days." Wade glanced around once more. "Is there anything else that needs doing?"

"Not down here, no. I've got some painting in the girls' room that I'd like to get finished before they come back. And I want to clean the carpets, but I've got a whole week for that." She was babbling and she knew it, but Wade's face looked so odd. He seemed to be in another world.

"Oh." He stood at the bottom of the stairs, waiting

for her to go first. By the time they were back in the kitchen the ominous rumble of thunderclouds could be heard rattling in the west. "We're going to get a storm."

"Good." Clarissa blew her bangs off her forehead as she poured them both a glass of iced tea. "It'll be that much nicer to work if it's cool." She pushed a glass across the table to him, then allowed herself to flop onto the closest chair, more tired than she was prepared to admit.

Wade sat across from her, fiddling with the moisture droplets on the outside of his glass as he stared at the ice cubes floating on the top.

Since she didn't know what to say, Clarissa remained silent, waiting for him to open up. The gap of quiet yawned between them, stretching her nerves taut. Something was wrong, she could feel it. Whenever he thought she wasn't looking, Wade stared at her as if she'd sprouted horns.

When she could stand it no longer, Clarissa cleared her throat, racking her brain for something to say. "Did you have anything—"

"Clarissa, would you mind if I left you alone for today? I need to do some thinking and it would help if I could get away from the phone for a while."

He didn't say "and you," but Clarissa was positive that's what he'd meant.

"Of course I don't mind! I suggested it, if you remember. Are you going to try golfing?" She flushed at her own obviousness. Why was it so important to know? Why was she still reminded of his uncle's insistence that Wade always ran away from his responsibilities?

"No, nothing like that. I just want to go somewhere quiet, get my brain straightened out. You have to admit that the past few months have been a little hectic." He smiled ruefully, as if to remind her of his words before they'd been married. "Unless you need me to help you with something around here? I could always go another time."

Clarissa heard the wistfulness in his voice and her heart melted. He just wanted a break, some time to himself. And why not? Hadn't he been working flat out since she'd met him? Wasn't this what love was all about—giving when the other person needed it?

She leaned across the table, her hand grasping his. "There's nothing that needs doing here," she told him sincerely, her eyes steady as they met his. "Go and relax. Take a break. You've earned it." She made herself summon a quirky little smile. "And to tell you the truth, it would be easier for me to get some work done if I didn't have to think about making you lunch and supper. Not that I'm trying to get rid of you, but…"

"Clarissa." His amused tone stopped her cold. "I get it. I'm in the way, and you wouldn't be averse to a little time spent on your own either. Nothing wrong with that."

It wasn't what she meant at all, but Clarissa let it go. Maybe believing that made it easier for him. So be it.

"No, nothing at all wrong with wanting some time alone," she murmured, shutting down the pestering voice in her brain.

"Right." He swallowed his tea in one gulp, then pushed away from the table. "I won't be late," he promised, bending over to brush his lips against hers. "Or if I am, I'll call you. Okay?"

She nodded, afraid to ask what was really going

through her mind. Why couldn't he talk to his wife? Why did he need to get away from her?

She watched as he picked up his sunglasses, the keys to his truck and then pulled out two cans of juice she'd put to cool in the fridge. "Are you sure you don't want to take some brownies along?" she offered, tongue in cheek.

Wade grinned, slicked a finger through the icing, licked it off with apparent delight, then slid the rest of the brownies into the trash. "Thanks, anyway," he told her seriously. "But I used all the antacids last night." He loped to the screen door and yanked it open. "See you later, Clara."

"Later," Clarissa repeated, wondering privately why it was that Wade always looked much happier to be leaving her than he did when coming home.

A few seconds later the rumble of his truck told her he was gone. She sighed and shoved to her feet, pushing a few straggling hairs back as a tiny breeze wafted in through the open window. Seconds later a light but steady rain began.

"Perfect painting weather," she told herself and leaned down to tug the cans out of the cupboard where she'd stored them. "Now get to work."

Chapter Eleven

The storm didn't hit Waseka directly. Most of the thunderclouds passed just to the south, bringing cooler air and life-giving moisture to the dry crops and wilting flowers. The lightning and thunder lit the sky from a distance, but Waseka sat calm and peaceful, as if in the eye of the storm.

Clarissa stood in front of the fan, letting it blow directly on her as she studied her work. The pink-tinged paint made a world of difference, giving the room a bright new look that was warm and inviting. She was considering curtains, bright candy-cane striped curtains she could make from that remnant of fabric she'd kept for so long, when the phone rang.

She hurried out in the hallway, wondering why painting one room was such an operation. "I'm out of shape," she told herself, with a dire look at her sweaty reflection. "Hello?"

"Is that Clarissa?"

"Yes, Mrs. Saltzburg, it's me. Is anything the matter?" Now she wished she'd let it ring.

"Yes, something is terribly the matter. My roof is leaking! Can you imagine? That storm rushed right by my place and took the shingles with it. I have buckets all over the place, and there's no end to it. Please have your husband come over immediately. I must have it fixed."

Ah, just desserts, decided Clarissa, stifling the tiny smile that rose to her lips. Then she gave herself a stiff lecture on loving those who needed it most.

"I am really sorry, Mrs. Saltzburg, but Wade isn't home. I don't expect him back until late tonight." She crossed her fingers for good measure, just in case. "Can you manage till tomorrow morning? Though I'm not sure he'll be able to do anything even then. I don't think they reroof when it's raining."

For the hundredth time Clarissa wished Wade had told her more about his business. How was she supposed to sound knowledgeable when she hadn't a clue about any of it?

"I don't see why he can't come over immediately. It's not as if he's doing anything special just because he's having coffee with that bunch of gossiping old men in the café. Saw him myself. If it were my day off, I wouldn't choose to spend it with those old fools."

Privately, Clarissa felt the same. She frowned. He'd wanted to get away to think, he'd said. Surely one couldn't do much deep thinking at the local watering hole.

"Well, either way, I'll let him know as soon as possible. Take care, Mrs. Saltzburg."

"Take care! Humph. As if I can with all these buckets lying helter-skelter. Beacock, this pail is full. Must I tell you—" The rest of the sentence was cut off with an abrupt click.

Clarissa whispered a prayer for the plight of poor Beacock as she replaced the phone. But her mind returned immediately to Wade. Some time with the boys, that's what he needed.

Her heart grew lighter as she reminded herself of the strawberries. They'd be all alone in the house tonight. Maybe she could…

Clarissa went back to the girls' bedroom and snapped the lids on the empty paint cans. It wouldn't be difficult to stitch up those drapes. Especially since she could set up her machine right here in this room. It wasn't a bad place to work at all, not with the breeze blowing lovely cool air in and the fan circulating air out the door.

She hurried down the stairs to get rid of the cans and wash out her supplies. She felt dizzy for a moment or two in the kitchen. It was because she'd bent down too quickly. Heat did that to you. Also hunger.

Her eyes widened as she noted that it was now after three. It didn't take a minute to help herself to a slice of ham and some of the potato salad she'd purchased that morning. She zapped the roll for a couple of seconds in her new microwave and licked her lips as the butter drizzled down into the soft fluffy flesh.

"Oh, this ham is excellent," she told Tabby, who strolled into the kitchen just long enough to sniff at her food. With a purr of disgust, the cat sauntered out of the room into the living room. Clarissa shrugged. "Be like that, then. I haven't had potato salad in ages."

Clarissa ate slowly, savoring each mouthful, her

mind busy with the curtains. It felt good to relax for a while, to enjoy food she hadn't prepared or cleaned up after. She tried to remember when she'd eaten last, but couldn't.

"It's been too hot," she rationalized, remembering how weak she'd felt earlier. "Nobody can eat when it's hot."

Her stomach jerked and quivered in revulsion and Clarissa hurried to the bathroom. When she'd finally recovered, she returned to the table, pouring herself a glass of cool water that she sipped as she reached for the phone.

"Hello, Gerda? This is Clarissa Featherhawk. I bought some of that potato salad this morning, and I'm pretty sure it's off. I just ate some and I've been quite sick. I thought you might want to throw it out."

"I only made it this morning, Clarissa." Gerda's German accent grew stronger, her voice more indignant. "I haf served it to all my lunch customers vith no complaints. I don't sink dis is de problem, Clarissa."

"Oh. Well, the only other thing I had to eat was the ham and the bun and they both tasted fine." She'd been trying to warn her, but now Clarissa felt like an idiot for saying a word.

"Perhaps it is zee heat." Gerda's harsh tones softened. "Eet makes us all sick."

"Yes, that must be it. Sorry to have bothered you." Clarissa hung up the phone, chiding herself for her impulsive act. Why had she disturbed that poor woman? Gerda was as careful of food poisoning as it was possible to be in a deli.

Once she'd finished her water, Clarissa felt better. It took only a few moments to set up the machine after she'd cut the material. Within two hours she had the curtains stitched and was just finishing hanging them when the phone rang again.

"Hello?"

"It's me." Wade sounded tired, dispirited. "I haven't gone anywhere yet. I'm waiting for someone. I'm not sure when I'll get home, Clarissa."

"Wade, it doesn't matter." She tried to be understanding, to cut him some slack, as Jared would say. "You don't have to check in with me. Just do whatever it is you need to do. I'm fine. In fact, I'm just hanging the drapes in the girls' room. Then I'm going to get the rug shampooer going."

"Don't wear yourself out. Maybe I should come home and give you a hand." He sounded depressed.

"It's your day off, Wade. Relax!"

She hung up the phone before he could argue.

After hanging the curtains and straightening the room, Clarissa took a coffee break.

She flopped into a kitchen chair and found herself drooping with fatigue. Eat something, her brain told her.

Clarissa moved to the fridge, her eyes moving from the cold cuts to the salad, to the strawberries. Ah, that was just the thing. With a little ice cream.

She leaned against the counter as she rinsed off several of the plump ripe berries and dished up a tiny scoop of lemon sherbet.

The berries were tangy, their flavor making her tongue come alive. She'd eaten three, and one spoonful of sherbet, before her queasy stomach rebelled.

"What a terrible time to get the flu," she muttered,

emerging from the bathroom, clutching a cold wet washcloth to her forehead.

She sank back into her chair, shoving the food away as the phone rang for the third time. "Yes?" she asked with a sigh.

"Ya, Gerda here. Das ist Clarissa?"

"Yes. Hello, Gerda." Clarissa forced her head to stay up when all she wanted to do was lay it on her arms and go to sleep.

"You are okay? No more sick?"

Clarissa wished a thousand times over that she'd never made that phone call. How embarrassing! Now the whole town would know she'd maligned the kind-hearted woman.

"I'm fine, Gerda. Thanks for asking."

"Ach, you do not sound fine." Gerda's snort of disapproval carried clearly across the line. "I think you haf been sick again, yes?"

"Yes," Clarissa admitted. "It must be some kind of flu. I only had a few bites of strawberries, but that was all it took."

"*Nein, das* is *nicht* flu." Gerda's harsh voice softened. "*Das ist eine* baby."

"I'm sorry, I didn't quite catch that." Clarissa shook her head, trying to stay awake. "What did you say?"

"A baby, Clarissa. You are waiting for a baby?"

Clarissa gulped, her eyes widening until she could see nothing but stars. She blinked once, then answered the urgent summons from the receiver in her hand.

"Yes, I'm here. But I think I have to go now, Gerda. I'm sure you're wrong, though." She almost replaced the receiver, then thought of something. "Have you seen Wade, Gerda?"

"Yah. He vas here mit zee pastor. Talking, talking." She called something out to someone else, then returned to the conversation. "He's gone. You rest, Clarissa. And get better. When babies come, you must be healthy."

"Yes, of course. Thank you. Goodbye." She hung up the phone, then went to stand at the screen so the evening air could cool her heated face.

It couldn't be? Could it? Clarissa tried to remember, tried to figure dates and such, but nothing would stay in her head. The plain truth was, she didn't know. It *could* happen.

Oh, but wouldn't it be wonderful if she was. A baby! A precious tiny baby she could hold in her arms, share with the children. A tiny prayer answered.

She touched her stomach with wonder. Could it be?

Of all the prayers she'd prayed, this was the one she'd been remiss in repeating. There hadn't been time to think about babies lately. She'd been too busy with the children, the library, learning to love Wade.

Wade!

The joy drained away just as the rain followed a little rivulet on its way to the gutter at the end of her walk. How terrible for Wade! He didn't want more responsibility, didn't want another person dependent on him, holding him back from the dreams that were far bigger than anything Clarissa had suspected.

Wade, who needed freedom, time to think, a place to be alone, how could she expect him to be excited about this? It would only be another burden, a burden she'd put on him. He'd feel trapped by their marriage, trapped by her. She and the baby could become another chore, another "to-do" on his list of "have-tos."

The whole, unbearable weight of it dragged her shoulders down, pressed against her forehead until it ached. Why hadn't she thought ahead, considered this? Done something to prevent it?

A little coo of sheer bliss echoed through her mind, the picture of tiny fat fingers reaching out flashed before her eyes. Such a precious thing, a baby. Such a joy to behold as it grew to know and understand its world.

She thrust it away, all of it, as Wade's dark brooding eyes swam into their place. The shuttered look he hid behind this afternoon when he'd glanced at the acceptance form from the admissions board. That desperate shove that sent an old and tattered blue bankbook with a zero balance into the trash box when he thought she wasn't looking. The hasty burial of drafting pencils and T squares under children's clothes.

That picture was replaced by one of herself, huge and ungainly as she tried to maneuver around the kitchen to get dinner on as Wade waited tiredly amid a mess that she couldn't get cleaned up. She saw him dragging in, day after day, handing over his paycheck before he went to wash up, jeans tattered and torn, filthy with plaster dust.

And his hair, his beautiful jet-wing hair, no longer glossy, but lackluster and thinning, more silver than black as it lay cropped and shingled against his head.

"Oh, Lord, help me." She let the tears fall then, hot bitter tears for a future that could never be. "Please don't let me be pregnant," she whispered, the agony of uttering those words tearing at her heart until her entire body mourned. "He doesn't want more responsibilities, more burdens to shoulder. He's such a good man and all he wants is to fulfill his dream. Is that so wrong?"

She stepped outside, onto the back step and let the little spits of rain dash against her hot cheeks.

"He's a good man, a wonderful husband and father. But he's nervous about responsibility. And no wonder. He had to take it on so young." She thought about the dream that had been stashed away under the stairwell. "I'd give almost anything for him to go back to school."

God is in control.

She looked up at the darkening sky, almost certain she'd heard a voice. "I know. And You always make the right decisions."

Trust in the Lord.

"I do, God. I trust You so much." She gulped down the huge lump in the middle of her throat and gave up what she'd always longed for. "But God, if You need me to, I can give up my dream for Wade's. It was a silly, fairy-tale dream anyway." She choked down the sob, but continued. "I've already got four wonderful kids to look after, to cherish, to raise for You." She squeezed her hands together, knowing what she had to do.

"I don't need a baby, Lord. What Wade needs is far more important than me and I don't ever want to make him feel I'm draining him."

Clarissa waited for an answer, a sign that would tell her what to do next. As she did, a scene from the past paraded through her mind. She was ten and looking forward to two weeks of camp. She loved camp and this year it would be doubly exciting because Gran was going to Scotland while she was gone. A sister still lived there, they'd corresponded for months.

Clarissa remembered the excitement she'd found gazing at travel brochures and watching her grandmother's eyes light up as she came upon a favorite place she remembered from her childhood. They'd spent hours pouring over maps, guidebooks, the letters, making sure each detail was carefully organized. It was the trip of a lifetime.

Then, the morning before Clarissa was to leave, the trip was off. Gran simply said her sister needed more time to prepare, but Clarissa knew it was more than that. She'd puzzled over it for hours, sitting there on the veranda as the rain spattered the garden. And then she'd heard the telephone conversation that had changed her life. Gran was explaining why she wouldn't be coming to Celia, her sister.

"I'm sorry, dear, but I just can't manage it this year. Clarissa has to have braces and there's only my savings to pay for them. No, don't cry, Celia. I will get there, I promise. Just not this summer. Clarissa's needs come first. The dentist says the bite must be corrected as soon as possible or she'll have lifelong problems." Her Gran's voice stopped, waited a moment, then continued.

"No, she doesn't know. And I won't tell her why. It's not her fault."

Clarissa remembered the choking sob, then the softly spoken words. "But, oh Celia, I wanted so badly to see you again. Just for a while."

That's when the truth had dawned. She, Clarissa,

was a burden. She was stopping Gran from doing things, from seeing the one person left from her family. How many times had it happened since she'd come here? How many other times had Gran done without, given up some dream she held so precious, just because Clarissa had come along?

As a child, Clarissa prayed and prayed for an answer, but none came. She'd gone off to camp with a sore spot on her soul. She'd stayed only one week that year. One miserable, lonely week while she made up her mind never to be a burden again.

Clarissa winced back to the present. "What am I going to do, Lord?" she whispered, pushing away her yearning for a baby.

The answer rumbled through her mind, a verse learned at camp.

Be still and know that I am God.

She knew that. She was confident that God could do anything. But how could He possibly straighten out this mess? Either way, she or Wade would lose the one thing they really wanted, wouldn't they?

How could she ever learn to live with that?

Chapter Twelve

"I'm sorry to bother you." Wade tugged off his cap and shoved it into the back pocket of his jeans. "I know you're busy with important things and I'm probably wasting your time, but…"

"But you needed to talk to someone." The pastor grinned and motioned toward a kitchen chair. "I'm just glad I got home before you left. Want some coffee?"

"Sure." Wade slumped into the chair at the same time as he ordered his weary body to get out of there. When had he ever spilled his guts to anyone? He sure didn't need to start now, at the ripe old age of thirty. And yet he did.

"Actually, I'm starving. Mind if I scramble some eggs? I can do some for you, too, if you're hungry." The pastor waited for Wade's nod, then pulled out a frypan and began cracking eggs. "So what's up in your busy family?"

"The kids are off at camp. Clarissa took a week off so she could get some housecleaning done. Everything's fine." Wade shuffled his feet nervously. "Look, Pastor—"

"It's Michael, or Mike to my friends. Which I hope you intend to be." He grinned in exactly the same way Pierce did when he was trying to con you into something.

"Okay, Mike." Wade squeezed his eyes shut, took a deep breath and blew it out on a sigh. "I don't know how to say this. No matter which way I phrase it, it's going to come out wrong."

"Why don't you just tell me what's eating at you and stop waiting for someone to judge?" Mike stirred his eggs with one hand while the other popped bread into the toaster. "I'm listening."

"It's Clarissa. No, it's me. Actually it's both of us." Wade shook his head, frustration welling up inside. "I didn't marry her because I loved her," he blurted out in a rush of air and then proceeded to tell the pastor the reason why they'd married.

Mike handed him the butter and the toast. "Here, you can do this." He turned back to the eggs. "So?"

"Well, the thing is, I think I committed a sin by doing that. A mighty big one." Wade knew his face was beet-red so he kept his head down, his eyes on his task.

"A sin?" Mike let out a belly laugh. "Well, brother, if you think making a home for four needy kids with a woman as loving as Clarissa is a sin, you've got a strange idea of God."

"I do?" Wade thought about that. "Yeah, probably I do. I never had much of a father figure in my dad, you know. I always kinda pictured God as this judge sort of fellow, who laid out a bunch of laws and waited to see who would keep them. I don't think even your kind of benevolent God would approve of my selfishness when it comes to Clarissa. No one would."

"What is this 'my God, your God' garbage?" Mike leaned backward, grabbed the coffeepot and filled two cups. "There is only one God, buddy. And He's the God of love."

"Love!" Wade flung down his fork. "That's what started this whole mixed-up mess," he sputtered. "I can't love anyone."

"Oh?" Mike quirked one eyebrow, his jaws crunching the toast. "Why's that?"

Wade felt a rush of anger like he'd never experienced before. Why was he here anyway? What good would it do to maul it all over with someone who so patently didn't understand?

"If you don't let it out, I can't help." The chiding voice got to him.

"Fine." Flinging down his napkin, Wade jumped to his feet, paced out the black-and-white kitchen tiles, then paced back again. He stopped right beside Mike's chair. "Anybody I love gets hurt. Doesn't matter that I don't want that, that I try to do the best. It always goes wrong."

"Mm-hm." Mike took a slug of coffee, helped himself to another lump of egg, then cocked his head to one side. "Why is that?"

"Because they always want something from me and I have nothing to give," he snapped out, angered by the other man's cavalier approach. "I get scared by all those demands and then I do something stupid or take off. I just can't handle other people's expectations."

"Running away?" Mike nodded. "I know about that."

Wade snickered. "Yeah, I'm sure, Pastor."

"Think not?" Mike was calm, his eyes steady. "Think about this. Ten years ago I was fourteen. I hot-wired a car and took it for a joyride. Crashed."

Wade flopped back down into his chair, his attention caught by the calm recital. "You?"

Mike nodded. "Me," he confirmed. "My parents had a cabin at the lake, and I hid out there as long as I could, knowing what the right thing to do was, but scared spitless to own up to my mistakes."

Wade wasn't exactly sure what protocol in this situation was. Should he ask Mike to continue, even though it was no doubt very painful?

"You don't have to look at me like that. I can talk about it now. It helps to know that at least I learned something from the incident." He grinned, his quirky mouth offering a wry smile.

"Okay, I'll bite. What did you learn?" Wade picked at his egg, but his interest wasn't in food. He reached for his cup, but his hand stopped midway at the response.

"I learned about grace."

He gulped. Now for the sermon, he thought to himself. "That was her name?"

Mike shook his head. "Uh-uh. That was the lesson. Her name was Margaret. Margaret Milton. She was seventy-one and about as big as a wasp. But could she sting!" He chuckled in remembrance. "The accident meant she had to take a cab to do meals-on-wheels. But that didn't slow her down one whit. She made her presence felt by contacting the police and the judge. She refused to press charges, said she'd drum up a real ruckus unless she could have some say in what my punishment would be.

"I was sure she was up to something, but she was so friendly, I hung around. Margaret insisted I'd been given an opportunity. She said she loved God, that He controlled her life and everything to do with it. She insisted that it had to be His will that I stole her car so something good could come of it." Mike grinned. "I figured she was off her rocker, but if it would keep me out of jail, I was all for it. I shut up and listened."

"She does sound a little loony," Wade agreed.

"But that's just it, she wasn't. She totally believed that God was in control and she did the best she could with what He gave her. She said she'd learned love that way and that evidently I was to be her next project. I laughed my head off, but I couldn't avoid hearing more of her theories. I had to keep going back there or wait in jail. I chose Margaret."

"I suppose she forced you to do a lot of stuff around her house or something, to pay off the debt?" Wade had met those kind of do-gooders before, those upright souls who were bent on exacting revenge.

"Nope, all she did was insist that I do a Bible study with her. I'd been to church, I figured I knew what most of it meant, so I agreed. We met three times a week, to talk over what we'd studied. But she wouldn't get off I Corinthians 13."

"The 'Love' chapter." Wade sighed, closing his eyes for just a moment as he remembered the night Clarissa had read those words to him.

"You got it. Love, love, love. That's all I heard for three long months. Every Monday, Wednesday and Friday evening I'd go over, and we'd talk about it. The more we talked, the more I realized that love isn't an action, it's a process. It's not something you do like speaking wisdom, or moving mountains. You see, you can do all those things without love."

"I get it. Like where it says giving to the poor, or having your body burned." Wade nodded.

"Yes. You can do all that, but if you don't love, it doesn't matter a whit." Mike leaned forward, his hand reaching across the table for his big black Bible. He flipped through it quickly, finding the passage he sought. "After he says that, Paul goes on to tell us what love looks like. It's long-suffering, kind, doesn't envy, isn't boastful or proud, doesn't behave poorly, can't be easily provoked. See here." He slid his finger along the passage.

"Thinks no evil, rejoices in the truth, bears all things, believes all things, hopes all things, endures all things." To Wade it sounded exactly like Cla-rissa. She lived what these verses talked about.

Mike pulled the Bible back in front of him. "But it goes on. It tells us that the only thing that will last is love. Everything else, even the good things, will pass away."

"I know all that. You spoke on it a couple of weeks ago." Wade wondered for the tenth time why he'd come here. It was an interesting story, but he was looking for help, not stories. "The thing is, I'm no good at love. I'm not dependable. In fact, I'm not any of those things you just listed." He made a face.

"I get to feeling like I'm boxed in and I can only think

of being free. What good would it do Clarissa if I loved her, Mike? She doesn't need me putting more demands on her. She's already working herself to a shadow trying to prove that running a home, keeping four kids on the ball and working aren't too much for her."

Mike opened his mouth, but shut it abruptly when Wade spoke again.

"I keep hoping we'll get a moment together, some time and space to work things out, to talk about what we want the future to bring, what she wants from me, what she expects me to do. But she's always got another job, another load of laundry, another little talk to have with the kids." He laughed bitterly. "Ironic, isn't it? That's exactly why I married her. Fool that I am, I thought that would be enough, for her and for me."

"And it's not?" Mike carried the dishes to the sink and ran hot water over them.

Wade was grateful for the break, it gave him time to organize what he was trying to explain.

"No!" he blurted out at last. "She says she loves me, and I believe her. But at the same time, I don't want her to."

"Why?"

"Because it makes me indebted to her. I only ever hurt the people I care most about. And I don't ever want to hurt Clarissa. She doesn't deserve that. No one does."

Mike flopped into the chair and hooted with laughter. "That's a crock, Wade, and you know it."

Wade flushed, stung by the reproof in those tones. "I don't know what you mean."

"Sure you do." He waited a moment, then sighed.

"Okay, I'll lay it out for you, buddy. You're a fraidy cat." Mike fixed his gaze on him and dared him to look away. "You want Clarissa to love you, you bask in all the attention she pays you. You like hearing the folks say what a wonderful couple you make, how the kids look so cared for and her house seems to hum. You love it when she tells people how careful you are at your job."

"I didn't know she did that," he mumbled, his cheeks burning, but then Wade recalled a certain telephone call and knew he lied.

"Oh, you know, buddy. You just won't admit it to yourself. Because then you'd have to respond and you're too wrapped up in yourself to reach out. At least, that's what you're telling yourself."

"You make me sound like a first-class creep," Wade muttered, grinding his back teeth together when what he really wanted was to hit something.

"Isn't that what you just told me you are?" Mike put a hand on his arm. "Listen to me, Wade. Love isn't about doing things. I know you've done a thousand things to repay her for taking you and the kids on. That's not the issue."

"It's exactly the issue!" Wade exploded. "Don't you see that it doesn't matter what I do! How am I supposed to repay her for the eyestrain she gets when she spends hours sewing sequins on a costume for school? How can I possibly do anything that will compensate her for the days she's spent building up Pierce's self-esteem or teaching Tildy to stop burning everything she touches? How—"

"You can't," Mike interrupted, calmly sipping his coffee.

Wade stared. It wasn't the answer he wanted. "I don't…"

"It doesn't matter how long it takes you or how hard you try, Clarissa will never get back those hours she's spent, or the words she's shared. You can't repay her, Wade. And if I know Clarissa, she wouldn't want you to try."

"Yes, but it's not fair."

"Love isn't fair. It goes above and beyond the call of duty. It does things just because. It's a heart condition, Wade. Not an outward show, just a steady glowing thing inside the heart that makes you take the second step, push a little harder, work a little longer."

"I can't accept that," Wade told him. "There has to be something I can do to repay her."

"You can do something."

"What?" At last they were getting somewhere. Wade moved to the edge of his chair and waited expectantly. "What can I do?"

"Accept it." Mike smiled. "It's called grace, Wade. And it works the same way as God does with us. Do you think it benefits Him to have human beings who keep running to Him for every little pimple? No. It's just more work. But He loves it when we keep coming to Him." He grinned.

"Do you think it benefits you to slave away like a fool so you can earn enough money for Pierce to be on the baseball team or Lacey to buy a new dress for the prom? Wouldn't you be far better off to keep your money and take yourself on a nice little holiday?"

Wade frowned. "But I want to do those things. I love doing things for them. They're my kids."

"I know. And that's exactly how God is with us. We bawl all over His shoulder, we nag Him for things that we shouldn't have, things that will make us sick or cause us problems, and He answers our prayers because He loves us. It causes Him more work to help us pick up the pieces after, but He stays right there."

"And you're saying that's how it is with Clarissa? That she only does what she does because she loves us." Wade thought about that for a moment.

"Well, maybe not everything. Some things just have to get done and you close your eyes, bite your lip and do them." Mike smirked as he jerked a thumb toward the sink. "That's how I feel about dishes. But I like to eat off clean plates so I wash them. Or cadge my friends to do 'em." His meaning was unmistakable.

Wade got up, ran some water and squirted in a blob of detergent. "So, how does this have anything to do with me loving Clarissa?" he asked finally, his brain whirling in confusion at these new concepts.

"It has everything to do with it. God sent you here, Wade. He sent you Clarissa, too. I'm convinced of that. He blessed you with a wife and a family that any man in this town would be proud to call his own."

"I know how great she is. And I'm grateful." Wade rinsed the plates and laid them on the tea towel. "But…"

"But you want to whine and complain because God went and put some love in her heart for you that you might have to accept. You want to dwell in the past, linger over your past failures, savor the hurt and the pain a little longer?" Mike stayed where he was, watching Wade as he began drying the few utensils they'd used. "You'd rather think about the past than face up to what the future could hold. Isn't that what's at the bottom of this?"

It wasn't a pretty picture, and Wade didn't dwell on it.

"What if something bad comes up?" he challenged. "What if I do or say something, hurt her somehow? What am I supposed to do then?" Wade couldn't tolerate the thought of Clarissa being hurt by his stupidity. "Isn't it just better to avoid it?"

"Avoid what? Life? Love?" Mike shook his head. "You can't do it, man. And if you try, you'd be telling the world a lie. Isn't your God big enough to handle whatever comes up in your lives? Can't He forgive you for past sins and teach you new things? Isn't it possible that God has a perfect plan laid out just for you, a blueprint of how your life should be from here on in?"

"I never thought of that." Wade tossed the towel onto the counter. He could imagine the analogy very well, he just didn't know how to find that blueprint.

"Read your Bible. Love is a state of the heart, Wade. But when love is there, actions follow. The things Clarissa has done have shown the love inside her. You can't see it, but you know it's there because of the way she acts. How about you? Have you shown her any love?"

Wade felt his face burn again, but he made himself say the words. "I can't seem to tell her what I'm feeling," he mumbled.

"She doesn't need the words as much as she needs to see what's in your heart. Look at this, Wade. Maybe it will help. Paul wrote it after the love passage. 'When I was a child I spoke and thought and reasoned as a child does. But when I became a man, my thoughts grew far beyond those of my childhood, and now I have put away childish things.' You see?"

Wade grimaced, but his heart felt twenty times lighter. "What you're telling me is that I need to grow up. Right?"

"Mm, basically, yes." Mike grinned. "Growing up means you give up some silly childish fantasies of what life should be like, give up the idea of getting even for past slights, and start making your life match God's blueprint. You build it into what He wants it to be."

"If I just knew what that was." Wade snagged his jacket and pulled it on slowly. "I thought I knew what I wanted, but now things look different to me. As if I can't quite see the whole picture. If only I could get my mind cleared and in tune with His."

"It just so happens, I have the perfect way for you to start doing that." Mike pulled a key ring out of his pocket and tossed it across. "Take this. I've got a little shack, a rough cabin, that's back in the woods a ways. Why don't you go out there for a day or two and sort things out with God?"

"Sort things out? You mean like fall on my face, or something?" Wade didn't think he wanted more emotionalism. He wanted good, rational reasoning, a way to handle his problems that didn't mean welching on his commitments.

Mike raised his eyebrows. "Well, buddy, if that's the way you think best, go for it. You just have to ask, and

He will make the path perfectly clear." He smirked slyly. "Personally, I always think He speaks more clearly when I'm sitting on the end of the dock, dangling a line in the water."

Wade wanted to go so badly, he could almost taste it. To be able to think things through, to consider what marriage to Clarissa really involved, to ponder the future—one without the architectural degree he'd craved so long. Some time alone to relax and listen for a heavenly answer to his earthly fears.

Then he thought of Clarissa home alone, waiting for him. She was sitting at home right now, carrying the load that was rightfully his. "I'd really like to go, Mike, but I'll need to check with Clarissa first."

"Of course. Here's a map. I drew it for a buddy of mine who never showed. Take as long as you need, Wade. I'll be praying for you."

Wade nodded, thanked him and hurried out the door. The rain was pouring down in sheets now, but he barely noticed as he headed for home.

Funny to think of that old monstrosity as home, to feel a little flutter of warmth amid the icy coldness that clamped his insides. But he did. He, who'd sworn never to settle down, couldn't remember when he'd last thought of a place as home. Was that because Clarissa was there, waiting?

"I don't know what You have in store for me," he murmured, as he pulled into the driveway and noted the light Clarissa had left burning for him. "But I'd like to. Please show me how to go about this. And remember I'm as dumb as a stump when it comes to women."

The house was dark, save for the stove light that cast glimmering shadows in the kitchen. Wade locked up, then climbed the stairs, marveling at the sense of rightness that settled on him with each upward step. He'd wanted to design homes with just this ambience, places where people could be exactly who they wanted. Places where people were loved, cared for, unafraid to say what they wanted, needed from someone else.

Was that dream totally dead? It was just another question that he needed an answer to.

In the bedroom, Clarissa lay curled up on her side of the bed, fast asleep. He showered, then climbed in beside her, his arms wrapping around her slim body, snuggling her against him. Clarissa shifted but didn't waken. Wade kissed her cheek, noting the shadows under her eyes and the lines of tiredness around her mouth. He wished he'd spent the day with her.

"We'll have other days," he promised softly. "I've just got to get a few things ironed out with God and then you and I are going to have a heart-to-heart—with no children to interrupt."

He didn't know exactly what he'd say, how he'd explain the roiling misgivings that churned inside his brain. But he'd pray about it. With his chin on her hair, Wade lay in the darkness and thought about his wife. He remembered how she'd cut his hair last week, her fingers light, tender as she'd snipped and cut, her bottom lip caught between her teeth as she concentrated.

The days he'd come home with his hands aching from tearing up a floor that should never have been laid, she'd insisted on setting aside supper preparations to bathe and bandage his bruised and battered knuckles, carefully removing the splinters and slivers as tears rolled down her cheeks. He could almost hear her soft eyes and sympathetic voice as she'd talked with Pierce and Lacey last night, answering their tearful questions about heaven and whether their parents were able to see them.

I want to be a part of that. I want to be there, to support her, to help her deal with them. They're my family. Clarissa is my wife. I don't know why, but she loves me. I can't let that go. Maybe I should, but I can't. It's too precious, too priceless.

He was going to fight off this restlessness, Wade realized as the raindrops spattered against the window. He was going to ask God some hard questions and he intended to listen until he got some answers.

Clarissa and her love are a once-in-a-lifetime gift that everyone doesn't get. And You gave them to me. It's time I realized what that gift entails and did something about returning it, or get out of her way. Clarissa isn't like anyone else. I can trust her, talk to her about my fears. She'll understand.

Clarissa's hand slid up his chest and cupped his cheek. "Wade?" she murmured, still mostly asleep.

"It's me, honey. Go back to sleep."

She smiled that angelic look that caught at his heart and made his breath catch. Her fingers brushed across his lips in a featherlight touch of assurance as she snuggled a little closer. "I love you, Wade," she murmured, her whispery soft voice trailing away into dreamland with the last syllable.

"I know," he told her quietly. "Thank you."

"Welcome." Her breathing returned to its regular pattern.

But Wade lay awake, cherishing this precious gift he'd been given even as he asked the Father how he could ever accept it.

He wasn't the kind of man someone like Clarissa needed. He was all wrong for her. And if he had any brains, he'd get out before he spoiled all their lives.

Before he ruined whatever bit of feeling she would have left if she knew how badly he wanted to run and keep on running.

Chapter Thirteen

Clarissa woke up the next morning when a sunbeam twinkled across her face. Bemused, she reached out a hand, but Wade's side of the bed was empty. As usual. Instead, her fingers crunched against a bit of paper he'd torn from the pad on the night table and left on his pillow.

She sat up, frowned, then unfolded the note.

Clarissa. I need to get away, just for a bit to think things through. I'm fine, I just have some important decisions to make. If you need me, contact the pastor. He'll know where I am. Wade.

Her stomach squeezed itself into a knot. He had to get away? From her? From responsibility? Which one? And why now? Why, when they could have spent some time together, had he taken off to a place he didn't even want to talk about?

"Lord, I don't want to complain, but this really isn't the kind of marriage I had in mind."

She swung her legs out of bed and then reeled as her

stomach issued an urgent summons. Suddenly yesterday's events came rushing back as she raced for the bathroom.

Half an hour later she was cleaned up and in the van, heading for the supermarket out on highway 97, where no one knew her personally. She purchased the pregnancy kit, two oranges and a quart of milk, then hurried home. Less than fifteen minutes after flying up the stairs she flopped against the bathroom vanity, the blood draining from her legs. She had her answer.

Pregnant! Oh, why hadn't Wade waited? Why hadn't he stuck around so she could talk this over with him?

The phone rang and she grabbed it, praying it was him.

"Hi, Clarissa. It's Candy at Dr. Baker's office. You asked me to let you know if we had a cancellation and we do. I know your appointment is for next week, but if you want to come in right away, we can get that physical over with today."

She'd completely forgotten the library board's insistence on her having a yearly physical to qualify for their medical coverage.

"Thank you, Lord," she whispered.

Perhaps she was wrong. Perhaps she'd done the test wrong. Surely the doctor would find something noticeable if she was pregnant.

"Yes, I'll come right over. The kids are at camp and Wade's away, so it happens that I'm free."

She decided on the drive over that she wouldn't say anything. If Dr. Baker noticed some changes in her body, surely he'd tell her. It would be a confirmation, and she wouldn't look a fool if she asked to have a test done. Especially if it came back negative. Her lips pursed. If she wasn't pregnant, she was going to ask the good doctor about preventing that in the future, in spite of her own almost desperate craving for a baby. Wade's needs came before hers.

Dr. Baker had been practicing for years. He took his time with each patient and she was no different. When Clarissa had been fully examined, he told her to dress and then come into his office.

"Clarissa, your body has undergone some changes. I have a hunch you know what I'm going to say. I think you're pregnant, but I'd like to do a test."

"I suspected as much." She kept her eyes trained on his face. She'd known this man for years and something was bothering him.

Dr. Baker scratched his forehead. "There's something odd that's twigging at me, sort of trying to get my attention. I can't put my finger on it just yet, but I'd like to take all the precautions I can."

"Of course." She waited while they drew blood, then sat in the office chair while his lab nurse did her work. By the time she was called back into his office, Clarissa was a bundle of nerves.

"Definitely pregnant," he told her with a grin, his weathered face wreathed in a grin of happiness as he pumped her arm up and down in a hearty handshake. "Congratulations. I've made an appointment for you to have an ultrasound. Will around two be okay?"

She nodded, thanked him for his good wishes and went back home, her mind twisting and turning over the information. It should have been the happiest day of her life and yet on the inside she wept for the loss of Wade's dream.

"It's not that I don't want the baby," she told the Lord. "I can hardly wait. But, oh, God, how can I tell him? How can I burden him even more, when he's obviously already in a lot of turmoil?"

She thought of going to see her pastor, but in the end she decided not to. She would wait on God. He would see her through.

"Would you excuse me just a moment?" The technician at the hospital flicked a switch that turned the screen off and put the paddle back on the table. "I just need to speak to someone."

"Is anything wrong?" Clarissa asked, but the woman merely smiled and hurried out the door, her manner distracted.

"Oh, Lord, please help me. I'm so scared." Clarissa scrunched her eyes closed and prayed as hard as she ever had. "I know it's not the best timing, and I know Wade isn't going to like it, but God, I really want this baby. Please, please, let everything be all right." She hardly dared ask, "Can't I have both Wade and the baby?"

She felt as if she'd lain there for hours before the door burst open. A tall thin man with thick bleary glasses and an impatient step followed the technician into the room. Behind them came Dr. Baker.

"Please tell me what's wrong," Clarissa begged. "Please."

"Now, now." Doctor Baker patted her hand. "There's nothing wrong. Our Penny only wanted to check something out with her boss. Since I was here anyhow, I thought I'd tag along. Just relax, Clarissa. Close your eyes if you want to."

But Clarissa kept them wide-open and focused on the screen, straining to see what it was that had the tall thin man studying it so intently. She knew Dr. Baker should be in his office right now. He had appointments. Penny had no doubt summoned him over, which meant that something was terribly wrong. Didn't it?

Finally, the ultrasound was done and Dr. Baker asked Penny to bring Clarissa to his office.

Clarissa sat in the office, impatiently fidgeting as she waited. Eventually the radiologist and Dr. Baker came in, heads together as they muttered indistinguishable medical words. Dr. Baker shoved the door closed, then sat down beside her and took her hands in his.

"Clarissa my dear, Dr. Grant and I are in agreement over your diagnosis."

"I thought I was pregnant," Clarissa mumbled, not understanding the knowing look that passed between the two men. "Is something else wrong?"

"No, no. It's not that. Is Wade here with you?"

"No, Dr. Baker. He's out of town for a while. Why? Please, will you just tell me what's wrong?" She was getting tired of this runaround.

"Nothing's wrong." Clearly Dr. Grant didn't hold with prolonging the suspense. "You're carrying twins. At least I'm ninety-nine percent certain it's twins."

"T-twins?" Clarissa sputtered, feeling her heart begin to race as the blood rushed out of her head. "Did you say twins? As in two babies?"

"We're fairly certain." Dr. Grant nodded at Dr. Baker.

"Oh, my! Oh, my goodness me." Clarissa let her mind drift for a minute, seeing two little cherubs flutter across the ceiling, the fat little hands entwined, their rosebud mouths grinning at her. "Oh, dear." She remembered Wade. "Ohh!"

"It is a bit of a shock, isn't it? I haven't delivered a set of twins in years. I'm rather looking forward to this. Will Wade be surprised, do you think?" Dr. Baker grinned like a cat who'd just spied some thick cream.

"Will he ever!" Clarissa's knees wobbled at the very thought. She glanced from one man to the other. "Do you think you can keep this quiet until I have a chance to tell him? I know what a hotbed of gossip this place is and I'd like to be the one he hears it from first."

"Everything that happens in this hospital is confidential," the radiologist told her, obviously upset by her accusatory words. "We do not gossip about our patients."

"Yeah, right." Clarissa gathered up her purse, her eyes on Dr. Baker. "Please? Will you keep it quiet? I'm not sure just when he'll be back."

"I'll speak to Penny immediately. We'll do the best we can, Clarissa, but I know I speak for the entire town when I tell you that it couldn't have happened to a nicer woman. You'll be just as wonderful with these babies as you are with Wade's kids. Your family will be the envy of everyone."

"Will it?" Clarissa thanked them and left the office, the hospital, with the words ringing around in her brain.

Her family. *Her* family. It was, wasn't it?

Twins? Twins! She wanted to jump for joy and praise God for answering her prayer. But at the same time she was so afraid of telling Wade, of seeing that dull, tired look wash into his eyes when he realized what she'd caused him to lose, what she was forcing him to accept. Wade wasn't a family man. Hadn't he told her that over and over?

"I will not doubt Your will," she whispered at last, leaning back in the recliner at home with a glass of iced tea nearby. "You have everything under control. You and You alone know how we'll manage, but I'll trust."

Wade had been gone almost two full days, and Clarissa was worried. She'd lain awake last night, her body craving sleep while her mind relived all the things she knew about Wade.

And one fact kept surfacing. Wade had left his mother and his sister, ran away when they needed him. He'd left again at seventeen.

Was he going to come back this time?

She spent her daylight hours accomplishing the items on her list, checking them off with no sense of satisfaction as one after the other was completed. The house gleamed from its polishing, the floors were spotless, the furniture without a speck of dust. The garden was weed-free, and the freezer held a host of ready-to-cook dinners and baking enough to last at least a week, even with four hungry children around.

Several ladies from the church brought over the baking and Clarissa accepted it gratefully, wrapping and freezing every bit. Evidently Dr. Baker's promise couldn't hold back the good souls of Waseka. It seemed that everyone knew of her condition and wanted to help.

Wade would hate it, call it charity, but she accepted each and every offer that was made.

Right now there was a crew of four workers outside painting the fence, and two more downstairs checking out the furnace and water heater. A young girl who'd sometimes helped her at the library offered to pick the peas while her boyfriend trimmed the hedge and mowed the lawn. For Clarissa there was nothing to do but sit and watch the hustle of activity around her home and wonder where Wade was, and what he was doing.

Chapter Fourteen

Half an hour later, Clarissa could have burst into song when her substitute at the library phoned to say she was having difficulty with the computer system. A little mental labor was just what she needed to get her mind off her problems.

Edna Morton had been the librarian before Clarissa and she didn't believe in computers. After all, she'd managed the library for years without it, why change?

"Just look at this pile of books I have to check out!" she shrieked when Clarissa finally walked through the big oak front door.

Thirty-five heads turned to stare at Clarissa. Thirty-five sets of impatient eyes watched as she stored her purse under the counter, then she picked up the stamp and waited for Bertha MacDonald to present her card.

"Back at work already, Clarissa? I thought you were on holidays or something?" Bertha shook her head, her double chins wagging her disgust. "I don't understand this new idea of taking separate holidays—Wade off at some cabin and you here, slaving over that house. Doesn't seem hardly fair. Especially not with you expecting and all."

Clarissa mentally groaned but forced a bright smile to her lips as a library full of interested parties widened their eyes and digested this newest bit of information.

"Oh, it's not really a holiday. And I'm not slaving over anything! Besides, we each have our jobs to do. We're married, but we're not siamese twins!" She giggled as if she had no more interest in being with Wade right now than fly to the moon.

"I guess." Bertha looked as if she didn't quite understand that reasoning, but thankfully she said nothing more. She stuffed her books into her bag and waddled out of the library.

And so it went, on and on, each one with a question, a hint, a suggestion on life after the honeymoon. By the time the last customer had left, Clarissa was hot and sticky and desperately tired. But the computer still sat, blank and useless. She had to get it running right away, or there would be a huge backlog of work when she came back. As tired as she felt now, it would only get worse.

With a sigh, Clarissa pulled out her book of emergency phone numbers and dialed. "Hello, Kyle. It's Clarissa Cart—I mean, Featherhawk. Yes, I got married."

Not that it's done me a lot of good. My husband is off in the boonies somewhere trying to get up enough nerve to come home and live with me! And just when I've heard the most important news of our marriage, I can't even share it.

She stuffed down the angry little voice and responded to the rush of questions.

Edna set a glass of ice water down in front of Clarissa, waited with one eyebrow raised until she took a sip, then picked up her purse and headed for the door.

"Sorry to have bothered you, Clarissa, but truth to tell, I'm plain tuckered," she called. "You go home and relax right at eight. I'll manage without that monster tomorrow. I did it for thirty years."

"Don't worry, Edna. It'll be working in a few minutes. Kyle is a genius when it comes to this stuff." She waved her hand and watched the other woman walk out, then took a deep breath and swivelled her chair around to face the screen once more. "Yes, I'm here. Okay, I can try that."

By the time the familiar library logo was in the upper right hand corner of the screen, Clarissa was starving.

"Yes, that's done it. Thanks, Kyle. Yes, I'll run it tonight just to be sure I didn't lose anything." She listened as he explained how to lock out any changes Edna might inadvertently make to the operating system. "I'll do that right away." A few keystrokes accomplished the task.

Her heart drooped a little at the next question.

"Wade? Oh, he's very good looking. Dark, tall, muscular. He builds things, beautiful things. I've never seen anyone who can transform a place the way he can." She swallowed a lump in her throat as she remembered his whittling at the lake during their family vacation.

Kyle's curious voice brought her back to reality.

"Yes, he's guardian of his sister's four children. That really fills up the old house." She nodded, eyes misty as she thought about the kids. "I love it. They make the place come alive. It's what I've always wanted." She laughed. "Yes, Wade is what I wanted, too. He's the best thing that ever happened to me.

"No, I'll stay here another half hour or so," she murmured, brushing the tears away from the corners of her eyes. "Till closing time. I can run the diagnostics while I wait. Thanks, Kyle. Yes, I'll be sure to tell Wade he's a lucky man. Uh-huh. Bye."

A lucky man? She almost laughed. So lucky, he was going to have to put his dreams, his plans, his future on hold. How lucky was that?

Clarissa pushed it all away and set to work keying in the loans for the day. Her fingers flew over the keys as she forced her concentration to remain on the screen. She had just finished her entries when a huge sheaf of red roses appeared in front of her eyes.

"Oh, my!" The scent of the flowers was overwhelming. Clarissa stood up, trying to straighten her vision and put out her hand to keep from falling. "Oh, my," she breathed, as her stomach rolled, her knees collapsed and she tumbled backward into mind-numbing blackness.

"Clarissa? Oh, God, what have I done wrong now?" Wade gathered the delicately boned body in his arms and carried her over to the thick plush rug in the story-time section. Gently he laid her out on it, then picked up a nearby book and fanned it back and forth above her face to create a breeze in the nearly airless room.

"Please, Clara, don't do this. I'm totally useless with fainting women. I have no idea how to make you wake up.

Clara, I love you. That's what I came to say. I wanted to court you, to do it the old-fashioned way. I wanted to make you feel special, loved. To make up for all the things you missed." He dropped the book and picked up her hand.

"I know about love now, Clara. I finally figured it out. I don't know exactly when it happened, I just know that you are the most precious thing in the world to me and I'm never going away without you again. Clarissa?"

Wade searched her face frantically for some sign that she heard and understood what he'd said. But her eyes remained closed, her transparent eyelids tinged with faint blue lines that hid the sparkle of fun he knew was cloaked in their depths.

"Oh, God, please give me another chance. I've messed up so many times. Now I've gone and waited too long, missed another chance to tell someone I love how much she means to me. I can't repeat that mistake again. Not with Clarissa."

He prayed desperately, his mind sending heavenward the words he couldn't begin to utter as he searched her face for some sign of life. "Come on, sweetheart. Please wake up. Oh, man! Now I make even my own wife faint."

He cupped the smooth skin of her cheek in one palm, tenderly caressing the curve of her lips, the stubborn lift of her chin, the tiny scar from so long ago.

"Clarissa darling, please don't do this. You're making me very nervous." He gathered her into his arms, pressed his lips against the coil of hair that was even now tumbling across his shoulder. "I love you Clarissa. You said you loved me. Please say it again."

Was that a smile on her lips? Wade leaned closer, felt the puff of air against his skin as she took a deep breath.

"Clarissa? Sweetheart, can you hear me?"

"I can hear something," she whispered, her voice bewildered, bemused. "Say it again, please."

"Say what? Blast it, if I didn't love you so much I'd be yelling right now! Wake up, will you? Please?" He wanted to squeeze her so tight, hold her so close that she'd never go away again. "Please?" he begged, his voice hoarse with worry. It wasn't normal for anyone to be out this long, was it?

The fist that held his heart in its grip loosened just a fraction as her gorgeous eyes blinked open.

"Oh, hi Wade. I just had the most wonderful dream." Clarissa squinted up at him. "You're back," she murmured, fidgeting just a little in his tight hold.

Wade refused to let her go. "Yeah, I'm back. I had it all planned out. I was going to show up here with those flowers, take you out for dinner and tell you how much I love you." He frowned at the drooping roses that lay strewn across her desk. Messed up again!

"You were?" She frowned up at him, ceasing her movements when his hand tightened around her shoulder. "Oh."

"Oh? That's all you're gonna say?" He glared at her, furious that all his careful planning was for nothing. This moldy old library was the least romantic place and he'd wanted something special for her, something really exceptional for this woman who'd wrapped her life around his and loved him so tenderly.

"I love you!"

"But—" She studied his face, her hand lifting to brush a lock of hair off his face. "I thought you weren't the type. You said you weren't a family kind of man."

"Yeah, well, what do I know?" He smiled, just to show he wasn't mad at her. "I guess I'm not a regular kind of family man. But then, heaven knows we're not a regular kind of family." He brushed his hand across her forehead. "Are you really all right? I've never been so scared in my life. You went down like a ton of bricks. I thought for sure I'd waited too long again."

"Again?"

Her eyes told him nothing. Her demeanor was the familiar watch-and-see attitude. Wade found himself wishing, no hoping, for some flicker that would tell him she still loved him.

"Yeah, again. I've always waited until it was too late to tell the people I care about how much I love them. I missed my opportunity with my mother and again with Kendra. I sure didn't intend to let it happen a third time."

"Well, go ahead and tell me then."

He blinked at the acerbic tone in her usually soft voice. "I'm not just saying it, Clara. I really do understand what love is. And I know that I love you. I'm not very good at it yet, but I can learn. See—" he checked to be sure she was listening "—it's different this time."

"It is?" She sounded as if she were withdrawing from him.

Wade hurried to explain. "Yeah, it is. This time I'm not running away. Not from anything. No matter what. This time I want to hang around and find out all about love."

"Why?"

"Why?" He swallowed. "What do you mean, why? Because I love you and I love the kids. Because you need me as much as I need you."

"Oh, Wade!" She burst into tears, wrenching herself out of his arms and pushing to her feet.

Wade grabbed her arm when she wobbled a bit, but she pushed him back, balancing one hand on a chair for stability.

"I don't want you to stay with me because I need you. I don't want a husband who thinks I'm a millstone, a burden, somebody who has to be looked after." Tears streamed down her cheeks and dripped onto her not-so-perfectly-pressed blouse. "I don't want to add to your responsibilities!"

He ignored her outstretched hand and gathered her into his arms, tenderly cradling her head against his chest. "But you are a burden, a very special burden! Don't you see, Clarissa. That's what love is all about. I *want* the privilege and the responsibility of taking care of you and the kids. I want us to share them."

She stepped back out of the circle of his arms. "You wouldn't say that," she mumbled, turning away. "Not if you knew."

"Knew what?" He turned her around and tipped up her chin so he could look into her eyes, see the truth for himself. Had she changed her mind? Didn't she love him anymore? Had he spoiled that, too? "Clarissa, what's wrong? Are you ill? Is that it? Something serious?"

She nodded slowly, her head jerked up and down twice. "Something very serious." She gulped.

Wade closed his eyes as the knowledge pierced his

heart. Oh, God, why had it taken him so long to see the truth? Why had he fought it? How long did they have?

"Wade?"

He opened his eyes.

"I'm pregnant." She stood there, tiny and frail, her eyes huge in that pale oval face that made him catch his breath as her words hit home.

"Pregnant?" His heart burst into a melody of praise. He grabbed her and whirled her around, then stopped when her face went a strange shade of green. "Sorry, darling. Pregnant with a baby? My baby?"

She rolled her eyes. "Yes, of course with a baby."

Funny, she didn't look that happy. Clarissa loved kids. She'd prayed for a baby of her own. Jared had heard her. Why wasn't she happy? Didn't she want to have *his* baby?

"What's wrong? Don't you want to be pregnant?" It cost him dearly to ask that question. He couldn't fathom her not wanting their child, couldn't imagine what he'd do if she rejected them both. At the stunned expression on her face, Wade had his answer. "Okay, you want this baby. So?"

"Babies," she whispered. "It's babies. Two of them. Twins."

Wade sat down. Hard. In the big oak rocking chair he'd seen her use for story time. He swallowed.

Two babies. His tiny little wife, delicate, fragile Clara, was going to have *two* babies? No wonder she'd passed out! He felt a little faint himself.

Clarissa knelt in front of him, her eyes brimming with unshed tears as a stream of worry poured out from her lips.

"You see? That's what I was trying to say. You said you wanted to share the kids, but this will make it six! It's far too much, far beyond the responsibility you ever expected. You'll want to run away every weekend. The house will be so crowded. And what will we do for money? The kids won't want to share the place with a baby. You'll have to take over when I get too tired, and I will get tired, Wade. I already am. Then there's your degree. You won't be able to get to college for years and years all because of me. I'll weigh you down and make you sorry—"

Wade laid a finger across her lips, stopping the litany of protests that she was rattling off. "Come here, Clarissa. You and I need to get some things straightened out." He pulled her closer, then down onto his lap. His arms tenderly cradled her against his chest as held the most precious thing in his life.

"Listen, sweetheart, above all else, I love you. Got that?"

She nodded slowly, eyes dark and troubled. "Yes, but…"

"No buts. I love you. Do you love me?" He waited only a moment for her nod, then heaved a sigh of relief. "Thank you, God! Okay, then, nothing else really matters, does it?"

"Yes, Wade it does. We have to figure out how we'll manage. It's going to be such a strain on you."

"No, it won't," he told her firmly. "It will be a delight and a pleasure every time I look at you and see those children growing inside you. Every time I hold one of our children, I'll know they are a special gift from God, just as you are. And I'll thank Him every day for permitting me to have another chance at love."

She frowned, unwilling to believe. "But it's not what you wanted. You wanted to be free."

"Did I?" Wade smiled, threading his fingers through the long shiny strands of silver-gilt hair. "I think I wanted to be exactly where I am. I just didn't know it. You see, honey, I spent a lot of years trying to avoid responsibility because I didn't think I could live up to the demands of having someone love me." Wade checked to be sure she was hearing him.

"Sometimes when you feel boxed in, you make up a dream so you have a reason to get out. Going to college, becoming an architect, that was my dream. It got me off the reservation, got me my high school credits, and gave me something to focus on when things got pretty rough after I left home."

"And now you'll never get that dream," she moaned. "Two more children mean we can't afford for you to go back to school, Wade. I've ruined that."

He pulled her tight against his chest and held her for a long minute. "No, my darling wife, you have given me the most precious gifts I can ever imagine. As it happens, I don't want to go to college. I don't want to become an architect. I like my life just the way it is."

Clarissa's voice rumbled against his chest, but the words were clear. "You're just saying that, trying to make me feel better for spoiling things."

"Honey, God is in control. Isn't that what you're always saying?" He tugged her head back and winked at her, his eyes daring her to answer back. He laid his palm very carefully on her flat tummy. "These babies are ours, something we will share with each other for the rest of our lives. I love them already because they'll bring us closer."

Her stare never wavered. "Are you sure?"

Wade nodded. "You wondered why I had to go away, didn't you?" She raised her eyebrows, her lips refusing to admit it. He grinned. "I know you did, Clara. Well, the truth is, I'd begun to realize that what I really wanted from life wasn't what I thought it was. I wanted to love you, I wanted us to be together in a real marriage and I wanted to tell you that, but I didn't know how because I was all mixed up."

"And it's straight now?" She looked dubious.

"I think so. You see, what I've always wanted more than anything is respectability. Pastor Mike pointed out to me that I liked having people comment on my lovely wife, our great kids, our happy home. And he was right. I did, I do. For once I wasn't the outcast, the poor dumb Indian who couldn't do things right. For once, I was the envy of other people. You gave me that and I loved it."

He grinned at her, hoping to ease the strain he could feel still holding her slender body in its grip.

"You made that possible, Clara. You. Your stalwart defense of me, your steady support and unwavering decision to pull your weight, to give me enough freedom to figure things out, made me realize that I was letting you do all the work and I was gaining all the benefit. I didn't want other people to think I was a great architect, a wonderful builder—I wanted you to think I was the greatest thing since sliced bread."

"I do," she assured him softly, her eyes downcast, reddened cheeks telling him she was embarrassed by the wealth of feeling that burst out in those words.

"I know." He kissed the tip of her nose. "So I figured if I worked my tail off proving myself, I wouldn't have to say the words. That you'd understand how much I cared."

"I didn't know," she whispered, the ache in her voice audible. "I wish I had."

"That's what finally drove it home. I was wimping out, hoping I wouldn't have to actually say the words and hang myself out on a limb." He shook his head. "Stupid!"

"Wade, I don't understand." She needed reassurance and Wade gave it to her.

"I didn't want to be rejected. I didn't want to take the chance that once you found out how selfish I'd been, you'd realize I'm to blame for Kendra's death and that I should never have been given the privilege of caring for her children. Kendra died because I was too self-absorbed to be her big brother. I failed her miserably. What's to show you I won't do it again?"

He sighed. "That's why I've always run away. I'm a chicken, Clara. A selfish chicken who disappoints even himself. I want to bask in the glory without giving up anything. Even for my own sister. How much worse could I get with you?"

She took his hand. "You *were* her big brother, Wade, and you protected her the best you could. She loved you. Besides, even then God was in control. If He'd wanted her alive, Kendra would be here now." Her eyes were swimming with emotion. "He was in charge, not you.

And He makes beauty come from sadness. Beauty like our family."

Wade closed his eyes, drew in a ragged breath of relief and told her the truth.

"Do you know what drew me back to you? I figured that if I can't manage the whole thing, can't be man enough to accept your love and love you back the way God loves us, then I couldn't keep accepting your love. That scared me so badly. I've finally realized that love is an all-or-nothing proposition, that it's a two-way deal." He cupped her face in his hands.

"I need your love, Clarissa. It makes me stronger, more complete. Without your love I'm just running away from life, from everything I've wanted for so long. I want to come home, Clarissa. I want to stand by your side and watch the kids grow, see the babies born, celebrate Christmas and New Year's in that big ol' house."

"It's going to be a lot of work," she warned, but her eyes sent a shaft of warmth straight to his heart. "It's not going to be easy."

"Running away is easy," he whispered. "But loving you is the most precious job I could ever have. Please tell me I'm not fired."

Clarissa's eyes roved over his face. He had the feeling she was imprinting the memory deep within. When her arms whispered around his neck, he let out the breath he didn't realize he'd been holding.

"You're not fired, husband," she whispered in his ear. "In fact, you've just received a promotion to father-to-be. Congratulations."

The sound of shoe leather tap-tapping over the

marble floor drew Wade's attention from Clarissa's kissable mouth. He craned his neck to see two elderly ladies peering first at the wilting roses, then at them. Their faces bloomed with curiosity.

"I'm sorry, ladies," he announced, his arms tightening around Clarissa, "the library is closed early today. My wife and I are celebrating."

Epilogue

"What is that awful smell?" Wade's voice rumbled from the depths of the satin quilt he'd dragged over his head the last time the babies' cries told him they needed changing.

"I don't know." Clarissa sat up, yawned and sniffed. She wrinkled her nose in distaste. "Should I go check?"

He lifted the quilt and peered one eye out at her. "Why? Can you make it go away?"

"I doubt it. It seems pretty strong." She giggled when his hand snaked around her neck and he tugged her head down for a quick kiss under her grandmother's hand-stitched quilt. "That isn't going to get rid of it, either," she laughed, kissing him back.

"Maybe not, but I sure feel better."

They both jumped as the bedroom door slammed open and four hearty voices joined together in a rousing rendition of "Happy Mother's Day to you."

"Déjà vu," Wade whispered in her ear. But he emerged just enough to lean against the headboard and watch as Tildy presented his wife with a breakfast tray.

"It's a good thing you're not pregnant," he teased, eyeing the glistening fish eye that gleamed out of a blackened body. "What is it, Tildy?"

"Kippers, of course. I ordered them in especially for today because Clarissa likes fish." The girl chewed her lip, her self-doubt obvious. "Did I cook them okay?"

From the next room, the babies made their presence known and the boys hurried out to collect the squalling infants. They returned, Jared with Kendra Lane, and Pierce with Andrew Lane.

Clarissa couldn't stop the tears that bubbled up from the fountain of happiness inside. They squeezed out from her eyes and tumbled down her cheeks as she surveyed the seven members of her precious God-given family.

"You did everything just right," she whispered, her heart overflowing with heavenly thanks.

Wade's arm curved around her shoulder, his lips gentle on her hair as he held out a small flat parcel covered in red hearts.

"Happy Mother's Day, sweetheart."

Clarissa searched, but couldn't read his eyes. All she could see was an overflowing love there, a quiet gentle love that told her he thought himself the luckiest man alive. She waited until he'd removed the breakfast tray, then slid a finger under the tape holding the triangular folds in place.

"I don't need anything, Wade," she mumbled, embarrassed by her abundance of tears. "I already have it all."

"Now you do," he whispered smugly as he watched the shock spread over her face. "Now you most certainly do."

"It's a miracle." Clarissa stared at the official legal document granting full and complete adoption of the children Tildy, Lacey, Jared and Pierce to Mr. Wade and Mrs. Clarissa Featherhawk.

"A Mother's Day miracle," Wade agreed. His finger scooped up her tear and kissed it. "For the most deserving mother God could have found us. We love you, Mom."

Clarissa clutched the document to her chest and held on for the sheer joy of it. "Come here you guys," she laughed as the kids tucked a baby into each of Wade's arms, then collapsed onto the bed around her in a group hug. Her eyes met his over the tumble of heads. "Each of you are my very own, personal, heaven-sent miracles. I love you so much."

Wade's earsplitting grin told her the feeling was mutual.

* * * * *

Dear Reader,

Thanks for picking up my latest book. I've had so much fun writing about Clarissa and Wade, and their four charges. Isn't it funny how God works? We pray and pray for something, He gives it to us and then we wonder if we can handle it!

In this story Clarissa thought her heart's desire was a husband and a baby. What she really wanted, what we all long for, is unconditional love. We yearn for somebody who will take us, warts and all, and hold us close on the bad hair days, on the cranky days, on the days when nothing seems to go right. Sometimes we can find love in another person, but true unconditional love comes from the Father. He wants us to seek His help, just as much as a mother wants her child to come to her when he hurts. We may think we're a nuisance, but not to Him. He thinks we're His beautiful children and He loves us.

I wish you great rewards as you start each new day with Him in mind.

Blessings,

HOW TO VALIDATE YOUR

EDITOR'S FREE GIFT!
"THANK YOU"

1 Peel off the FREE GIFTS SEAL from front cover. Place it in the space provided at right. This automatically entitles you to receive two free books and two exciting surprise gifts.

2 Send back this card and you'll get 2 Love Inspired® books. These books have a combined cover price of $11.00 for regular print or $12.50 for larger print in the U.S. and $13.00 for regular print or $14.50 for larger print in Canada, but they are yours to keep absolutely FREE!

3 There's no catch. You're under no obligation to buy anything. We charge nothing—ZERO—for your first shipment. And you don't have to make any minimum number of purchases—not even one!

4 We call this line Love Inspired because each month you'll receive books that are filled with joy, faith and traditional values. The stories will lift your spirits and warm your heart! You'll like the convenience of getting them delivered to your home well before they are in stores. And you'll love our discount prices, too!

5 We hope that after receiving your free books you'll want to remain a subscriber. But the choice is yours—to continue or cancel, anytime at all! So why not take us up on our invitation, with no risk of any kind. You'll be glad you did!

6 And remember... just for validating your Editor's Free Gift Offer, we'll send you 2 books and 2 gifts, *ABSOLUTELY FREE!*

YOURS FREE!

We'll send you 2 fabulous surprise gifts (worth about $10) absolutely FREE, simply for accepting our no-risk offer! Don't miss out - MAIL THE REPLY CARD TODAY!

® and ™ are trademarks owned and used by the trademark owner and/or its licensee.

Order online at:
www.LoveInspiredBooks.com

YES!

PLACE
FREE GIFTS
SEAL
HERE

I have placed my Editor's "thank you" Free Gifts seal in the space provided above. Please send me the 2 FREE books and 2 FREE gifts for which I qualify. I understand that I am under no obligation to purchase anything further, as explained on the opposite page.

☐ I prefer the larger-print edition **121 IDL EVG6**
321 IDL EVHU

☐ I prefer the regular-print edition **113 IDL EVGU**
313 IDL EVHJ

FIRST NAME	LAST NAME

ADDRESS

APT.#	CITY

STATE/PROV.	ZIP/POSTAL CODE

Thank You!

◄ DETACH AND MAIL CARD TODAY! ►

© 2008 STEEPLE HILL BOOKS

(LI-EC-09)

If offer card is missing write to: Steeple Hill Reader Service, 3010 Walden Ave., P.O. Box 1867, Buffalo, NY 14240-1867

BUSINESS REPLY MAIL

FIRST-CLASS MAIL   PERMIT NO. 717   BUFFALO, NY

POSTAGE WILL BE PAID BY ADDRESSEE

STEEPLE HILL READER SERVICE
3010 WALDEN AVE
PO BOX 1867
BUFFALO NY 14240-9952

NO POSTAGE
NECESSARY
IF MAILED
IN THE
UNITED STATES

BLESSED BABY

Before they call, I will answer.
And while they are still speaking, I will hear.
—*Isaiah* 65:24

This book is for two blessed babies—C and J.
May you never outgrow your dreams.

Chapter One

"It's fifteen months too late, but I'm here, Bridget."

Briony Green brushed away a tear of remembrance, the whispered words echoing through her car. Reluctantly she tore her gaze away from the rugged mountains of Banff, still snow-capped in June.

It was time.

Bri parked on the side street marked Bear, searching for the address. It wasn't that she *wanted* to do this, she *had* to. She owed it to her sister.

She counted down the numbers. There it was—a pretty stone cottage. Number 132. According to her information this was the place.

"Oh, Lord, please help me," she murmured, scrunching her eyes closed as she drew a deep breath of courage.

Then, with the resolute determination Bri applied to every difficult task she undertook, she climbed out of her car, walked up to the solid oak door and gave two hard raps.

The man who pulled open the door wore a blue

flowered apron spattered with a variety of foods. That feminine bit of cloth did absolutely nothing to diminish the masculinity of his lean tanned face. His chocolate-brown hair stood up in wild tufts, adding to his craggy manliness.

He was *not* what she'd expected.

"Yes?" He waited impatiently for Bri to state her business. A quick glance over one shoulder indicated his harried state.

It was obvious to Bri that she'd interrupted his dinner.

"Are you Tyrel Demens?" Briony's voice scraped out in a nervous squawk.

"Yes." His brows lowered fractionally, his attention concentrated on her fully now.

Briony huffed out a sigh of relief. At least she had the right house. Now for the hard part.

"My name is Briony Green," she told him, offering a tentative smile.

He didn't smile back.

"I understand you have a daughter, Mr. Demens."

The glower hardened into an outright frown as suspicion swirled in his brown stare. In one all-consuming assessment, his gaze took in her plain face, her ordinary blue pantsuit and the handbag she clutched against her stomach to stop the nerves.

Reaction was immediate. Eyes narrowed, darkened to coal chips. Lips pinched tight. Hands bunched at his sides.

"What do you want?"

"I think—no, I'm certain that I'm your daughter's aunt," she blurted out, eager to remove the worry from his face.

A wail from inside the house diverted his attention for just a moment.

"I can see you're busy," she offered, fidgeting from one foot to the other. "And I really don't want to intrude. It's just that Bridget, my sister, never told us she'd had a baby."

"Look, I haven't got time—" The wails were getting louder now.

"Please, just hear me out."

Oh, how she longed to be back in her lab! At least there, she was alone, comfortable. Here, she was butting into this man's house, interrupting his day. The big man towered over her, brimming with tension. It was obvious he longed to ignore her by slamming the door. Bri couldn't let that happen.

"I'm keeping you from something and I'm really sorry. It's just that with Bridget gone, I felt it was my duty to make sure her daughter was well taken care of." She stopped, worried herself now by the high-pitched sobs she could hear. "I just wanted to assure myself that the child is all right—"

The unmistakable sound of shattering glass cut through the words. Briony's voice died away as the man in front of her wheeled around, his attention elsewhere. His low rumbly voice brooked no argument.

"Wait here. I'll be right back."

She stepped backward into the porch, watched as he closed and locked the door carefully behind him. Through a pane of etched glass, muffled voices from the other room drifted toward her. She could hear Mr. Demens's low soothing tone and the softer voice of a woman. His wife?

Determined not to eavesdrop, Briony couldn't help seeing what was in front of her. She glanced through the glass, assessing, filing away details. It was a small kitchen, homey with its flowering window plants and bright yellow walls. It could have been pretty, but the mess made her wince. Dishes strewn everywhere; pots piled high in the sink; plates and glasses on the table; an open loaf of bread on the counter. Stains and spills obscured the floor.

The entire room set her back teeth jangling. Surely a little organization couldn't hurt.

A minute later, Tyrel sauntered back into the kitchen carrying a small child clad only in a diaper. With one hand he snicked the lock off and tugged open the door.

"Sorry. When Cristine calls, she doesn't like to be ignored, especially after a nap." He waved Briony inside.

"Is she all right? I heard the glass break." Though she searched, Briony could see nothing to indicate injury on that pale, perfect baby skin. Gingerly she stepped over the threshold.

"Oh, Cristine's fine. Getting more active every day. She reached out from her crib and managed to knock a lamp on the floor. I'll have to move things around again." He brushed his lips against the glossy gold curls and smiled. "This is my daughter." His pride was unmistakable.

Briony's breath snagged in her throat as saucer-wide blue eyes winked down at her from the security of Tyrel's wide football shoulders. She didn't need blood tests or any formal papers to identify the mother of this child. She could see Bridget in the small tilted nose, the firmly pointed chin, the long, slender fingers.

Cristine Demens *was* Bridget's daughter.

"Now, you were saying something about your sister?"

He stood silent, playing with the little girl's fingers as Briony explained how she'd found her sister's diary—about the words that had shocked her parents.

"We had no idea she was going to have a baby, you see. We knew nothing about her life before she came home." Briony tried to explain her sister's tumultuous existence in as few details as possible.

"She ran away, demanded to be left alone. She only returned a few months before she died. She said she needed a place to crash. By then she was so ill we didn't dare question her about her past."

"And you believe Cristine is your sister's baby?" He frowned, obviously not happy with the idea.

Bri nodded. "I'm almost certain she is. I found this tucked inside the cover of Bridget's diary." She held out the legal paper by which Bridget Green had forfeited all rights to her daughter. Some nagging memory twigged at her brain.

"But you must have known Bridget," she murmured, studying the confusion on his face. She reviewed the sheet in one quick glance. "A Mrs. Andrea Demens signed this paper."

Tyrel stared at her, glanced down at the paper for one interminable second, then shook his head in a firm, decisive jerk. "That's impossible! The adoption was closed. We weren't allowed to know the birth mother."

Briony thought for a moment. "Isn't Andrea Demens your wife?" she asked softly, and wondered at the stark despair that immediately washed over his face.

"She was. She died over a year ago."

"I'm so sorry." The pinched lines around his eyes deepened, and Bri wished suddenly that she hadn't probed.

"It's all right." Tyrel turned away to tuck his daughter into her high chair, then handed her a biscuit. He waited until she began gnawing at it, he turned back to Briony. His face blanched a chalky white. "May I see that again? Please?"

She handed over the document, puzzled by his words. How could he not know? Bridget wrote that she'd studied the family very carefully before she'd agreed to give up her child.

Tyrel Demens was a tall man, six feet at least. He appeared exactly as she'd expected a forest ranger to look: lean, muscular, powerful. But more than that, he seemed completely capable of any challenge father-hood could bring.

What Briony hadn't expected was the glint of hurt she saw lingering in his eyes.

He studied the signatures at the bottom with an intensity that frightened Bri. Was he going to dispute her claim, pretend the signatures were forged? A brooding fear clutched her heart.

She suddenly wished she hadn't felt obligated to do this, hadn't allowed herself to believe she could make it up to Bridget by checking on her baby. Her sister had made a lot of mistakes, but she'd always been a perfect judge of character. She wouldn't have given her child to these people unless she was certain they would make good parents.

"I'm sure it's all quite legal," she murmured, watching the carved lines around his mouth deepen.

"Yes, of course it is. I wouldn't have tolerated anything else where Cristine was concerned." His smile eased the harshness in his voice as he handed back the paper. "I'm sorry. I wasn't questioning you. It's just...strange that I didn't know about this. Andrea said..." His voice died away, leaving an empty silence that stretched between them.

Briony couldn't think of anything to say. There were no words for a situation like this. She stared at him mutely.

He shook his head as if to clear it. "Never mind. It doesn't really matter now, does it?"

"No, you're right," she agreed with a twinge of relief. "The past isn't important. And I haven't come to cause you any problems." She hurried to assure him. "I just wanted a chance to see the baby, to make sure she was well. I felt I owed that to my sister."

"Of course." Every feature altered from protective to adoring as he bestowed a tender smile on his daughter. "Well, here she is. Say hello, Cris. This is your aunt—" He turned to look at Briony. "I'm sorry, I've forgotten your name."

"Briony Green. Auntie Bri," she murmured, bending to meet the child on her own level. "Hello, sweetheart," she whispered, tentatively stretching out one hand to touch the fair silky skin. Cristine studied her aunt very seriously for a moment, then she grinned, her baby teeth shining proudly out between her chubby lips. She reached to curve her fingers around Bri's.

"Up," she demanded in a bell-clear tone, pushing for all she was worth against the rungs of the high chair.

"She can talk already?" Briony stared in awe at the chubby little miracle before her. "Isn't she smart."

"I think she's a genius, but then again, I may be biased." Tyrel laughed as he wiped the sticky crumbs off Cristine's fingers, then unfastened her from the high chair. He held her out to Briony. "Actually, she favors three words at the moment. *No, up* and *Nan.* Not a lot, but they're effective."

Briony awkwardly cuddled the little girl to her body, her hands fumbling as they sought a secure hold. No matter how much she'd dreamed of holding Bridget's child, she obviously wasn't any good at this!

"Nan?" she asked, glancing up at Tyrel for a second.

"My mother. She's been helping me out with Cris since Andrea died." He adjusted Cristine on her lap, grinning at her look of panic. "It's intimidating at first, but you'll get the hang of it soon enough."

Briony doubted that. It felt as if she were holding an eel. The soft downy skin was so silky smooth, it was almost slippery, and that was complicated by Cristine's churning legs and waving arms.

"Does she always wiggle like this?" Bri asked, biting her bottom lip as she fought to hold on while the baby bounced up and down.

"The only time Cristine stops moving is when she's asleep," a proud voice from the doorway informed them. A tiny woman with gray-streaked hair and crutches under both arms hobbled into the room.

"I'm Monica Demens, Ty's mother." She made a face. "I'd shake your hand but I'm not sure I can do it without falling down."

"You're supposed to be sitting down, Mother." Ty pushed a chair forward, then held out one hand. "Come on. The doctor said to keep that leg up as often as possible."

Mrs. Demens eased herself into the chair, then tilted her head back and glowered at her son. "It isn't possible to keep my leg up and move around," she told him grumpily.

Briony hid her smile as Tyrel sighed. He took the crutches and placed them out of the way behind a door.

"So don't move around," he advised laconically.

Monica ignored him, her eyes moving from Briony to the baby and back again. She peered up at Ty, obviously awaiting an introduction.

"This is Miss Green. She believes she's Cristine's aunt. She has an adoption paper signed by Andrea to prove it."

"But I thought that you didn't know…"

Briony watched the silent interplay between mother and son. Whatever message Tyrel telegraphed his mother, she seemed to understand. She nodded once, took a deep breath, then turned her attention on Briony.

"Have you come to take Cristine?" she demanded frankly.

Briony blinked in confusion.

"Come to— *Me?*" She shook her head vehemently. "No!"

The idea was so ludicrous it was laughable. Her? Look after a baby?

"Good gracious, no!" She gulped down the unexpected rush of emotion. "No, I'd never dream of doing that."

Relief washed over their faces, almost lifting the dark cloud of fear from Tyrel's eyes. Why *was* he so afraid?

"My sister wanted her baby to live here, and I would

never go against her wishes." Bri explained again about her sister's death and the diary.

"I'm starting a new job in a month, you see," she added when Mrs. Demens frowned. "I just finished my studies and I thought I'd use the next few weeks to make sure little Cristine here was well cared for. Once I get back into the lab, I forget everything."

"Lab?" Mrs. Demens's eyebrows rose enquiringly.

"I'm a research scientist—a botanist. I've just taken a job in Calgary." She smiled up at Tyrel. "Actually, my first assignment is some work for the park service. They want to introduce a disease-resistant spruce tree." She shifted Cristine just a little, gaining confidence the longer she held the wriggling bundle of energy.

"I've heard some talk about that." Tyrel watched her closely, his words guarded.

Bri understood his reserve. The park service preferred its ideas to be kept under wraps until fully developed. She was used to the solitary nature of the work. It wouldn't be a hardship not to discuss it. After all, she mused with a sadness that wouldn't be silenced, who would she discuss it with? She didn't have anyone in her life anymore.

"It's rather intense work. I don't expect to have much freedom once I start, so now seemed the best time to visit. I hope that's not a problem." Would he understand that she had to be certain Bridget's daughter was all right?

"No, not a problem at all."

Tyrel shook his dark head once, his words stilted but polite. He turned away and began loading the dishes into the dishwasher.

"I'm afraid I know less than nothing about babies." She volunteered the information frankly. There was no point trying to hide it. "Bridget and I were the only two in our family."

"Was she older than you?" Mrs. Demens obediently laid her leg across the chair her son had placed nearby, her fingers rubbing her knee. "You seem so young to be a scientist."

"Everyone says that." Briony laughed. "Actually, we were the same age. We were twins. Just not identical." She glanced down at the shiny head tucked beneath her chin.

"I'm not sure I was as good a sister as I should have been," she murmured softly, staring at the features so like her sister's. "Bridget was—a free spirit, I guess you'd say. She had to experiment, find her niche. I always loved nature. I knew pretty early on that was my direction."

Mrs. Demens reached out and patted her hand.

"I understand, dear. Children are often quite different from their siblings, twins or not. Ty is bossy and a tyrant," she teased, with a smile in her son's direction, "but he'll fight you for his forest. It's like his best friend. His brother got hooked on engines and never looked back. My daughter doesn't resemble either of them, thank goodness."

"No, Giselle's a perfectionist who thinks she knows everything." Tyrel's dry voice broke into their conversation. "Which is why I want you to get to her house and take a vacation before she decides to pay me a visit. Can you imagine how she'd view this kitchen?" He rolled his eyes. "She'd close me down."

"Don't start that again. I can't possibly leave you with no one to care for Cristine." Mrs. Demens fidgeted nervously. "We've explored all the options, Ty. There isn't any other way unless you're willing to let the child go. Don't worry, I'll manage with this ankle."

Briony frowned. Let Cristine go? What did that mean?

"No, you won't 'manage,'" he said, his voice hard and cool. "I'll find another solution. There's no way I'm letting anyone else raise my daughter. It's my one chance to be a father, and I'm not handing that off to anyone."

His "one chance"? What a strange thing to say. Had he loved his wife that much? Bri couldn't figure it all out, but she could see his face tighten up into a mask that hinted anger as he bit off the words.

"But Ty—"

"No, Mom. You know how I feel about Cristine staying here, in her own home. I don't want to shuffle her around from one caregiver to another."

Bri watched him study his mother's anxious face. Her skin prickled when his brown eyes softened, the glow of love darkening them to a rich chocolate that melted his mother's worry. He reached out a hand and touched her shoulder.

How would it feel to be loved like that?

"You've done more than enough, Mom. If you weren't already worn to a frazzle, you would never have hurt yourself."

"Such a silly accident." Mrs. Demens clucked her disgust. "Surely I'm not so old and tired that I must trip over every single toy the child drops."

"You wouldn't be so tired if you'd go to Giselle's

and rest for a while. As I've asked." His voice held a hint of teasing.

Briony politely tried to pretend she couldn't hear a word of their conversation. But it wasn't easy, sitting there in the middle of the kitchen, smack-dab between the man and his mother. It was obvious that Tyrel wanted his mother to go, and equally obvious that the older woman felt she couldn't. Still, it was none of Bri's business.

Briony concentrated on Cristine, bouncing her gently on her knee. When a burst of giggles erupted, she tried it again, pleased at this small success.

"You're good at that. She loves movement of any kind." Tyrel stood beside her, watching his daughter reach for the gold chain around Bri's neck. "But don't let her get hold of that. She'll either try to eat it or wreck it completely."

"Oh." Bri tucked her necklace safely under her shirt collar. "It's rather special. Bridget gave it to me when we were kids—the first piece in my antique jewelry collection. Thanks for warning me."

"Where are you staying, dear?" Mrs. Demens's gray eyes glittered with suppressed excitement. "You did say you were staying?"

"Well, I intend to see more of Banff, in preparation for my work, so I rented a room at a bed-and-breakfast," she told them, secretly hoping they wouldn't think her too forward. "I actually have a month before my job starts. I thought if everything with the baby was all right, I'd spend some time hiking the area, get a feel for the kind of reforestation the park is looking for."

Did Tyrel's hands hesitate just then? Briony wasn't

sure. Perhaps he hated the idea of her butting into his family, of her just walking in and assuming they'd let her see Cristine. Mrs. Demens, at least, seemed to have no problem with her staying.

"Aha. Perhaps you wouldn't mind stopping by for the next few days, then? It would be nice to have a helper to lend a hand looking after Miss Cris," she added, one eyebrow lifting as the little girl pumped her legs with glee.

"Mother! You can't ask a perfect stranger to baby-sit my daughter!" Tyrel stared at his mother as if she'd taken leave of her senses. He pivoted on his heels, cheeks dark with embarrassment as he faced Briony.

"Don't feel obligated to agree to anything Mother says, Miss Green. Though, you're more than welcome to visit Cristine whenever you like. It seems she's taken a liking to you."

His eyes glowed with fatherly pride. They all watched his daughter brush her baby fingers reverently over Briony's bright hair. For once she was glad she'd left it loose.

"She's so precious," Briony whispered. A thrill of pure delight trickled through her body when the baby fingers cupped against her cheek.

She wanted to stay, to watch Cristine, to store away the memories of babyhood that she would never share with a child of her own. In a flash of longing she made the decision.

"If you're sure you don't mind, I would like to see her again. I'd be happy to help out however I could. I've been told I'm quite good at organizing."

Tyrel froze, his eyes unfathomable as they studied her. Time dragged.

He questions my motives.

She should have seen that earlier, should have shown him the documents before now. One glance at Tyrel Demens with his daughter was enough to prove that he wouldn't willingly allow a total stranger to care for his beloved child without some assurance.

Bri shifted the baby's weight into one arm, hung on tightly, then reached down for her purse.

"I thought you'd probably want references for me to see her," she explained, holding out a sheaf of papers. "These are from my parents' lawyer. He handled their estate last year. I've known him for twenty years. This is from the professor who recommended me for the job at Bio-Tek."

She sat silently as he carefully read through each one.

"If you need more, I have a friend who works with the Royal Canadian Mounted Police in Calgary. You could phone him." She waited, breathless until he finally nodded.

"No, this is fine." He glanced at his mother, then back at Briony. A tired sigh reverberated through his chest. "All right, we'd be glad to have you. But don't let Mother bully you. She likes to have her own way."

Once more Briony witnessed the glow of love in the glance he bestowed on his mother. She felt warmed by it, thrilled that Cristine would know that same love in her own life. Bridget had chosen these people very well.

"Tyrel! I don't bully. I merely suggest." Mrs. Demens worked hard to hide the note of weariness in her voice, but her pinched cheeks and wince of pain when she shifted in her chair gave her away.

"Go and lie down, Mother. I'll take care of Cristine. You need to get your bearings back after that fall." He helped her stand, watched as she moved her crutches into place.

"You've taken too much time off as it is, Ty. You should be at work, not babying me." She reached out to brush a hand over the baby's hair. "You sweet thing," she whispered. Her eyes shifted, met Bri's.

"It was a pleasure to meet you, Briony Green. I'll look forward to seeing you tomorrow. Is seven-thirty too early for you to visit your niece?"

"Mother!"

"Of course it's not too early. I'm always up with the birds." Briony ignored Tyrel's loud protest and smiled her acceptance. "I hope you have a good rest, Mrs. Demens."

"I knew God would work this out," Mrs. Demens mumbled as she hobbled over the dirty floor and around the corner. Her voice whispered back. "It just takes a little faith."

Tyrel waited until his mother was well out of earshot, then he snorted his disgust. "It takes nerve, she means." He shook his head at Briony. "I'm sorry about that. It's presumptuous of her to assume you can just drop everything to help us out."

Bri smiled down at the baby in her lap who was studying them with her huge blue eyes.

"I came to Banff to meet my niece, Mr. Demens," she said quietly. "If I can help out in any way, I'm very pleased to do so. After all you've done for Bridget's daughter, I think a few hours lending a hand with her care is the very least I can offer. It can't be that difficult to care for a child."

Cristine galloped her agreement, her legs churning with excitement as she waved madly.

But Tyrel clearly was not thrilled by the prospect of Briony's arrival in his household. He looked grim, out of sorts.

"I still don't understand all of this adoption business," he muttered. "My wife handled most of the details, so I wasn't involved with every step of the process. But I do know what she told me. Surely there would have been some papers, something she'd have shown me or told me about if she'd known the birth mother." His forehead pleated in a frown of concentration.

"You knew nothing about Bridget?" Briony's heart ached for his pain. How hard it must be to raise a child, even a beloved one, on your own.

"No, nothing," he murmured. His long black lashes drooped closed as he thought it through. "I asked about the mother several times, in case of a medical emergency or something. The lawyer mailed us a medical record, but that's all. My wife said he insisted the mother was adamant that we not know her name." His eyes pierced Briony with their questions.

"But my sister specifically left this certificate so I'd know about the adoption. And she certainly knew your wife," she murmured.

"No, my wife never met the baby's mother," he contradicted her.

"Perhaps you feel that I'm lying, that Cristine isn't my niece?" Briony tried to keep the frustration out of her voice. Why was he making this so hard?

"I have some of Bridget's baby pictures. If you saw

them and compared them to Cristine, you'd see the similarity."

"I can see it just by looking at you. You have the same eyes, the same hair, even the same little cleft in your chin." A wry grin twisted his smile. "It's obvious that you are related to her. I have no valid reason to doubt your paper or your word. It's just...odd."

"I suppose it seems that way," she agreed quietly. "I can only tell you that Bridget knew you by name, both of you. I haven't read her whole diary, just the first few pages where she talks about coming to Banff, getting a job, her pregnancy. I skimmed parts, but it seems obvious that she was determined her child have parents she'd handpicked. You and your wife obviously met her specifications."

He digested that for a moment, then sank down onto the chair across from her, long khaki-covered legs splayed out in front.

"She names *me?*" The caustic words hissed out between his teeth, as if he could hardly bear to say them.

"No." Briony shook her head. She held Cristine under her arms, letting her legs dangle between her knees as she spoke. It was easier if she didn't look at him, didn't see the confusion and pain in his eyes. "I haven't seen your name in there yet. Just your wife's. 'Andrea's husband is a forest ranger. They seem like good people' is what it said."

"I see." He tented his fingers and studied the configuration for several moments. Then his head lifted, those glowing brown eyes searching hers.

"I'd like to read her exact words for myself," he

said in clear and crisp tones that brooked no nonsense. "I'd like to know exactly what she said about us. In fact, I'd like to keep that diary for Cristine, to give her when she grows up."

Briony gulped. She hadn't expected this, though she probably should have.

"I haven't read it all myself yet. I, uh, was hoping to get through it while I was here, to understand why she didn't come home, why she didn't ask us for help." She couldn't let go of it, not yet. It was her last tangible link with the sister she'd never understood.

"You make it sound like there's a lot to read." He watched her follow Cristine as she took several steps across the room to rescue a plush toy behind the door. "Surely a diary isn't that long?"

"This one is. Bridget poured her heart and soul into that book. I don't want to just casually flick through it. I want to examine everything she wrote down."

I have to understand how my sister could have given away her own child, the one thing I will never have.

"Yes, of course." His face softened as he took Cristine onto his lap, the bunny firmly clasped against her chest. "Believe me, I know exactly how hard it is to lose someone." His voice changed, hardened. "It's just that I'd like to make sure that Cristine has all the information there is about her birth mother." His eyes glittered with fierce possession as his hands closed protectively around the energetic little body. "I don't want her to be hurt by the past. I won't allow that."

"No. Of course you won't."

The love flooded into his face once more as he

cradled the baby in his arms, swinging her back and forth as she giggled her glee. What an abundance of love he had to shower on this precious little girl.

How she envied him that.

Tyrel glanced up at Briony, his eyes intent on her face. "It's her father I'm thinking about, too," he murmured, a roughness catching at his low voice. "What if he comes back, makes some prior claim?"

It was clear to Briony that the very idea only added to his misery. She shrugged helplessly. Tyrel's worry and concern for his daughter were painfully obvious, even though she'd only known him for mere minutes. She owed it to her niece and to him to find out all of the truth, to leave knowing nothing could separate them.

"I don't know about the father," she murmured, gathering her purse into her hand as she stood. "But I promise I'll read more tonight, try and figure it all out. I'll let you know what I find."

Tyrel rocked to his feet in one lithe roll and followed Briony to the door, Cristine perched high against his broad chest. He stood there for a moment, one big palm over the doorknob.

"May I ask you something?" He didn't look at her.

"Sure." Briony stood still, hands squeezed tight against the leather of her bag, hoping he wouldn't ask her to not come back.

She couldn't explain it to him, couldn't define the reason she felt drawn to this house, couldn't rationalize how her cool-headed scientist heart was inexplicably lured to the fragile child he held.

How her colleagues would laugh. Dr. Briony Green

with emotions? No one would believe it. But that's the way she wanted it.

"Go ahead. Ask me whatever you'd like."

"Why didn't you read the diary through before you came? Why read only enough to learn about Cristine?" He blurted out the words in a rush of controlled agitation. "Why not learn all you could before you drove here?"

"I suppose it must seem odd to just walk into your lives." How could she expect him to understand? The need to see this precious baby had gripped her heart the day she'd found her sister's letter. Briony tried again.

"It's just that—" She stopped, lifted her head and looked him directly in the eye. "Bridget was never particularly spiritual. She scorned most things about God when we were teenagers. But before she died, she told me she'd found God here. That she came to understand His love when she lived in Banff."

He nodded slowly.

"You wanted to be in this special place when you learned what changed her." He smiled, his face soft, understanding. "Of course. I'm sorry I probed. It must be hard for you to understand how God could have let something like this happen. I know I've often asked myself the same thing."

Briony blinked away the tears, her eyes widening in surprise.

"Oh, no, I've never wondered that at all." His frown surprised her. "I know that God has everything in His hands. If He allowed it, it's because it's for the best." She brushed a hand down Cristine's bare leg.

"Then, why—"

"Why do I want to read her diary here?" She smiled at him. "It's really quite a selfish reason. I want to read it in the place where she finally came to feel His tender touch. I want to read how He softened her aching heart and molded it to His will."

Briony pretended to move a wisp of hair out of the way, but in truth she needed a moment to organize her words.

"Once I know, then I want to praise Him for doing all that for my sister, a child He loved enough to let stray from Him, and then lead back to His heart." She tugged open the door and stepped across the threshold.

"I guess I want to see His love at work in Bridget's words," she confessed in a sudden rush. "Goodbye."

Before he could laugh at her foolishness, Briony pulled the door closed and hurried over to her car.

But later that evening as she sat in her bedroom and stared at the thick leather cover of her sister's diary, she wondered if coming here had been the right thing to do.

"How could he not have known about Bridget?" she asked aloud. "Didn't he care enough to be involved?"

But that didn't make sense. For whatever Tyrel Demens was, he had clearly demonstrated that he went out of his way to love, protect and care for his family. In every way that counted, Tyrel was Cristine's daddy.

"Something about this whole situation just isn't right," she confided to the Father. "I just hope that I don't make it worse."

Chapter Two

D-d-ding, dong.

Ty lifted one sleep-glazed eyelid and peered at the clock. Seven-fifteen. Couldn't be the alarm. Anyway, he hadn't set it.

The noise intruded again.

Ah, the doorbell.

He squeezed his gritty eyes closed and tried to remember if someone was supposed to ring his doorbell at this hour of the morning. He couldn't think of a single soul.

When the noise bonged through the house for the third time, Ty lurched out of bed, grabbed a robe and flew down the stairs, tying the sash around his waist as he went.

"Please stay asleep, Cristine," he begged in a whisper. That plea turned into a yowl when he stubbed his toe on the sofa. Ty quashed a second howl of pain as he passed through the living room, temper inching upward as the doorbell pealed again.

"What?" He yanked the door open and glared.

"Good morning. I was beginning to wonder if I was too early."

Ty took a cool refreshing breath of the dew-laden air and frowned. It looked like Miss Mary Sunshine had come to visit.

Dr. Briony Green stood on his doorstep, face freshly scrubbed, long blond hair flowing loose and shining down her back, her navy jeans and jacket clean and pressed. In one hand she clutched a battered briefcase that bulged.

Her face beamed a happy smile at him as she saluted. "Ready, willing and reporting for duty, sir." Briony sing-songed the words as she clicked her heels together.

Ty blinked, the events of the night before tumbling in a cloudy mixture through his brain. She *was* supposed to be here, he thought vaguely, though he couldn't remember exactly why. So much had happened since he'd last seen her.

He was without a baby-sitter for Cristine. That thought reigned paramount in the confused babble of his brain. Ty rubbed his sore toe and sighed. He wasn't up to entertaining.

Still, he couldn't just leave her standing there.

"Oh. Yeah. Sure. Uh, come on in." He held the door open even as he wondered how fast he could get rid of her. He needed—no, craved sleep. Mind-numbing, body-refreshing sleep.

Briony took a careful look around, nodded.

"If you're sure. It looks like no one's up yet. I thought your mother said everything would be clicking by now." She stepped through the door, closed it and peered up at him. "You look awful."

"That's nice to know," he mumbled, rasping a hand against his jaw. "Thank you very much for sharing." He waved a hand around the room. "Help yourself to whatever you need. I'll go have a shower. Then I've got to start hunting for a sitter."

He'd almost made it out of the kitchen before his little gray cells rearranged themselves.

Wait a minute! Baby-sitter? That was her, wasn't it?

He pivoted, bare feet squeaking on the linoleum, and stared at her, wondering if he dared ask her to help. Just for a day. Or two.

"Was it a rough night?" Briony set her handbag down on the only bit of counter still visible, then tucked her brief-case under a chair, bottom lip caught between her teeth.

Ty grinned. Her expression didn't require transla-tion. The good doctor preferred the sterile conditions of a laboratory. His kitchen did not pass the test.

Ty needed a few minutes to get everything function-ing. Just a little bit of time to decide whether he dared trust her with his most precious possession. He raked a hand through his hair, mentally assessing Briony Green.

She stood silent under his study, feet together, hands folded in front of her, eyes quirked in a semi-frown as she studied the remains of his last meal with distaste.

She was smart, she was educated, she wasn't disabled with crutches and she'd already met Cristine. But most of all, she was here, ready, willing and able to pitch in for one solid month.

Ty sighed. The sum total of his scrutiny was a definite "yes." It might not be the holiday of her dreams, but she *had* wanted to see her niece. It was too good to turn down.

"I've had a horrible night," he told her solemnly. "I'll tell you about it as soon as I get that shower, okay? Maybe hot water will wake me up." He waited for her assent. "Cristine's not awake yet so we might get a moment to talk."

He knew it was underhanded, tantalizing her with the baby like that. But he was desperate. He breathed again when she nodded.

"Go ahead and shower. Take your time." Her big blue eyes glowed with sympathy. "I'll listen for her." She glanced around, nose wrinkling at the messy room. "In the meantime, I believe I'll just straighten up a bit."

"Bless you." Ty sighed with heartfelt thanksgiving. He headed for the stairs before she could change her mind. "If you could put on a pot of coffee, that would be wonderful. The grounds are in the fridge."

With superhuman strength, Ty forced himself to ignore the beckoning warmth of his king-size bed and walk straight past it to the shower. Ten minutes later, shaved, bathed and optimistically dressed in his uniform, he was wide awake and almost ready to plead for heavenly help as he started downstairs, glad that, for once, Cris had missed her usual six a.m. wake-up call.

On the main floor of his home, all traces of the night's activities had been erased. The furniture sat fluffed and prim, the tables polished, the lamps straight, and the blinds open to the morning sun. The kitchen looked just as neat, though an odd smell permeated the room.

"Ah, coffee," he sighed, spotting the full carafe. "That's exactly what I need. Thanks so much for helping out, Briony."

Ty grabbed a mug and poured himself a huge amount of the potent black brew. He noticed Briony frowning at him, and lifted his mug in acknowledgment.

"I don't usually drink this much coffee," he told her with a grin. "But I need it today."

"I'm not sure it's…"

Her voice died away as he took a swig. She stood, fingers knotted together, studying his face with a worried frown as he tasted the bitter burnt liquid.

There was nothing Ty wanted more just then than to spit the horrible acrid stuff into the sink and wash out his mouth with antiseptic. In all his years with the other park wardens, he had never tasted anything quite so awful as her coffee!

"Oh, my—" He swallowed his words, refused to gag.

Briony had come to his assistance today, and he desperately needed her help. He wouldn't offend her—not for the sake of coffee.

"It's very…unusual," he told her, setting his mug on the counter. "Thanks for doing that." He grabbed a chair and sat down, throat still burning with the awful taste.

"It's bad, isn't it." She sighed, her big eyes, so like his daughter's, brimming with apology. "I didn't think it smelled right, but I wanted to at least try. Usually I'm quite good with measurements, but I couldn't find the directions anywhere."

"How much coffee did you use?" he asked carefully, praying he wouldn't offend her.

"Just half a cup." Her eyes blinked innocence.

Half a cup of grounds? Ty swallowed, no longer surprised at the darkness or the bitter aftertaste.

She was speaking again, blue eyes pensive as she methodically sorted through the process. "The numbers are worn off the carafe, and I wasn't sure exactly how much it made, so I thought it must be about the same as the one in the lab at the university."

"Ah." That explained it. Coffee from a lab. Some scientific experiment, no doubt. "Your pot was probably larger," he offered.

"Do you think so?" She considered that for a moment. "Perhaps that's it. Though, to tell you the truth, I haven't made coffee for a long time." She frowned, her forefinger tapping against her chin. "The other students seemed to prefer making it themselves. Mine never tasted quite the same as theirs, though I tried all their secret tricks."

"Secret tricks," he repeated stupidly, stunned by her beauty. The sunshine poured in, turning her hair to a golden halo. He shook his head, focused on the present. "What secret tricks are there to making coffee?"

"Well, I added the salt. One teaspoon for a full pot, they used to say. Your pot does look a little smaller." She peered at the glass carafe. "Perhaps it should have been less."

"Salt." He nodded, rolling his tongue around in his mouth. What in the world was salt doing in his coffee?

"Yes. It's supposed to keep the scale off or something." Briony shrugged. "I can't remember the reason, but it sort of made sense. And a pinch of pepper, too. To enhance the flavor, I think. I forget what pepper does." Eyes downcast, she played with a ringlet that drooped over one ear.

"Actually, it might have been more than a pinch," she

admitted, lifting her eyes to meet his and giving an apologetic smile. "The lid came off."

"Uh-huh." Pepper? Now Ty knew why his throat burned. He coughed discreetly behind his hand, trying to hide a smile at the ridiculousness of adding pepper to coffee. Surely these "friends" must have been fooling her!

"I take it you don't drink coffee."

"Oh, I love a good cup of coffee." Her eyes opened wide. "I just can't seem to make one. I usually buy instant," she told him cheerfully. "And I never put salt or pepper in it. I think it tastes funny." Her nose scrunched up at the remembered smell.

Ty choked back a laugh and mentally made a note to purchase a new coffeemaker. That pepper would be a long time dripping through.

"Do you want me to try again?" she asked, head tilted to one side, eyes glazing over as she delved into some mental calculations. "Maybe if I used twenty percent more grounds—"

"Never mind," he said hastily. "I don't really have time, anyway."

"Did something happen last night?" Briony's voice was quiet, hesitant. As if she were worried he'd boot her out for snooping.

If she only knew!

"My mother fell again last night." As he sank into a chair, his mind relived that awful *clunk*.

"Oh, no!" Briony clapped a hand over her mouth. "Was she badly hurt?"

"Well, she didn't help anything." It hurt to say it,

pained him even more to know it was all his fault. "Cristine cried out in her sleep. I didn't hear her right away. By the time I did, Mother was already going to her. She stumbled over something and fell."

"How awful! I'm really sorry." Briony reached out a hand to touch his arm. "I suppose she's in the hospital now?"

He shook his head. "She's at my sister's. In Calgary. After they fixed her up, I drove her there. Giselle's guest bedroom is on the main floor. Mom will be able to rest there. Finally."

"Calgary?" She stared. "But that's over three hours of driving! Not to mention how long it took to x-ray and treat her."

He nodded, one hand massaging the back of his neck. "Believe me, I know exactly how long it took. I got to bed about four-thirty. I would have stayed but my sister had company—her son's teenage friends took over the basement."

"I'm very sorry."

It was just a whisper, but Ty could hear the heartfelt meaning in her words.

"I am, too. Though I've been trying to get my mother to take a break for months now, I would have preferred she didn't take it in the leg."

Briony's solemn look didn't alter.

Ty sighed. "That was a joke."

She didn't even crack a smile. One finger tapped against her chin as she stared at the jam-spattered cabinet door. "It leaves you in the lurch, though. Doesn't it?" She fiddled with the crease in her jeans now, obviously deep in thought. "You'll need to find someone to watch your daughter."

Something inside Ty gave a twist of relief at her words. "His daughter," she'd said. She obviously didn't think of Cris as anything else. That was reassuring. For a while last night he'd wondered if she was seeking custody of the little girl for her own reasons.

"Yes, I'll need to find someone right away." He took a deep breath and plunged in. "I was hoping maybe you could help."

"Me?"

Briony gawked at him, her blue eyes expanding into huge sapphire pools that reminded him of the untouched mountain lakes tucked away in Banff's remote valleys.

She swallowed, her long, pale throat clearly defined in the opening of her shirt. Her shoulders went back.

"Of course, I'll help all I can." The little wobble in her voice quickly disappeared. "I told your mother that last night. But I don't know anything about child care. I'm afraid I wouldn't know where to begin."

Ty empathized with the helplessness flooding her face. He'd felt the same way when Cristine had come into their lives, even more so after God had taken Andrea. That was when he'd realized he was responsible for a tiny helpless baby.

He reached out and touched Briony's delicate hand, stilling its fluttering motions with a squeeze. A tingle of electricity shot through him. Her silky smooth skin radiated a warmth he saw reflected in her eyes.

"It's not really that hard, though it takes a lot of energy." How strange that she should affect him like this—make him nervous and unsure of himself. He was never unsure. Ty tried to sound confident. "You just have to meet her needs."

Briony's glance flew from his hand on hers to his face. "But I have no idea what those needs are." She sounded as if children were from another world.

Ty grinned. Perhaps in her lab they were. Just the thought of Cristine in a pristine sterile environment for more than ten seconds tickled his funny bone.

"Pretty basic needs at her age," he answered. "Clean, dry and fed. A hug now and then. Protection from dangerous situations. Didn't you ever baby-sit?" He studied her curiously.

"No. Never."

That was all. No explanation, no reason. He sensed there was something behind that, but now wasn't the time to question her.

The telephone rang, breaking the silence.

Ty answered and listened, his heart sinking at the news. "I'll be there as soon as I can," he told his boss. "I'm just not sure when that will be." He sighed as he listened to the lecture on his multiple absences over the past few months.

The reminder chewed at his pride.

"I know I've asked for a lot of time off, John. But my daughter comes first. Always." A few more directions, a plea to handle it, and Ty hung up the phone.

"More problems." Briony sat primly in her chair, waiting. She was not asking a question.

Ty nodded. "A child is missing. She wandered away from her campsite early this morning." He wondered if he should tell all of it, then decided it couldn't hurt. No doubt Briony already knew all about his job. "I'm supposed to lead a search party."

"But you don't want to leave Cristine." She kept her eyes on her hands. "Especially not with someone like me who doesn't know the first thing about parenting. I understand."

She'd refused before he could even ask. Ty turned away to pick up the phone book, shoulders slumping in defeat.

"It's all right. I'll find someone to look after her. The kids are still in school, of course, but maybe…" He bent over the pages, his mind busy.

He dialed a number and explained his problem. Then did it again. And again. By the sixth time, frustration held him tight in its grip.

"I'm sorry, Ty, but I just can't. Herb's away and the twins have chicken pox. I wouldn't dream of exposing Cristine to that." Mary MacGregor apologized profusely. "I'm sorry I can't be more help. It's made things really difficult with that flu that's going around. They even had to close the day-care center."

Ty's heart dropped to his shoes as he thanked his talkative neighbor, then hung up. The day-care center had been his last hope.

"Oh, boy, am I ever in trouble." He dropped his head into his hands, feeling as desperate as a man on death row.

"Is everything all right?"

Ty glanced up. The gorgeous scientist stood in the doorway, her arms wrapped around Cristine. Nervous expectation washed over her face as she met his stare. Ty swallowed, his heart thumping with pride as his baby played happily with Briony's necklace, cooing her pleasure as she stroked her hand over the shining sapphire that hung suspended from an antique gold chain.

"Cristine woke up a few minutes ago. I didn't want to disturb your phone call so I got her up myself." She frowned, her eyes on the puffy bottom of the fuzzy sleeper. "I'm not exactly sure I got her diaper on right. It looks a little baggy."

"It looks fine."

At the sound of his voice, Cristine turned her head toward him. Her chubby face broke out in a delighted smile as she stretched her arms toward him.

"Up!"

Ty scooped her into his arms and held her close, pressing his face into her neck. He kissed the downy skin, feeling the love surge inside him. This perfect joy made everything else bearable.

"Good morning, sweetheart. How's Daddy's girl?" He froze as her baby lips brushed against his cheek, thrilled beyond measure by that delicate touch. "I love you, sweetheart," he whispered, his throat hot and tight with emotion.

"Did you find someone?" Briony pulled the high chair close to the table, watching every move as he set the little girl in it and fastened a strap that prevented her from slipping out.

"No. There's no one." The hopelessness of it overwhelmed him as he admitted the truth. "It's my own fault. I should have hired a full-time caregiver ages ago, before I used up my sick leave and holidays."

"Oh."

What else was there for her to say? How could she possibly understand how difficult it had been?

"I've taken so many days off, asked someone else to fill in for me so often, that I'm in danger of getting laid off, instead of bucking for the promotion I wanted. And now I can't find anyone to look after Cristine."

Ty knew he should have managed better, should have conducted his affairs in a more organized fashion. Most of all, he should have found someone to replace his mother long ago. He'd depended on her for too long, and now his job was jeopardized.

"There's me."

His head jerked up at her words, his hand stilling against Cristine's soft curls.

"I know I have no credentials to offer, no experience at this at all. But if you show me the basics, I ought to be able to handle it." Her shoulders thrust back, her chin jutted out. "I'm a competent scientist with a PhD, Mr. Demens. Surely I ought to be able to care for a little girl, my own niece, for a few hours."

"It's Ty." He could see how much the words cost her. Worry and fear hung like shadowy specters in the back of her eyes, waiting to pounce at the first sign of failure.

And she would fail. They all had. It was only natural. But Ty had a hunch Briony Green had contemplated that possibility and offered anyway. Even now her hands shook as they smoothed Cristine's bib into place.

"I can do this," she whispered, her face pale but composed. "I can do this. For Bridget." She stood, small and defenseless before him, determination surrounding her like a cloak.

"I wouldn't dream of asking," he explained kindly. "It isn't your problem. If you did stay, all you'd be doing is prolonging my problem. You have to go to your new job in a month, and I'd be back to square one."

Briony nodded thoughtfully. He could see her mind sorting through the possibilities.

"I know it's not a full reprieve," she agreed at last. "I don't have all the answers. But I know Someone who does, and I'll be praying that He will make all things work together." She smiled. "In the meantime, if you can bear to allow me to care for your daughter, I promise you I'll give her all my attention."

"You're sure?" Did he dare take her up on it? Did he dare believe that God had answered the last prayer he'd vowed ever to pray?

"I'm positive." Briony stared down at Cristine, eyes pensive. "Bridget never asked me for help while she was alive. But maybe, through her daughter, I can help her now."

Ty studied her for several moments, as she turned her attention to Cris. How tenderly she spoke to the little girl, offered her a toy, smiled at her giggles of joy.

Hadn't he once believed that God cared for His children in all circumstances? Hadn't his mother told him over and over that God would answer in His own good time? Maybe, just maybe…

Ty took a deep breath. "Very well, if you're willing, thank you. I appreciate your help more than you can possibly imagine."

He launched into a description of Cristine's day, the foods she ate, the toys she loved, what she couldn't

have, slowing down only when Briony missed scribbling something on her notepad and asked him to repeat.

"She's very healthy. No allergies we know of. But she
does keep you moving. You can't let up your guard for
a moment," he warned, setting a bowl of cereal in front
of his daughter. He fed her a spoonful.

Briony studied his movements clinically, as if it were
an experiment she would have to replicate in order to meet
some criterion. Ty wondered for the thousandth time if he
was doing the right thing, but he shoved the doubts away.

If God was who his mother said, if He truly cared
about them, He'd come through. Maybe, just this once,
He'd come through.

Ty concentrated on giving her his numbers. "Everything's written down on the list on the fridge. If you need
me, I've got my cell phone. It generally works in the
mountains, but if there's a problem, any kind of trouble,
just call the park office. If I can't get here immediately,
they'll send someone who can."

"Yes. Certainly. Got that."

Ty could see her absorbing every detail, organizing
and filing each tidbit of information in precise, logical
order. He tried to be patient while he waited.

The phone rang again, and he answered.

"They've found some bear tracks in the area," he
told Briony after he hung up several moments later. "I
have to report in now." He studied her pale face. "Are
you sure you can do this?"

"Maybe not exactly the way you've been doing it,"
she quipped, her voice shaky. "But I think Cristine and
I will manage. You go ahead." As if to prove she was

capable, she took his place beside the high chair and began spooning the cereal into Cristine's rosebud mouth.

"She sometimes—" Ty swallowed the words as his daughter puffed out her cheeks and blew her oatmeal all over her new caregiver.

"Yes?" Briony peered up at him through the milky-white goop running through her lashes. With pinched fingers she removed three globs from her shirt and laid them on a napkin she'd carefully placed nearby.

Ty shook his head. Sometimes experience was the best teacher. "Never mind. With kids there are some things you just have to encounter firsthand." Ty snatched up two bananas, his knapsack and his jacket. He leaned down to press a kiss against Cristine's head, skillfully avoiding her dirty hands.

"Bye, darling. Be a good girl for Auntie Briony." He walked to the door, took one last look around, then met Briony's bright gaze.

"If there's anything…" he repeated.

"…I'll call you," she promised. "Don't worry. We have God on our side."

Ty headed out the door to his Jeep, wondering as he went how he was supposed to *not* worry. That was his daughter back there. His one and only child. A gift more precious than life.

"I know we haven't exactly seen eye-to-eye on things," he murmured as he steered through town to the checkpoint he'd been directed to. "I can't figure out why You do things and I don't like not knowing, or not being in control. But could you please send an angel to watch out for my little girl?"

He spared a thought for the small blond woman who had no idea what she'd gotten herself into.

"Maybe You'd better send one for Briony Green, too," he added, pulling in to the site now teeming with people. "She's kind and generous and smart, but I'm pretty sure she had no intention of spending her holiday looking after her sister's child."

Briony's words about Bridget and Andrea returned to haunt him. Andrea's signature under Bridget's on that adoption order burned into his brain. How could he not have known such a vital piece of information? Had Andrea hidden a friendship with Bridget?

"But why?" he asked himself. "Why? I was her husband. I wanted the child as much as she did."

The questions had to be stored away. For now.

But Ty knew he would find the answers. He had to.

Chapter Three

Five-and-a-half long hours later, Briony clutched the phone to her ear like a lifeline.

"Please, Clarissa, help me! I can't seem to stop her from crying." She felt the tears wet on her own cheeks and sniffed in misery. "I know she's tired, because she almost nods off. Then her little head jerks back and she starts all over again. You've got to think of something else to try."

Bri waited desperately for her friend's suggestion, never more conscious of her own helplessness than at this moment.

"Wait a minute, Bri. Blair just arrived. Maybe she's got some suggestions." A murmured conference in the background waffled over the telephone, then Clarissa returned. "I don't really know what else to tell you, honey. I've used up all my best baby-quieters. Hang on."

Bri stared at the beet-red face that glared furiously at her. About two more minutes of this and she intended to call Tyrel Demens back home permanently—bear and lost child notwithstanding. At this point she'd even *pay* for him to stay here.

Motherhood was not her forte. Hadn't she learned that lesson years ago?

"Bri?" Blair's pure clear voice sounded in her ear. "Clarissa tells me you're having some baby-sitting problems. I can't wait to hear how this came about. You, the woman who intended to devote her life to science? Baby-sitting?"

"Not now, okay, Blair?" Briony moved the phone a little nearer to Cristine's screaming mouth. Her old college buddy laughed, then surrendered.

"Okay, Bri. I get the message. Listen, does she have a stroller?"

"I don't know." Briony cast a quick glance around the room. Something navy and white was folded behind the door. "I think so. It's all flattened out, though."

"That's to make them easier to stow in the car. Usually if you push the handles apart, the seat folds down and *presto!* a stroller. Do you want me to hang on?"

"Yes." Bri carefully set the sobbing child on the now-pristine floor and moved across to grasp the stroller in both hands. Fortunately, it snapped apart with little effort. She picked the phone back up.

"Okay. Now what?"

"If she's as mad as she sounds, she's not going to settle for a few pushes in the house. You'll have to take her for a walk. The fresh air usually knocks them out in seconds." Blair stopped, said something to Clarissa, then came back on. "Make sure the seat belt holds her in securely. You don't want her to take a tumble."

"So I just get her in it and go strolling down the street?" Briony cast a dubious glance at her niece's writhing body. "I don't think that's going to do it, Blair."

Blair chuckled. "Oh, you don't stroll, honey. Not at first. You walk fast, pushing her along as quickly as you can. The bouncing and changing scenery usually do the trick. Either that or a car ride."

"A car ride?"

"Uh-uh. Scratch that. You can't take her unless you have a child seat, Bri. So for now, I'd bundle her into the stroller and take a walk. Probably do you good, too."

"Silence would do me the most good," Bri mumbled glumly. Silence, or a visit with her two best friends. Why hadn't she chosen to spend the month with them, at the lake, instead of getting herself tied up with a screeching bundle of contrariness?

Bridget, that's why. Bri sighed.

"Thanks a lot, Blair. I'll have to hang up, but stay near the phone, will you? I may need more help."

"I'll be here, kid. And we'll ask the Father of us all to lend you a little support, too."

Clarissa came on the line. "Don't worry, Bri. If she's dry, full, and not pushing a fever, she's just tired out and can't relax enough to sleep."

"But she's crying so hard!"

"Kids cry. It's the only way they can tell us they need something. But crying's not fatal. Okay?"

"Okay. Bye." Briony sighed, then bent down and picked up the kicking baby. "Listen, sweetie. You and I are going to take a walk. It's nice outside and you need to have a nap. A very long nap. Okay, darling?"

It took ages to get Cristine fastened into the stroller. And even longer to find a light blanket to lay over her when she fell asleep—if she ever stopped crying, that is.

"This house needs some serious organization," she muttered, finally dragging a flannelette square from between the sofa cushions.

Bri stuffed down her urge to organize, and followed Blair's directions. She wheeled the little girl outside, closed the door behind her and quickly walked down the path that led along the river.

Several people turned to stare as Cristine's wails reverberated across the water, echoing far louder and longer than Bri considered strictly necessary.

"Please, God, make her go to sleep. Please? Or even just stop bawling. She's so tired and she wants her grandma and I don't know how to help her. Please make her stop."

It took a minute to realize that Cristine was indeed silent. Briony slowed her walk, heard a whimper and immediately resumed her pace, trying to peer around the top of the stroller to see if the child was sleeping.

Four blocks later, she decided she couldn't wait any longer. She had to know if Cristine was all right, and if that meant risking waking her, well, then, she'd do it.

But Cristine, it seemed, had no intention of waking. She lay fast asleep in her soft flannel nest, her face turned to one side in a cherubic pose that sent little thrills up and down Briony's spine. This baby was so precious.

"Thank you, Lord." With a breath of relief, she rearranged the blanket so no chilly mountain breeze could touch that delicate skin, then continued on her way, absorbing the sights and sounds as she went.

Banff in June was God's creation in all its glory. The river tumbled past, cloudy blue-green water testament to its glacial origin. Beyond the town site, craggy, ice-covered peaks blazed white in the noonday sun, nestling the steep roofs of the alpine town in their embrace.

A little bench sat tucked behind a tree, just feet away from the water's edge. Briony sank down on it with a sigh of relief.

"You're useless," she chastised herself as the weariness stole over her. "One tiny little girl, and you're like a dishrag."

She checked to be sure Cristine was still asleep. How was such a miracle possible? Today she'd witnessed Bridget's daughter falter across a toy-strewn carpet just to be held. She'd watched that little mouth consume tiny amounts of food with relish, then come back for more. And now, that sweet soul lay resting so quietly, as if she'd never given anyone a moment's trouble.

"She's a darling, Bridget," Briony whispered as she gazed across the river at the old stone bridge. "Thank you for telling me about her. Thank you for letting me share the blessing."

A *thud* on the bench beside her made Briony start.

"You scared me half to death." Ty Demens peered at his daughter, then, seemingly satisfied that she was all right, glared at Briony. "I went home to check on you and nobody was there. I thought for sure you had to go to the hospital."

"I'm not quite that incompetent!" Briony grimaced at him, secretly relieved that she hadn't been forced to use the medical facilities. "It's such a lovely afternoon, we decided to take a walk."

"And everything is all right?" He frowned, studying her as if to find a telltale sign that she was incapable of looking after his daughter. "No problems?"

"Oh, sure. There were a few things. But we worked them through." She tossed it out airily, pretending she hadn't been scared of doing something wrong. "It takes time to learn a baby's routine."

Bri smugly repeated Clarissa's words without a single qualm, then hastily changed the subject before he could ask more.

"How did your morning go? Did you find the child?"

"Yes." He nodded, a smile tugging at the corners of his mouth. "She climbed a tree when she saw the bear, but she couldn't figure out how to get down. Smart little thing."

He leaned back against the bench and tilted his face up to the sun. "I'll miss lunch if I don't take a break now."

Lunch? Briony's stomach rumbled a loud, insistent complaint at the mention of food. She offered Ty an apologetic smile. "I guess I missed breakfast."

He studied her. "I thought you were staying at a bed-and-breakfast."

"I am. I just didn't feel like bacon and eggs this morning. Nervous, I suppose. Then Cristine and I were too busy playing for me to notice the time, until now." She blinked at her watch in surprise.

"There's a fast-food place not far away. What if I picked up a couple of burgers? We could eat our lunch here. Cristine will sleep longer, I'm sure. And I know you could use the rest."

Burgers? How long since she'd eaten red meat? Briony barely kept her lips from smacking. Burgers sounded fantastic. "That would be nice," she told him demurely.

"Okay. Be right back." Ty loped off across the park, intent on his mission to secure food.

"Your daddy is a very nice man, Cristine," she whispered, watching Ty's lean body dodge tourists as he jogged across the intersection and dashed inside the fast-food place.

He's also very good-looking.

She ignored the hint from her subconscious. She wasn't interested in a relationship. But even if she were, a man with a child certainly did not merit placement on the list. She'd learned her lesson there—learned it well. Only stupid people repeated their mistakes.

"I'm sorry, Bri, but I don't think I ever really loved you."

The remembered words stung almost as fiercely now as they had six years ago. She relived those awful minutes.

"I think I was subconsciously looking for a mother for my son. I wanted to be certain he wasn't deprived of a loving home and I thought you could help me provide that. But you're not really the mother type, are you?" Her husband-to-be had smiled, as if to soften the horrible words that dripped from his lips.

"You're too obsessed with your lab and your microscope to be the kind of mother a child needs."

She'd been stunned by the comment. How could he know her so little? Her heart fractured as he continued.

"His real mother has come back, Briony. She's the only woman I'll ever love. No one can take her place. She's agreed to marry me."

And just like that, Bri's engagement was over, the wedding canceled, the groom gone. And with him—or rather, with his son—had gone Briony's dreams.

She'd fallen in love with that little boy, given him the secret place in her heart that poured out all the love and affection she'd never known she possessed. She'd invested herself in getting to know the six-year-old, and in doing so had come to realize she wanted to be a mother.

Worse than that, she'd begun to think of them as a family.

And then, suddenly, father and son were gone, and she wasn't part of their lives anymore. She felt the sting of it even now.

"It was a good lesson to learn," she reminded herself as she studied the sleeping baby beside her. "You can't get involved with this child. She's his. All you're doing is helping him out. When the time comes, you need to be able to walk away."

Yes, that was it. Remain unemotional. Don't get involved. Do the job, then leave.

Hadn't she accepted that God had His hand on everything in her life? He'd given her a career instead of a family. She had to accept that He always knew best.

Bri stared down at Cristine. Her throat pinched closed, her breathing stuck in her chest. One month and then she'd leave. But for now, it couldn't hurt to just look, could it?

"They weren't very busy." Ty plopped down on the

seat beside her. "I hope you like chocolate milk shakes. I bought the largest."

He handed her a paper cup with a straw poking out the top, and a sack. Then he paused, holding his own. "You looked awfully pensive. Is anything wrong?"

"No, nothing." Bri offered him a weak smile. At least he'd brought her a milk shake. She didn't think she could drop her defenses enough to swallow a soft drink *and* a burger.

"Rough morning, huh?" He grinned, patted her hand, then dug into his own lunch. "I know the feeling. For the first six months of her life, I don't think I slept more than an hour at a time."

"Was she sick or something?" Bri looked up from sipping her shake. "I've heard stories about newborns that don't sleep."

Ty laughed. "Oh, this little miss slept like an angel. I'm afraid the problem was me."

"You?" She waited for his response, her gaze riveted on the family sharing a picnic on the grass just a few feet away. There was a persistent ache in her heart. Bri turned away.

"Yeah. Me." Ty unwrapped his burger, took a bite and chewed thoughtfully. "I was a nervous wreck. I had to keep checking if she was breathing, that she wasn't smothered, that she didn't need a dry diaper or fresh air. She was too warm, she was too cold." He shook his head. "It's a wonder I didn't drive everybody nuts."

"A little overpossessive, were you?" She grinned, unable to visualize this in-control man at the mercy of a tiny baby.

"A lot overpossessive." His gaze slipped far away, into the past. Some emotion—dark, brooding—slipped through his eyes until they glowed almost black.

"She was so tiny, so precious. We'd wanted to have kids for ages. Then we accepted we never would."

"I'm sorry."

In front of Bri, Tyrel's face lost the grim look and glowed with joy. "One night I came home from work—and there she was. My very own daughter. I couldn't quite believe in that miracle. Sometimes I still can't."

Briony nodded. "I felt the same way when I found that paper." She laughed. "My sister a mother? It just didn't compute."

"And yet it does. Sort of." He studied her from beneath his lashes, hiding his expression. "From what you've said, Cristine is definitely her daughter." Just the hint of a question dangled in those words.

Bri couldn't leave him hanging. She nodded. "Yes, she's the spitting image of our baby pictures. And from what I read last night, Cristine is certainly Bridget's daughter." She took a deep breath and admitted the truth. "I read on in my sister's diary last night. The dates Bridget indicates all seem to correlate with Cristine's birthday—March first, isn't it?" She waited for his nod.

"And then there are the signatures." She almost hated to remind him of his wife's part in this.

"Yes, the signatures." He folded up the wrapper from the fries, shoved it inside the bag, then dumped it and the remains of his shake into the nearby garbage can. "I still can't understand that part. Andrea was so certain the

birth mother would never allow herself to be revealed."
He glanced at her. "I'm not making that up, you know."

"I know." Bri had no answer to the question in his
eyes. "Maybe if you told me a bit about what was going
on back then, you'd remember something that would
explain it," she offered, fully aware that his past was
none of her business.

He frowned.

"If you're not comfortable with that, it's all right,"
she reassured him hurriedly. "I understand that it's
painful to dig into the past."

"It's just that it's all such a blur. We had a huge forest
fire in the park last year. Everyone was working extra-
long shifts with not much time for sleep or anything
else." His expression turned grim. "Not enough snow
and a very warm winter."

"I remember." Bri closed her eyes. "Several rangers
got caught in a back draft."

He nodded. "No matter how many people they
brought in, we couldn't turn the tide. Sometimes we
didn't even make it home, just took a sleeping bag and
sacked out for a few hours." He glanced up through his
lashes. "I came home as often as I could, but with the
fire threatening the town, I'm afraid I was preoccupied
with work."

"Of course." Bri finished her lunch, savoring the
last smooth swallow of her cool milk shake. "So your
wife would have had a lot of time on her own. If she
met someone, made a new friend, she may not have
told you about it."

"Andrea didn't go out a lot." The words slipped out

on a soft murmur, as if he felt he was maligning his wife by admitting that.

"Oh." Bri waited.

"She was nervous about tourists and the strangers that always come to town. It was worse then. It would have been…unusual for her to have made a new friend," he said after a pause.

"But not impossible?"

"No. Not impossible."

But something in his voice told her he thought it very unlikely.

"Bridget found a job working in the Banff Springs Hotel. She'd worked in Reservations before, so that wasn't unusual. She loved those fancy, historic hotels."

"When did she arrive?"

Bri frowned. "I can't really tell that, but from her diary entries, it seems as if she'd been here for a while. She writes a bit about her doctor telling her to rest. A local doctor, apparently."

"I don't know any. I haven't seen a doctor in years." He shrugged. "Andrea always insisted on seeing someone in Calgary. Sometimes my sister would coax her to stay for a day or two, but my wife never spoke of meeting anyone."

Silence hung between them, punctuated by the gurgle of the river, the conversation of passing hikers and the rumble of traffic as it crossed the bridge. In the distance, Briony could see tiny, glass-enclosed gondola cars lifting up Sulphur Mountain.

"And Cristine's father?" He seemed to ask in spite of himself. "Did you find any mention of him?"

Pity welled inside her. How difficult it must be to wonder if the child you'd come to adore would be claimed by someone else.

"I'm sorry, I don't know that. Bridget doesn't mention him at all. So far."

His head jerked in a nod of understanding. His big hands twisted and tore the paper napkin into puny shreds. "But there is hope that she might. Maybe once you've read more?"

She didn't want to dash his hopes. "Perhaps." She remembered the notations she'd read. "Bridget wrote about a support group she met with."

"Support?" He stared at her. "For what?"

"I'm not sure. Alcohol, perhaps. I don't think she was ever into drugs. Anyway, I think the group met every week. She writes of several people in the group." Briony took a deep breath. "I thought perhaps I'd go to the hotel and ask if anyone remembers her, or if the group is still going."

"It's a good idea," he agreed, but a hint of warning shaded his voice. "Just don't expect too much. The population here fluctuates with the seasons. It's quite possible that many of the people she worked with last year have moved on."

"Of course." Briony nodded, her eyes on the diminutive form now stirring in the stroller. "I think perhaps I'd better start walking again. I don't want Cristine to wake up just yet." She jiggled the stroller in hopes of calming the little girl.

"I've got to get back soon, but I'll walk a little way with you." Ty adjusted his stride to match hers as they meandered back down the river walk. "Soon these streets will be overflowing with tourists," he murmured. "July is frenetic."

She followed his glance. Three buses unloaded their passengers, each of whom scurried in a different direction. She knew what Ty was thinking: how would he ever find information about his daughter in such a quickly changing community?

Briony chanced a look at him. "Don't worry, Ty. We'll find out more about Cristine. It just takes time for God to work out all the kinks."

"You have a lot of faith in God, don't you?" He stared down at her intently.

"It's the one thing that's kept me going through some pretty tough situations."

"You sound like my mother." He stopped for several moments, saying nothing as he skipped a rock across the water. When she kept going, he caught up, then offered her a timid smile. "I wish I had faith like you two. I guess I'm just one of those people who has to see to believe."

"No, you aren't." Briony shook her head. "You don't see the air, do you? But you keep right on breathing, all the same. You don't know for sure that you'll be alive and healthy next year, but you keep on planning for the future." She grinned at him. "You have faith, Ty. Maybe it just isn't developed enough."

"Like my muscles?" He huffed out a laugh.

Briony couldn't seem to keep her eyes off him. His lopsided smile tugged at her heartstrings.

"I don't think you need to worry," she whispered, her cheeks burning with embarrassment as she stared at his brown muscular arms, bare where the short-sleeved shirt ended.

He laughed. "Thanks, I think." Then his face grew serious.

"I have tried, you know. To have faith. But nothing turns out the way I expect."

She knew he was thinking about his wife. "It isn't easy," she agreed. "But if 'faith is the evidence of things hoped for,' then you can't give up. You've got to keep trusting that someday you'll understand why."

Her steps slowed, then stopped as a small stone church came into view. "First Avenue Fellowship." The name sounded familiar. Bri's mind clicked through the information, then flew back to the diary in her room.

Ty frowned at her. "Is anything wrong? You've the strangest look on your face."

"No." Bri shook her head. She pointed. "There's the church."

"The church?" He followed her gaze, a whimsical grin crinkling his eyes. "That's nothing new. It's been there for a long time, Briony. Over a hundred years." He must have sensed her excitement. "Does it mean something to you?"

"Not a thing," she assured him, hurriedly wheeling the stroller to the intersection. She waited until the coast was clear, then scooted across, fully aware that Ty was trailing behind her.

"Then, may I ask what you're doing?"

"Bridget mentioned that church in her diary. I didn't make the connection right away. I thought she was talking about a fellowship group that met someplace on First Avenue."

Bri marched up the sidewalk and stood staring at the huge sign beside the front door.

"You think this is where she came?" he asked as he ambled up beside her. All at once a sudden crush of people flowed out from the side door, and his arm curved over her back to shield Bri.

Bri's breath forgot to move. Jolts of electricity radiated from his hand to her body. Power and steely strength emanated from that touch. What was it about Ty Demens that affected her so much?

Bri took a calming breath. "I don't know if this is the place. But I think I'm going to find out." She pointed to the sign. "Look. 'Fellowship meetings every Tuesday afternoon for those who need a friend,'" she read out loud.

He looked unconvinced by her find. "But how would that connect Bridget with Andrea? We never attended this church."

"I don't know how. Yet." Bri tugged open the side door and wheeled the stroller inside. "But maybe we can find out."

They followed the long narrow hall back to a room that was obviously behind the sanctuary. A man stood rinsing out cups in a small kitchen to the left.

"Oh, hello." He smiled, his eyes moving from them to Cristine. "A bit of rest for everyone, is it?" He winked. "I'm sorry, but the meeting is over for today."

"That's all right. We didn't come for the meeting." Ty cast a dubious look around the room. "Is it for AA or something?"

The man in the kitchen shrugged, wiped his hands on the towel, then moved toward them. "Something like that. Really, I suppose it's a support group for anyone who needs a hand up."

Bri waited for Ty to ask the obvious question. But when he remained in front of a cork board, staring at the small felt handprints that decorated it, she took the bull by the horns.

"Do you ever have any expectant mothers come?" she asked in a rush. "Unwed mothers?" It seemed shameful to call Bridget by that horrid demeaning title, and yet, wasn't that exactly what she'd been?

"Sometimes we do." The man frowned. "Is there something in particular you'd like to know, Mrs...."

"Oh, sorry." Bri grinned at him. "My name is Briony Green. This is Tyrel Demens. He's a park ranger, and I'm the sitter for his daughter."

"I see. I'm Tom Winter. I'm the minister here." He shook hands with them both, then motioned toward the chairs. He waited until they'd seated themselves, his open gaze moving from one to the other. "How can I help you?"

When it became obvious that Ty had no intention of speaking, Bri took a deep breath and related their story, without going into details.

"So you see," she finished, "we've been trying to figure out how Ty's wife could have met my sister, and the only clue seems to be a meeting here. Bridget wrote that she attended it each week. Maybe Ty's wife came, too."

Ty shook his head. "It's not likely."

"It's all we have." Bri focused on the minister.

Tom tapped his finger against his chin. "I see. And when was this?"

"About a year ago. We're not sure of exact dates."

Once again the frustration rose. Bri watched Tyrel's face tighten up with nervousness. If only she'd kept better track of Bridget, paid more attention to her needs instead of spending all her time in the lab to get the details lined up for that dissertation. Maybe then she'd have known all the facts that Tyrel longed to hear.

A motion in the corner of her eye drew Briony's attention away from the handsome forester and back to the minister.

"Oh, that's too bad." Tom shook his head, his face sad. "There's no way, then. I'm sorry."

Bri frowned. "You don't remember her?"

"I'm afraid I don't. But then, I wouldn't. I'm new here, you see. Since last Christmas. I'm afraid I wouldn't have any information about your sister." He offered an apologetic smile to Ty. "Or your wife."

"It doesn't matter." Ty heaved himself to his feet, his face impassive.

But Briony could clearly read the message in the glance he telegraphed to her. *Why bother? There are no answers here.*

His hopelessness and despair ate at her confidence. This was a clue, she was certain of it. Years of conducting painstaking research and tracing every lead always yielded results. Why hadn't she stayed awake last night, pored over that book and found him some shred of hope?

Please, Lord. I need a little help. If he could just catch a glimpse of Your hand working, maybe he'd be able to trust just a little longer. Couldn't You just send me an idea?

Stalling for time, Bri shuffled to her feet, her mind

working furiously. As she slowly pushed the stroller, her glance fell on the list tacked to a nearby bulletin board.

"Come on. Cristine will be awake soon." Ty stood in the doorway, shifting from one foot to the other. It was obvious he wanted out.

"The group." The glimmer in her brain grew. "Maybe someone in the group would remember her." She turned to the minister and begged with her eyes. "It might be worth a shot, don't you think?"

He nodded, contemplating the idea. "It might indeed. People come and go all the time, but someone may remember your sister." He chewed on his bottom lip. "I won't be able to ask them until next week, though."

"Next week?" Ty repeated.

Bri wanted this mystery solved as badly as anyone, so it came as no surprise when Ty blurted out his disappointment. But truth be told, she had far less at stake than him right now. Bridget had given her child to the Demens by signing the adoption form and ensuring the paperwork was done correctly. But if she hadn't notified Cristine's biological father, Ty Demens's position could be threatened. Of course he was apprehensive!

She turned back to the minister. "We're very anxious to speak to anyone who might have known her."

"I understand." He patted her hand. "But the group only meets once a week. Some of them come from a distance and some have to make special work arrangements to be here."

"Maybe we could phone them, one by one." As soon as she said it, Bri knew it wouldn't work. Tom's words only confirmed her fears.

"I'm sorry. The membership is private. In fact, the group is closed to new members after the second week. Only those who keep up a regular attendance are allowed in, and we never divulge names. It would threaten the confidentiality, you see. No one would feel secure in sharing."

"Of course." Ty's arm curled under her elbow, his other hand gripping the stroller handle. "We never meant to suggest that you should break any confidence. Goodbye." He hurried his daughter down the hall, ending the discussion abruptly.

"I'll stop back in," Bri called over her shoulder as she followed Ty. "Thanks for your help."

They emerged into the afternoon sun, with Bri rushing to match Ty's long-legged pace. "Slow down," she puffed at last, too tired to keep it up. "Where is the fire?"

"Sorry." He slowed slightly after casting her one dark look. Then he stopped. He lifted his hands off the stroller. "I need to get back to work. I'd better go."

"Oh." She gulped, wondering at the anger she glimpsed in his eyes. "Is anything wrong?" she ventured, when he didn't immediately walk away.

"Yes!" Ty drew her off the walkway and onto the grass, pulling the stroller with him so that they were out of sight of curious onlookers. His face loomed mere inches from Bri's as he growled at her.

"I know I wasn't the best husband in the world. I failed at a lot of things. I probably didn't have the happily-ever-after kind of marriage you women always read about."

From the look on his face, Bri guessed his marriage was probably a long way from that.

"But there is no way I want to talk about it with a bunch of strangers on the off chance one of them knew Andrea or your sister and can explain what they *might have been* doing together."

Briony peered up at him. The flecks in his eyes stood out, showing his anger. But she saw something else there, too.

Embarrassment? What on earth did he have to be embarrassed about? Wasn't it Andrea, his wife, who had kept the details of the adoption from him?

Or was Tyrel Demens hiding something? Something that he hadn't shared with her. Something that made him afraid.

Bri reorganized the information she had in military precision, but the question would not disappear.

Was Ty worried about other people learning some secret?

Cristine stirred, then let out a whimper.

"She'll wake up soon. I'd better get back." Bri stepped forward, grasping the stroller handles firmly. "I guess I'll see you when you've finished work," she murmured, keeping her eyes downcast.

"Yeah. I guess." Ty took one last look at his daughter, brushed the golden curls off her forehead. He leaned over to place a tender kiss across her eyelids, then sighed. "Bye." He headed down the street without a backward glance.

Briony walked back to the stone cottage slowly, her mind racing a hundred miles an hour.

"I believed him," she murmured, puzzling it out in her mind. "I accepted that everything he said was fact.

But what if it wasn't? What if he's the one who's not telling the whole truth? What if he's hiding something?"

That didn't seem right. Ty seemed as upright and straight-shooting as anyone she'd ever met. And yet, it would explain his fear. It would explain why he seemed dogged by worry.

But what could possibly be so awful about his marriage that he didn't want anyone to know?

Bri rolled the stroller into the house, removed the smiling little girl and changed her diaper, before offering her a drink. Then she spread a blanket on the floor and sat next to little Cristine while she played with her toys.

"He loves this child," she said aloud. "Anyone can see that. He adores the ground she crawls on." She thought for a moment, remembering the sad look that washed over Ty's face whenever he spoke of Andrea.

"I believe he loved his wife, too. So what in the world would Ty Demens have to hide?"

The first day she'd met him, he'd been so certain that Andrea had told him the truth about Cristine. What if, by probing the relationship between Bridget and Andrea, Bri had made him remember another time his wife had lied to him? Or was it simply that Ty didn't want to tarnish her memory by digging into a past that couldn't be altered?

Was she hurting him unnecessarily by being here, by uncovering secrets that might be better left alone?

Bri built a tower of blocks and watched as Cristine giggled her glee, knocking them over with a brush of her chubby hand.

What if Ty felt that something in his and Andrea's

past could lead to questioning of the adoption, or of their ability to be parents?

Suddenly a dark thought clouded Briony's mind. *What if all her probing into the past cost him his daughter?*

She didn't know how it could happen, of course. Bridget had certainly taken steps to ensure that her baby stayed where she put her. But the fact remained that Bri didn't know the whole story.

"By poking at it all the time I'm hurting him," she whispered, the knowledge causing a pang in her heart. "And I don't want to hurt him. He's had too much pain already. He and Cristine deserve to be happy together."

It didn't really matter what had happened. Briony knew Bridget, knew the kind of awful things she'd done when they were kids. And yet, she'd loved her sister in spite of it all.

"Perhaps Ty can't bear for his love for Andrea to be put to that test. Perhaps he wants to keep the image he has of her intact, unblemished."

Who was Briony Green to question his wishes?

For the next three hours Bri tossed the problem around in her mind as she played with Cristine, read her a story and took her for another short walk. Ty arrived home just as Bri had almost finished feeding the little girl her dinner.

"Hi." She studied his face anew. It was an honest face. That devoted look when he studied his daughter wasn't fake.

Bri made up her mind. Whatever was wrong, she wouldn't add to his pain. Her investigations would have to wait, or at least bypass him.

"Is anything wrong?" Ty placed his knapsack on a chair and hunkered down to tickle Cristine, whispering sweet nothings as he nuzzled against her neck. The little girl giggled and wiggled with sheer pleasure. He looked up from his play and caught Bri staring.

"Briony? Has something happened?"

When she didn't speak, he picked Cristine up out of her chair, holding her tightly in his protective embrace as his eyes scoured Bri's face.

"What is it?"

"It's nothing. I just wanted to let you know that I'm not going to be sticking my nose into your past anymore." Bri smiled to reassure him. "We scientists sometimes get caught up in digging for the truth. I can see that asking so many questions, puzzling over the past, hurts you," she said honestly.

"I see." He stared at her, his dark gaze roiling with confusion. "Why did you decide this?"

"When I look at Cristine, see how sweetly she smiles, how her eyes light up whenever you're around, I realize that the past and my sister's reason for being here, for choosing you—none of that matters." She brushed her hand over Cristine's bare foot, then her eyes rose to meet Ty's.

"This is what matters. The present and the future for this sweet little soul. Anyone with eyes can see that she'll be perfectly happy with you, Ty. Nothing else compares to that."

Ty studied Bri for a long time.

Eventually he set Cristine in her chair, straightened her bib and waited for Bri to resume feeding. Once the baby had begun slurping up bits of peach with pudgy fingers, Tyrel pulled off his tie, unbuttoned the neck of his shirt and raked one hand through his hair so that it stood straight up.

"That's where you're wrong, Miss Green. Dead wrong."

His glacial voice sent her head jerking upward in surprise. Her eyes met his, searching for an answer.

"I don't understand," she whispered, aghast at the agony that pulled his handsome features taut.

"Cristine's past may well affect her future in a way that none of us can control, unless we prepare for it." He raised a hand when she would have spoken. "I know you're concerned for me and that's very noble of you, but believe me, I can take it." His mouth creased in a wry grin. "I figured out this afternoon that I can handle anything that we may discover, so long as it means my daughter's future is with me."

Briony hated to say it, knew how much it would hurt him. But she had to ask, had to know. "And if it isn't?" she whispered.

He stood ramrod straight, his shoulders thrust back, his chin jutted out. It was his combat stance.

How wonderful to be loved like that, Briony marveled. How incredible to know that you had someone on your side who would stand behind you no matter what.

Ty's words snapped out in harsh resolve. "Cristine's future is with me. There's no discussion about that. But I need to be prepared. I need every bit of information there is out there, good or bad. Can you understand?" His eyes beseeched her.

"I have to do everything in my power to ensure no one will take her away. So if you have to dig into the past, dig. As long as it helps me keep Cristine, I don't care about anything else. Her welfare is primary."

She stared at him, awed by the fierceness in his voice. At the corner of his eye, a bit of moisture glimmered in the light. Bri swallowed, hard.

"And if I find something unpleasant?" she said at last.

"You keep digging," he told her. "Whatever my wife did, she had a good reason. I'd like to know what that reason was." A bleakness washed over his face, then disappeared.

His fingers closed around Bri's arm, forcing her to look at him.

"Do you hear me, Briony? Talk to people, ask questions, find out all you can. And if I ever again tell you to stop, ignore me. I need to know the truth. Cristine deserves it."

"The truth often hurts," she reminded him.

"I've been hurt before." His voice crackled with ice. "I'll live. As long as you don't lie to me, I'll be fine."

"I'll never lie to you," Bri promised solemnly.

But as she walked home half an hour later, she wondered how dearly that promise would cost him.

And her.

Chapter Four

A few days later, Briony took advantage of the baby's naptime to do some household organizing and review the information she had thus far.

It wasn't much.

Bridget's diary was slow reading. So many of the entries revealed a longing for God's love. Often Briony had to put it away, lest her emotion blind her to the information she was seeking. She had gained only one clue so far. Bridget cared deeply about the opinion of a man named Kent.

"I need to find him," she told herself, setting the last of the spices on the shelf.

That's when she realized she'd just emptied and then refilled Ty's cupboards using the precise alphabetical method she'd used in her own apartment. "At least he'll find everything quicker." She hoped.

She was thankful that the phone rang, so she didn't have to rationalize it all out.

"Hello?"

"How is my granddaughter?"

"Mrs. Demens!" Bri smiled into the phone. "I should be asking how you are."

"Bored silly," the older woman complained. "All I do is sit around and crochet. My daughter won't let me do a thing except watch the flowers grow. I wish I were there with you and Cristine."

"We do, too." Sometimes Bri desperately wished someone was here to confide in, to reassure her that her mistakes wouldn't permanently harm Cristine.

"Are you finding it too difficult?"

The soft-voiced concern soothed Bri's battered heart. Maybe she wasn't so alone.

"I usually end up putting her outfits on backward," Briony admitted. "When Ty comes home, he always changes them around with this strange glower, as if he's fed up with my stupidity." She gulped, then decided to say what was in her heart.

"It's not that I'm not trying, Mrs. Demens. But reason tells me the buttons and snaps should be in the front to make it easier to change her. I listened and tried to do as he did. The one time I put them in the back, I was wrong then, too. It's so confusing and totally illogical."

"Oh, dear." It sounded as though Monica Demens was laughing.

"The only time I get it right is when she wears a dress."

"Is Cristine happy?"

"She seems all right. She giggles and laughs most of the time she's awake." A warmth flooded Bri's heart. "She's got a funny little smile that she uses when she makes this particular shriek. I think she's teasing me."

"If you were doing something wrong, she wouldn't be smiling," Mrs. Demens pointed out. "Stop worrying so much. I'm sure Ty thinks you're doing a marvelous job. He seemed quite pleased when I spoke to him last night."

"Did he?" Bri could hardly imagine it. "Well, I'm trying, even though I feel like a fish out of water."

"You'll do fine, dear. And remember, I'm praying for you."

"Thank you. I can use that."

"Have you, er, found out any more about your sister?"

Bri swallowed. She'd felt Ty's irritation with the subject on several occasions and had learned to keep her own counsel.

"Not much. I've been trying to dig into her diary, but the company who hired me also asked me to do a little preliminary reading on some studies they've already conducted, so my evenings have been pretty full."

"I can imagine. Don't overdo, Briony. Whatever the truth of the past, Cristine is healthy and happy and has a family that truly loves her. I don't think anything can change that."

Bri nodded. "I know. I just want everything cleared up before I have to leave. I want to make sure nothing can change Bridget's plans or take Cristine from Ty. Then I'll be satisfied."

After a few more minutes of chatter, Mrs. Demens said, "I'd love to drive out for a chat, Briony, but my daughter lives on the far side of Calgary and she works such full days. Asking her to drive an hour-and-a-half into Banff for a little visit then turn around to go home seems so demanding, especially after all she's already done for me."

"But you're supposed to keep your leg up! You can't do that in a car." Bri hurried to reassure her. "We're fine. Truly."

"I'm glad." A faint sigh. "Things seem so rushed here. I guess I'd gotten used to the serenity of the park. Giselle and her husband are always on the run to soccer and baseball games."

"That must be lonely for you."

"Actually, I rather enjoy the calm after the storm." Mrs. Demens laughed. "You'd have to know Giselle to understand, Briony. She's like a whirlwind that just can't sit still. I shouldn't complain so much."

"Sometimes we just have to share, don't we?" Bri wished she had someone she could share with. She'd never been really good with people. Perhaps that's what made it so easy to fall back into her books and studies.

"If you're looking for a friend, you can't do worse than Ty's church. Such a lot of dedicated young souls. They're really friendly."

"I'll try it on Sunday, if Ty doesn't need me," Bri said. "I'm not ready to take a child to church just yet— Oops, there's Cristine. I'd better go. She doesn't like to be kept waiting."

"How well I remember!" Mrs. Demens laughed. "I'll be praying." Then she said goodbye.

Bri hung up and climbed the stairs to the little girl's room. "Thanks," she whispered. "I can use all the help I can get."

Once Cristine was changed, she was raring to go. Unfortunately an earlier light mist had now turned into a steady drizzle that diminished the options for playtime.

Bri checked over her baby-care schedule and knew there was no way around it. Cristine needed this free time to work off her energy. If Cristine didn't get enough exercise, the little girl turned into an imp.

Briony surveyed the living room, crowded with furniture, playpen, baby swing and a host of plush toys that spilled all over everything. The chaotic mess irritated her more now than ever before.

Time for a change.

"Cristine, my love, you just sit in here for a minute while Auntie Bri makes you a play space."

She popped the little girl in the playpen, rolled up the sleeves of her crisp white blouse and began shifting things around until the furniture was arranged around the periphery of the room and Cristine's play blanket and toys sat in the center.

"Now you've got lots of room to toddle, if you want." Bri hugged the powdery-soft body close until Cristine wriggled to get down. "And no tables to bump this nose."

Cristine immediately tested the theory by rushing across the carpet as fast as her chubby little legs would carry her. She smacked into the cushions of the sofa, sat down with a thump and grinned.

"You like that, huh?" Bri moved the swing out of the way, behind the love seat. Then she tossed the extra toys into the playpen, while Cristine fiddled with the toy lawn mower that purred when she thrust it across the floor, gobbling up anything in its path.

"You and I think alike, my dear."

Bri stood, watching the little girl babble as she played with her toys. If Ty wanted to entertain, all he had to do was remove the playpen full of toys, and the room would look like a normal living room again.

"Except for those awful towels." She leaned down to tuck yet another edge under the cushion. "I suppose they're to protect this thing from your drooling," she mumbled, tickling Cristine. "But they're always coming off."

Cristine apparently agreed, for she began to tug on one corner. When it finally pulled free, she pulled the towel over her head and giggled.

"Peek-a-boo." Bri knew this game. She dragged the towel off and grinned. "There you are."

Off came the next towel, and the next, until the furniture sat completely uncovered.

"We'll leave it that way for a while, sweetie, but I've got to put them back before your dad comes home."

"No." Cristine mowed the towels, sturdy little legs propelling her across the room.

"I wish you'd learn another word," Bri told her, crouching down to pick up the towels.

"No." Cristine tugged one free and mowed it again. "No."

"How about 'yes,' Cristine? Yes, yes, yes."

"No." She pulled on the drooping edge. "No."

"You win." Bri let the entire bundle drop. "If your dad gets angry with me again, I'm going to tell him Cristine made me do it."

"No."

Bri shook her head and collapsed on the floor, her back against the sofa. It was going to be one of "those" afternoons.

By five-thirty Briony was ready to dial 911.

"Cristine, this is good. Mmm. Potatoes are nice. Here, see?" She pretended to eat some off the tiny baby spoon. "Mmm." She held the spoon to Cristine's lips.

Cristine opened her mouth for just one reason. "No." Her eyes darkened, her chin jerked up and her tiny feet pummeled the footrest on the high chair. "No!" she bellowed shoving the spoon directly into Briony's shirt.

"Cristine—"

The little girl shape-shifted right before her eyes. Gone was the sulky look, the angry tilt to sweet pink lips. Bri gaped, stunned by the sudden change in the child. Cristine dropped her hands, her face lost its furious red tinge and a huge smile transformed her face.

"Mmm." Cristine held up her arms. "Up."

"Hey, sweetie." Ty swung through the door, his face lighting up at the sight of the child. He bent down to brush a kiss over her potato-laden hair. "You look pretty grubby, kiddo." His scrutiny moved to Bri.

Bri looked grubby, too. She knew he itched to say it.

Her braids had come loose and bits of hair now drooped and clung to her face and neck in the messiest way. Most of Cristine's lunch and almost all of her dinner clung to Bri's body in various spots, including her shoes.

"Don't hold back on my account," she muttered.

"You look worse than she does," Ty told her bluntly as he picked a pea out of her hair. "What're we having, a food fight?"

Bri kept her smile with great difficulty. "She's not happy about staying inside today." Which was the understatement of the year! The most rigorous day of research had never left Bri as drained as she felt right now.

"So why didn't you take her outside?" He stood frowning as she scooped potato off herself.

"It's been raining."

"She won't melt. It's far better for her to get some fresh air than to be cooped up inside all day. Next time put her coat on and take her out."

It hurt to be criticized when none of it was her fault. Bri knew she wasn't good at baby-sitting. She often felt uncertain and useless. Cristine seemed to understand that, for she chose just those moments to act up.

"I'll clean her up and go," she murmured, blinking away the rush of tears that blurred her vision. She took a washcloth and held it beneath the tap. "I think she's eaten all she wants for the moment."

"Good thing, too. Another ten minutes and we'd have total destruction." He tweaked the little girl's ear, then hurried away to change out of his uniform.

Cristine was not thrilled with being left in her chair, and she fought Bri's efforts to remove the food as hard as Bri fought to keep her emotions in check.

What was wrong with her? Bri had never been emotional; she hated that kind of display. She liked to assess the situation completely and then act accordingly. But this situation continually tested her theories and her logic. Neither seemed to work with the miniature bundle of energy in front of her.

"Come on, Cristine. We've got to get this mess cleaned up if you're going to see Daddy. Hold out your hand." Bri forcibly unfolded the little fingers and wiped away the mush inside. "Good girl," she muttered. "Now the other one."

"No!" Cristine grabbed a few loose strands of Bri's hair and yanked for all she was worth.

It was the last straw in a long and trying day. Bri backed away, her hand to her aching head, fighting to keep the tears from coursing down her cheeks.

"What happened to the living room?" Ty Demens sauntered into the kitchen, clean, pressed and frowning. "Why is the furniture rearranged?"

"Cristine needs more room to move around." Bri turned her back on him, huddling over the sink as the tears welled in her eyes. Her scalp stung like crazy, and now she had a headache, too. She gulped, made her voice firm. "If she runs, she bumps into the table. I tried to give her room to move."

"It's kind of awkward coming down the stairs," he told her with a growl. "I banged my shin on the swing."

"Sorry." It was the best apology she could scrape together.

Bri concentrated on washing the pans that wouldn't fit in the already full dishwasher. Most of them came from Ty's dinner creation of the night before, and she'd had to soak them all day to get the spaghetti sauce and burned meat loose.

Finally she had the entire mess scrubbed and draining on the board. She wiped down the counter with a sigh.

"Hey, Cris. You're all mucky. I think you need a bath." Ty's voice brimmed with love as he spoke to the now cooing child. "Briony, are you almost finished with the sink?"

"Yes, almost." Bri surreptitiously dried her eyes with the dish towel, scoured the last pot halfheartedly and then began stowing everything in the neat precise style she'd arranged earlier.

"Hey, what's this? I can't find her shampoo." Ty began hauling things out of the cupboard with no regard for their arrangement.

"Stop it!" Bri could no more have stifled that response than she could have made her hands move from her fierce clasp around his arm. "I spent half the morning organizing that. Kindly don't undo my work!"

He blinked. "But nothing's where it's supposed to be."

"It's all in order. Cristine's things are here, in this cupboard near the sink so you can reach them easily while bathing her. Her bathtub is under the sink, where it's out of the way."

"What was wrong with the way it was?" He jammed his hands on his hips belligerently.

"It wasn't that it was wrong, exactly. It's just more efficient this way."

"Huh?"

Bri felt a slow burn creep up her neck. "It is more efficient to do it this way. If everything has a place and is kept in it, things can be done in half the time. I spent forty minutes searching for the dish detergent this morning. It didn't occur to me you kept it in the bathroom."

He grinned. "I don't. I was using it to clean my binocular lenses."

"And Cristine's diapers? I found the new box in the broom closet."

"I always keep them there."

"Why? Wouldn't it make more sense to keep them in her room?"

He shrugged, his eyes wide with confusion. "I guess. I just go get them when I need them."

"When I needed them, I didn't have time to go hunting." She decided not to tell him that she'd used one of his T-shirts as a stop-gap measure.

"You're making this into a big deal." He yanked out the tub and flopped it on the counter, adding water as he continued. "It's not as if I'm totally disorganized. I've been doing this for fifteen months and I think I've managed pretty well."

Now who was criticizing? Bri took a deep breath, handed Cristine a biscuit and then scrubbed down her high chair.

"I'm sure you've done a wonderful job, Ty. It's just that this is all new to me." She straightened the cupboard he'd messed, then stood. "I'm used to working in a lab. If you want a swab, you go to the place where swabs are kept. Then you get back to what you were doing."

"This isn't a lab, it's a home," he countered, opening and closing drawers until he found the one where she'd laid the baby's bath towels.

"That doesn't mean we can't utilize a system of order." She lifted the baby out of the high chair and stripped her clothes off before setting her in the bath. "You see, I can hold her with this hand and reach everything I need without losing my grip."

To demonstrate, Bri handed Cristine the rubber duck from the window ledge, squirted out a tiny bit of shampoo from the bottle she'd set on a nearby shelf, and then washed it off, all without letting go of the slippery little girl.

"It's safer," she murmured stepping back when his hands closed around the child's soft skin. She watched him for a few moments.

"I was trying to do the same thing in the living room," she murmured. "I wasn't trying to disrupt your system or imply you weren't doing your best."

When Ty didn't say anything, she gathered up her briefcase, shoved in the information she'd organized about her sister and stepped toward the door.

"I've got to get going. I promised someone I'd meet them and I'll be late if I don't hurry." Avoiding Ty, Bri managed to brush a kiss across the baby's cheek. "Bye, sweetie. See you Monday." Then she hurried out the door, closing it firmly behind her.

As she stepped outside, Bri thought she heard him call her name. But she didn't stop. Instead, she hurried toward her favorite spot by the river. Thankfully the little wooden bench was empty, though tourists strolled past constantly.

She collapsed onto the bench and stared out over the rippling water, absorbing the peace and serenity with every pore. Now and then a trout jumped up to catch a fly. The rain had long since stopped, leaving the trees, wildflowers and grassy bank glistening, as if God had just finished dusting.

Ty made her feel as if she were a child again—a misfit, an oddball. Now, as she sat watching, Bri felt awkward and out of step with the rest of the world. All around her couples held hands, whispering, laughing, sharing the beauty together.

As usual, she sat on the outside looking in.

"You gave Bridget peace and solace here," she whispered to the pink-kissed sky. "Can't you do the same for me? I like structure and orderliness. I was just trying to help. Why is that always wrong?"

Cars rumbled past on the stone bridge to her left. In the mist of evening shadows it looked like the troll bridge from Cristine's book of fairy tales. Across the river, a mother elk with her baby munched on the long grass, tail swishing in perfect four-four time. Every so often the mother lifted her head and stared at Bri. Then she went back to chewing.

"Hi. I'm sorry I'm late. I'm Sandi Harker."

Bri glanced up, surprised.

"From the hotel? We talked on the phone yesterday."

"Yes, of course. I'm so glad you could meet me so quickly, especially since I only found your name in my sister's diary last night," Bri apologized. "I guess I just got lost in thought."

"Good place to do it." Sandi flipped her black shorn head back with a grin. "Bridget used to come here quite a lot."

"She did?" The knowledge cheered Bri somehow, made her feel not quite so alone. "Did you know my sister well?"

Sandi shrugged. "Not that well. We roomed together for a while, then Kent helped her get her own place."

Bri sat up straight. "You knew Kent?"

"I knew who he was. Lots of people did." Sandi snapped her gum, her eyes busy assessing the outlandish costume of an Alpine yodeler. "Look at them. Anything for the tourists' dollars. Pathetic!"

Briony couldn't have cared less about the man, but she couldn't let the criticism go.

"He's not out for a dollar. He's here from Austria. There's a yodeling contest in Lake Louise, I think he said." She grinned at Sandi's stare. "We're staying at the same bed-and-breakfast."

"Oh. Anyway, like I said, lots of people knew Kent. Not many liked him."

"Why not?" At last she was finding out something about the man Bridget had cared for.

"He was a creep."

"A creep? What do you mean?" Dread niggled at her. She'd been so afraid of this, so worried that Cristine's father would be the kind one didn't want to tell one's child about.

"He was, like, preaching all the time. You know." Sandi snapped her gum while she sought the appropriate words. "You gotta be saved because Jesus loves you, an' all that stuff. He just kept harping on it."

"Oh." What relief! Bri couldn't stop the grin of joy. "I was afraid Bridget had hooked up with someone into drugs or something."

Sandi frowned. "Maybe she did. I wouldn't know about that."

"Do you know where I could find this Kent? What his last name is?" Hope kept Bri from breathing.

"Sure." Sandi nodded. "Kent Young. Usually teaches up at Sunshine in the winter. He's on the ski patrol there, too."

"And in the summer? Now? What does he do in the off season?" Anticipation shivered over the nerves in her fingers as she clutched her briefcase close. "Do you know, Sandi?"

Sandi frowned. "I think he went to Africa or somewhere on some mission trip. Building churches, maybe?"

Briony closed her eyes as hope drained away. She was normally a patient person, willing to wait whatever time it took to get results. But Cristine's parentage was in question. For Ty's sake, she'd wanted it all cleared up.

"You wouldn't know how I could reach him?" she asked hopefully, then sighed at Sandi's negative response. "I didn't think so."

"Why do you want to talk to Kent so bad? Is something wrong?" Sandi snapped nonchalantly, her eyes curious.

"Not wrong, really. But as the father of Bridget's baby, he should have signed off on the adoption." Bri tented her fingers together, then let them fall into her lap.

"Kent? The baby's father?" Sandi burst into loud laughter. "No way! He preached all the time about how sex before marriage was a problem the world didn't need. That kind of stuff was his favorite sermon." She snapped again, her black head twisting from side to side.

"No way!" she repeated, then she winked. "Besides, Bridget was pregnant before she met him."

"She was?" Bri didn't know what to think. This was more information than she'd dared hope to gain. She didn't like asking these questions of a virtual stranger, of course, but she had to know. She'd have to go back over the few pages she'd read, try to find some other answer. "She wrote so much about Kent that I figured…"

"You figured wrong. I don't know who the father

was, but last time I saw her, I got the impression she was done with the guy. She was pretty upset."

Sandi had to go. Bri thanked her, offered to buy her lunch another time, and watched the girl walk away, jaws snapping in time to her feet.

With a tired sigh, Bri lugged the briefcase off the bench and started toward the bed-and-breakfast.

"Back to square one," she muttered to herself. "Thank goodness tomorrow's Saturday. I can get a chance to really dig in to the diary. There's got to be a clue somewhere. There's just got to be, God. Ty needs to know for certain that his rights won't be challenged."

But that wasn't the only reason Bri wanted to know more.

I've got to get out of his house, she thought several hours later, as she sat on the window seat and watched the mountain sky fill with stars. *I'm getting too involved. I'm getting too close to Cristine. I have to remember that she's not mine. She won't ever be mine.*

The moon flickered out from behind a silvery-gray cloud, daring her to tell the truth.

"But she could have been," she whispered to the darkness. "I would have cared for your daughter, Bridget. If only you had let me know."

The hurt blossomed inside.

"I'm trying to be satisfied, Lord," she whispered as the tears she'd kept bottled up for so long finally rolled down her cheeks. "Please help me to be content with whatever You give."

This time the peace was a long time coming.

Chapter Five

"Your father is a jerk, Cristine Demens. A first-class, award-winning jerk."

Cristine grinned her agreement, her pudgy hands battering Ty's chest as if to punish him. She shrilled her delight as the Saturday morning cartoons flickered across the television.

"So what's the next step, kiddo? Got any ideas?"

It wasn't that Ty didn't know the answer. His mother had spent the past fourteen months complaining about his habit of pushing too hard, riding roughshod over others to get his own will done. She hadn't minced any words, either.

"'Do something or get out of the way' is not a philosophy that will win you friends, my boy," she'd told him only last week when he'd complained about someone at work. "It's about time you learn that there are some people in this world who simply refuse to be pushed into doing things your way, no matter how right you think you are."

From the glare she directed his way, Ty got the impression she was one of those people.

Judging by the precise organization of his house, Briony Green was another. Look at the way she'd arranged the spice rack.

"Alphabetical spices?" He rolled his eyes at Cristine. "Who arranges their spices alphabetically?"

"Bee." Cristine blinked her big blue eyes, staring at him like a wise owl. "Bee." She wiggled to get down off his chest. "Bee," she yelled again, tottering over to her stroller.

Ty let her go, his mind busy reviewing the previous evening.

As he watched, his daughter knocked his coffee cup over, drenching the sofa—which no longer bore the protective towel coverings.

Ty sighed and mopped up the mess with a perfectly folded rag from the neatly arranged linen closet. Was the woman going to chart and graph his entire life?

Not that it should have mattered what the provocation was. Ty knew he'd hurt her feelings, had complained when he should have been on his hands and knees thanking her. He closed his eyes and winced at the memory.

He'd have to apologize to Briony, and sooner would be better than later. Maybe something would come to him out by the lake. Ty got up to finish what he'd started, thrusting Briony Green and her penchant for order out of his mind.

"Bee."

"What's that, kitten?" Ty placed the last of the lunch he'd prepared inside the picnic basket, quickly slid in a bottle of juice for Cristine and two others for himself. "There, that should hold us."

"Bee." Cristine wasn't giving up easily. Whatever this new word meant, she wanted it. Now.

"Ready to go fishing, sweetie? A nice fat pickerel would be good for dinner, wouldn't it?" Where had he tossed her jacket last night after stomping up and down the streets trying to get her to sleep? "Here we are." He tugged it from behind the high chair, conscience pricking him.

Briony was right. Organization beat bedlam any day. He was organized at work. Why was it so hard at home? One look at the kitchen she'd left pristine last night and he understood. He was a slob because his mother had let him get away with it.

"I'll start making the change tonight. Okay, sweet pea?" He swung the little girl up high in his arms, catching her when she let out a peal of giggles. "That's better. Come on, baby girl. Let's go fishing."

"Bee."

"Well, you might see some bees." He hoped that would satisfy her. It didn't. Ty spent far longer than he should have loading fishing gear, a picnic basket and one small child into his Jeep. He was tired by the time they pulled out of the yard. No wonder Bri had rushed away last night!

Ty turned right twice and was heading down Banff's main street when Cristine resumed her complaints from the back seat.

"Bee," she yelled, fists pounding on her car seat. "Bee!" It was a demand he couldn't ignore.

Ty turned his head to say something, and caught a glimpse of Briony as she strolled down the sidewalk. For the first time since the day she'd shown up at his door, she had let her hair down. Now it flowed in a river of gold to well below her shoulders.

"Bee! Bee!"

Briony. *Bee.* Ty pulled over to the curb and turned to grin at the red-faced child behind him.

"Bee," she yelled again and pointed. "Bee."

"I've got it, honey. Stop screaming." He leaned over the passenger seat and called through the open window. "Good morning, Briony."

She stopped immediately, but waited a few minutes before she turned and acknowledged him. Her eyes were cool glacial blue, maybe even frostbitten.

"Bee. Bee." Cristine was jerking back and forth in her seat, trying to get out.

When a host of Japanese tourists turned to frown at his screeching daughter, Briony took pity on him, crossed the sidewalk and leaned in the window.

"Good morning. Hello, Cristine." She reached over to squeeze the little hand. "How are you today?"

"Bee."

Briony glanced at him, one eyebrow arched.

"I think it's her name for you. She's been yelling it for almost ten minutes." Ty shifted behind the wheel, wondering how he was going to sneak in an apology without admitting his off-the-cuff method didn't work.

"Really?" Bri's face lit up, the ice melted and her eyes glowed a brilliant blue. "A new word? And she used it to call me?"

"I think so."

Briony pulled the back door open and slid across the seat to hug the little girl. "Sweetie, that's wonderful. A new word!"

Ty noticed the way Briony winced, then carefully edged away from the curious hands that grabbed for her hair. Like a movie, his mind reversed tape to last night and the long blond hairs his daughter had clutched while he bathed her.

Cristine had pulled her hair, hard enough to loosen a baby fist full of the glossy gold. It must have hurt incredibly. He could have kicked himself for his ignorance.

Bri had spent a long, hard, *thankless* day with his very demanding daughter, and he'd added to her stress by complaining about a couple of pieces of furniture and some cupboards. What a jerk!

For the first time Ty began to visualize what acting as caregiver had done to Briony's world. Everything about her was fastidiously correct, in place, categorized and classified. But nothing was meticulous, organized or reasonable when it came to a child. He'd had fifteen months to figure that out, but he'd expected Briony to know it from the start. Why? Because she was a woman?

Ty closed his eyes and swallowed. Had he become what his sister always claimed—a bossy boor?

Just yesterday he'd seen copies of three bestselling baby books tumbling out of the briefcase Bri always brought along. She had probably read them all, even believed it when they listed the frequency with which Cristine would need to be fed, changed, played with. Unfortunately, Cristine had never read the books!

Ty could have groaned at his pigheaded stubborn-ness, but that wouldn't have done any good.

What he did do was apologize.

"I'm really sorry about my bad attitude last night, Briony. Please feel free to make whatever changes you think will be best for Cristine. You're doing a wonder-ful thing for us, and I have no right to question or complain about any of it. I'm just so thankful you're there for her."

"It's your house. I should have checked first." Her voice oozed studious politeness. She refused to look at him, busy with Cristine and a game of pat-a-cake.

Ty reached over the seat and put his hand on hers, stilling the game. She had to look at him then.

"No, Briony, you shouldn't have to check at all. And I don't want you to feel you do. You're in charge. Feel free to change whatever you like. Okay?" He sat, waiting, hoping.

Long pause. "All right. Thank you."

"And you'll forgive me for being so cranky?"

She smiled grimly. "Everyone gets tired."

"That wasn't tiredness. That was sheer bad manners. Cristine reminded me of it this morning." He had her at-tention now.

"Cristine did?"

He could see her trying to reason it out, sift out the facts and line them all up in neat, precise rows. Appar-ently they didn't compute. She frowned.

"How could Cristine do that?"

Ty wanted to laugh. She was so methodical, so pre-dictable. He suddenly itched to show her that there was a whole world of things she was missing out on by being so analytical.

"Cristine thumped me on the chest this morning. And she wasn't playing around. You know how outspoken my daughter can be."

"Trust me, I do know that." She grinned at him.

Ty couldn't breath, he couldn't swallow. He could only stare. Why, she was gorgeous! When Briony Green forgot to be so reserved and polite, her true radiance shone through.

"I know this is your day off, and feel free if you want to say no, but I was wondering if you'd like to come along with us. We're going fishing." Now what had made him invite her on his favorite, most longed-for escape?

"I don't think so. I don't know how to fish." She beat a quick retreat into her shell again, blond head shaking a definite no.

"Don't know how to fish, huh?" He copped an amazed stare. "You visit Banff and don't fish? I don't think so."

She frowned at him.

"I'll help you. It's simple. You throw in the hook, they bite—bingo! You fish." Suddenly he wanted to show her that he wasn't the sourpuss he'd acted all week.

"I somehow don't think I'd be very good at it. I could watch Cristine for you, though." She straightened Cristine's sunhat and retied one shoe.

"Nope." He wasn't going to let her get away with it. "Cristine doesn't need a sitter today. She just needs to see her auntie Bee."

"Bee," Cristine yelled in support.

Briony burst out in startled laughter. "All right," she

agreed at last, holding up her hands in mock surrender, "I'd love to go with you. Fishing it is."

He insisted she climb into the front seat, and before Cristine's angry bellows could change her mind, he steered out of the town and onto the overpass.

"I suppose you have a secret fishing place," she murmured, reaching back to bind her hair into a wide barrette. The golden strands burst out and down her back like a geyser.

"Briony, I'm very sorry Cristine pulled your hair," he murmured, forcing his eyes back to the road. "It must have stung."

"How did you know?" Briony averted her gaze.

"She was clutching a fist of that gold of yours when I bathed her. I'm afraid it only clicked when I saw you with your hair loose." He swallowed, unable to tear his eyes from her. "It's very beautiful hair."

Her head jerked around, her eyes huge as she peered at him. "My hair is beautiful?" she squeaked.

Ty frowned. What was this about? Briony seemed totally unaware of the striking picture she made sitting in his truck in her navy chinos and matching navy shirt. She was all cool efficiency, brimming with capability.

Compared to her, he was all thumbs. As she lifted one perfectly pressed sleeve to remove a bit of something from Cristine's jacket, Ty remembered the state of his kitchen and winced. Better not to think about it right now.

"Your hair is lovely," he repeated. "Don't you like it?"

"I—I never really thought about it." Her cheeks sported matching flags of hot pink. "Braiding it keeps it out of the way, but sometimes my scalp gets sore and I have to wear it down."

"It's very nice down. And up." He barely caught the flash of pleasure in her eyes before she ducked her head.

"Th-thank you."

"You're welcome." He turned off the highway and onto a gravel road. "How long did it take you to get your doctorate?"

"A year longer than it should have." With that one sentence her face closed up, all pleasure drained away.

Now what had he done?

"I'm sorry. I didn't mean to pry."

She said nothing.

Ty sighed. He'd been a fool to ask her to come. It was going to be a long day.

"This project you're going to be working on—" He tried again. Surely she wasn't touchy about work. "What's behind it?"

"With the number of tourists and vehicles traveling in the parks these days, diseases are spread far quicker than they would have if left to themselves."

Ah, now she was in her comfort zone. Ty drove, listening as she explained how she hoped to genetically alter some of the species currently being damaged.

Then the talk turned technical, and he got lost. Fortunately, Cristine didn't like being ignored.

"Bee."

Ty couldn't help but stare as Bri emerged from her technical world. It was like watching Sleeping Beauty wake up. Briony blinked, her eyes opened wide and she glanced around the Jeep as if she'd never seen it before.

The baby yelled again, bringing her world back into focus. A funny smile tugged at her lips. She turned, checked Cristine.

"I'm sorry. I was babbling. I tend to forget that not everyone is as enthused as I am on this subject." Her face glowed bright red as she stared out the window. Her hands knotted in her lap. "Sorry to bore you."

Bore him? It was obvious to Ty that Briony carried scars from her past. She'd mentioned before that her sister was different. It wasn't that difficult to imagine some remembered hurt from their past echoing through her mind.

"I guess it would be boring to someone who didn't make their living from the trees and the forest," he assured her quietly. "But I wasn't bored. Sometime I'd like to see your facility."

"Really?"

There it was again, that soft inner light that infused her skin with a breathtaking luminosity.

"Perhaps after I've been there for a while, you and Cristine could come for a visit."

Ty laughed. "Somehow I can't quite see Cristine placidly looking around a lab. Can you?"

Her lips curved in a tender smile, which she bestowed on the babbling little girl. "Well, maybe not."

"Definitely not." He braked the vehicle and waved a hand at the vista before them. "This is Cristine's kind of lab."

"It's gorgeous."

Ty was certain Briony wasn't even aware she'd left the truck. She stepped into the meadow, face thrust into the sunshine as she surveyed the blue-green water and surrounding grassy meadow.

"It's a perfect playground," he heard her whisper. "She chooses well."

"Bee!" Cristine's urgent summons forced Ty to abandon his study of the small blond professor.

"Come on, darling. It's playtime."

Cristine bounced and jiggled in the car seat, smiling like a cat offered cream when she spied the water. "Up, up!"

"I'm trying, honey. Just settle down."

At last he had her free. Ty couldn't help his grin of pure pride at the way his daughter charged ahead, intent on catching up to Briony.

It took a few minutes to unload the truck, spread out an old quilt and organize his fishing stuff. He'd play with Cristine first, he decided. Then, when she was tuckered out, he'd cast a line and contemplate.

Cristine wasn't waiting. She'd already tugged off her shoes and now thrust one fat toe into the lake, screaming with delight at the chill. Ty poised on his toes, ready to charge forward, until he saw Bri crouch down beside the little girl. She'd also removed her shoes, he realized, surprised by the move. Her pants were rolled up past her knees, and she, too, dabbled in the water.

He walked over slowly, enjoying the picture of the two of them, so fair against the vivid water. They could have passed for mother and daughter.

As fast as it came, Ty thrust the thought away, anger burning in a tight hot spot deep inside. His daughter didn't have a mother. God had taken her away in some kind of cruel divine joke. Fine, he'd deal with that. But no one, including an aunt who made him feel things he shouldn't, or some biological father who'd never even met her, was going to part him from his little girl.

He'd play the hand he was given. Alone.

"Going swimming?" Two shining heads twisted to grin at him. "It's still pretty cold." He held out Cristine's pail and shovel. "How about if we build something?"

"A sand castle?" Briony cast a dubious glance at the coarse beach. "I don't think it will work."

"She hasn't any faith in us, sweet pea." Ty picked up Cristine and whirled her around. "She doesn't know that we can build something out of anything. Shall we demonstrate?"

Cristine babbled her response and squirmed to get down. Ty let her go, pail in hand, to gather whatever treasures she deemed appropriate. She didn't wander far, but he kept his eyes glued to her, anyway.

"You're very good with her." Briony smiled as Cristine dumped her pile of stones at Ty's feet. "I'm glad Bridget chose you as her family."

"No more doubts about her safety?"

Bri smiled, her face soft, reminiscent.

"Actually, I didn't have any doubts after the first hour," she said. "I just pretended I did because I wanted to get to know her. She's so precious."

"You'll be a good mother to your own kids one day," he murmured, piling stone upon stone with Cristine's help. "You're patient, calm, loving—all the things a child needs."

The silence surprised him. Ty glanced up and stared.

Bri's face was frozen in a mask of blanched whiteness. Her blunt fingernails were blue from clenching Cristine's shovel.

"Briony?"

"I won't ever be a mother." Her voice was icy.

That didn't make sense. She was great with Cristine. Ty ignored the warning note in her voice. "Why not? You'll meet someone. Fall in love. Have kids."

"No." She shook her head. "I have my work. That's enough."

"Are you kidding?" He frowned at her. "Work doesn't compensate for love. Not ever."

"I'm not saying it does. I'm simply saying that God has other plans for me. I've come to terms with that."

Ty watched the pain sift across her face and wanted to know why she was so ready to give up on a family. He itched to ask her about her past. But he didn't dare. Something in her expression, some dark specter at the back of her eyes warned him that Briony Green didn't allow anyone to see inside her heart, to the hurting part she kept locked away.

"Cristine does need a mother, though. Any thoughts in that direction?"

Ty grimaced, fully aware that she'd twisted the focus of the conversation away from herself and onto him.

"I was married once. I won't marry again. Cristine will be just fine."

He stared directly at Bri, daring her to ask any more on the subject. He'd respected her privacy. She would have to respect his.

"You must have loved Andrea a lot."

"Do you want a drink, honey?" Ty ignored the comment and turned his attention on Cristine. "Juice?"

She nodded, her hands clapping with joy. Ty swung her up into his arms and settled down on the quilt. He pulled out the juice and poured some into her sipping cup. Cristine grabbed on with both hands and sucked greedily.

Ty laughed at her. "You sound like a piglet."

"She goes into everything with gusto, doesn't she." Briony stood staring down at the little girl, a flicker of love shining in her eyes.

"Would you like some juice? I packed plenty. There's also a thermos of coffee, if you'd rather have that." He waited for her to sit down.

"I should have brought something along. I never even thought of it." She flushed with embarrassment at the oversight.

"We've plenty. Here—" he said, handing her a bottle of orange juice. He cuddled Cristine and began to gently rub her tummy, watching as her eyelids drooped. "She'll nod off pretty soon," he murmured. "The fresh air just zonks her out."

"I think it has more to do with your touch. She's a daddy's girl." Bri looked at the two of them. "You're the kind of father most kids dream of. She's fortunate."

"I'm trying." He liked knowing she approved. "If only I can stay her daddy, I'll be content."

"You don't want more children?" she asked, then hurried to cover her lapse. "I'm sorry, that was very rude."

"Cristine is the only child I'll ever have. I don't intend to lose her." Ty saw a shadow flicker through the blue eyes so like his daughter's. "Is something wrong?"

"Not wrong, really. But not right, either." She played with the baby's fluttering hand as she related her meeting from the evening before. "I'm afraid my investigations aren't progressing. I have no clue who Cristine's biological father is now that this Kent is out of the picture. I even went through the diary very quickly last night, looking for another name."

"Nothing?" His heart plummeted. "Not even a hint?"

She shook her head.

"Well, thanks for taking it this far." Ty almost wished she hadn't told him. With every step Briony took in her research, he felt less and less secure as Cristine's father, legal adoption papers notwithstanding.

"Oh, I'm not letting go completely. I still have a couple of other avenues I'd like to pursue while I'm here."

"Such as?"

Ty liked the way she sat there calmly, not panicked, not tense, as he was. Briony had a certain inner peace that seemed to settle like a cloak about her shoulders. It seemed she could weather any storm. Ty envied her that serenity.

"I'd like to talk to a few other people at the hotel. Maybe visit Sunshine."

"The ski hills are closed," he reminded her.

"I know, but there might be someone hanging around who knew Bridget, or this Kent Young." She sat quietly, hands folded in her lap, eyes pensive as they studied the sleeping child.

He shook his head, his fingers tightening around the baby. "I hate this! Why can't we just call up the lawyers and demand they open the file and tell us? Why do we have to pussyfoot around? It'll take forever!"

She stared at him, eyes wide with surprise.

"Sorry," he muttered, feeling the heat sting his cheeks as Cristine jerked awake. He soothed her, then apologized again.

"I didn't mean to yell. It just gets to me. I feel so helpless. My whole future rests right here," he muttered, staring down at Cristine. "How am I supposed to just sit and wait to see if someone pops up who will claim her?"

"I know it must be very difficult." Briony's soft hand covered one of his, just for a moment. "I'm sure you must wish I'd never come here, asking questions, probing into things."

"No." He shook his head, only then realizing that he was glad she'd persisted. "It's better to know up front than to have it sprung on you. Besides, I'd rather deal with this now, while Cristine's too young to understand, than later when she would experience the insecurity of not knowing where she belongs."

Briony smiled, shook her head, then glanced down. "I don't think Cristine will ever doubt where she belongs."

"I hope not." He felt his heart pinch with love for the tiny bundle of joy he held. "I guess I'd better get to it if I'm going to do some fishing." He lifted Cristine and settled her down in the playpen he'd placed next to the quilt. A soothing hand on her back stilled her fretful motions. Minutes later the mosquito netting was in place.

"Okay, Professor. Wanna learn how to fish?"

Her eyes expanded exponentially. "Oh. I'm not actually—"

"Aw, come on, Briony. Live it up. Try something different for a change."

"How do you know I don't try something different every day?"

"Yeah, right." He laughed. The prof? Take a risk? It was unthinkable.

Bri bent over, tying up her shoes as she spoke. "Believe me, Tyrel, caring for Cristine is a life-altering experience every single day I'm with her."

He chuckled. Now that he could believe. "Then you're ready to branch out. Come on."

"I have a feeling you're not going to give up on this." She sighed, nodded and lurched to her feet.

"Correct." He checked Cristine once more, then led the way to the edge of the water.

"Now, the first thing we do is hook on one of these little worms."

She winced, but gamely forced the worm onto her hook.

Ty made fun of her. "The prof is squeamish? A scientist? Who knew?"

"I'm a botanist. I don't work with worms very much," she told him. "If I did, I'd change professions. These things are slimy."

"You did it! All right, now cast like this—" He demonstrated.

She cast. And snagged his shirt.

"Not quite." Ty freed himself, wincing as he tore the fabric. "Try again."

She did. This time she hooked his shoe.

"I don't think this is my forte," she muttered.

Ty considered her comment an extreme understatement. Still he persisted. For some reason it seemed important to him to show her she could do it. "Don't give up yet. Give it another try."

The third time, Briony finally struck the water— about two inches offshore. Water splashed up and caught him in the face. Frustration nipped at Ty's heels. He wanted to grab the rod from her hands, do it for her.

He wanted to get on with it.

Ah, yes. His mother's words tinkled in some distant cell of his brain. He choked down his impatience through sheer will.

"Good. Keep at it."

"The worm's gone." She peered at the end of her rod as if it consumed her attention. Her eyes switched to blink up at him in confusion. "What do I do with the fish when I catch it?"

Since there was a less-than-infinitesimal chance of her ever catching a fish, Ty snorted. He caught the downcast look on her face and quickly changed that to a cough.

"We'll take care of the fish when the time comes," he said. "Just keep practicing."

Ten minutes later Briony squealed her delight as the line flew across the water. The hook barely caused a ripple.

"I did it! I did it!"

"Wind it in," he yelled, envisioning his favorite red- and-white hook two hundred feet down in the glacial lake. "Slowly. That's too slow. Not that fast."

"Stop telling me what to do!" She glared at him.

Ty clamped his lips together and returned to his own pole, sneaking glances from the corner of his eye. She wound placidly for a few minutes. Then her face turned a ghastly pea green.

"Something's pulling back," she whispered.

"Just keep winding. Slowly." His own hook was so far out, he didn't dare stop to help. Instead, Ty tried to be encouraging. "Easy, just go nice and slow."

"I am going slo-o-w— Oh!" She yelped as the line ripped out, making a zipping sound.

"Don't drop it!" Why hadn't he given her the cheaper pole? That was his Father's Day gift from Cristine! Well, okay, so Ty had bought it himself, but still—

"It's coming in!"

Ty stared. Briony stood perched knee-deep in water, her clothes spattered by the scramble she'd made down the rock to catch the rod and reel she'd dropped.

"It's a fish," she squealed in a voice that was nothing like her usual solemn tone.

"That's what we keep in this lake, Briony. Fish. That's why it's called *fishing*." Ty, his own line finally secure, put down his pole and sauntered toward her, issuing directions as he went. "Just keep slowly winding. He'll tire out. No, don't lift it. Don't lift—"

Smack!

Seven pounds of cold, slimy fish caught him square in the mouth, slid down his shirt, then dropped to the ground. It was the biggest fish Ty had ever seen come out of these waters. And *she'd* caught it.

"Oh, my! Oh, mercy! What now? It's wiggling all over the ground, Ty. What do I do?" She was beside him now, dancing from one foot to the other as she stood guard over the pickerel she'd landed.

Ty picked up the fishing line, caught the fish by the gills and walked over to his tackle box.

"What are you doing?"

"Knocking it out. Then I'll put it on a stringer and—"

"Knocking it out? Don't you dare!" She stood in front of him, one hand on her hip, one finger wagging in front of his nose. "You're not going to hit my fish, Tyrel Demens. No way."

He stopped what he was doing and stared at her. "Well, how do you want to kill it, then?"

"Kill it? I'm not killing this poor defenseless animal!" She glared at him as if he were Jack the Ripper. "I hate animal abuse. I refuse to tolerate that kind of behavior, especially in a forest ranger." Her eyes clouded. "I thought you would be different."

"It's a fish, Bri! How do you think we eat the things if we don't kill them first?" Ty couldn't believe what he was hearing. She'd turned into a wild, illogical woman.

"Give me that!" She snatched the line out of his hands, marched back into the water and dropped the fish back in. It wiggled, mouth securely snagged on the hook.

"Oh, you poor thing. Move a little bit, that's it. You can get free if you try. You're not hurt, baby. Just try, okay. Just try." She crouched beside the water, encouraging all the while. When the fish didn't get free, she stepped right into the water and led it back and forth. "Go now. Go!"

"You'll kill it if you keep that up." He saw the pain in her eyes and gave up trying to figure out this woman. He also tossed any notion of fish for dinner.

"Give me the line. I'll release it."

"You won't hurt it?"

He clamped his lips together, tasted the fishy slime and grimaced. "No more than I have to," he promised.

After several soul-searching moments, she handed him the line. Ty quickly unhooked the fish, waggled it back and forth in the water, then glanced up at her. "You're sure?" he asked, hoping she'd change her mind.

"I'm sure. Let it go, Tyrel."

He let it go, staring mournfully after it. Then he walked back and stared at his own pole. Fishing had suddenly lost its allure. What Ty really wanted was a shower!

He glanced over at Bri and found her perched on top of the rocks, her shoes and socks laid out to dry. As he watched, she zipped off the bottom legs of her pants and laid them beside her shoes. Her long legs, perfectly visible in the blue shorts, were stretched out on the rocks, soaking up the sun.

"That was fun, wasn't it." She chirped it out as if they'd just finished tea. Her face glowed. "I guess you were right. It is good to try new things now and then. What should I try next?"

Ty had several responses, none of which were remotely appropriate. Instead of answering her, he whipped off his hiking boots and socks and waded into the frigid lake, vigorously scrubbing to remove all signs of fish from his clothes.

Some time passed before he noticed that the sun had disappeared. Ty glanced up, saw the dark clouds pushing up over the mountains and groaned. With his luck he'd come out of the lake just in time to get rained on.

His fishing day was ruined, he stunk to high heaven, and he'd missed out on the catch of the season because that coolly logical scientist didn't want to hurt a fish!

The sharp rock cutting into his foot did nothing to improve Ty's temper.

What did I do wrong this time, God? An icy droplet smacked him in the face, his only answer.

Chapter Six

"I like these ideas of yours to broaden my horizons."

Bri pretended her lungs weren't burning as she puffed up the long steep hill to the Upper Hot Springs.

"I've seen more of Banff in two weeks than I'd ever have seen on my own. I've never been here before, though I once visited Miette in Jasper. Is it the same?"

"Our Upper Hot Springs are older. No major renovations have been done here for a long time." Ty pushed Cristine's stroller with no obvious exertion, the mid-June sun emphasizing his dark good looks. "I haven't been here with Cristine for several months."

"The water isn't too hot for her?"

"It isn't this year. We had so much precipitation with the heavy snow pack. Then all the rain caused a runoff that's affected the temperature in the pool. That doesn't happen often. Let's just hope we're here before the crowds. It can get a little tight."

Ty insisted on paying for this excursion. "After all, I might need help with Cristine."

He and Cristine went one way, while Bri went off to change in the women's dressing room. She bundled her hair on top of her head, hoping she wouldn't have to dry it. It took so long, and she hated the dampness on her neck.

As she lowered herself into the spring, the warm water slid up her body like a silken sheath, enfolding her in its mineral softness.

Half a dozen bathers lounged in the water, and most of those seemed content to bask on the sunny side where they could stare out over the spectacular valley below them. Bri joined them, closing her eyes as the sun's warmth compensated for the cool breeze off the snowy mountaintops—

"Isn't that cute?"

Bri opened her eyes and found everyone's attention fixed on the big bronzed man murmuring to a tiny child as he carried her down the stairs. Ty nestled his baby girl against his chest, her frilly pink suit magnifying the richness of his dark chest hair. All the while he murmured soothing words, Ty walked deeper and deeper, until Cristine was completely wet.

He was so gentle. So tender. What would it be like to be cared for like that? How proud you would feel, to walk beside a man who loved like that, who lavished such care and attention on a little girl.

Just for a moment Bri's heart longed for that companionship, ached to share in that tender look of love and concern he gave Cristine.

"I'm sorry, Briony. I guess I never really loved you. I just thought you'd make a good mother for the boy."

The words stabbed at her, reminding her of her one

foray into love. What a disaster! The shame and embarrassment of falling for someone who didn't love her had been nothing compared to the indignity of canceling the wedding and knowing he was going to remarry his first wife.

All those years ago. And yet, her determination was the same today as it had been then. She would never be a stand-in mommy, never be an add-on to a family simply to fill an emptiness inside herself. Never again would she allow herself to be tricked by soft words or soothing kisses.

The simple truth was, Briony Green was not the kind of woman men married. God had given her a brain. It was up to her to use it.

"Bee." Cristine spotted Bri and held out her arms, her grin wide.

"Hi, sweetie." Bri took the baby from Ty, her hands brushing his. That simple contact sent the blood rushing to her cheeks, so Bri concentrated on the child and her kicking legs. "You like the water, don't you, Cristine? Me, too."

"So you did call her by that name." An old man beamed from his perch on the big cement mushroom in the center of the pool. "I always wondered if you would."

"I beg your pardon?" Bri stared at him blankly, then sought Ty's interested gaze. He shrugged.

"You don't remember me, do you? I'm not surprised. You've had a busy year." The older gentleman reached out a hand and brushed Cristine's shoulder. "She looks just like you, as I predicted. Beautiful mommies always have beautiful babies."

Ty's grasp on her arm held Bri immobile. She couldn't have moved, anyway.

This man had known Bridget, had talked to her about the baby she would be having. In that split second, Bri made her decision. For now, she'd play the part of her sister.

"I'm sorry, I don't remember you," she murmured, gently swishing Cristine back and forth in the warm water.

"I suppose I'm not very memorable compared to your husband." The old fellow winked at Bri and thrust out a hand to Ty. "Rick Vicker," he bellowed, pumping Ty's hand as if he were grinding an organ. "I met your missus some time ago when I was here soaking. Arthritis, don't you know?" He leaned close to Ty. "Always worst in the winter."

"I'm sorry." Ty raised his eyebrows at Bri, obviously begging for help.

"I am, too, but it comes and goes. Not much you can do, 'cept try to ease the pain." Rick shrugged. "I drive up for the weekend sometimes and just sit and soak. Always helps." He smiled at Briony. "This one used to come and soak to get out the kinks that baby caused. We got to be friends when I kept reminding her that babies don't like their mommies in hot water."

Cristine kicked and splashed water at Rick and Ty. Rick simply laughed.

"Before they're born they don't like it. Not that I needed to remind her." He shook his head, eyes fondly remembering the past. "Your lady took real good care of that baby, talked to it when she thought nobody was looking. She'd be in and out ten times, either warming up or cooling down." He grinned at Briony's bathing suit with male appreciation.

"I 'spect that's how you got rid of the baby fat, isn't it?"

Briony gulped. What was she supposed to say to that? Apparently nothing. Rick simply kept on talking.

"My wife never did get rid of hers. Every kid she'd complain she kept ten pounds. We had six of them."

"Oh." Ty took Cristine back, leaving Bri free to talk with Mr. Vicker. Ty's eyes issued some kind of a warning Bri didn't understand. Rick was speaking.

"So you decided to keep her, eh? I'm glad. She's a little sweetie, this one. Too precious to give away. When was she born?"

"March first." Bri ignored Ty's frown. She intended to clear up the misunderstanding, but not until she'd found out everything she needed to. This opportunity was heaven sent, and she didn't intend to waste it.

"Is that a fact?" He scratched his bald head. "Why, that's the day after I last saw you. I remember 'cause the twenty-ninth of February is my birthday and coming here was the birthday present I gave myself."

"That was—"

"The other one didn't come that day, did she?" He frowned, trying to remember. "No, she wasn't here. I'd have remembered that bright red bathing suit of hers."

"Mr. Vicker, I think I should—"

"Say, you must be the young man she was waiting for back then!" Rick studied Ty from head to foot, his face less friendly now. "Don't know why I thought you were smaller. Fellows in the Forces aren't tiny little weasels."

The Armed Forces? Briony tucked that away.

"You should have married her before you left, young man. Never take a chance is my motto. Those peace-keeping missions sound safe, but you never really know when your time is up."

"No, I suppose you don't." Briony spoke for Ty, who seemed lost by the verbiage. "Mr. Vicker, I should apologize. I think the woman you're talking about is, was, my sister Bridget."

He frowned. "Was?"

Bri nodded. "She died not long ago. I only found out she'd had a baby after she died, and so I came to Banff to meet Cristine. This is Cristine's father, Tyrel Demens."

"I'm sorry to hear about that." Rick was silent only a moment. "She was a real nice girl. Your hair's longer than hers was," he announced. "Other than that, I can't see a whole lot of difference. Same eyes, same build."

"Well, we were twins."

"Humph!" Rick glared at Ty. "So when did you get back?"

"Get back?" Tyrel glanced up from trying to keep Cristine off the cement mushroom. "I, uh, didn't get back."

"Ty is Cristine's *adoptive* father, Mr. Vicker. We were hoping you might know something about her real father."

"Not the father?" The old man looked disgruntled, then pinned Ty with a frown. "Why didn't you just tell the truth up front?"

"I'm afraid that's my fault. I've been trying so hard to find out about my sister's life here that I thought it wouldn't hurt to let things slide. I hope you'll forgive me?"

"I guess. Though I don't like liars." He glanced sideways at Ty, then leaned nearer to Bri. "Always thought that fellow your sister got mixed up with was a liar. Air Force doesn't use bungee jumpers. Leastways, not that I ever heard of."

"You don't think her boyfriend was in the Air Force." Bri wished he would contradict her, but she didn't think it was likely judging by the scowl on the old man's face.

"I think he was a cheat and a liar. Never said it out loud, but I thought it all the same." His mouth tightened. "Just dumped her here, you know. She stayed, working every day, while he took off on some jaunt. Told her to wait, that he'd be back. Never came. Never even wrote."

"Did you ever hear his name, Mr. Vicker?" Bri held her breath and prayed harder than she ever had before.

"His name?" Rick scratched his chin. "Don't rightly know. It was so long ago. She never talked about him much after that first time. We talked about the baby, though."

Mr. Vicker explained how he'd come back to the pool periodically and met Bridget on several occasions. They'd even shared lunch a couple of times.

"Later on we didn't talk as much, not about that stuff. It seemed like she always had this woman with her. They'd laugh and talk. They were good together, chased the shadows away. Andrea, her name was. That's all I remember."

Ty stopped playing with Cristine, his body stiffening. "Andrea?" His voice barely carried above the voices of the group now entering the pool.

Bri moved closer to him, one hand covering his. "We already knew that," she reminded him.

Ty nodded. "I know what you said. It's just that—" He swallowed; his shoulders jerked back.

Bri understood what he was going through. Ty clung to his conviction that she was wrong about Andrea, hoped she had confused his wife with someone else, some other woman. It was too painful to accept that the person he'd completely trusted had gone behind his back.

"Thank you very much for telling us all this, Mr. Vicker. We really appreciate it." Bri ordered her brain to think, to remember if there was some clue she'd missed. But her brain was too busy recognizing the effect Ty had on her.

She ached to hold him close, to comfort him, to offer some tiny crumb of hope that would wash away the confusion and bitter pill of deception. But Ty yanked his hand away from hers and turned his back on them.

"No problem at all." Rick studied Ty curiously. "I hope you find the information you need. Say, if I remember anything, how would I get in touch with you?"

Bri told him where to contact Ty, then watched Rick leave. Her glance flew to the big man with his precious child.

Please give me the right words that will help heal his hurt, Lord.

She gave him some time with Cristine, watching them surreptitiously as she swam back and forth across the deep end of the pool. His manner toward his daughter hadn't changed, but his eyes—black, hard— glittered with anger.

Briony couldn't let him deal with it alone.

"It doesn't really change anything, Ty. She gave you

Cristine. She obviously wanted her as much as you did. What does it matter—"

"What does it matter?" He gritted his teeth, stemming the anger that simmered just below the surface. "My own wife lied to me. That matters."

"She just wanted a baby, Ty." Briony brushed her hand over Cristine's hair. "She just wanted a child."

"Do you think I don't know that? We were married for six years, Briony. After the first year, all Andrea talked about was a baby. I figured that much for myself." He held out Cristine. "Can you hold her for a minute while I get our towels? We can sit over there in the sun and dry off."

Bri took the baby and watched as he strode across the pool and up the steps. He returned minutes later with his ever-present video camera and some towels. He shot miles of footage of Bri with Cristine, then packed it away in a bag that he set in a dry corner.

By the time Bri fetched her own towel and claimed the lounge next to his, she knew they had to talk it out. At least some of it. He couldn't carry this burden for long.

She was thankful that the busload of Japanese tourists chatted loudly enough to drown out her words.

"You can tell me to butt out if you want to, Ty. And I will. But I really would like to understand."

He didn't yell at her, so Bri continued. "Why would Andrea have kept all this from you? Are you certain you didn't miss something she said? You admitted you were busy, tied up with a fire. Maybe she did tell you about Bridget and you brushed it off or something."

"I didn't brush anything off where Andrea was concerned." A muscle in his jaw flexed. He handed Cristine some beads. "I couldn't afford to."

"What does that mean?"

He sighed. "Andrea and I grew up in the same neighborhood. She used to come to our place a lot. Her home life wasn't the best and it bothered her. She sometimes stayed with my parents while I attended college. Then we got married. I don't think she ever really recovered from the abuse she suffered at home."

"I'm sorry."

"So was I. I tried everything I could think of, but despite the doctors and the medications, Andrea had very bad days when she wouldn't talk. All she wanted to do was sleep." He smiled as Cristine bopped him in the chest with her beads. "I thought I knew her, knew the best way to care for her. I thought our marriage was what God wanted."

"Maybe it was." She hated that look of self-castigation on his face.

"I'm beginning to think everything I ever believed about her was a mistake." He stared at the water. "When Cristine came, I thought God had relented, given her a bit of peace. She loved to sit and watch Cristine sleep."

"I guess most new moms do."

"And then she died. No warning. No notice. Cristine was six weeks old. Six weeks! We didn't have time to share her. Six weeks wasn't long enough to build a family." His face tightened into a rigid mask of control.

"I've asked myself what I did wrong, what mistake I made that God would dump me in a situation where I had to raise a child alone. And now it's worse. Not only do I not know if Cristine's father will show up at some point and try to claim her, but now I've discovered my wife deliberately lied to me."

The grief and anger spilled out in a wash that grabbed at Bri's heart. She prayed silently for a moment, opening her mind to God's leading, as she watched Ty lift his daughter up to look out over the parapet.

"You're speaking as if God is after you, as if He's punishing you." She spoke softly, willing him to listen.

"Funny." He tossed her a mocking smile. "That's exactly how it feels."

"But God isn't like that. He doesn't get His jollies from ruining your world." She could hardly believe he'd said it.

"Doesn't He?" Ty pointed out the snow-topped mountains, his face softening as Cristine clapped her approval.

"No, He doesn't." Bri touched his arm. "God doesn't make mistakes, Ty. He doesn't have to go back and fix up some oversight. He works everything together for good. Everything."

"I used to think like that. I used to believe that I understood what He wanted for my life. But I don't think that anymore. Now everything just seems like a big mess."

He stood suddenly, lifting Cristine to his shoulders, where her view of the valley was unobstructed by the wrought-iron railing.

"It doesn't matter what it looks like, Ty. All we have to know is that God has everything organized, and then we proceed from there."

"Maybe His will is clearer to you than it is to me." A short huff, then the angry words burst out. "Apparently I didn't even know my own wife, Briony! And how can I possibly understand God's will or follow some nebulous plan for the future when I don't even know if I'll be able to keep Cristine?"

Bri prayed nonstop as she listened, aching to help him. The Japanese tourists eventually filed out, still chattering as they climbed the stairs. Only five people remained in the pool. It was the opening she sought.

"Give me Cristine," Bri said determinedly. He frowned. "It's all right. Just give her to me."

He handed over the little girl.

"Want to go swim again, sweetie?" Cristine's arms and legs flapped madly as she tried to gallop toward the pool. "Okay, come on." Bri glanced at Ty. "You, too."

Back in the water, Cristine squealed with delight. A lifeguard handed them inflatable arm bands, and Bri slipped them on Cristine's chubby arms. Slowly, carefully, Bri released her hands, just for a moment, and let Cristine float on her own.

Bri regained her hold before Ty could grab his daughter.

"How do you know Cristine won't drown?" She watched his face work, the emotions fluttering across. Anger, frustration, fear, hurt. Longing.

"She will if you let her go for too long." He grated out his answer, voice gruff with emotion.

Bri shook her head. "No, she won't, Ty." She let go again, watching carefully as the child kicked her legs. "You're not going to drown, are you, sweetie?" She cuddled the little body close. "Wanna try again?"

Cristine shrieked with joy, fist pummeling the water, sending up a spray that caught her in the face. She blinked, then let out a howl of dismay. Ty snatched her away from Bri, snuggled her close and whispered comforting words as he brushed away the water.

"You see, she's well protected. Her daddy is right there watching all the time. The minute she gets into trouble, he'll help her. But he also wants her to try new things, to learn about all the wonderful things she could enjoy if she'd just take a chance." She waited for him to absorb the idea.

"So I'm supposed to think that God snatching Andrea away when we needed her most was a—what? A learning experience?" He snorted his disgust.

"Ty, when Cristine was on her own in the water, did she notice what you or I were doing? Did she see the lifeguards change when their shift ended or hear that truck change gears?" Bri shook her head. "She was focused on the water in her eyes. She didn't understand that the lifeguard had to change before she got too tired, or that the truck had to slow down in order to speed up. It's all in the focus."

"So I should focus on the greater good?" His eyes were penetrating. "A motherless child is for the greater good?"

Bri smiled, unable to take offense when the words were so obviously torn from his heart.

"A father who adores you more than anything in this world is a wonderful thing to give a child," she whispered. "Maybe someday she'll have another mother. But through Andrea's actions, for whatever reason, you learned a depth of love and commitment you'd never known before. And despite what you thought at the time, God *was* in control. He was and is right here. You just have to trust."

Some of the bleakness drained out of his eyes. "Is it so easy for you to have faith, Briony? Are you so certain of your path in life?"

"I guess I am certain of my path—now. But it wasn't always that way." She debated whether to bare the whole truth, then decided that she'd poked and probed into his personal life, so he had the right to know about her. It was only fair.

"Trust is still an issue I deal with almost daily."

"I don't know what you mean," he said. Little by little Ty was teaching Cristine that she could float on her own.

Bri took a deep breath. "When I was working on my master's thesis, a new professor took over my supervision. He lived on the same scientific planet I did, we shared our work every day." Now for the hard part. "And he had a seven-year-old son that I adored. I was certain God had sent me a man and a child I could love. A family of my own. I devoted myself to them, took time from my studies to care for the child. We decided to get married."

He stared at her as if he couldn't imagine her married.

"Three days before the wedding Lance called me. I'd been speaking at another university and I'd barely arrived home. He couldn't wait to inform me that his ex-wife had returned and that they'd just been remarried." She gritted her teeth and forced out the humiliating words.

"Apparently, Lance decided I'd make a good wife not because he loved me, but because he thought I'd make his son a good mother. Now that the boy's real mother was back and willing to work things out, he realized he'd always loved her. There was no need for a stand-in."

"Ouch!" Ty made a face. "I don't suppose he had the good grace to move away and leave you in peace?"

Bri shook her head. "No, I did that. After I canceled the wedding, there were still a lot of bills. I had to get a job to pay them off and in the process I lost a year's worth of work." She swallowed hard, then admitted the truth.

"But the worst of the whole thing was facing the fact that God had never intended for me to be a mother to that wonderful little boy."

"Oh, but—"

She shook her head, a grim smile tweaking her lips. "No, Ty. You've never seen me in the lab, or you'd understand how impossible it really is. I forget everything, including meals, other people, appointments."

"You could get an alarm clock or a timer."

Bri laughed. "That's just part of the problem. I hate a mess. I like everything organized, clean, precise. You've seen that for yourself. How do you think a child would grow up with a mother like that?"

It hurt to say it, but as Briony had learned, the truth was a painful beast.

"You're very good with Cristine!"

His frown eased some of her heart-hurt. "Only as a substitute, a temporary stand-in." No matter how tempting, Bri couldn't, wouldn't ever allow herself to imagine she could be more than that. As it was, leaving Cristine was going to be so hard.

She laughed as Cristine splashed again, spraying water over both of them. The gloom lifted.

"How did we get on this maudlin topic, anyway?"

He raised one eyebrow. "As I recall, you brought it up to explain faith and trust. I don't think you can call it trusting God just because you don't want to get hurt again. The guy was a flake. There are others."

"You misunderstood." Okay, she'd go through this once more, then it was history. "The trust part came because I didn't give God enough credit, I didn't let Him handle things. I grabbed on to Lance because I wanted his son, because I thought I would miss out on that experience."

"Huh?"

"I substituted real love for like-mindedness between two people with compatibility, Ty. I thought his son was the bond that would keep us together. God knew it wouldn't. I had to learn that a stand-in mommy is no substitute for real love."

Ty played with Cristine for several minutes, whooshing her back and forth. Finally he spoke, his voice devoid of emotion.

"She's tired. Shall we go?"

"Okay."

But later, as they trundled down the street to the pizza place Ty loved, Bri wondered if she'd helped him at all.

"What I was trying to say back there was that Andrea's friendship with Bridget may have been God's hand, leading them to find comfort and solace with each other. And from that friendship came Cristine. *All things work together for those who love God.* All things, Ty. You've just got to have faith."

"Maybe that's enough for you. But I'm not going to stop asking for answers." He guided them into the restaurant, his hand firm on her back. "I need to know why my wife was so secretive. What was she hiding from me?"

Chapter Seven

"I'm sorry, Bri. I just can't make it back in time to get to the gondola rides by six. Can we reschedule?" Ty dragged a hand through his hair, turning his back on the interested stares from the other rangers. "What about Friday?"

"Someone told me recently that I should stop being so tied to a schedule." Briony's voice brimmed with laughter. "I'm trying to take his advice."

"I meant it in the nicest possible way," he muttered, ashamed of his quick temper.

"I know. Actually, I'm, uh, busy with something here. Let's just see how things go, okay? There's no hurry to go on the gondola. No hurry at all. Do whatever you need to at work, Ty. We'll manage. Bye."

She sounded distracted, and Ty was pretty sure he knew the reason why. Briony had decided to get to the bottom of Bridget's mystery before she left town in thirteen days.

If he closed his eyes, Ty could imagine her sitting in his kitchen, glasses perched on the end of her nose as she analyzed the diary in minute detail. He wondered if she'd even remember he'd called.

"New lady in your life giving you a hard time, Tyrel?" His buddies harangued him constantly these days, especially since they'd seen Briony hiking with him and Cristine one evening last week. Briony had been collecting samples for her Calgary lab.

"Wish my wife would give me a hard time like that." The chief ranger batted his eyes, his voice hitting a wobbly falsetto. *"I'll take Cristine home if you'd rather do something else, Ty."*

"Yeah, Darlene's always nagging me to get home on time. If it isn't that, then it's the garbage or the kids. She never tells me to just take off and have fun."

Ty laughed. "But Darlene's a first-rate cook. That cake she sent over yesterday was a killer. Mmm."

The other rangers agreed, then fell to discussing their own families. As he listened, the bee of envy buzzed in Ty's mind. They grumbled a lot, but there wasn't one of his co-workers who'd willingly change places with Ty. They had the kind of marriage his parents had shared. Joy, anger, pride—they all flowed together, creating a loving unity.

He'd never had that with Andrea. From the beginning he'd known their marriage was about getting her away from her parents and the horror of her home life. He never doubted she loved him, not then and not now. What he'd begun to question were his own choices.

What made him think he could help her? Why had he been so certain that was the only way?

He'd prayed, that's why. Constantly. He'd believed God would get them through anything as long as they trusted.

The chief called the meeting to order and launched into a list of priorities. After the first five minutes, Ty fell into his own thoughts.

It was his fault Andrea's depression had worsened. All the classic signs were there, everything he'd been warned about. But he'd chosen to ignore her manic talk about babies, the pictures, the magazines, the books she collected in huge stacks.

Ty's skin crawled as he remembered their last trip to the fertility clinic—the day his dream had died.

He'd hated the place, hated the indignity of it, the aura of frenzy that clung to the very air. He'd hated the quiet desperation of the couples huddled in the waiting room, hope shining in their eyes, had shuddered at the disappointment that followed as they trudged away.

He'd gone through it twice. But the cost of the trips, the days off, the evaluations and medical procedures—all took their toll. In a way he'd been glad when Andrea finally agreed they weren't going back. Of course he'd felt sad at the pain teeming in her eyes, but inside relief reigned.

And then the sledgehammer felled him—he would never be a father. Adoption was their only recourse.

Tough weeks of intense heavenly questioning followed. Gradually, though, they'd found new promise in the Bible. Ty told himself he'd accepted God's will. Andrea worked herself out of the slump, concentrated on her therapist's instructions. They'd filled out form after form, hoping, always hoping. Five long years of waiting—for nothing.

"Ty, you can handle that, can't you?"

He blinked up at the chief, saw the pity in the other

man's eyes and knew he understood that Ty had been focused on the past.

"I mean, you don't have to actually climb Castle Mountain. We know that little girl of yours keeps you climbing enough." They all laughed. "Anyway, the tree line doesn't go very high and the bears won't be hard to track, if they've moved that far."

Ty caught on immediately. Bear checks. He nodded. "Sure, no problem. Anything else?"

"Yeah. It's your turn to bring the goodies for coffee time. That does *not* mean we want you to bake."

They spent a good ten minutes teasing him about the state of his brownies. By the time he was leaving, the sun and surrounding mountains were completely obliterated by a thick heavy mist.

Ty walked out, then stuck his head back inside the door. "Hey, Chief. If it pours tonight, that footbridge over by Maligne Lake is going to be washed out. There's a group of hikers scheduled to go through there over the weekend."

His boss nodded. "Thanks. Almost forgot your report on that. I'll get someone to check it out. You head on home now."

Ty nodded and left, his eyes automatically scanning the parking lot and surrounding streets for unpredictable elk. The herds were fond of roaming the town for food whenever they pleased. Ty had no intention of surprising a cow and her calf enjoying a late-evening lunch beside his Jeep.

All clear.

He drove toward home, planning to stop by the tiny

bakery ahead. Unfortunately, it was closed, and he'd have to come up with some other idea for the guys' snacks.

At home, Bri and Cristine lay sprawled on the floor in the living room, the fire crackling behind them. If ever Ty had visualized a homey scene, this was it. Blond heads snuggled together, they were studying the animal book Cristine loved.

Both females looked up at the same time, smiles mushrooming across their faces until two sets of vivid blue eyes glowed. The problems of the day evaporated. He was home.

Cristine was the first to move. She wiggled herself upright and tumbled headlong toward him. "Da!" she screamed at the top of her lungs.

Ty stared at her in delight. He gathered her plump little body into his arms and hugged tightly. His eyes met Briony's.

"She said 'Dad,'" he whispered, emotion welling up inside.

Bri nodded, eyes shining with pleasure. "She's been practicing all day. I videotaped her. I noticed you've been doing it quite a lot. I hope you don't mind."

Mind? He wanted to hug her for thinking of it. Cristine was his only chance at fatherhood. Ty intended to record every second of her childhood. Then, when he was old and alone, he'd watch it and be warmed by the memories.

"No. I don't mind." He shook his head stupidly. "Not at all. Thank you."

"Da. Da. Bee."

"She's building quite a vocabulary."

Bri's voice was quiet. Too quiet. Ty frowned. There

was something about her eyes. He felt a shiver of apprehension.

"What happened?"

She gathered herself up and perched precisely on the edge of the sofa, her feet together, hands clasped primly in her lap.

"I did something you may not approve of," she told him, eyes meeting his without pause. "I ran an ad in several newspapers asking anyone who knew Bridget to contact me."

"Contact you? Here?" Ty couldn't believe she'd done it. This was asking for trouble, bringing it right to his door.

Bri's shoulders lifted as she deflected his questions. "No, I used my former address and had all mail forwarded to me here. I received a response today."

He forced himself to sit because there was nowhere else to go. You couldn't run away from pain, escape the hurt that God meted out. Whatever justice He demanded had to be done.

Ty set down his squirming daughter. He took a deep breath. "Go on."

"There is a woman who worked with Bridget. She lives in Vancouver now, but two-and-a-half years ago she was working in Reservations at the Banff Springs Hotel."

"That's where your sister was employed." The words came out in a dull, flat voice that he had no control over. Ty waited for the ax to fall.

"Apparently Bridget trained her." She glanced once at Cristine, checking, then focused on him. "Are you all right?"

"I'm fine." That was a lie. He wasn't fine. He was

more afraid than he'd ever been in his life. One adver-
tisement, and Briony Green could tear apart his life. "Go
on," he said through clenched teeth, handing Cristine the
small doll she'd dropped.

Bri scrutinized him before she continued. "Apparently Bridget knew this woman for several months.
They talked a lot about their lives."

"Her name?"

"Isabelle. Isabelle Edwards." She quirked an
eyebrow. "Does it mean something?"

Ty shook his head.

"Oh. All right. Well, then." She took a deep breath.

"Briony, get to the point, will you? I don't care
about all the details. I don't need to know every single
word she wrote." He held on to his temper by a thread.
"I hate all this preamble. Just tell me what this woman
had to say!"

"I wasn't deliberately—"

Ty glared at her, white-hot fury dancing through his
veins.

"She knew Bridget's boyfriend. They double-dated
a few times." She spilled it out in a rush of words. "Peter
Grant. The name of Bridget's boyfriend is Peter Grant."

"And does this know-it-all woman have any idea
where we might find Mr. Peter Grant?" He crossed his
arms over his puffed-out chest. "Well?"

"She thinks he had his own business, but at the time
she knew Bridget, Peter worked for a bank in Calgary."
Briony licked her lips, her face flushed.

She hated being pushed like this, he knew, hated the
disruption in her logical presentation. But Ty couldn't

stop the words. Every cell in his body urged him to snatch up Cristine and run as far and as fast as he could, away from the threat, away from the danger of losing his child.

"I took the liberty of calling the head offices of several banks. Peter Grant worked in the downtown branch of the Bank of Montreal, but he's no longer employed there." Bri lifted her head, her eyes brimming with tears. "I'm sorry, Ty. So sorry."

"I'm not." He felt a bitter glee well up inside. "I wish he were gone for good. I wish no one could ever find him." He saw her stare and shrugged. "I know it's not the right thing to say. But that's the way I feel."

"But he may not know about Cristine," she reasoned.

"Get real! If this *boyfriend* saw Bridget even eighteen months ago, he could hardly miss the fact that she was pregnant. It's obvious he didn't want the responsibility so he just walked away."

Suddenly Ty was sick of it, sick of the whole mixed-up, confusing mess. He wanted it settled. Now. Before he lost more time.

"I'm taking tomorrow off. I'm going to Calgary." The minute he said it, he knew it was the right thing.

"To do what? I told you, Peter is no longer at the bank."

"But someone there may know where he is, what he does, how to contact him. I intend to get to the bottom of this." He surged to his feet. The decision lifted an enormous weight off his shoulders. For now.

"While I'm there, I intend to check with my lawyer. Perhaps he'll have some suggestions." He dared her to argue.

"I did phone the lawyers that were named on the

adoption certificate," she murmured. "They don't seem to have any information on Peter."

"Then, they can find some. If it's there, I intend to know about it." He swung Cristine up into his arms and hugged her close. "Daddy's not letting you go, sweetie. Not ever," he whispered, brushing her downy head against his cheek.

He felt Bri's hand on his arm.

"I wasn't trying to hurt you." Tears clumped her lashes together, poised to fall from the corners of her gorgeous eyes. "I was trying to help. I want you to keep Cristine always. I know how much you love her."

Ty lifted an arm and hugged her close against his side. She smelled like baby powder and lemons and just a hint of spice. And she fit into his arm as if she were made to be there.

"I wasn't blaming you," he murmured, watching as Cristine played with Briony's braid. "It's just that—"

"You're an action man. You've got to be up and doing while I like to mull everything over." She nodded, her smile misty. "I know. I tend to think that my way is the only way there is. I forget that there are other ways."

Ty stared down into her eyes—eyes filled with compassion and caring. She was so generous, so sensitive. He'd have to tread carefully. Ty set Cristine down, watched for a moment as the little girl settled in to play with her blocks. Then he turned back to Briony.

"I haven't got your patience, Bri. I've spent too many hours wondering when the ax would fall, when something would happen to ruin what I've got. I can't live that way anymore."

"Don't say that!" She brushed her hand over his chest. "Why should you be afraid? You believe in God, you know He's going to do what's best."

Ty had to smile. She was so naive, so trusting. It hurt him to shatter her illusions, but she didn't realize the ramifications of Peter Grant's existence. He did. Ty cupped her cheek in his hand, his thumb brushing over her jawline.

"Briony, you've got your beliefs, and I respect that. But I'm not sure God and I agree on what's best for Cristine." He spoke frankly. "I told you, I don't understand His ways. I don't have the faith you do."

Her eyes widened. "But you could have," she whispered.

He shook his head. "No. I can't. Not anymore."

She studied him, puzzled. "Why?"

"Because I think I hate Him." There, it was out. Sheer relief to have finally said it.

"Oh, Ty, you don't hate God. God is love." She looped her arms around his waist and leaned her head on his chest, exhibiting the trust she spoke of.

Ty drew away, just enough so he could look straight at her.

"He took everything, Bri. My hopes for a family, my future with Andrea. Now Cristine is threatened. I can't just sit back and wait for it to happen. Do you understand? I have to do something."

"You're going to fight God?" A tender smile fluttered over her lips. "You're taking on the Almighty Builder of the Universe because you don't like the way He's handling things?" She shook her head, her expression full of mirth. "Sounds like pretty poor odds to me."

He would have drawn away then, would have reverted to acting like a boss would, but she wouldn't allow it. She kept her arms in place, wrapped tightly around his waist, her eyes focused on his face.

"He doesn't want to hurt you, Ty." Her voice wove over him like a web of calm. "He wants the best for you. He aches to give you the delights of your heart. He loves you far more than you can even imagine." She leaned back, just a little, her face shining with joy.

"How much love can you imagine, Ty? A couple getting married, a new baby born, sharing a birthday with your best friend? What?" Her eyes dared him to answer. "Go ahead, try."

"I don't know," he muttered at last, irritated by her dog-with-a-bone persistence.

"Think of Andrea and of how much you loved her," she murmured, head tilted to one side. Then her gaze swept to the carpet. "Now, think of Cristine. Yes, I can see your love for her. It blazes in your eyes. Can you feel it here?" Her palm covered his heart. "Can you feel the warmth of that love spilling through you, touching everything with a bright glow?"

The beauty and wonder of her words caught him in a spell, weaving the fantasy around him with silken threads.

"How much will you love her when she starts school? Tries out for basketball? Starts ballet classes? Won't that love grow and deepen even more?"

He nodded, the pictures building, gaining momentum in his brain.

"And when you walk her down the aisle on her wedding day, won't your heart be full to bursting with love for her?" Bri brushed back his hair, her eyes glistening as she nodded. "Yes, it will. But even then, Ty, even then at that most special moment, you won't feel the tiniest fraction of the love God feels for you right now."

"Then why, Briony?" he whispered, pressing his cheek against her hair as he tried to comprehend. "If He loves me that much, why must I go through all this pain and heartache?"

She hugged him close. "I don't know, Ty. I simply don't know. I'm certain of only one thing. Nothing can separate us from the love of God—"

The words came faintly to his ear, muffled by his shirt.

"If you ask me, that's a pretty powerful love."

Ty held her for a long time, savoring the strength and comfort he found in her presence. It surprised him that she fit so perfectly—not just into his arms, but into his life.

She drove him crazy, of course. Her perfectionist attention to details, her nitpicky insistence on order and organization, her constant analyzation of every option made him nuts.

But he couldn't fault her dedication to Cristine or her unwavering commitment to finding the truth, no matter what. Her staunch determination to do the right thing, to be sure her sister's child was well cared for, touched him.

Briony Green might be meticulously organized and efficient to the point of tediousness, but she had a quiet loving heart that was unstinting when it came to caring for someone else.

She deserves to have a family, God. She deserves a

chance to be a mother to her own child. She has such a capacity for love when she lets herself go.

She'd be a wonderful wife.

The thought came from nowhere, blindsiding him. When had he started thinking of Briony as anything other than Cristine's caregiver?

Ty stood with her head resting on his shoulder and asked himself what had prompted him to see Bri in this new light. Was it her understated beauty? The quiet way she waited for him to speak first? Or was it her faith and assurance that God would do exactly as He'd promised?

When had this attraction built into something stronger, something he dearly wanted to explore? She had brought calm and peace to his life in just a few short weeks, made him believe there was still a chance for happiness.

Marry again?

The idea barely popped into his mind before he tossed it. It could never be. It was impossible. God had taken Andrea because He wanted Ty to manage alone. Very well, he'd manage. Alone. On his own. If he lost Cristine, he'd handle that, too. But he couldn't, wouldn't make the mistake of involving anyone else in his pain. Not again.

Carefully, he moved his hands, wrapping his fingers around Bri's arms as he edged away. Ty avoided her eyes, detoured around her to pick up Cristine.

"I'm going to Calgary tomorrow," he said, pretending nothing had happened. "I'm going to check out Mr. Peter Grant. If there's a clue to unravel this, I intend to find it." He glanced up, saw the confusion cloud her eyes, and softened just for a moment.

"I have to know, Briony. I have to get answers."

"You may not find them," she reminded him.

"Then, at least I'll have tried. Sitting here, waiting for God to respond, hoping He'll send down something from heaven—it just isn't working."

He sank into the armchair, cuddling Cristine against his chest. The little girl snuggled close, her eyelashes drooping with tiredness.

"I've got to do everything I can. Everything," he said.

Bri walked across the room picking up toys, straightening things, until she'd made her way in front of his chair. She studied him for several moments, then nodded.

"Yes, I can understand that. I'd like to go with you."

Ty frowned. He'd expected to handle it alone.

"I want to know as badly as you do, Ty. Besides, I promised Bio-Tek that I'd stop in their office and fill out some paperwork before I start my new job." She bent to brush her lips over Cristine's head. Her eyes met his. "We could stop by your sister's so your mother could see Cristine. She's phoned almost every day. I think she's lonely."

Ty considered it for a moment. "Okay. We'll leave at eight-thirty." He watched as Bri gathered up her ever-present briefcase.

"You're a fraud, Dr. Green," he murmured, never stopping in his rhythmic caress of Cristine's back. "You'd like everyone to think you're a cool, dispassionate scientist who's only interested in the facts."

She stopped what she was doing to stare at him. "But that's exactly who I am!"

Ty shook his head, eyes twinkling at her confusion.

"Uh-uh. Deep inside that busy brain you're a marsh-mallow, Prof. You go out of your way to help, from taking on a child you've never met, to looking for your sister's boyfriend, to meeting my sister. You just can't help it, can you?"

Her cheeks blushed red. Bri turned so that her back was to him as she repacked her lists and charts.

"I don't know what you're talking about. I just happen to want things neatly tied up before I leave, that's all."

Leave. Ty mentally winced. How could he have forgotten? He'd been acting as if Briony would be around forever, and she had less than two weeks left. The thought hurt on some level he didn't even understand.

Alone again.

"Ty?" She stood at the door, umbrella in hand, waiting for his response.

"Yeah?"

"You're okay? There's nothing more I can do?"

He shook his head. "I'm fine. Thanks. I'll see you in the morning. We'll pick you up."

She hesitated, then nodded. "All right. Good night."

Ty glanced up just long enough to see the questions fill her face. His eyes met hers, locked and held, as the memory of that embrace simmered in the air. If only…

"Good night, Briony," he whispered.

She was already gone.

He was alone. As God intended.

"But I've still got Cristine," he whispered. For once, Ty found no assurance in his own words.

Chapter Eight

"I'd rather be arriving than leaving Banff." Briony glanced over her shoulder at the receding mountains and sighed. "It's going to be hard to leave, to go back to the city."

Ty checked on Cristine in his rearview mirror, then gave Bri a mocking smile. "Ah, but you'll be in your lab, Dr. Green. Oblivious to the world."

She thought about that for a moment. It sounded deathly dull compared to her time with Cristine. "I suppose" was all she said.

"Where do you think we should start?" he asked, passing several RVs as they rolled down the highway through the foothills. "At the bank?"

Bri shook her head. "No, actually I thought it might be better to stop at Bio-Tek first. They're on the far side of the city. We'll work our way back from there." She tugged out her city map and a pencil. "What's your sister's address again?"

Ty told her. She eventually found it on the map and noted it with a bright red marker.

"Yes, you see if we work our way across the city we can end up near her house and not have to backtrack." She smiled at the simplicity of it.

"I might have known you'd say that. Always organized." He glanced at the briefcase. "What else do you have in there?"

Her cheeks betrayed her, burning bright with embarrassment. "Just a list of a few questions I thought we might ask. Also, perhaps we could check the hospital where Cristine was born, see if they remember anything."

"That's a long shot."

"I know. But long shots are all we seem to have." She wished it weren't so. If only Bridget had told her *something,* confided in her before she died. "I read some more of the diary last night."

"Oh." His eyes narrowed. "Anything?"

"Well, nothing specific, perhaps. But I feel the tone of her writing changes at one point. She's talking about work, about the baby. She seems excited. It sounds as if she intends to raise Cristine herself. It's hard to read dates—to know if she means day, month, year or month, day, year—but apparently a week passes."

"And?" Impatient as usual, Ty's fingers gripped the wheel. "What does she say then?"

"She talks mostly about making sure 'the baby' has a good home."

"'The baby'?" He frowned. "Why do you say it like that?"

"Because up to then it was 'my baby.'"

Ty's words brimmed with kindness. "This is hard

for you, isn't it?" He rolled his eyes. "Now, that was a stupid question."

"Yes," Bri agreed after a moment's thought, "it is hard sometimes. My parents would have loved Cristine."

"Would have?" He frowned.

"They died several weeks after Bridget. A car accident."

His hand covered hers, squeezed, then continued to hold it on the leather seat separating them.

"I'm very sorry, Briony. You've had a really tough time."

"Thanks." She sat and absorbed the comfort he offered, content to accept it without feeling guilty.

Though at first she'd thought Ty unemotional and harsh with everything except his daughter, she'd come to appreciate that this man possessed a wonderful ability to empathize. He had no patience with tales of woe, but when someone mattered to Ty, he was fiercely protective. She'd seen pictures of Andrea wrapped tightly in his arms, as if he could protect her from the world.

What would it be like to be loved like that? To know that someone would tackle anything to keep you safe, that they loved you that much? It was Bri's secret fantasy to be loved like that. An aching little dream she kept tucked away inside, where no one could see that the scientist was a dreamer.

Ty, of course, wouldn't believe it. To him she was Cristine's caretaker, a necessary nuisance whose oddball foibles had to be tolerated for exactly thirty days, until his mother returned. He probably assumed that his life would return to normal after that.

But Mrs. Demens's return was not at all assured. Bri

knew she'd be better able to assess the situation today, when they stopped by. Perhaps she'd also be able to persuade Ty's sister to help her come up with some other scenario. If Bri found Cristine a taxing responsibility, what would she be like for Mrs. Demens?

"What are you thinking about?" He turned as indicated and followed the Crowfoot Trail. "You've been quiet most of the way. Like someone else."

Bri glanced back, smiling at Cristine's sleeping face. "Actually I was thinking about you," she admitted, surprising herself.

"Me? That's pretty boring."

"I was wondering if you'd ever had to rely on someone else."

He frowned, his eyes full of questions. "I suppose we all rely on others to some extent."

"That isn't exactly what I meant." Bri thought for a moment, rewording it in her mind. "Have you ever been in a situation where you've had to let go and just trust that someone else would do the best they could for you?"

He shook his head once, decisively. "I've usually managed pretty well on my own steam. I get a fix on the problem and then find a solution."

It sounded so simple. Briony had to smile.

"So you just set your goals and go for it?"

He nodded.

"What happens when it doesn't work out?"

He pulled up in front of Bio-Tek, then gave her an odd look. "Why are you asking me this?"

"I'm a little concerned about today," she admitted. "There's no guarantee that we'll find anything that will help us. What are you going to do if it turns out this was a dead end?"

It was obvious such a thought had never even entered Ty's realm of thinking. He puzzled over it for a moment, then shrugged.

"Reevaluate and form a new plan," he replied. Then he climbed out of the truck to free Cristine.

"Oh, boy! Move-or-get-out-of-the-way Tyrel Demens is in charge." Briony unclasped her seat belt as she whispered a prayer for help. "But what if you can't change it," she insisted, walking beside him toward the sprawling white complex. "What if there's not a single, solitary thing you can do to change what God's given you?"

Ty jerked to a stop, his mouth tight, lips pinched. His eyes chilled Briony as they glared into hers.

"Then you deal with it and move on to something else. Any other questions?" He jiggled Cristine, hushing her complaints. "Look, you don't have to give us a tour of Bio-Tek today if you don't want. Maybe some other time would be better."

Hurt pinched her heart. Bri pretended it didn't matter.

"If you don't want to waste time today, it's perfectly all right with me," she murmured, tugging open the solid glass door. "I'll try not to hold you up."

"Briony." His hand came out to stop her hurried pace toward the receptionist, his fingers squeezing her arm. "I truly didn't mean to say it like that. Cristine and I would love to see everything. I guess your questions just got to me."

"Why?" She simply stood, waiting.

He hesitated, his eyes on the floor. "There's only been one time in my life when I've faced a situation I desperately wanted to change and couldn't. I don't much like talking about it." His lips clamped together like a clam about to spill the pearl.

It was probably rude, but Bri asked, anyway. "Why not?"

His fingers tightened on her arm. But Ty didn't even seem to notice. As she watched, he hugged his daughter closer. His eyes softened, melted, an overwhelming pain washing through them as he gazed down at Cristine.

"Because it hurts," he admitted at last, his voice a whisper of regret. "It still hurts, Bri. And probably always will."

"I'm sorry." Bri yearned to know what cut through his implacable assurance to wound so deeply. She wanted to offer—what? Something to make it go away?

"Thank you." The moment stretched between them. Their gazes caught, held. His hand relaxed, his fingers brushing the skin he'd clutched.

"I wasn't just probing, you know," she said, conscious that all around them people were watching. "I was trying to prepare you for today, for the disappointment."

"I'll be fine. But thank you. Again." He lifted his hand away and brushed it against her cheek, fingers sliding over the skin, past her jaw and down her neck.

"Miss Green? How wonderful to see you here today. And you've brought the little girl! She's delightful." Her future boss stood beside them, waiting to be introduced.

"Dr. Natelle, I didn't expect you to stop your work just to show us around." Bri introduced Ty and Cristine, but remembering Ty's wish to hurry she didn't offer any explanations.

The doctor insisted on a full tour, pointing out Bri's

office and her portion of the lab, and then spreading out a map outlined in dark blue, the area of Banff National Park where she'd be collecting samples.

"All of the collection has to be done first, of course. Then we'll begin testing to see which strains we can alter enough to withstand the bugs."

After three-quarters of an hour, Briony insisted they had to go.

"As long as you're staying in Banff, you might want to scout out a place to live while you do your fieldwork." Dr. Natelle tapped the end of his nose with his pencil. "The summer months are often busy, and I'd hate to see you stuck in limbo, Miss Green. After all, your real work can't begin until the samples are collected and tested."

A minute later the doctor's assistant carried him off with news of a problem in the lab, leaving Ty and Bri to exit the building without fanfare.

"So you'll be coming back to Banff," Ty murmured, fastening Cristine back into her car seat. "I didn't realize that."

"I expect it will take some time before the actual genetic altering takes place. Of course, it would be simpler if they'd set up a temporary lab in Banff, but the doctor wants everything in-house. Makes for a lot of traveling." She waited for Ty to close her door and climb in the other side.

"Okay, bank first?" she asked, after he'd started the truck.

Ty shrugged. "I guess. We have to start somewhere. Which way?"

They tried three branches before they found someone who actually remembered Peter Grant.

"Oh, Peter. Sure. He hasn't been here for a while, though." The bank clerk shrugged. "He was only temporary."

Ty tossed an I-told-you-so look at Bri.

"What did you want to know?" The woman admired Cristine, her eyes soft. "Your little girl is so cute. She looks like her mom."

"Yes, she does." Bri smiled, thinking of Bridget. "Actually we'd like to know anything you can tell us."

"Okay." She thought for a moment. "Peter was an extreme type. You know, on the edge."

Ty frowned. "I don't think I do know. Can you elaborate?"

"Eight-hour jogs, bicycling Borneo, that kind of thing. When he was here, he was planning some sheer-face mountain climbing. I forget what he called it."

"Rappelling?"

Ty's intensity bothered Bri. He was scaring their only contact.

The woman took a step back, her face wary as she sputtered a half laugh.

"Well, it was repelling to me, that's for sure. Letting yourself fall down the edge of a mountain?" She shook her head. "Not my idea of a good time."

"Mine, either." Bri stepped in. "Did he tell you where he was going to do this? Or when?"

"He was in training, I remember that much. He spent his lunch hours at that new gym around the corner. Claimed he had to get in shape for some eco-challenge he wanted to enter." The teller rolled her eyes. "I should be as out of shape as him."

"He was good-looking?" Bri took the baby from Ty and leaned closer to hear the answer. "All muscles?" Bridget had always preferred fit men, and edgy men.

"Yes, but not bulky. He was a little taller than me. Lean, sleek looking." She laughed. "Peter always reminded me of a panther. That honed muscular look, I guess. The blond hair didn't hurt any, not with that tan."

Ty, clearly impatient with this physical assessment, interrupted. "Do you remember when he last worked here? Or where he was going when he finished?"

"Let's see. It was summer, I think." She considered for a minute. "Yes, during summer vacation. I remember because Peter worked extra hours so some of the others could extend their leave."

"And then what did he do?"

"Hmm, good question." She tapped her lip. "After that, I'm pretty sure it was heli-skiing on Shuswap Lake. Or maybe the rappelling thing." She shrugged. "Sorry, but that's the best I can do after so long."

Bri saw her eyes move to the clock.

"You've been wonderful. Thanks so much for talking to us." But as the woman turned to leave, Bri asked her most pressing question. "Did you ever see him again? Hear from him or of him?"

"No. Sorry. He's probably in South America somewhere, though. Peter lived for a challenge."

"You don't happen to know if he had a girlfriend." Bri held her breath.

The teller nodded. "Yeah, now that you mention it, he did talk about someone. I never knew her name, just that she liked the same stuff he did. She must have lived in the mountains because they hiked together a lot." She glanced at the manager. "Look, I've really got to get back to work."

"We understand. Thanks a lot for speaking to us."

"I hope it helped." She tweaked Cristine's cheek. "Bye, honey."

Bri linked her arm through Ty's and walked him out of the bank. He stopped, refusing to budge one more step, the moment they cleared the door. His chin jutted out in grim determination.

"I had more questions, you know." His eyes flashed his anger. "Maybe you asked all you needed to, but—"

"We couldn't hold her any longer, Ty. She'd already done us a favor by talking to us. Besides, what else could we have asked?"

"About Cristine." He was indignant over her refusal to understand. "We're no closer to knowing the truth than we were."

"She barely knew about even Bridget," Bri reminded him. "Besides, when he left here, Peter may not have known about the baby."

"If you hadn't hurried me, maybe we could have found out." He stomped over to his vehicle, unlocked the door and fastened Cristine inside. "Where next?"

Bri climbed in and waited for him to join her.

"Just a minute, Ty," she began, when he shoved the key into the ignition. "We need to talk about this."

"What's to talk about? I want answers and I intend to get them." His belligerence dared her to argue with that.

"I want answers, too. But you can't force them out of people. They have to talk it out, go back in their memories. We're asking about two years ago. Can you remember what happened two years ago? Just like that!" She snapped her fingers.

His eyes flared, his mouth tightened. He was furious.

Bri laid a hand on his arm in a silent plea. "We're on the same side here. We both want answers. I just don't want to alienate anyone along the way."

"How am I alienating?" Fury laced his voice.

"You stomp in there with your list of questions and demand they answer you." Bri's frustration grew. "We have no legal status, no means to compel anyone. We just have to hope they'll remember something."

"She didn't." He motioned with his head toward the bank.

"She remembered quite a lot." Bri ticked the details off on her fingers. "Peter worked just long enough to support his habit of extreme sports. He went hiking with his girlfriend a lot."

"Big deal." He thumped the steering wheel with his palm. "Where does that get us? Exactly nowhere nearer to my goal."

"You are such a control freak!" Bri glared at him. "Stop focusing on *your* goal for a minute, slow down and think. If you spent almost every dime you made, how would you live?"

"Cheaply." He nodded. "Okay. So what?"

"Rappelling, heli-skiing, cross-country biking. All that stuff takes gear. Expensive gear. You wouldn't haul it around with you."

Ty's eyes opened wide. "So maybe he lived with some buddies?"

"Or maybe he stayed with his parents when he came to Calgary."

"We could ask the bank for his last known address." He grinned at the brilliance of it.

Bri smiled. "I already tried that. They won't give out personal information on employees." Briony dug out a biscuit for Cristine to munch on.

"So what now?"

Bri grinned, her thumb motioning back over her shoulder. "Lunch, I think."

He laughed. "Good idea. I know just the place."

Bri had to admit, the restaurant was perfect. Cristine pranced around the children's play area as if she owned it, inspecting each toy with a crow of pleasure.

Bri smiled as she sipped her coffee and watched the little girl work off some of her excessive energy.

"Makes you tired, doesn't it?" Ty cupped his mug in both hands. "I need to apologize. Again."

She could hardly believe it. "For what?"

"For trying to barrel ahead. For trying to force you and the rest of the world to conform to my way." He thrust out his hands, palm up. "I'm beginning to realize that you've given this whole search thing a lot of thought."

"Yes, I have. And each time I think I've found an answer, I run into another roadblock." She held his gaze. "It's just as frustrating to me as it is to you, Ty. But I think if we can plan ahead, try to anticipate the finer points of this situation, we can save ourselves some grief."

He frowned. "I don't know what you mean."

"I'll tell you." Bri sucked in a breath of courage. "But you're not going to like this," she said.

His eyes darkened. "Your point is?"

"I want to phone all twelve of the Grants listed in the phone book."

His eyes lit up. "Hey, great idea. We should be able to get through it in no time. I'll take the first six." He jerked his cell phone off his belt.

Bri reached out to stop him. "I meant that *I* want to do it."

His face froze into that same angry mask.

"Just listen for a moment, will you?"

He shrugged.

"What if we end up reaching his wife? Are we just going to blurt out that we think Peter had a child with someone else? Or what if he and his family are estranged? We've got to be careful about how we handle this, Ty."

"You're not very flattering, do you know that? It's kind of hard on my ego." He sipped his coffee thoughtfully. "All right. I'll admit you're somewhat better than I am at beating around the bush."

"That wasn't—"

"So go ahead and start phoning. I'll watch Cristine and take lessons from a pro. Or should I say 'prof'?"

Bri wasn't sure how to take his comments. Ty often kept his emotions bottled up inside. She took her list and her phone from her purse.

"I'll start with the only 'P. Grant' listed." She dialed. "Hello, is this the Grant residence? My name is Briony Green. I'm trying to reach a Mr. Peter Grant who formerly worked at…" She gave just enough information to make her enquiry sound official.

"Thank you so much for your time. I'm sorry I bothered you." She clicked off her phone, then placed a little *X* by the name. "No relation. Don't know him. This P. Grant—Philip, is eighty-four."

Ty nodded, his eyes steady. "Go ahead."

She phoned six more, all with the same response. No one had heard of Peter Grant.

For the third time in as many minutes, Cristine fell and burst into tears.

"She's tired," Ty murmured as he consoled her. "I think we'd better get out of here."

They gathered up their things, paid the bill and left the now-crowded restaurant.

"There's a park, just over there. Maybe she'd sleep if we spread out a blanket."

Ty frowned. "I didn't—"

"I did." Bri reached into the bag at her feet and drew out an old quilt. "I keep this in my car for just these emergencies. Something told me to bring it along today."

Ten minutes later, Cristine was cuddled up in her daddy's arms, fast asleep. Ty kept up his rhythmic stroking of her back, his face soft as he watched her.

"You know, it occurs to me that all of this is an exercise in futility." Bri smiled at his curious glance. "You are Cristine's father as certainly as I'm sitting here. She doesn't want or need any other. There's nothing anyone could give her that you haven't, Ty."

"Except a mother." The words whispered so low, barely penetrated the rustling trees surrounding them.

"I'm sure you could find her a mother if you set your mind to it," she teased.

He lifted his head. Bri caught her breath at the wealth of defeat, the glimmer of regret she saw in his eyes.

"I can't marry again. Not ever."

"You think that now," she murmured, hiding her own pain at the words. "But someday, when Andrea's loss isn't quite so sharp, you'll look around and realize you've met someone who has taken root in your heart."

"It won't matter how I feel. I'll never marry." His voice, hard-edged, chewed out the words. "I can't," he muttered, his chin resting on his chest.

Bri didn't know what to say, couldn't think of the words that would reach him. She'd assumed that he and Andrea were happy, that he was bereft at her death.

But now, listening to him here, she heard yearning.

Bri leaned over to press her fingers against his. "I don't understand, Ty."

He lifted his head, smiled wryly and nodded. "No, you probably don't." Like a mantle, his eyes shuttered out their emotion, closing his thoughts to her. "Go ahead and phone, Briony."

"Okay."

She wanted to reach out so badly, ached to understand what he was thinking. But she wouldn't pry. Ty was a private man. He handled his grief in his own way.

And she wasn't part of his world.

The knowledge pricked her, reminding her how foolish she was to let herself get drawn into their lives. Cristine was her niece, but Bri would be leaving soon.

Ty was the child's father. He would do what was best for the little girl, regardless of the cost to himself.

But as Bri snuck a second look, watched him sitting on the hillside, alone, with only his daughter for comfort, she felt the bleakness of his soul reach out and touch her.

Ty Demens touched a chord in her heart that had never been heard before. He was true to himself and his daughter. He didn't hide the truth, or pretend.

But he was a single father, and no matter how much Bri loved Cristine, she could never again allow herself to be a mommy substitute. If she couldn't be loved for herself, she'd do without. One thing she'd learned from being dumped at the altar—she couldn't live with second best, not in her work and not in her personal life.

Slowly Bri dialed the number. And the next. And the next.

"There's no point," Ty hissed, as she kept making *X*s on her list. "We're getting nowhere. We need to move on to the next step."

"This *is* the next step." Her frustration mounted. "You heard me on the phone, talking to the lawyers. They don't know anything. To their knowledge there was never any mention of a birth father."

"And none of these people know Peter." He sighed. "It's a dead end. We might as well toss in the towel."

Bri shook her head. "No, I'll see it through. I know you think I'm nitpicky and obsessed with details." She nodded. "I am. In my work you have to analyze every option."

He kept observing her, his face impassive.

"Believe me, Ty, I know my way isn't the only way. It's just the only way I know."

He lifted an eyebrow.

"When I'm in the lab, I don't toss out anything. I note every detail, run thousands of tests, until I'm absolutely certain my conclusion is correct. If I don't, I run the risk of missing a clue, a detail that could change the results."

"And you think checking out every one of those phone numbers will put us a step closer to figuring out whether or not I get to keep my daughter?" He shrugged. "Go ahead. Personally, I've given up hope."

Bri smiled, then leaned forward to brush the hair out of his eyes. "Don't ever do that, Ty. Remember, our God is a God of hope."

His hand reached up, grasped hers and clung. "Your faith shames me. Here I am, always demanding quick fixes. I want the answers to my questions now." His thumb brushed against her knuckles. "And here you are, quietly taking care of the details, waiting."

He stared down at their entwined fingers, his face brooding. "How do you do that, Briony? How can you let go of the controls and let God take over?"

"Oh, Ty, you do ask the toughest questions." She smiled, breathy at the intensity of his gaze.

"Well?" He waited, impatient to hear her answer.

Bri used both hands to cup his face, holding it so she could stare directly into his eyes.

"The truth?" She stroked her thumb against his cheek. "The truth is, I never had the controls in the first place, Ty. There is only one God. I'm not Him."

After a single surprised moment, he leaned forward and kissed her, his lips softly sweet as they touched hers.

When he drew away, Briony could barely breathe. She saw a glimmer of humor lurking behind his solemn stare.

"Always so logical," he murmured.

"Can't help it. That's who I am." Bri wished he'd kiss her again, yet she knew she couldn't let it happen. Her hands fell away.

"I know, and I'm glad." He bussed her nose. "Finish your list, Briony. Then we'll go see my mother."

Briony tore her gaze from his and concentrated on the last three names. She got a nibble on number two.

"William? I see. No, sir, I didn't know that. Married? Oh, no, I didn't know that. I see. Yes, I'm sure it was." She felt Ty's interested glance but deliberately kept her focus on her list as the words flowed across the phone.

"I'm so sorry. And that happened when?" She scribbled down the information, listening as she did.

"I'm terribly sorry to have bothered you, but I thank you for your help. Yes, God bless you, too, Mr. Grant. Goodbye."

"Well? Aren't you going to finish the list?" Ty gathered Cristine's tiny body as if he meant to rise. He stopped when he caught sight of Bri's face. "What is it?"

"*William* Peter Grant died a year ago last August in Peru when he fell down a mountain."

Ty collapsed back onto the quilt. "Died?"

Bri watched as he assimilated the information, added up and came to his conclusion.

"He died before Cristine was born?" He waited for her nod. "But how do we know he's our Peter?" he murmured. "There has to be more than one Peter Grant in the world."

"He's the one we want. Apparently his fiancée used to call him Will." Bri held his gaze, her voice emphasizing the detail. "This fiancée worked in a hotel in Banff. They hoped to be married when Will/Peter returned after his *August* climbing stint."

"He didn't know about Cristine!" Ty stared at her, trying to work it all out. "He never knew he was going to be a father."

Bri nodded. "Apparently it took the authorities some time to verify who he was and notify the next-of-kin. That's why Bridget's diary talks of them being a family. She didn't find out until well into the winter. She must have been so worried."

They fell silent, thinking of the young man whose life had ended too soon.

"This means that there's no one to stop me from being Cristine's father." Ty's eyes lit up with excitement as he gazed lovingly at his daughter, then gently laid her on the quilt. "If I hold her, I'll wake her up. My hands are shaking."

Seconds later, Bri watched the thrill of it drain away.

"His parents. Do they want Cristine, Bri? Do they even know about her?"

Relieved that he realized the influence Cristine's biological family might want to exert, Bri freely told him the rest of the story as she stood to ease the cramp in her legs.

"Peter's parents died when he was a little boy. His aunt and uncle raised him. The aunt died a couple of months ago. His uncle is moving into a senior's complex soon. I'm sure he'd be delighted to get to know Cristine, but I can't imagine that he'd try to seek custody."

Ty struggled to his feet, hesitating to voice the words that had so long been denied. Bri reached out and hugged him, her heart brimming with thanksgiving.

"She's yours, Ty. All yours. She always has been. You just didn't know the secrets God had in store."

His arm looped around her waist and held her clamped against his side. He bent his head and buried it in her hair, nuzzling the softness as he spoke.

"Thank you, Briony. Thank you for persisting and insisting and showing me the way. Thank you for giving my daughter back to me."

They stood holding each other, peering down at the sleeping child.

"I didn't do it, Ty," Bri whispered after a long time. "It was a God thing."

She felt the rumble of laughter shake his chest before it burbled out.

"I'm just beginning to understand that, Bri. Thanks to you." He lifted his head, his eyes glowing. "Let's go tell my family, okay? We can have a party!"

Bri smiled and nodded, her eyes misty, as he picked up his daughter and kissed her awake.

She was happy for him. She was! Ty's world glowed new and full of joy. At last he was free of the worry that had plagued him for so long.

He had everything he needed to be happy.

But for Briony, the world was still the same. And she was still standing on the sidelines, watching.

Alone.

Chapter Nine

"Ah! At last I meet the infamous Dr. Green." Ty's sister thrust out a hand. "I'm Giselle. My husband and son are away for the week, or I'd introduce you to them. I'm guessing you remember Mom."

Giselle led them into the living room, where Mrs. Demens sat perched on a recliner, her bandaged leg evident beneath the cuff of her brown shorts.

"Nan!" Cristine wriggled out of her father's arms and scrambled across the room to climb up beside her grandmother.

Bri smiled as the two rubbed noses, hugged and chattered nonstop.

"Please sit down, Dr. Green. You won't get a word in edgewise once those two have started." Giselle reached up to wrap her slim tanned arms around her brother's neck in a hug. "You look good," she told him, frankly appraising his blue jeans and shirt.

"Thank you. So do you." He leaned back and took a second glance. "Are you putting on weight?"

"Ty! What a thing to say." Bri immediately wished she'd stemmed her sputter of disapproval. Mrs. Demens and Giselle both turned to glance curiously at her.

"Ignore him, Briony. Can I call you Briony?" Giselle didn't wait for a nod. "Ty always blurts out the first comment that comes into his doddering head."

"Doddering?" Ty glowered at her. "I'm not yet doddering, thank you very much."

"Well, you will be soon, Uncle Ty." Giselle grinned at him. "We're having another baby."

"About time, too." Ty's gruff voice couldn't hide his pleasure as he hugged her again. "Congratulations, sis."

"From me, too." Bri held out a hand. "It's wonderful news. Do you want a girl this time?"

Giselle patted her still-flat tummy. "I want whatever God gives me," she said simply. "I'll leave that decision up to someone with more knowledge than I possess."

Bri sipped her tea, smiling and nodding as the three of them teased one another, watching the family interactions, while she tried to hide the persistent ache in her heart.

"I understand you're starting a new job soon." Giselle sank down beside Bri, her elegant sundress flaring out around her bare brown legs. "That must be exciting."

"I've worked toward it for a long time." Bri couldn't say more without divulging how she dreaded leaving Ty and Cristine.

"Still, you jumped from the frying pan into the fire when you finished school and then took on Cristine." Giselle's eyes sought her niece, a glow of love lingering there. "I love Cristine dearly, but she's a handful."

"Yes, she is." Briony smothered a laugh when Cristine

tested her father's "no" by trying to ride her grand-mother's leg like a horse. "I've grown very fond of her."

"Is she a lot like your sister?" Giselle's big eyes held no guile. She was honestly curious.

"Quite a bit, actually. But I think she's more like Ty."

"Really?" Giselle frowned, lips puckered in a moue of displeasure. "That's too bad. How?"

A blush stung Bri's face as she realized Giselle knew she'd been studying Ty. She shrugged.

"I don't really know how to explain it. Her focus, I suppose. Once she sets her mind on something, she will not be dissuaded without a very good reason."

"Well, that's exactly like Ty and don't I know it!" Giselle winked at Bri, fully aware of her brother's interest in their conversation. "Hardheaded. Not to mention pushy, stubborn, intolerant and inflexible." She grinned at his frown. "Not that Cristine is like that. Yet."

"Cristine is sweet and innocent." He grinned at them. "And she's mine."

"You found out something!" Giselle squealed with excitement, folded her legs up under her and leaned forward. "Spill it."

He explained about their day.

"What an answer to prayer." Mrs. Demens heaved a relieved sigh. "Briony, my dear, you were sent straight from heaven."

"Bee." Cristine pulled herself onto the sofa and flopped into Bri's lap. "Bee," she hummed over and over, her fingers careful, delicate as they touched Briony's unfettered hair.

"She certainly loves you." Giselle exchanged glances with her mother. "If I leave my hair down, she pulls it."

Bri brushed her hand over the little girl's soft cheek. "She's learning that causes pain," she murmured, touching the bright curls so like her own. "Most of the time she's very careful."

"You've done wonders for her." Mrs. Demens's voice rang round the room. "I think it's time we did something for you. I doubt you've had a minute's peace with Ty's schedule." She tapped her forefinger against her chin. "Let me see."

Giselle got into the spirit of things.

"Why don't you take her dancing, Ty? You haven't been out in ages." She turned to Bri. "You like dancing, don't you? Ty's great at ballroom stuff. Don't ask me why. All he ever did was step on my toes when I tried to teach him."

"That's because you always had to lead." Ty laughed at Giselle's inelegant snort. "You're more of a control freak than I am."

"Worse?" Bri couldn't imagine it. She wasn't even aware she'd spoken until she caught Giselle's smug little smile. "I mean—"

"Never mind, honey. We all know Ty. And we love him in spite of his tendency to boss us all. Most of the time, anyway." Mrs. Demens ignored Ty's interruption. "Dinner and dancing, I think. Yes, that should give you both a break. Now, where, Giselle?"

"Montague's." Giselle didn't need a moment to think. "They've got a lovely dance floor. Friday is their best night."

"And you guys have the nerve to call me bossy?" Ty glared at them both. "We didn't bring clothes to go dancing. We were in town to do business. We simply stopped by to let Cristine have a visit."

"Oh, Tyrel, do be quiet. I'm thinking." Mrs. Demens motioned her daughter over and the two of them began a lively discussion on whether Giselle's husband was Ty's size. "I'm sure it will do. There now, that's settled. I'll call for reservations. Giselle, you take Briony and find her a dress. You're about the same size."

Two minutes later Bri found herself in the master bedroom, standing in front of a massive closet with no clear idea of how she'd arrived there.

"This, maybe? No, wait." Giselle rifled through the hangers and pulled out a long white gown with a tiny matching jacket. "This is perfect."

"I can't wear this." Bri fingered the seed pearls stitched to the jacket, her eyes huge. "What if I spilled something on it?"

Giselle shrugged. "Then we'll get it cleaned. Here's the matching bag. Now, what about shoes? I think my feet are bigger than yours."

"Not by much." Bri touched the filmy chiffon, longing to try it on yet knowing she shouldn't. She was a scientist. This gown belonged on a model, or a movie star.

"How about these?" Giselle held out a pair of strappy white sandals.

"They're lovely," Bri said honestly. And far too high. Bri's shoes never had heels that high.

"They're ridiculous, really. I never did wear them

much." Giselle kicked off her sandal and thrust out one foot. "I have ugly toes."

Bri didn't see anything wrong with Giselle's toes. But there wasn't really a nice way to say that. Anyway, she didn't have time. Giselle immediately launched into speech.

"You and my brother seem to get along. He doesn't usually respond well to my teasing." She settled onto the middle of her vast bed, full of questions. "Is it hard for you to deal with him?"

Bri blinked, sat down on a nearby chair and studied Ty's sister. "Hard?" she repeated.

"Does he get mad at you when everything doesn't happen exactly as he wants it?"

"No. Not usually." She smiled. "Though, to tell you the truth, I'm not sure I'd have noticed if he did. I'm pretty focused myself."

Giselle laughed merrily. "Good," she cheered. Her smile faded. "He had to be pretty controlled with Andrea, be the strong, sensible one. You know?" She tipped her head to one side like an inquisitive sparrow. "It's good to see him respond to another woman."

Bri had to stop this. "Oh, but I'm not—" Hmm. How *did* one tell Ty's sister that she wasn't interested in being a stand-in for her niece's mommy?

"Not what? Another woman?" Giselle blinked. "Of course you are. And it's very clear that my brother is fond of you."

Fond of her? Bri shook her head.

"I simply help out with Cristine. Nothing more."

"Do you really believe that?" Giselle's kind glance

stopped any response Bri would have made. "I can see that you care for him, Briony. It's in your eyes whenever you look at him."

"Giselle, I like your brother. I think he's doing a wonderful job with Cristine, managing a difficult situation more adeptly than a lot of men could." She took a deep breath. "But come the end of the month, I'm leaving to start a new life. It's one I've dreamed of for years. I'll see Cristine and Ty, of course, as often as I can."

"But that's it?"

"That's all it can be. I love my niece. I care very much about her future. But I can't pretend to be her mother. I've got to move on with my life, just as Ty will move on with his."

"To move anything, Ty will have to be prodded." Giselle chewed on the edge of a nail. "He doesn't talk about Andrea a lot, but I know it wasn't an ideal marriage."

Bri knew she shouldn't listen, but how could she escape? Giselle seemed set on pouring out her heart.

"I'm not sure there are any ideal marriages."

"Maybe not. But it works far better when you're pulling together rather than apart." She broke off her discussion to smile at her mother, who was peeking around the doorway. "Hi."

"Find anything spiffy?" Her mother picked up the hanger with the glistening white outfit and nodded. "Yes, this is perfect."

She laid the dress back down, then turned to Bri. "Thank you so much for standing in for me. I'm quite sure I've never told you how much I appreciate all you've done. These past weeks have been so nice. I've done nothing but laze around."

Ty's mother wrapped Briony in a hug that made her feel warm and cared for.

"I'm glad I could help. I'd do more if I could…"

"I know you promised to be at work the second of July. We wouldn't dream of asking you to put your life on hold any longer." Mrs. Demens sat down on the bed, easing her heavy cast up onto the pretty peach quilt. "Cristine's taken everything in her stride, and I'm sure that's due to you. She's going to miss you."

"I'll miss her, too." Bri didn't dare think about that now. She was grateful when Giselle motioned her out of the room, one eye on her mother's lined face.

"You relax for a minute, Mom," she said before she closed the door. "Briony and I will help Ty with Cristine."

Since Ty didn't object to his sister and mother organizing their evening, Briony didn't feel comfortable about protesting. When the time came, she slipped into Giselle's gorgeous dress and shoes, then obediently sat and let Ty's sister fiddle with her hair.

"There. You look lovely, Briony. Ty's going to be so proud to escort you."

Bri stared at herself in the mirror and swallowed. She felt pretty, as if she were a beautiful woman going out with a wonderful man. She wasn't beautiful, of course. But Ty was handsome. How long had it been since he'd dated?

She realized she'd attended only group functions since her almost-wedding six years ago. Of course, her studies meant she devoted hours to her career, but still—

was this truly the path she would tread for the rest of her life? Always alone, always on guard.

The thought scared her.

"Is there someone special in your life?" Giselle put away the brush and spray, her conversation casual.

Special? Bri shook her head.

"No. I was just thinking to myself that it's been a long time since I've been out with anyone."

"Oh." Giselle plopped down on the bench beside her. "Why?"

How much should she tell? Bri decided the bare bones were enough.

"I was engaged once."

"Really? What happened?"

"My fiancé decided his ex-wife would make a better mother for his son than I would." The bitterness behind those words surprised her. Surely she'd forgiven Lance?

"I'm so sorry." Giselle's hand covered hers in a gentle squeeze. "But you can't let that stop you from opening your heart to someone else."

"I haven't." Bri smiled at her raised eyebrow. "Well, not really." She explained about the child. "Of course, I eventually realized that God expected me to use the talents he's given me. That means concentrating on my work, excelling at what I do best."

"But—"

"I'm not really very good at motherhood, Giselle. People always say it's instinctive, but it's not for me. I have to have it all charted out or I mess up." She rolled her eyes. "Do you know that I gave Cristine a whole apple once?"

Giselle burst out laughing. "Knowing Cristine, she probably sunk in her teeth, too."

"She did."

"I can just picture it." Her smile faded, her eyes serious. "But don't you see, Briony? You've been a wonderful mother for Cristine. I'm sure it hasn't been easy, but you've figured out what you need to know. Cristine certainly hasn't suffered. God has blessed you. He can use whatever you do if you hand it over to him."

"I suppose."

"It's not only that, is it? There's something else about caring for Cristine that bothers you."

Bri simply stared at Giselle and let her figure it out for herself.

A moment later, Giselle's eyes widened. "It's not the same as before, Bri. Ty won't yank Cristine out of your life, forbid you to ever see her again. He knows how much you love her."

"I know. After today, he'll never worry about losing Cristine to someone else. She has her fat little fingers wrapped tightly around his heart." Bri kept her head bent, her eyes on her plain unvarnished nails.

"Then, what's bothering you so much?" Giselle waited patiently, while Bri sorted through her thoughts. "I'd like to help if I can."

"I know. And I appreciate it." She stopped, then after a moment said, "It's hard to explain."

What was she afraid of? Bri wasn't sure she knew anymore. She was only aware of a deep persistent ache and a feeling that moving to Calgary wouldn't cure it.

"I guess I'm afraid to let myself want anything too much," she admitted at last.

"I'm sure that's perfectly natural. You've lost a sister, your parents, all your connections." She studied Briony. "What else?"

"You're an awful lot like your brother, you know." Bri sighed. "I'm not sure I can explain this without sounding smugly superior."

"I don't think you're smugly superior."

Bri smiled. "You will," she promised with a sigh. "You see, I was always the brain. I found my studies incredibly easy. Bridget didn't. It—caused a lot of strife. I always felt 'not normal.' Bridget had tons of boyfriends, lots of dates. She was the life of the party. I never figured that stuff out. Didn't want to, if the truth were known. I was totally focused on my books."

"So you hid behind your brains?"

Bri nodded, cheeks burning. "As I look back now, I realize that I avoided trying to be part of her circle because that was where Bridget excelled."

"And you didn't want to steal it from her." Giselle nodded. "I think that's commendable."

"Not really. I never let anyone see that I wanted more from life than to be the class valedictorian, the university's top student, the professor's pet project." Her voice dropped to a whisper. "I never let them see me."

"Not anybody?"

"Well, two others knew." Bri smiled, remembering. "There were three of us who roomed together in college. Each of us got dumped at the altar and so we banded together." She glanced up at Giselle. "Clarissa and Blair are happily married now. They've made peace and moved on. I'm the only one who's still out in the cold."

"But you don't have to be! I'm sure there are any number of men willing to take you out." Giselle straightened a drooping curl. "You don't have to be alone, Briony."

"Don't I?" She couldn't afford to cling to the hope Giselle offered. "That's the crux of the issue, you see. All these years I've focused on my work and been perfectly happy. It wasn't until I met Ty and began to care for Cristine that I even questioned my future. I'd just accepted that God meant for me to handle life alone. It's what I'd always done."

"Uh-huh." Giselle's lips curled up in a knowing smile. "And now that's not enough?"

"It has to be!" Bri concentrated her thoughts, organizing them so she could clearly express something she wasn't sure of herself. "I'd make a lousy mother. I get too focused on work because that's my purpose. That's where my strengths lie. That's where God wants me to be—in the lab."

Giselle stood, her hand gentle on Briony's shoulder. "Are you certain of that?"

"Yes."

"Then, I have only one thing to say. Sometimes we believe God is sticking with the tried and true, when in reality He wants to branch out and treat us to something special. But He can't, because we're stuck in our fear."

"I'm not sure I understand that. I believe God has a purpose for everything. I know there's nothing He'll give me that I can't handle."

Giselle snorted. "Of course He'll give you things

you can't handle!" she insisted. "If He didn't, why would we ever have to call on Him for help?"

"Well, that's sort of what I meant. I was trying to say I believe God has everything under control."

"Hmm. Yes." Giselle nodded slowly. "But you're trying to understand his control from your earthly viewpoint. Just as Ty has always done. My brother is so certain that Cristine is the only child he'll ever have that he clings to her out of fear. He can't see beyond that." She shook her head.

"God isn't that small, Bri. He's bigger than anything we can imagine, and sometimes, every once in a while, he wants to surprise us with his magnificent abundance. We simply have to let him."

"Are you guys ever going to be finished in there?" Ty's low voice rumbled through the closed door. "Our reservation is in fifteen minutes."

Giselle tugged open the door, motioned to Bri and said, "Ta-da!"

Ty scrutinized every move, as Bri stood and glided toward him. His dark eyes glowed with admiration. "Wow!"

"Doesn't she look great?" Giselle rose on her tiptoes to kiss his cheek. "You look nice, too. For a brother. It's a good thing my husband is your size." She brushed a speck of lint off his shoulder. "Though I do believe he's just a tad more handsome than you."

Ty ignored her. "Ready?" he murmured, one hand outstretched to Bri.

"Yes." She let his fingers wrap around hers, warming them. Then she caught Giselle's knowing look.

"Remember what I said, Briony."

Bri nodded. "I will, and thank you. For everything."

Cristine didn't even notice their departure, she was so busy with the crayons her grandmother was laying out on the table.

Ty helped Bri into an unfamiliar car, which he said was his sister's. Once on the way, he tuned the radio to some soft music, then glanced sideways at her.

"I'm almost afraid to ask," he muttered. "But what, exactly, did my sister say?"

She laughed. "Worried?"

"Yes. I've learned over the years to be worried whenever Giselle locks herself in the bedroom with a woman I'm about to take to dinner."

"Ah." She hid her smile. "Have there been so many?"

He frowned at her, but answered. "Some. Not that many." He shrugged. "Andrea and I grew up together. I didn't date a lot."

"You knew she was the woman for you from the beginning?" Ty's hesitation made her study him more closely. "Did I say something wrong?"

He shook his head. "No, but tonight I'd rather forget the past and concentrate on enjoying ourselves. We probably won't get another break like this for a long time."

I won't, anyway. I'll be gone in less than two weeks, and you'll have Cristine all to yourself.

The thought stung Bri into silence.

"Do you like to dance?"

Bri blinked. "Um, I guess. I don't think I'm very good at it." Something twigged. "You ballroom dance, they said."

"I use to. Haven't done it for a while."

Bri choked. "I'll embarrass you terribly."

"We're not in competition, Bri. We're just going to enjoy ourselves."

She sat, mulling that over. "How did *you* ever get interested in ballroom dancing?"

He grinned at her, his eyes twinkling. "Doesn't seem like a macho thing, does it?"

He laughed out loud as the color rose to her cheeks. For once he looked free of the memories, happy to be in her company.

"Believe me, I didn't think so, either, until my football coach pointed out how fast those guys moved, how intricate their footwork was. Coordination was a problem for me back then."

She stared. "I don't believe it."

He nodded. "Oh, yeah. I grew so fast, I couldn't make my feet and my body move in sync."

Bri got lost in the picture of Ty's lean, lithe body ever stumbling.

"You didn't answer my question." He held her gaze. "What did Giselle say?"

"We were talking about me, mostly. I'm afraid I'm not very good at the social stuff," she explained.

He frowned. "You do that a lot, you know."

"Do what?"

"Put yourself down. As if being smart is somehow bad or less than optimal. There's nothing wrong with using the mind God gave you, Bri."

"Especially if that's all He gave me." She muttered the words to herself, wishing she'd never agreed to go out. How was she going to make light conversation when she felt so out of place?

"It isn't all He gave you." Ty's soft, assured voice penetrated the radio's violin concerto. "He gave you true beauty, inside and out. He gave you insight and understanding for others. He gave you love for your sister, enough to ensure you would check up on her daughter. You've been royally blessed, Briony."

She stared. She couldn't help it. His words brimmed with sincerity. He wasn't trying to flatter her; he really believed what he was saying.

"I—I never thought of it like that before." She swallowed. "I guess I have been blessed."

"Yes." He nodded, certainty swirling in his eyes as he sat waiting for the traffic light to turn green. "And so have I. Cristine is the best thing that's ever happened to me. I'll be eternally grateful for her in my life."

"And you don't want anything else?"

His eyes dulled, the shine disappeared. He turned back to concentrate on the traffic. "We don't always get what we want, Briony. Sometimes we have to be happy with what we have."

"That's funny."

"Funny?" He looked grim. "Why?"

"Giselle just finished telling me that I settle for too little. She basically told me that I was afraid to accept what God wanted to give me because I won't look beyond my preconceptions." Bri frowned. "At least, I think that's what she was saying."

Ty made a face. "Giselle is thrilled with her life right now. She wants everyone to be as happy as she is. She doesn't understand that God doesn't always give you what you ask for."

"I think she was implying that He wants to give more than we could even ask or think." Bri contemplated that, while Ty found a parking spot, opened her door and helped her out of the car.

"Let's forget about my sister for a while," he muttered as he guided her to the restaurant's front door. "She always thinks she knows best—and that bugs me."

"By all means, let's not have you bugged." Bri grinned at him, hoping to tease him out of his grumpiness. "If you think God wants you to be happy with your life the way it is, who am I to question it?"

He gave her a hard look, then turned to speak to the maître d'. Once they were seated, however, his manner changed completely.

"You're very beautiful, Briony. I don't have the right words to tell you how lovely you look tonight."

"Thank you." She fiddled with the little evening bag, screwing up enough courage to meet his stare. "I suppose you want to dance?"

He shrugged. "If you do. The music is good and the floor's not too crowded." A dreamy romantic ballad underscored his words.

Bri sighed. "Just don't expect me to follow any fancy moves," she said as she set down her bag. "Plain and basic, that's me."

He held out her chair, then slipped a hand around her waist as he guided her to the floor. As she moved into his arms and began to sway to the music, her footsteps following his lead, Bri relaxed. It felt so right, so good, to be here like this.

"I don't think I've ever known anyone less plain or less basic," he murmured into her ear, his lips grazing the skin laid bare by her upswept hair. "You're an amazing woman, Briony Green."

She tilted her head up. Her eyes widened as they met the intent look in his. "Tonight, with Giselle's finery, you mean."

He shook his head, his eyes never leaving hers. "Tonight, last week when you got caught in the rain, the first day with carrot goop splattered all over your clothes. Yours is the kind of beauty that withstands all the tests."

She didn't know what to say, so she said nothing.

When the third song started, Ty enfolded her in his arms and danced her out onto the patio. The rich blackness of the night provided the perfect backdrop for the tiny white lights scattered across the hedge surrounding them and flung high up into the sheltering cedar trees. A hundred miniature lanterns swung gently in the breeze.

"Cristine and I were blessed the day you came into our lives. I'm sorry you have to go, but you'll always be welcome to come and visit."

Visit? Bri closed her eyes as the truth slammed into her heart.

She was totally, completely and stupidly in love with Tyrel Demens—a man who could not forget his dead wife.

How could God have let this happen?

Chapter Ten

Briony's sudden silence mystified Ty. He finished the dance, ordered their meals and kept up a light patter of conversation, hoping she'd come back from whatever place her mind had journeyed to.

Tonight he realized just how exquisite she was. Every time he held her, every time her cheek grazed his chest, every time her breath brushed across his neck, another stab of pain darted into his heart.

Why had God brought Briony into his life now, when it was too late?

"Is anything wrong?" He studied the delicate way she held her fork, blinked as it gleamed in the candlelight, observed her face softened by the shadows.

"Wrong?" She swallowed, staring at him in confusion.

"You seem distracted, worried. Is the salmon not to your taste?"

"It's fine. Thank you."

He watched, saw how desperately she searched for a topic to keep him busy, something deep enough that he wouldn't question her about her irregular breathing, or the odd stares she tried to hide.

"I was just thinking about this afternoon."

"Cristine's father, you mean." He frowned. He set down his fork; his appetite had suddenly fled.

"You are Cristine's father, Ty. Her only father." She reached out to touch him, then quickly pulled her hand back, as if afraid. "Yes, I was thinking about Peter. I remembered something Bridget wrote—'Will isn't enough.'" She shook her head.

"I didn't understand it then. I thought she was referring to something else. But now I believe she was talking about her relationship with Peter. Remember his uncle said he was really William?"

"Yes, I see. So there may be several other references to him that you didn't pick up on." He sipped his coffee thoughtfully, hating to rehash that time again, but knowing there could yet be answers they hadn't uncovered. "You think it was only after she found out he was dead that she decided to let Cristine be adopted?"

Briony nodded. "I'm fairly certain of it, now that I consider what I've read. She writes at length of her desire for a 'real' father for her baby. That must be why she connected with Andrea. She believed the two of you offered the most opportunity for her daughter."

It made a weird sort of sense to Ty now. Andrea must have known Bridget was having second thoughts about keeping her baby. Reality hit him squarely between the eyes.

"But that means she must have told Andrea that Peter was dead!" Ty glared at the tablecloth, his face grim as he fit the pieces together. "Why wouldn't Andrea have told me? Why make me go through this hell of wondering?"

"I don't know, Ty."

Her soft voice shamed him.

"I'm sorry, Briony. None of this is your problem, yet I keep dragging you into my messed-up life." He tossed down his napkin. "Would you like to go for a walk before dessert? They have lovely grounds here."

She placed her own napkin on the table and stood immediately.

Ty led her out onto the patio and beyond, down the tiny path that followed a brook. He said nothing as his mind raged over the injustice of it.

Why hadn't Andrea shared the truth? Why deceive him? There was no benefit, no possible good to come of keeping the truth from him. Except to keep him hanging, worrying, wondering.

"Are you all right?"

They'd stopped beside a little stone bridge. Briony stood in front of him, one hand on his arm, her face sad in the wash of moonlight.

"I'm so sorry, Ty. If I could, I'd erase it all, take the pain myself."

Her words unleashed a torrent of longing that Ty stemmed by crushing her against him, hanging on to her as if she were a lifeline in his confused, upset world.

"Thank you," he whispered, breathing in the sweet flowery scent that clung to her. Long ago, when he'd first thought about marriage, Ty had imagined life with someone like Briony.

She was everything he'd ever dreamed about in a

woman. Able to stand up for herself, but still capable of helping someone else. She didn't play games, didn't pretend, didn't prevaricate. Briony lived truth. She dealt in facts, not half truths.

"Ty?" She lifted her head, her sapphire eyes glittering with unshed tears. "I'm sorry I brought all this trouble on you. I wish I'd never gone to Banff!"

"Don't say that." He lifted a finger to brush it across her wet lashes. "You've done so much for us. You've given me the security I needed with Cristine."

"But I've caused you so much pain." Her voice whispered across his skin as her lips touched the hand lingering near her mouth.

"Not you, Briony. Never you." Ty bent and swept his mouth across hers, offering a kiss of reassurance. But that wasn't what he wanted at all, he realized the moment his mouth locked on hers.

He wanted to erase the shadows in her eyes, to kiss away the tears and pain he saw on her face. He wanted to ease her loss over her parents' and Bridget's deaths.

All of this and more Ty sought to convey with his embrace. But more than that, he tried to show her how much he cared for her. He tried to express the joy she brought to his life with her delight over accomplishing the simplest things. He caressed her for her patience and understanding with Cristine.

But by the time he finally pulled away, Ty knew that he'd kissed Briony Green because of something far deeper than simple appreciation. As he cradled her small, compact body in his arms, felt her fingers tangle in his hair, heard her sigh of pleasure as she nestled against him, Ty knew that he'd kissed Briony Green because he loved her. And that was a mistake.

So now what did he do?

Ty stood transfixed, holding the woman of his dreams in his arms as the evening surrounded them like a dark velvet cloak. He pretended to consider his options. In reality, he had only one.

The truth.

He refused to play games, to lead Bri on, to pretend that there could ever be anything between them.

"Briony?" He eased her away, his heart wrenching the rapturous glow on her face. "I need to talk to you."

"Talk?" She leaned back, her arms clasped behind his neck. "You kiss me like that and then you want to talk?"

"We have to." He removed his hands, then gently led her toward a bench that sat sheltered under the drooping shelter of a weeping birch tree. "Here. Sit down."

"All right."

Slowly, her natural reserve reasserted itself. Perversely, Ty was glad. She'd need that calm reserve in a minute. He sat down on the other end of the bench and placed his hand over hers where they lay clasped in her lap.

"I shouldn't have kissed you, Briony."

"Why not?" She frowned, her eyes darkening. "Is it because of your wife?"

"In a way." He searched for a way to tell her. "But it's more that I have no right to kiss you."

"I understand. You loved her too much. Kissing me is like a betrayal." She drew her hands away, hid them under the folds of her skirt. "I'm sorry."

His heart contracted at the pain in her eyes.

"I did love Andrea," he admitted. "Perhaps not the way you mean, exactly, but in my own way I cared deeply for her."

"You don't have to go on. I've said I understand." She would have stood then, but he stopped her with one hand on her arm.

"You don't understand, Briony. But I'd like you to." He waited until she subsided, fully aware that she now sat as far from him as possible. Time to tell the truth.

"Andrea had problems. To compensate, she made herself a dreamworld and she made me a part of it. She wanted children. She would be their mother, love them, care for them, do all the things her own mother never did. She was going to be different. She pulled herself out of her depression with a huge effort, and we got married."

He sensed that it hurt her to hear this. And why not? It hurt him to rehash this sad story. He plodded on.

"In the beginning we were very happy. I loved my work and Andrea was busy fixing the house. It didn't dawn on me, at first, that anything was wrong. I was a fool!"

She laid a hand on his arm. "Don't blame yourself, Ty."

"It was my fault."

She simply shook her head. "Go on."

"Every month she'd be so full of hope. And every month those hopes would be dashed when she learned she wasn't pregnant." Ty's face burned with shame. Was it right to tell her all this? But how else would Briony understand his determination never to marry again?

"It was like living on a roller coaster," he whispered, as all the old ache and regret he'd thought long buried swept back over him. "High hope, then crashing disappointment. She was devastated each time it happened."

"As were you."

He nodded slowly. "Yes, I guess I was. I'd always wanted kids. I agreed to see a specialist, agreed to have tests, agreed to try whatever they suggested." He stopped, searched for an appropriate way to explain.

"When our last hope was gone, we crashed for a while and tried to move on with our lives. Then Andrea decided we should adopt."

"You didn't want to?"

He looked at her, saw the commiseration and empathy in her eyes. The words poured out of their own volition.

"I just wanted to get off the roller coaster. I compensated with work, lots of it. I know that didn't help her, but I couldn't stand to see her immobilized by the horrible world of pain she suffered. I couldn't stand to watch the love in her eyes die, to see the blame she tried to mask."

"Why should she blame you? You both wanted children."

"It was my fault. I'm the one who made it impossible for my wife to be the mother she'd always dreamed of. Do you understand, Briony? I killed her dreams because I can never be a father."

"Oh, Ty." Her arms came around him then as she scooted across the bench to hold him. "I'm so sorry."

Ty let himself revel in her compassion for just one precious moment. Then he carefully drew away.

"We filled out all the papers for adoption, only to learn that it could take up to five years. Andrea begged me to take her overseas, to adopt a child from one of those countries you hear so much about." Ty raked a hand through his hair.

"I wouldn't do it. I couldn't! She had so many problems already. How would she deal with a foreign child who couldn't immediately do and say all the things she'd dreamed about? She was so fragile, emotionally drained, living on the edge." He shook his head. "Even if we could have afforded it, I couldn't take the chance."

"What did you do?"

He knew she knew. He could hear it in her voice.

"I buried myself in work. I got her the best help I could, made sure she went to every appointment, watched her take her medication. And I prayed. Desperately. I begged God to help." The shame of it still ate at him.

"I wanted out, Briony. I wanted to forget it all. Failing that, I just wanted her to be happy, to make the best of what we had. If an adoption worked out, okay. If not, we had each other." He almost laughed at the stupidity of those dreams.

"Andrea was furious, said I'd never cared about what she needed. We argued constantly. Then I had to leave for the fire."

"And she found Bridget."

"I guess." Ty clasped his head in his hands. "We'd spent every dime we had trying to get a baby, and we were left scrounging. Nothing was the way I wanted. I took every overtime shift I could to get the bills paid off. I was bitter that we'd spent so much and gotten nothing." He swallowed. "I hated God for doing that to us."

"Ty!"

"I did. In a way, I still do." He implored her to understand. "He's the God of everything, Briony. He could have eased her through it all without the loathing and pain. He could have given her a child—sent us a baby."

"He did." Briony's tears fell unashamed onto her cheeks. "He sent you Cristine."

Ty shook his head, fury burning in the depths of his heart. The anger and bitterness had never died. It welled up now with a fierceness that grabbed him and hung on.

"God didn't send Cristine," he told her. "Andrea went out and found Cristine. Do you think they would have met if Andrea hadn't been so actively seeking a child?"

He could hardly bear to think it even now. All that time she'd kept it a secret from him, kept Cristine's true identity and parenthood a secret that he should have shared. Why? Revenge?

Ty couldn't deal with that now. He shoved it away.

"God did nothing, Briony. Nothing!" The words spilled out in an angry tirade. "He let us hang there for years, vainly hoping. And I've spent another year-and-a-half wondering if Cristine would be ripped out of my arms. Is that love?"

He glared at her, willing her to understand. His fingers closed about her arm in a tight grip.

But Briony didn't flinch, didn't look away. Her blue eyes stared calmly into his, her face wet with tears.

"Yes, Ty. That is love. God's love. I don't understand why it had to be like that, I don't understand why He didn't alter the circumstances, but He had a reason."

Ty knew his face reflected his disgust at her answer. He didn't even try to mask it. Just this once he wanted it out, all of it. He wanted someone else to understand how betrayed he felt by the God he'd trusted day after day for most of his adult life.

But not anymore. He would never hope again.

"Some love! And was it also this divine love that took Andrea after she'd had only six weeks with the child she'd always wanted? Was that an expression of this *godly love?*"

She nodded, eyes never leaving his. "Yes, Ty."

His lips twisted at her quiet response. "Well, I don't want that kind of love, do you hear me? I don't need some kind of judge standing over me, ready to snatch away anything I set my heart on." His fists clenched uselessly as anger surged through him.

Bri's soft voice shattered the hate. "Do you think you can stop God from doing His will by refusing to accept it?" She smiled gently. "It won't work, my dear."

He wondered at the endearment, but didn't stop to question it. "Then I don't want any part of Him."

"What do you want, Ty?"

The words threw him. He knew she wasn't blaming, wasn't trying to convince him. Maybe she didn't understand.

"Look, I know I didn't handle things well. I know I messed up and disappointed Andrea when I should have been there for her. If I could change it, I would. But I can't."

"So you're going to press on to the future and hope you manage better next time?"

She didn't understand. He'd have to lay it out plainly. "There won't be a next time, Bri. I'll never marry again. I won't watch another woman go through what Andrea did, hoping maybe God will relent, believing things will be different." Ty shook his head. "I won't take that chance again." He clenched his jaw, stemming the rest of his bitter tirade. Briony didn't deserve it. "I'll raise Cristine and be happy with that."

She studied him, amazement pleating her smooth forehead. "Do you realize what you're saying, Ty? You're telling God that if He won't play by your rules, you won't play with Him!"

He sat silent, refusing to debate the issue.

"You can't do it, Ty. God is in control, not you. He's not going to apologize for running His world the way He wants it run. He's the boss, He's *God!* You're not. Just because you decide He was wrong doesn't change the facts. He wants you, He loves you. He has the best in store for you. What you do with that is up to you."

Ty got up and paced, his mind racing over what she'd said. "When you put it that way, it sounds childish," he muttered in disgust.

"It is childish!" Bri grinned at his sour look. "But we're His children. I guess we're entitled to act like it once in a while."

He couldn't let her brush it off so easily. "I don't accept that, Briony. He didn't have to let it happen. He could have stopped it, all of it."

She rose slowly, the white gossamer fabric floating around her as she stood in front of him. Her blue eyes glowed with an inner fire.

"If God had changed it, I'd never have met you," she whispered as her fingers drifted over his cheek. "I'd never have known how wonderful Cristine was, I'd never have understood my sister, I'd never have fallen in love with you."

"No!" Ty reared back, aghast at her words.

"Yes, it's true. I only realized it myself tonight. I had no intention of telling you because I was afraid."

He frowned. Afraid? "Of me?"

"Of your using me. Of being nothing more than a convenient caregiver for Cristine. Of letting myself love and then get hurt."

She brushed her fingers through his hair, her touch gently addicting. Ty froze at that soft caress. Bri's gentle fingers said more than any words she might whisper on the night air.

"I believed God didn't want me to know anything about love, Ty. After my fiancé dumped me and I couldn't see his son anymore, I figured God intended for me to devote myself to my career. And I have." She smiled. "Sometimes too much."

"There's nothing wrong with that." He shifted so her hands fell to his shoulders. Just for a minute, Ty let himself relax.

"Actually, I've realized there is. God doesn't do things poorly. He doesn't withhold His blessings to those who love Him."

Her fingers soothed his throbbing head.

"God's ways are perfect and He wants well-rounded people in His kingdom. Locking myself away because I was afraid to get hurt wasn't healthy. Pretending my career met all my needs wasn't, either."

Ty wanted to protest, but something silenced him.

"Can I tell you something? A secret I've never shared

with anyone?" She didn't wait for his nod. "I know it doesn't jibe with my image at all. People think I'm strong and self-sufficient, that I don't notice others."

Her tremulous smile lifted the corners of her generous mouth. "I notice, Ty. I always have. When my friend Blair had to leave school to raise her little boy, I was envious. Her fiancé had taken off, but she had someone who loved her just because she was his mother." A faint smile touched her pale pink lips.

"This was your college roommate?"

She nodded, eyes misty.

"My other roomie, Clarissa, married a man with four kids. I thought she was the luckiest woman in the world to have her house full of people who always needed her for something."

Ty closed his eyes, sucked in a breath for control. Here it was again. The same female need to have a baby. Briony was no different from Andrea, though he ached to pretend otherwise.

If he'd had any doubts about the need to push Briony Green away, they were gone. Things would be the same with Bri. If he took the love she offered, if he dared to care for her, she would end up agonizing just as Andrea had, wasting her life craving for something he couldn't give her.

"You're not listening to me, Ty."

He opened his eyes, stared at his feet, nodded. "Sure I am. You were saying how much having a baby meant to you. Which is exactly why I started out by saying I have no right to kiss you."

"Shut up, Tyrel."

He blinked, caught a glimpse of her face and swallowed.

"It isn't about babies," she hissed, blue eyes spitting sparks. "It isn't about parenthood. It's about being loved. Unconditionally. It's something Cristine offers every time she hugs you or sees me or greets her grandmother. That's what I longed for, that's what my sister found and that's what I want from my life."

Ty needed to get away. He ached to turn tail and run like a coward, but Bri's intense gaze wouldn't permit any backing down. All he could do was stand there.

"I think I've finally figured it out," she whispered, her eyes wide with understanding. "I love you. Next to that, my career comes a distant second."

He opened his mouth, but she forestalled him. "I know you can't or won't love me back. I know you think you're mad at God and you want to tell Him how to manage His world. I know you're scared and hurt and, most of all, angry." She wrapped her arms around his waist and hugged him so tightly he felt it straight through to his heart.

"But that doesn't change a single thing, Tyrel Demens. I still love you."

She leaned back, arms still hugging his waist, eyes sparkling with a joy that would not be suppressed.

"You can't control it. You can't quash it or make it go away, or pretend it isn't there. There's not a single thing you can do to stop me from feeling this way. I love you, Ty Demens. So there!"

Ty unwrapped her arms, set her gently away. He stood and walked to the edge of the water, stared into its tumbling froth.

"It won't work, Briony," he whispered, shaken at the havoc in his mind, his soul. "I can't have anything to do with you."

"Okay."

He turned to stare at her, stunned by her acceptance.

"All these years, Ty, I've never even met anyone I specially liked, let alone fell in love with."

"And?"

She spread her hands wide. "This love, it's a God thing, Ty. He brought me to Banff, He organized Cristine's adoption, He's been in it all along."

"So now what?" Ty wished he could steal some of that hope that glowed in her eyes and claim it as his own. But he couldn't. He was powerless.

"So now I'm going to wait and see what God wants to do with it," she told him with a cheeky grin.

"You'd dump your career, just like that?" He couldn't believe it. "Give it all up, just to be a wife and mother? All those years of work?"

Bri shook her head, tapped one finger against his brow. "Ty, think about it. He's God. I keep telling you, He knows what He's doing." She laughed at his scowl. "God didn't send me to school for all those years so He could ignore me. He's got a plan, He'll work it out. I just have to trust."

Ty stared at her for a long time, trying to wrap his brain around what she said. But he couldn't. The fear, the hurt, the pain—they all crowded out whatever little faith he'd once enjoyed.

Briony made him consider things he had no right to imagine. He didn't want to go back to being that empty man he'd once been—beaten, broken, helpless. He wanted to keep his life on the track he'd set, care for Cristine, get the promotion at work. He wanted to know what tomorrow held.

Pretending he would get what he wanted without striving for it was a pipe dream.

"Come on, it's time to go. We still have to drive home."

Bri followed him from the restaurant without a word. They drove through the city to Giselle's, changed and said their farewells. Then, with a sleeping Cristine firmly belted into her car seat, Ty drove back toward Banff.

Unless directly questioned, Briony remained silent, eyes watchful on the road ahead. Ty turned the radio on, glad for the distraction. But as he caught a glimpse of Briony's serene profile in the flash of lights from an oncoming car, he decided he was glad tomorrow was Saturday.

So many questions boiled in his mind. Maybe she was right, maybe he did need to give God a chance. But the hard lump of hurt had lodged deep in his heart and it was so hard to let go, to see anything other than Andrea's suffering.

He needed a break from Briony's steady assurance and that solid faith in a God he didn't know. Ten more days of watching over Cristine and she'd be gone.

Ty had no idea how he would manage when Briony left, but he'd figure something out. That was the least of his problems. What bothered him most was that maybe she was right, maybe…

Ty groaned silently. If he was to find his way, he'd have to do it without any help. Hadn't it always been that way?

God expected him to manage, and he would.
As he always had.
For Cristine's sake.

Chapter Eleven

"I'm sorry. Did you say immunization?"

Briony pressed the phone tightly against her ear, straining to hear the conversation over Cristine's cantankerous protests.

The voice on the other end explained that Cristine would soon be due for her eighteen-month shot. "She's already behind. She missed her yearly checkup, and we like to keep on top of things."

"I'm just her sitter," Bri explained. "But I'll speak to her father and I'm sure he'll call you back. Can you give me the number again?" She scribbled it down, hung up the phone and glared at Cristine. "I don't like that noise," she told her little charge plainly.

"Neither do I." Ty stood in the doorway, a quirky smile on his handsome face.

Six days later and Briony still couldn't get over it. He was so handsome, so wonderfully kind and gentle. When he wanted to be.

But every day for the past week, he'd also been

guarded, restrained and intent on keeping out of her way. Which wasn't easy. Briony often deliberately brushed his shoulder, touched his cheek, squeezed his hand—whatever it took to keep the contact between them going.

He was softening. She could tell.

"What are you doing home?" she asked, lifting Cristine down from her high chair. "We've just finished snack time."

"*We* have? Or Cristine has?"

"Well, actually Cristine. I don't often eat snacks." She couldn't gauge the glint in his eye. "What's up?"

"I just got my promotion." His ear-splitting grin couldn't be suppressed.

"Ty, that's wonderful." Bri threw her arms around his neck and hugged him enthusiastically. "We should celebrate."

She didn't miss the fact that, just for a second, he hugged her back.

"Up, Da," Cristine demanded, and laughed when her father swung her up in the air.

"I thought we'd take that gondola ride you missed. It's a perfect day. There's not a cloud to mar the view."

"Oh, yes. Gondola ride. Uh-huh. Well, that's an idea. We need some fresh air, don't we, Cristine?" She smiled absently when the little girl flapped her arms and kicked her feet.

Bri searched for another topic, then remembered the telephone call and explained. "I could take her in for the shots if you'd like."

"But the doctor's in Calgary." He frowned.

"I know."

"That's a long drive for one person with a baby. What if something happens?" He shook his head. "I wish I'd changed doctors way back when, but Andrea liked this fellow and I just kept taking Cristine there. They have her whole medical history." He shrugged. "Or, at least, as much as we received."

"Nothing's going to happen, Ty. And if it does, I'll deal with it." She smiled to reassure him, love flooding through her as she watched him cradle Cristine. "Try to trust just a little bit," she whispered.

He glanced at her, then the baby. Then he nodded. "All right, if you're sure you want to. With the holiday season and tourists flooding the place, I could ask for a day off, but I'm not sure I'd get it. We're all on call now."

"We'll be fine." Bri telephoned and made an appointment for Cristine. "We'll go Friday," she told Ty. "That works out great for me because I'll have some preliminary reports to hand in to Bio-Tek then. It'll be my last day with Cris."

He ignored her reminder. "Reports? On what?" He studied her.

"Oh, a few assessments I've made." She began packing a backpack with Cristine's necessities. She guessed he wouldn't give up on the gondola idea. "I went out hiking again last weekend."

"Alone?"

She nodded. "Of course. Overnight this time. It was great." She gasped when his fingers closed around her arm. His face was white, taut with strain.

"Don't do it again," he ordered.

"Ty—"

"We've had three more bear scares, Briony. You should be traveling in a group. Don't camp alone."

"All right." She felt a shiver of pleasure. He cared! She knew he did, no matter how much he pretended he didn't. "I won't promise to not go, but if I do, I'll phone and tell you first. Fair enough?"

His eyes blazed, but before he could answer the phone rang. He grabbed it. "Hello."

Briony went back to her packing, oblivious to the conversation as she mused on Ty's response.

Please God, keep working on him. He'll come to trust, I know it.

The wonder filled her soul with a glow that would not be quenched.

I love him, God.

"Briony?"

At the touch on her arm, she glanced up.

"It's the minister from that church—First Avenue Fellowship." Ty thrust out the receiver.

Briony felt a flutter of hope grow inside her. *More answers, Lord?*

"Hello, Mr. Winter. Yes, I remember your group." She listened, her heart racing. "Thank you so much for calling. Yes, I certainly will. God bless you, too, sir. Thanks again." She hung up, her fingers clutching the phone number he'd given her.

"Are you going to share whatever is making you stare off into space like that?"

Ty's droll tone penetrated her musing. Briony blinked, focused, then spilled the news.

"One of his group members knew Bridget. This person doesn't mind talking to me, since I'm her sister. She'll be available tonight."

Ty's forehead furrowed. "What more is there to talk about? We already know Cristine's father is dead."

She knew what he was doing, could see it in his eyes. He wanted to avoid the issue, pretend everything was fine. Bri understood that, but she couldn't go along with it. Too many questions lingered in the back of her mind, too many unresolved details. She had to know.

"Maybe it's nothing. Maybe it's something. Either way, I intend to talk to her." She finished stocking the backpack and set it by the door, her mind made up.

"I thought you knew enough. I thought you were prepared to let it go. At last."

The hurt she glimpsed in his eyes almost undid her resolve. But thoughts of Bridget's diary, the heartfelt writing Bri had poured over last night, would not go away.

Briony laid a hand on his arm.

"Try to understand, Ty," she begged. "Bridget loved her baby. I'm positive of that. She knew Peter wasn't coming back and she still wanted the baby. Then one day it all changed and she went searching for adoptive parents. I have to know what made the difference."

"Why?" His eyes were penetrating. "Why hash it through again? She did it, isn't that enough? Why do you have to go snooping through the past?"

Tears pooled in her eyes.

"I'm not deliberately trying to hurt you, Ty. And I would never dream of taking Cristine away. Do you believe me? Will you trust me, about that, at least?" She held his gaze, willing him to see her heart.

At last he nodded. Bri sighed with relief.

"Okay, then. Try to understand. This is my last chance to do something for my sister. I'll be gone soon. I'll be wrapped up in work with no time to go back and reconsider. Before that happens, I want all the information on the table, I want to know every detail." She saw him swallow and knew it was time to beard the lion. "If you were honest with yourself, you'd admit you want to know, too."

He simply stood there, staring at her.

"You're afraid, Ty," she whispered, heart aching to comfort him. "I understand your worry and your fear. But that might be stopping you from gaining some piece of vital information that could help Cristine. Isn't it better to know?"

His lips pinched in a tight line of frustration. "I'm trying to believe what you say. I'm trying to believe God wouldn't kick me when I'm down. But you're asking me to trust blindly, to close my eyes and free-fall."

She watched the hesitation crowd out the fragile thread of trust that had almost surfaced.

"I'm not sure I can do that."

"Oh, Ty, God didn't kick you. He *blessed you* with Cristine! For whatever reason, however He worked it, He sent you a gorgeous daughter. Isn't that proof of His love?"

He didn't answer. Bri knew she had to leave it alone, let God handle it, in his time. Very well, she wouldn't push. But neither would she stop questioning. Surely God had sent her here for just this purpose.

"I guess I'm as ready as I can be, if you are."

He nodded his head once, shook it, then threw up both his hands.

"Yes, I'm ready. No, I'm not! I'll change first. It won't take a minute." He glanced at her light shirt and shook his head. "You need a warm jacket. It's cold up there. And bring a camera. The view is unbeatable."

In fact it took him several minutes, but that gave Briony time to shuffle her sister's diary into her briefcase and snuggle it into a corner of her car where Ty wouldn't be bothered by it.

First, Briony had to go back to the bed-and-breakfast for a warm sweater. Then Ty remembered his video camera, and they trekked back to his place for that.

They didn't leave town until well after six due to the congratulatory phone calls of the other park rangers who teased Ty about his promotion.

"We're later than expected, but at least your mood has improved," Bri teased, as he drove them up the hill through town to the parking lot. She wished the butterflies in her stomach would stop tap dancing.

"They're a nice bunch of guys. It's good to feel like I'm pulling my weight again." He snagged the spot nearest the building and turned to face her. "That's due to you, Briony. If you hadn't come along when you did—"

"God would have sent someone else." She grinned at him cheekily, then climbed out of the Jeep and unfastened Cristine's belt. "Come on, sweetie. We're going way up there." She pointed up the treed slope. "And I hope I don't get dizzy and do something embarrassing."

"Up!" Cristine pointed up the mountain, her eyes shining with excitement.

"That's right, baby. We're going way up there." Briony laughed when Cristine slid her chubby fingers into hers and Ty's. The child frowned at them both.

"What do you want, sweetie?"

"Up!"

They swung her high between them, sharing a smile as Cristine giggled delightedly.

"Up! Up." They kept swinging her until they reached the lower terminal.

"Great! No lineup. We timed this right."

Ty rushed to purchase tickets, while Briony nervously watched another car swing into the terminal.

"Oh, boy," she whispered to Cristine. "I think your auntie needs her head examined."

"Okay, let's go." Ty shepherded them over to the loading area, grinning with delight as the three of them clambered into the gondola car. "We'll climb for eight minutes to the top of Sulphur Mountain, a distance of 2,292 feet. It's a steep track, over five thousand feet long."

"Uh-huh." Bri gulped, then deliberately chose the seat facing the mountain.

As they swung around the cable and left the security of the terminal, the car swayed in a light breeze. Briony sucked in a deep breath and prayed as hard as she could.

"Why don't we switch places?" Ty motioned behind her. "You can't see the panoramic view from there."

"Oh, no! I mean, this is fine," she hissed, her lips pinched together as the gondola dangled in midair, slowly gaining height.

Ty made a motion as if to stand. Bri thrust out her hand. "No! Just stay there. I'm fine. I can see just fine."

He raised his eyebrows. "You've turned a peculiar shade of green," he told her, tongue lodged firmly in one cheek. "Is that normal?"

"Only when I don't have my feet firmly on the ground." Her fingers gripped the seat edge as Cristine danced on the seat beside her, stretching to see everything. Her motion set the car in a rhythmic sway that did strange things to Bri's stomach.

Ty studied Briony's face for a moment longer, then took his daughter and held her so she could see out the windows. "There you go, pumpkin. You can see just fine from here."

"Bee!" Cristine's face crumpled in angry mutiny.

Ty shook his head, his hold tight on her wiggling body.

"Nope. Bee needs some space." He began pointing out the no-doubt fantastic view of the Bow Valley, the peaks of the famous Banff Springs Hotel—anything that would distract Cristine.

Bri kept her eyes front and center. If she bent just a little, peeked out the very top of the window, she could see the treetops falling away underneath them. She made herself relax, inhale, and appreciate the beauty of the forest pressing toward them.

"Oh!" She grabbed the seat again and held on for dear life. "What was that?"

"Just a tower." His eyes darkened in concern. "It bumps a little when we go over some of the supports. Are you all right?"

"No." She took air into her lungs, then grinned. "But I

will be. I can see the building." Relief shot through her veins. Soon, please God, her feet would be on solid granite.

"I'm glad you're enjoying it," he commented dryly.

"Oh, I really am." She forced a smile, back teeth clenched tight.

"I can see that." A mocking grin twisted his lips. "You're supposed to glance at the view once or twice, Briony."

"Oh, I will. Later. When I get off this glass-and-metal toy car and stand on a firm foundation."

Bri squeezed her eyes closed for a minute, and held her breath as the car swung up onto the metal support system and into the summit building. Only when they'd finally come to a stop and the attendant had pulled open the door did she exhale.

Ty lifted out Cristine, then held out a hand for Bri, watching as she gingerly stepped onto the cement walkway.

"We could have hiked up, if you'd told me you were afraid of heights," he muttered as he guided them into the visitor complex. "It's primarily switchbacks, but your feet never leave the earth."

"I am not afraid of heights."

He held the door to the outside deck open, his expression carefully blank.

"I enjoyed it." Bri thrust her chin out. "Well, most of it."

He burst out laughing at her grim insistence. "Oh, Briony. Your nose is growing." He shook his head. "What you really enjoyed was getting *out* of the gondola. Admit it."

But Bri was too busy staring over the railing, gaping at the spectacular scene below. "It's gorgeous," she whispered, awe filling her soul. "God has the best view of all."

She felt Ty's eyes on her, but couldn't look away from the vista below. "It's like that old hymn about Mount Pisgah's lofty heights. Look, Ty!" She grabbed his arm, the one that wasn't holding Cristine. "It's like being on top of the world. Those purple-blue mountains seem like a dream. Oh, my, look how the snow glistens such a blazing white on the jagged edges. And the water—did you ever see such turquoise water?"

She couldn't stop gawking.

"I never knew a scientist could wax so poetic." He waited a few minutes, then took her hand and led her toward a metal gate. "Come on, we can hike to Sanson's Peak. It's an old weather station building that's been restored."

Bri exchanged "ohs" with Cristine as they laughed at the mountain sheep that came to explore them during the climb up the steep path in the crisp, cold air.

"I'm glad you told me to bring this sweater," she mumbled as her feet sought a grip among the crumbling bits of granite that littered the trail.

"You're lucky there's no real wind. It can be icy, even in the middle of July."

At last they made it to the hut, where Bri endured Ty's usual photo opportunity. Bri posed the two of them and took a few snaps with her own camera. She had just climbed down off her perch, thanks to Ty's helping hand, when someone tapped her on the shoulder.

"Why don't you go stand with your husband and

daughter? I'll take a family picture for you." A woman wearing a toque and mitts smiled generously, her eyes admiring Cristine's blond good looks.

"I'm not—"

"That's a good idea." Ty slipped Bri's camera from around her neck and handed it to the woman. "Where do you think would be a good place?"

Bri couldn't understand what he was doing, why he was pretending that they were a couple, a family, when it wasn't true. Given the number of curious tourists constantly passing them, she had no intention of creating a scene. She simply followed his lead. But her mind swirled with questions.

The woman organized them so that Ty stood behind Briony, his arm around her waist. Cristine stood on the rock beside Bri, her cheeks pink, eyes shining.

"What a gorgeous family!"

Bri heard the comment as a group meandered past them. Her heart clenched at the words. She could no more stop herself from glancing up at Ty than she could stop breathing.

To her amazement, Ty stared back at her, eyes alight with emotions Bri could only guess at. But somewhere underneath, she knew there was love, knew that he cared for her, even though he would never allow himself to say the words.

Oh, Lord, help.

"That's going to make a lovely photo." The woman handed back Bri's camera. "It would make a perfect Christmas card, the two of you gazing into each other's eyes, your daughter clasping her hands like that."

Bri glanced down. Cristine stood beaming up at her, chubby palms together.

"Thank you very much." Ty's voice came out hoarse.

"Oh, you're more than welcome." She beamed a happy smile, stepped back and grabbed her husband's hand. "Do you remember when we were all starry-eyed like them?" She giggled and gave a coy smile as they strolled back to the visitor's center.

"Up." Cristine held up her arm, demanding her father carry her.

"There's a restaurant here. You can sit by the window and look into the valley while you're eating." Ty stared down at Briony, his dark eyes brooding. "We could eat there, unless you're in a rush to get back home."

"I'd like to share dinner with you," she murmured. "Thank you."

Who knew what God had in store? Bri wasn't going to miss an opportunity to spend a few more hours with Ty, no matter what the reason.

But as she sat across from him in the circular glass terrace, Bri couldn't help wondering at his thoughts. He listened as she said grace for them all, helped Cristine with her soup and ate his own prime rib, all without looking at her.

"Do you come here often?" she asked finally. Someone had to say something!

He shook his head. "Usually just once per season, to watch the mountains change their colors. I don't often work in this area of the park." He kept his eyes down.

"I wish you'd tell me what you're thinking," Briony

burst out, exasperated by his silence. "If I'd wanted to eat without conversation, I could have come here alone."

"I was just thinking." His eyes flew to hers, offering a glimpse of the emotions warring there, before his lids came down to shutter them.

"About what?" She pounced on it like a cat on a mouse.

He shrugged. "Just thinking."

"About those people believing we're a couple?" Her cheeks burned at his startled look. "At how right it felt to pretend, just for a minute, that we really are together? That you care about me as much as I care about you?"

There! She'd said it. Now let him make of it what he would. Bri stabbed her salmon fillet until it lay scattered in flaky pink bits across her plate. She laid her fork down with a sigh, the hunger draining away.

"I do care about you, Briony." The words seemed torn from him.

"Yes, in your own way, I believe you do." Bri held out Cristine's glass so the little girl could take another drink. "The problem is, you won't admit it to yourself." She held his gaze calmly, her face sad.

"I can't love you, don't you understand? It wouldn't work." The words came out harsh, bitter.

"So you've said." She placed her napkin near her plate. "I'm finished, if you want to leave."

"You don't want to see the sunset from the observation terrace? It's two floors above this."

She pushed back her chair. "By all means, Tyrel, let us visit the observation deck." She looped her camera and her purse around her neck, wiped down Cristine and gathered the little girl into her arms.

"Let's stop by the gift shop, too, and get a souvenir so I can remember my time in Banff. Let's pretend everything is just wonderful."

She turned her back and walked out, hugging Cristine tightly. They spent a few minutes freshening up in the bathroom, then Bri walked back outside. Ty stood waiting for them.

"I'll take her."

Bri turned away. "She's fine. You lead the way."

He sighed, pulled open a door and motioned to the steps. "It's quite a climb."

"Fortunately, I'm not quite dead." She couldn't stop the sarcasm from spilling out.

Hot tears poised, ready to tumble down her cheeks, but Bri gulped them back, stomping up the stairs as if they were the enemy. She ignored Ty as she stepped past him and through the door.

The freshened wind pummeled them as it whistled around the deck, dragging at their clothes, carrying away Ty's comments.

"Pardon?" When he didn't respond, Bri handed him Cristine, who snuggled tightly against his chest for warmth. "If you want to go back, go. I'm going to stay here for a few minutes."

As she walked away from him, the icy wind tore through her thin sweater, biting her skin with the same bitter disregard she attributed to Ty.

"Why, God? Why can't he love me?" Once she knew she was alone, Bri let the tears flow. "Why does the past have to be so important?"

I can never be a father.

The words echoed in her head. She stared out over the verdant valleys with their thick forests and stunning water, and asked herself the question that had hidden in the back of her mind ever since he'd told her the truth.

Even if the impossible happened and Ty somehow agreed to marry her, she would never have a child of her own, never know the thrill of carrying a baby inside her body as Bridget had. She would never know the pains of labor, never feel a tiny mouth nurse at her breast, never watch for the first step.

"It was only ever the slimmest of dreams, anyway," she whispered as the sun drooped down ever lower, nearing the craggy precipices. "I didn't really expect to be a mother any more than I expected to climb those mountains. It was just a dream."

But loving Ty means that dream is dead. It can't happen.

She swallowed as the truth rolled over her in cold waves of implacable fact. Maybe there were treatments available, but even if it were possible, she could never ask Ty to submit to that. She'd seen his face as he talked about the fertility clinic, knew how emasculated he'd felt. He would only end up hating her if she asked him to go through it all again.

"Okay, no baby."

She let the tears flow unchecked as the dream slowly died. The sun slipped a notch in the sky, nearing the rocky horizon. Peace stole upon her in a quiet calm.

"All right, Father. I'll never be a mother. I can learn to live with that. But how can I learn to live without him?"

"Briony?" Ty stood behind her. His hands rested on

her waist as he turned her to face him. Cristine sat at his feet, content, for now, to peer through the iron bars.

"Why are you crying?" he whispered, one finger smoothing the tears from her cheeks. "I'm sorry. I didn't mean to make you cry."

She stared up at him, unafraid to let him see all the love that welled up inside. "I love you, Ty. I've never loved anyone like I love you. How can you just ignore that?"

His arms tightened around her, drew her into the warmth of his embrace. "I can't ignore it," he whispered, his lips against her ear. "But I can't accept it, either."

"Why? Just tell me why." It was a cry from the heart. "Do you hate me?"

"God, no!" His mouth pressed against hers in a kiss of desperation, telling her far more than words could ever do.

Bri poured her soul into that kiss. As she did, she begged heaven for help.

"I can't do this to you." Ty drew away suddenly, bent to gather up Cristine, then nestled her in the space between their two bodies, his arm hugging Bri into the circle. Cristine heaved a sigh, laid her head on his chest and closed her eyes.

Bri brushed a curl off the sweet face. "You're not doing anything to me," she whispered. "I love you. And I love Cristine." She dared him to refute it.

"But you've got plans, a career. Your life is ahead of you." He shook his head. "I have nothing to offer."

She tilted up his chin with one finger. "You have the only thing I want," she whispered. "I can change my career, adapt, move."

"How?"

"I don't know! It's a detail, Ty, it can be handled. It was something I pursued so single-mindedly because I had nothing else. It filled a hole I wasn't willing to admit existed. Don't you understand?"

"No." He met her stare. "You spent years pushing for that goal. Are you suddenly going to throw it away, because of me?" He shook his head. "I don't want to be responsible for that."

"You're not." Bri glared at him. "I'm not throwing anything away. I am a scientist. That isn't going to change." She let her fingers slip beneath his collar, cradled the back of his neck.

"I can work anywhere, Ty. As long as the equipment is there, I'll manage."

"But—"

"The only thing I can't do is reorganize my life so I don't love you. It's here—" she pointed to her heart "—inside me. Part of me. If I wanted to, I couldn't tear it out without tearing out a part of myself."

The wind shifted, brushing past them as if to isolate them in their own little world. Ty stared down at her.

"You tempt me," he whispered as his fingers brushed the golden strands off her face. "This afternoon, when that woman said we were a great family, I wanted to grab that and hang on for all I was worth. I wanted to make the dream reality."

"So why don't you?" she coaxed. "Why can't you accept that I love you and Cristine, that I want to be part of your lives?"

One finger traced her bottom lip.

"You'll always be part of our lives, Briony." He

rested his chin on Cristine's head. "But I can't let you give up your whole life for something that could change at any moment."

She frowned. "What are you talking about?"

"I have this terrible fear, Briony. Apprehension, terror. Call it whatever you will." He bowed his head, his forehead pressing against hers. "For a very long time I've tried to pretend that Cristine's adoption was perfectly ordinary."

His daughter shifted in his arms. He glanced down, his face glowing with tenderness and love that Bri could see included her, too.

When Ty finally spoke, one lonely tear hung suspended from the end of his long dark lashes. "The truth is, I fell in love with Cristine that very first day. I refused to believe there was anything wrong, anything strange in Andrea's sudden silences or the way she avoided answering me."

"Oh, Ty." Love squeezed her heart.

"When Andrea died, the fear multiplied. I ignored the truth about Andrea, pretended everything was all right when it wasn't. Then she died. In the back of my mind, I always wondered when God would make me face the reality about Cristine." He took a deep breath.

"That's why I don't want you to contact that woman from the fellowship group, that's why I didn't want to ever find Cristine's biological father, and that's why I can't let myself love you." The white lines radiating around his mouth testified to his dread.

"I always lose the thing that matters most, Briony. It's only a question of when. Losing Cristine will be hard

Chapter Twelve

Ty stonewalled that dreaded phone call with every possible means he could find to delay the truth.

But once Cristine had been bathed and put to bed, once he'd re-tidied the immaculate kitchen Briony always left, once he'd brewed a pot of coffee and poured some for both of them, there was nothing more to do.

"You might as well go ahead and call her."

And thus Ty gave Briony permission to start the nightmare he knew would end in grief.

He sat in his living room with his hands clasped between his knees, watching as Briony punched in the number. His senses screamed at him, ordering him to get out while he could, to refuse to let her call, to send her away. His mind told him he was a fool to dance so close to the edge. His heart told him that the truth would come out eventually.

It was time to face the music.

If he could have, Ty would have prayed. As it was, he sat numb, cold, immobilized by dread he couldn't explain.

enough, when the time comes. I can't—I won't—let myself fall in love with you, only to lose you, too."

Briony stood there with her arms around him and knew there was nothing she could do, nothing she could say. God would have to handle it.

"I love you, Ty," she whispered, as they stood watching the sun dip behind the mountains in a wash of baby-soft pink. "I'll keep on telling you that until the day that I die, but I think it's something you'll have to trust in."

His shoulders slumped. The tender-soft eyes dulled, lost their chocolate glow. Her heart winced at the haggard fear washing over his beloved face.

"I don't have any faith left, Briony. I'm sorry."

Ty's words were carried away on the wind, their plaintive sound tearing at her insides. She watched him turn and walk away from her, cradling Cristine, the last of his hopes and dreams for the future, against his chest with heartbreaking tenderness.

"Then, I'll have to have enough faith for both of us, my darling," she murmured as she walked to the stairs, climbed down to the main deck and followed him out to the little cars waiting to carry them down the mountain.

But later, as Ty drove them back to his cottage, the foreboding he'd only mentioned followed like a specter.

It was only a matter of time until the truth came out.

And only God could control what happened after that.

Bri switched to the speakerphone. Ty tensed as a woman's voice answered on the fourth ring.

Oh, God, please…

Please what? Make it go away?

"Mrs. King? My name is Briony Green. I believe you knew my sister, Bridget?"

Too late for that now.

Ty sat frozen as Bri explained how she had found the fellowship group, had read her sister's diary, was trying to understand what Bridget had been going through almost two years ago.

"Yes, indeed! I met her just after she learned her boyfriend had died. She was very confused." Mrs. King's confident voice left little room for doubt. "I became quite friendly with her, though I must say, I had no idea Bridget had family. Other than Will, of course. He was her rock and she loved him dearly."

"Will? Oh, Peter. Yes, we've just recently learned about him."

"So tragic when he died. Poor Bridget didn't know what to do. I think that's what drew me to her, made me want to help her. She wanted that baby so desperately, but she knew she couldn't raise it. She'd been told she had a very serious disease. Her pregnancy meant she couldn't seek treatment because the medication would impact the baby." Mrs. King tut-tutted. "Terrible thing. She wanted so badly to believe she would recover, but she was also afraid she wouldn't."

Ty hadn't known about the disease, but it was obvious Briony had. She simply kept plying the woman with questions, her scientist's mind absorbing the facts in neat, precise order.

"You got to know Bridget quite well?"

"As I say, we were friendly for the first few meetings. Four, I think."

"Then what happened?"

Ty closed his eyes.

A sour note crept into Mrs. King's voice. "A woman named Andrea started attending. After the first meeting, those two were like peas in a pod. Then it seemed Bridget wanted to speak only to her. I didn't like to interfere."

Ty wanted to be anywhere but here. He could just imagine his wife's envy of Bridget's pregnancy, her constant hovering, her whispered comments about single mothers. He opened his eyes and faced reality, whatever it might be.

"I'm sorry, I don't understand." Bri frowned at the phone, her eyes moving to Ty. "Why was Andrea there?"

"Something about her nerves, I think. We don't always give exact reasons. It's more just a venue to share if you want." She coughed lightly. "I was having a bit of a rough go myself. Perhaps I didn't always pay a lot of attention to Andrea's ranting. I'm afraid I mostly avoided her."

"I see."

Andrea's ranting. Bri's disappointment touched him all the way across the room. He knew she'd expected more concrete information, something specific.

Ty fumed at his own inadequacy. He couldn't help her now. He hadn't even known Andrea was attending a group.

"My dear, it was obvious to me that Andrea needed

more than we could give. She needed professional care. She had these mood swings. Sometimes you could talk her out of them, sometimes not." Mrs. King sighed.

"Please continue."

"Up, down. Up, down. I felt sorry for the woman's family, I'll tell you. Five minutes after meeting Bridget, *zip,* her mood was sky high! It was very hard to deal with. You never knew when she was going to blow."

"I understand." Bri chewed her bottom lip, her fingers busy scribbling notes on the white pad in front of her. She swung her legs up underneath her and hunkered over the phone. "Do you happen to know when or why Bridget decided to give her baby up for adoption?"

"Of course I know! I remember the afternoon well. Someone mentioned that their daughter was driving them nuts and they were thinking about boarding school." Mrs. King chuckled. "My dear, we all had problems with our kids at that time."

Silence stretched, yawned and finally snapped.

"But our Miss Andrea stood up and said that people who had problems raising children shouldn't be allowed to have them, that they were too self-centered to devote themselves to their children's needs instead of their own pursuits."

"But what about my sister?"

"The very next week Bridget announced that she was going to give her baby up for adoption."

"I see."

Ty leaned forward. Time to clear the air.

"Mrs. King, I'm the person who adopted Bridget's baby. My name is Ty Demens."

"Oh, you're Andrea's husband." Stern disapproval clouded the formerly friendly voice.

"Yes, I am. Did the entire group know that Andrea was to be the baby's new mother?"

"Oh, no. Bridget took me aside one night and told me she was having second thoughts about the adoption. She wondered if Andrea's hus—er, if the baby would have a good home."

Embarrassment and anger raged inside, but Ty choked it down. He *had* to know. "Did she say why?"

Silence.

"Please, Mrs. King, we really need to know. You can be frank." Ty gritted his teeth and waited.

"Well, it was just that from the stories, I guess Bridget wasn't sure how suitable he—you would be. I'd really rather not relate what she said. Everything is supposed to be in confidence, you know."

Bri's commiserating eyes told Ty she knew how much the words stung him. What on earth had Andrea intimated?

"I can reassure you, Mrs. King, that Ty is the best possible father any little girl could ever have."

"Oh." A sigh of relief. "That's all right, then."

"Could you please tell us some of what Andrea said? Specifically?" said Bri.

"Well, it's rather personal."

Ha! Ty stifled the ready response. His character, his personality, his beliefs had been discussed in that room, and she was afraid it was *rather personal?*

"We have to know so that we can understand several things that have happened since. Please tell us." He waited.

"Andrea wanted a family. We all knew that. I gathered that there was some, er, problem. On your part."

He winced at the baldness of it.

"Andrea said you refused to consider any of the new things the doctors can do these days. She said you seemed perfectly happy to go on as things were, but that her heart was breaking to have a baby." The woman's starched tones softened.

"We could see that for ourselves. She doted on children, fawned over several other ladies' wee ones. When she was with them, her moods were gone and she was a different person. That's partly why I agreed to convince Bridget."

"Convince?" Ty sat up straight, every nerve in his body on red alert. "I thought she *wanted* to give up the baby."

"She did. She did! Bridget was just confused. I reminded her that Andrea had a settled home, a marriage that seemed fairly stable. Andrea said you—they'd discussed adoption and that her husband was agreeable, so I convinced Bridget she'd made the right decision."

Bri's quiet voice broke in. "When did this conversation take place, Mrs. King?"

"Oh, we had variations on it several times. But the last time Bridget got really upset was when she was in labor. She kept saying she'd have to see the baby first, hold her, then decide." Mrs. King sniffed. "Well, I just didn't see the sense in her fussing over that while she was dealing with labor pains. Besides, everything had already been arranged."

"Arranged?" Ty couldn't believe what he was hearing.

"Why, yes. Andrea had the papers all drawn up ahead

of time. In fact, I believe you'd signed them that very morning. I witnessed the signatures of the others. Andrea said everything had to be signed and sealed, a done deal, or her husband wouldn't allow it. I thought it a mite callous to rush everything through like that, but Andrea was so desperate."

She didn't say anything for a minute, as if only then realizing to whom she was speaking.

"Go on." Ty didn't know how he choked the words out. Anger burned inside with a deep, penetrating grief. Why had Andrea done it? Why?

"You have no idea how nervous I was when they left for Calgary that afternoon. Mercy, the poor girl was already in labor! I could only hope and pray they made it safely."

"Why didn't my sister have the baby here?" Briony's pale face looked lost, forlorn. Ty watched her fingers snap the pencil she held into two pieces.

"Oh, honey, Banff is far too small for that. Everyone would know about it, wouldn't they." She tut-tutted. "No, it was better to be in Calgary. If anything happened, the facilities were right there. Besides, Andrea had a nice little hotel room all arranged for Bridget after she got out of the hospital."

Ty cast his mind back, remembering the credit card statements he'd questioned and Andrea's glib answer that she'd had to be near the lawyer's office while the adoption process was negotiated. A sour taste filled his mouth.

"She was such a smart woman, so organized." Admiration shone through her words. "Do you know, Andrea even phoned the hotel and told them Bridget had been rushed to the hospital and wouldn't be in to work for three weeks?"

"No, I didn't know that." Bri's voice barely carried. Her face shone wet with tears.

Ty couldn't stand it any longer; he got up and moved to sit beside Briony. He wrapped his arm around her shoulder and hugged her close, wishing he could take away some of the pain she must be feeling.

"They named her Cristine. That was the one thing Bridget insisted on. We never knew why—she never said." A soft sigh washed over the line. "She was such a darling child, so pretty. Newborns often aren't, you know."

Ty swallowed the bile that rose in his throat. "You— saw the new baby?"

"Of course. The very night she was born. Andrea insisted the child spend her first night in her very own home. The doctors found nothing wrong, and besides, there was an awful pileup from that snowstorm the day before. Remember? They needed every bed."

Briony's hands were icy cold as they grabbed at Ty, her face a stark gray-white.

"Did Bridget ever see her baby?" she whispered, her fingers clutching Ty's. "Did she get to hold her at least once?"

"Oh, yes. They'd agreed that Bridget could hold the child after she gave birth. But that was the only time."

"And my sister was happy with that?"

Ty's heart ached for the pain in her voice, shadowing her eyes. It hurt to know he'd been a part of it.

"Why, I believe so, dear. She made the deal, after all."

The careless words bit at Ty. "Did she know that she

had a period of grace? That she could change her mind if she wanted?"

"I don't know." Mrs. King's voice came across the line less assured now. "Andrea dropped out of our group after that. Well, she had to, with the baby and all. And, of course, Bridget never came back. She transferred out of the hotel a short time later, I understood."

His mind screamed. Why had God done this? Why such misery, such pain?

"And you never saw her again?" Ty had to ask it, had to force out the question he knew Briony longed to ask, but to which she couldn't bear to hear the answer.

"I didn't see Andrea again. Someone told me she'd passed away. But now that you mention it, I did see Bridget again. I'd almost forgotten." Mrs. King's voice softened. "The end of that summer, as I recall. She was standing at the corner of Bear Street."

"Doing what?"

"Nothing. Just standing there. Staring at a house. Then she turned around and left. That's the last time I saw her."

Briony gulped, then nodded, her face awash with tears. "Thank you, Mrs. King. Thanks for all your help."

"I'm sure you're welcome as can be. I hope I haven't said anything out of turn."

"Don't worry about it." Ty added his thanks, then punched the speaker button off with a vicious jab. "I should have known," he groaned. He jumped to his feet and paced the room, filled with impotent rage that would not be quieted.

He couldn't stand to watch the grief and loss overwhelm Briony, couldn't bear to see the agony tear her apart. Neither could he bear to face the truth.

"I'm not her father," he whispered at last, staring at Briony as he admitted the truth. "She was never mine. Andrea committed a terrible sin by taking her."

He flopped into his chair, head in his hands. "I should have known. I should have guessed that's why she was so secretive. Why didn't I question her more, demand to know all the answers? Why didn't I force the issue?"

"It wouldn't have mattered. Bridget knew what she was doing." Bri's voice sounded ragged, distorted. "I'm certain she did what she felt best."

He jerked his head up, glared at her. "After having just given birth?" he demanded, shocked that even now she refused to lay blame. "You really believe she understood that she would never see her child again when my wife ripped her baby out of her arms and carried Cristine away?" He snorted in disgust.

"Ty, we don't know exactly what happened."

He shook his head, eyes bitter as he watched the tears form white tracks down her cheeks.

"I know, Briony. I know exactly what my wife would have done under those circumstances, given the slimmest chance for adoption." He groaned, only then assimilating the whole truth.

"And I was a party to it. I let it go because I was too cowardly to demand answers."

Every bone, every muscle, every nerve in his body ached as the truth washed over him in a tidal wave of pain. God was stripping away the last thing he cared about—his beloved child.

He'd lost it all—Cristine had never really been his.

"She's not my daughter," he whispered, speaking the truth he'd always sensed deep inside. "What Andrea did, what she coerced your sister into doing, was terribly wrong. Cristine should have been your child, Briony. You should be raising her. Not me."

Briony's blond head lifted. Her eyes widened, darkened as she stared at him. "What?"

"You have to take her, Briony. I have no right to deprive you of that child. She isn't mine. She never really was. My life with her is based on trickery and deceit. She should never have borne my name. I just got to look after her for a while."

"Ty, no!" Bri couldn't believe what she was hearing. She surged to her feet, her fists clenched at her sides.

"You listen to me, Tyrel Demens, and you listen hard." She squatted in front of him, her face mere inches from his. "Don't you tell me Cristine's being here is a lie. Don't you dare say it's a mistake!"

She picked up his hand and held it tightly between hers. "Maybe it didn't happen as we would have liked, but God knew exactly what he was doing. He placed my niece in a home where no one—" she met his gaze head-on, her eyes blazing "—and I do mean *no one* could have loved her more. I believe Bridget knew what she was doing. She believed God's perfect plan was for Cristine to be with you."

"But—"

"There was no mistake, Ty. Not one. I think God led her to Andrea because he knew your love would make up for anything else Cristine lacked in her life."

"I do love her." Ty nodded, his eyes glassy. "That's why I'm turning her over to you. I love Cristine enough to do the right thing for her."

Bri peered up at him. "What do you mean, *the right thing?*"

"You're the person she should be with, Briony. You're strong and courageous, you keep pushing until you find the truth. You don't have any horrible shameful actions in your past. You're open and honest. You'll make Cristine a wonderful mother." His face was closed up like a mask, hiding his emotions.

She stared at him, unable to believe what she was hearing. "What are you saying, Ty? You mean you love me? You want us to be a family?"

His sad eyes shimmered with tears he refused to shed.

"I can't love you, Briony. With every fiber of my being I long to, but it wouldn't work." He smiled gently. "I ruin everything I touch. I get so self-involved, I drive people to do the wrong thing. I've offended God, and he's taking away what I most want."

"That's foolishness, Ty."

He shook his head, his eyes deadly serious. "No, it's the cold hard truth that I've avoided for too long."

"But I told you, I explained—" She stopped when he held up a hand.

"You have a wonderful faith, Briony. Don't let anyone ever spoil that." His voice dropped to a whisper. "I envy you that unfaltering confidence. But it's not for me. It just doesn't work for me."

Tears poured down her face. "It could," she whispered, praying he'd understand.

Ty shook his head. "No," he said. "You're so full of love. Once you let yourself step out of the cocoon you build around yourself, you'll find yourself longing to share that love with a family." He squeezed his eyes closed.

"I can't give you children, Briony. No matter how much I want to, it's not possible. God knows, if I could I would do anything to alter that, but it will never change. And I won't make the same mistake twice."

"What mistake? Andrea's problems were not your fault, Ty." She prayed as she spoke, begging the Father of all children to heal the hurt she saw shining in Ty's eyes.

"Weren't they?" He shook his head. "You can't erase the guilt, Briony. You can't change the truth. Twice in my life I've ignored someone else's needs and it's cost them dearly. I will not repeat my mistake, especially not with you."

He bent toward her, brushed his lips across her eyelids and smiled. "Please don't cry, my darling. This one unselfish thing I'm doing is for you."

Bri pulled back, worried by the tone of his voice. Desperately she searched his face for answers.

"What, exactly, are you doing, Ty?"

"I'm giving you Cristine." His voice wobbled, broke. He forced a rigid control on himself.

"I don't understand. How can you give me Cristine?" Bri couldn't fathom the funny-sad little smile that touched his lips, couldn't discern the meaning that glimmered in the depths of his dark chocolate eyes.

"Please. Just tell me what you're saying."

He stood then, straightened his shoulders like a soldier preparing for battle. His hands dropped to his sides, his chin thrust upward.

"I'm having the adoption nullified. You will be Cristine's mother. You are the rightful parent."

Bri gasped, horror filling her soul with panic. "No!"

Oh, Father, what have I done? What damage has my poking and probing inflicted?

Tyrel nodded, eyes hard. Cold. "Yes. It's only proper that Cristine be raised as your child. I have no right, no claim to her. I will never be her father."

There was something wrong here, something she didn't understand. Ty's self-blame came from something in the past. Bri knew she had to find out what it was. Sometime. Not now.

Now Briony wanted to rail at him, to scream her denial until he took back what he'd said. Of course he was Cristine's father! How could he ever deny it?

But the outrage blocked her throat, as a strangled cry jangled around the silent room from the baby monitor sitting on a side table.

"Cristine!" Ty spun toward the stairs and raced up the risers three at a time.

Bri followed him, her feet less nimble, her mind still rejecting his words. When she arrived in Cristine's room, the little girl was sitting up in bed coughing desperately, fighting to draw another breath. Ty's big hands tried to soothe her.

"What's the matter?"

He turned tortured eyes toward Bri, the brown orbs brimming with stomach-clenching fear.

"He's taking her away," he whispered, as Cristine gasped beneath his hand. "I told you, I mess up and God takes away everything I love. It's a punishment."

"Stop it!"

Bri knew nothing about medicine, even less about childhood diseases, but she knew God, and she knew He did not punish innocent children for the error of someone else's ways.

With energy born of desperation, she shoved Ty out of the way and assessed the situation. Cristine was choking. Briony didn't know how or why she knew that, she just knew.

"God, please help me now," she whispered, then she swabbed the baby's mouth with a damp washcloth, searching for something, anything that would ease Cristine's breathing.

Ty's whitened face sought reassurance. "Her color's returning a little. Isn't it?"

Briony grabbed a couple of blankets, wrapped them around the beloved body and snatched Cristine into her arms.

"We have to get her to the hospital, Ty."

He stood there, paralyzed by the fear that consumed him.

"I love her so much," he whispered, eyes almost black in his pale face. "But He's taking her, anyway."

"Ty!" She grabbed his arm, jerked it hard. "I'm taking her to the hospital. Either help or get out of the way."

He looked at her dazed, then glanced down as Cristine cried out. She help up her arms, wiggling in Briony's embrace, begging for her daddy to carry her.

"Are you going to abandon your daughter now?" Bri whispered.

Without a word, Ty grabbed the little girl into his arms and left the room. Bri followed him down, joy filling her soul as quickly as the worry.

Okay, God, she prayed silently as she drove the Jeep toward the hospital. *You've got something wonderful planned here. Help me to be a part of it. Whatever it is, whatever it costs, let me help Ty to find you.*

She drove through the town as fast as she dared, weaving in and out of the evening traffic. Ty directed her, and within minutes she was able to pull up at the emergency entrance.

As she followed Ty into the building, Bri's nonstop prayer continued.

I love Ty, you know that. But if I can't have him or Cristine, please take care of them for me. Please show Ty that Your plans don't include taking away everything he loves.

As she dashed into the first cubicle, Briony caught the doctor's low-spoken reaction.

"It might be meningitis."

"Oh, God!"

Her eyes met Ty's.

"Faith," she whispered. "Just a little bit of faith, Ty. Like a grain of sand. Trust him. What have you got to lose?"

"Everything."

Chapter Thirteen

"You'll have to leave. Now. You're only impeding our work." The nurse held the door open, waiting.

Though Ty resisted the tug on his arm, Briony pulled even harder, until, finally, he followed.

"Come on, we'll go out on the patio."

"But Cristine—"

"Is in the best hands she could be in. They'll find us if anything changes."

He followed Bri through the small hospital. When they reached the red-bricked patio, she pressed him down onto a bench, grasped his hands in hers and began praying out loud, pouring her heart out to the only One who could heal the entire mess.

After a while a nurse brought them each a glass of orange juice. The doctors were still working on Cristine. There was no change and no firm diagnosis. Bri slipped out of the room long enough to dial Clarissa's number and ask her to pray.

"It's bad, Clarissa. And it's more than Cristine's illness. Get Blair to pray, too, will you?"

"Of course. Heaven's gates will be flooded, honey."

"Thanks."

"Briony?"

"Yes?"

"Is he the one?"

Bri swallowed, her mind brimming with all the reasons Tyrel Demens believed he couldn't let her into his life. But then the peace of God, the assurance of His love, swept into her heart.

"Yes, Clarissa. He's the one. God willing."

"I believe God's willing, honey. Otherwise He wouldn't have led you there in the first place. Go to him now. I'll get Blair and we'll start praying."

"I love you."

"I know." Clarissa laughed gently, her voice soft with reassurance. "I love you, too, Bri. I still expect to be invited to your wedding."

"From your lips to God's ear." Bri hung up the phone and hurried back to Ty.

He sat staring at the water that spilled quietly into the fountain. His eyes seemed riveted on the flood of light that shone down on a small cement sculpture of a shepherd with a sheep cuddled in his arms.

"It reminds me of Cristine," he whispered, when Bri slipped into the seat beside him. "Only He's doing a better job than I ever could." His fingers knotted.

"Ty, I need some answers." It was time for the whole truth. Bri swallowed and plunged ahead.

"Why do you feel so guilty? Why do you think it's your

fault, that bad things have happened because of something you did? What *two* things were you talking about?"

"Things happened because I didn't measure up. Not ever." The words came out coldly unemotional.

"I don't understand that." She waited patiently, praying as she did.

"I don't want to talk about this."

She took his face in her hands and forced him to see her. "We have to talk about it. Now. Tell me."

After a moment, he nodded.

"Andrea died because of the strain of having Cristine around. She should never have had to deal with that. If I'd been doing my job as her husband, if I'd stuck to my guns and looked after her interests by refusing to consider adoption, she might still be alive."

A derisive smile tugged at his mouth. "But no, I made my own life easier by going along with this adoption, quelled my own conscience when I knew there was something wrong. That's what killed my wife. Me."

Bri thought for a minute. "Andrea might be alive today, but would she have been happy without Cristine in her life?"

He frowned, tilted his head and looked at her.

"She wouldn't, would she? She craved a baby, longed for a child. Cristine must have been everything she dreamed of."

"And a lot more, besides." He shook his head, his eyes straying to the past. "She was up all the time, worried silly that she'd do something wrong. Neither of us slept much, but she hardly slept at all. She said it was her only chance to be a mother and she couldn't miss anything."

"She loved Cristine."

"Uh-huh."

"That's what matters, don't you see?" She laid her palm against his jaw and turned his face toward her. "God doesn't expect perfect people. He expects people who love Him and do their best. He can manage all the rest on His own."

"But I should have—"

She put her finger to his lips. "Answer me honestly, Ty. Did you love Andrea?"

"Yes, but—"

"Good. Do you love Cristine?"

His eyes darkened, his mouth trembled. "Yes."

The firm clear ring of those words gave her courage.

"Do you love me?"

It took him a long time, but he finally exhaled and nodded. "Yes."

Bri couldn't believe he'd said it so casually. "That's it? That's all you're going to say?"

"No." He pulled her into his arms, kissed her, then spoke.

"Sometimes, like today on the mountain, I let myself think what it would be like if we were a family, if I could wake up every morning and see your gorgeous hair spread across the pillow. I daydream about Christmas together, in front of the fire, about Cristine playing with Giselle's new baby." His hands trembled as they touched each feature on her face.

"It's like a mirage, Briony, shimmering in front of me, too beautiful to be true. Just for a moment, for a tiny second, I'm tempted to reach out and grab it."

"And then?"

"Then I realize what kind of a life that would be for you." His hand smoothed her hair. "You once told me your secret desire was for a baby. You couldn't have that with me, Bri. Not ever."

"But—"

It was his turn to silence her, one lean finger stopping the words.

"Listen to me, my darling. Please?"

She nodded.

"At first you'd say it wouldn't matter. You'd put a brave face on, try to compensate in a thousand different ways. But it would eat away at you, you'd start to look around you at other women who were having babies and you'd realize that you'd made a mistake. You'd want out."

Bri shoved him away, fury building inside. "Stop it, Ty!"

"What did I do?" His shocked gaze met her angry one.

Fighting for control, Bri prayed for patience.

"Before you were married, Ty, before you knew you couldn't have children, did you look at every woman you saw and rate her on whether or not she would make a good birthing machine?"

"Of course not." His face reddened, his eyes shone with hurt. "That's horrible."

"Suppose it was me, then. Just suppose I could never have children. Would that stop you from marrying me, from loving me, from caring about me?"

"No." He wrapped his arms around her and hugged her close. "I care for you because of who you are, not because of what you could or couldn't give me. God help me, I love you."

Tears welled in her eyes. "Don't you see? It's the same with me. I love you because you're you, warts and all." She kissed his nose.

"Thousands of people marry and then find out they will never be parents. They marry because they love each other, because they want to be together. That's the prerequisite for marriage. And we've got it because God brought us together."

He hugged her tightly for a minute, then frowned. "But I failed Cristine. Now God will take her away, too." His hands shook as they held her.

"You're making me very angry with this illogical argument," she told him pertly. "Would you please explain how you failed Cristine? Don't you love her?"

"Of course." His eyes glowed.

"Don't you care for her, meet every possible need, give her the very best you can no matter what it costs you?"

"I try."

"Well, then, you and God have something in common because that's exactly what He does for you. Only He does it a lot better."

At last Ty spoke the fear that had lain buried in his heart for too long. "But what if He takes her away from me?"

"My darling Ty, God would only do that for a very, very good reason. And all your fussing and arguing and worrying won't change His plan one iota." She combed her hands through his hair.

"He brought her to you when she needed someone strong who could survive when her mommy died, He blessed you with her bubbly life and joy, He made sure you were the kind of man who didn't think it was foolish to care for a tiny baby when other men were out with the guys."

Bri shook her head, daring him to contradict her. "I love you, Tyrel Demens, but you're making me crazy with this ridiculous fear. God went to great pains to choose a wonderful daddy for Cristine because He loves her even more than you do."

He shifted uncomfortably, but Bri wouldn't let up.

"Are you now telling me God messed up when He picked you? Are you telling me you're not up to the challenge, that you think your plan is better than His?"

"Well, when you put it like that—I guess not." He smiled sheepishly.

"Well, hallelujah! A light at last." She'd pressed this far, but something still eluded her. "Who was the second person you said you let down?"

His face froze.

"I have to know." She sat and waited for him to empty himself of all the pain.

A sigh shuddered through him.

"He was my friend, my partner. We were on a rescue together." The flat hard tone offered the facts in cold, brisk precision. "Some hikers got lost in a blizzard. We were assigned to bring them out."

"And this friend of yours got hurt?" It was beginning to make sense. Bri covered his hand with her own. "Just tell me, okay, Ty?"

"It was rough, really rough. He wanted to go around, take an easier route. I was worried about the hikers suffering from exposure. I insisted we do it my way, march straight in and bring them out. It had to be my way. I knew best. I always know best."

The self-condemnation in his words tugged at Bri's soft heart. How long had he carried this burden?

"What happened?"

"I pushed him too hard. He was tired, needed a break. I said we'd take one when we got across the river." Ty's voice broke, then resumed, rough, intense. "He never made it."

"I'm sorry."

"One minute he was there, telling me to slow down. The next he was slipping away. He fell." He stopped, took a deep breath and continued. "The current was too fast. I couldn't reach him, and he couldn't reach my rope. Three days later they found his body six miles downstream."

"And the hikers?"

"I got them out, all of them. They were fine, no problem. They had enough provisions that they could have lasted at least another day. Certainly, fifteen or twenty minutes of rest time wouldn't have made a difference. I just had to have my own way. I had to be in charge." He turned to look at her.

"When Andrea's depression got worse, I decided I would never push her as I had him. I'd let her find her own solutions, see the doctors she wanted. If she asked, I went. If she didn't, I let her handle it. I figured that later, once she realized there wasn't going to be a baby in our immediate future, she'd settle down, find another interest."

"There was nothing wrong with that."

He smiled sadly. "Wasn't there? I was jealous, Bri. Jealous that a baby would take my place with her. I wanted to be the center of her world, I wanted us to be strong together, like a team. I gave her all the love I had, and it fell short. I didn't do enough."

"She was sick, Ty."

He nodded, his eyes slipping back to focus on the shepherd. "I know. I knew it then, too. But that didn't make it any easier to take. I wouldn't take more tests, pretend it could be changed, trail around to doctor after doctor. I knew it was hopeless and I refused to do things her way. I drove her to it, Briony. Because I was so stubborn, she found a way to get her beloved baby."

Bri didn't know what to say.

"When Andrea died, I realized Cristine was my last chance. I couldn't mess up again, I had to get it right. I think I knew He'd take her, too. I just didn't know when." The lines around his eyes deepened. "I never told another soul, never let anyone even see what I knew. But it was always there, hidden away in a place I wouldn't have to look, to see my own culpability."

"Ty, you were not in control." How could she make him see? "You didn't know how Andrea got Cristine. I'm not sure we know even yet. Maybe that's the way it's supposed to be. Maybe it's a mystery we will only know when we get to heaven."

His lips pinched together. "It isn't enough."

She smiled. "It has to be. I haven't quite finished Bridget's diary, but I've read enough to know that she was all right with her decision. She felt she'd done what God wanted her to do and she was ready to go on to face her illness." The certainty filled her heart, calmed her soul, gave her strength to meet his painful gaze.

"That's exactly what we have to do now. We have to face Cristine's illness with faith and trust that somehow, behind all the mystery and confusion, there is a reason. There is a plan."

Like a tonic, Bri felt God's assurance healing her. "Bridget was led to Banff, led to Andrea. She didn't get hoodwinked, she trusted in her Father and believed He knew what He was doing." She hugged him.

"And boy, did He! Cristine got a loving father, Ty. She got a daddy handpicked from heaven itself."

"But I'm not really—"

She placed a finger across his lips.

"Don't say it again," she told him firmly. "You're demeaning what God planned when you try to change His way. Don't you think the God of the universe could have brought Bridget home to me if He'd wanted me to have Cristine? Don't you think His master mind could have found a way, if that's what He intended?"

Ty frowned, then slowly nodded. "Maybe. I guess."

"Don't you see, my darling man? God took what could have been a bad situation, and He turned it into something fantastic. He introduced us through Cristine, and then made it possible for me to stay around long enough for my heart to be filled with love for you."

Finally Ty relented, moved by the tenderness in her voice. His arm crept around her shoulder, hugging her close to his body as the wonder of it filled his mind.

"Next, you'll be claiming He helped my mother trip," he murmured, eyes bright with hope.

Bri shook her head, her face warm with love. "No, but I do think He used that. He knew I only had a month here, so He worked fast." She grinned.

Ty kissed her nose, then frowned. "What about your job, Bri?"

She waved a hand. "He can work that out, too. I don't see why I should spend my time second-guessing Him."

"That faith of yours!" Ty shook his head in wonder. "I'm beginning to believe your faith could move those mountains out there."

She smiled. "It all starts with trust, Ty. Once He's got your trust, He can do anything."

"You're sure that you won't accept my offer, you won't be Cristine's mother?"

Bri shook her head slowly. "No, Ty. There's only one way I could ever be a mother to Cristine, and you know it."

He leaned forward and kissed her nose again, his eyes dark with emotion. His fingers squeezed hers in a promise that echoed in the depth of his eyes.

"One miracle at a time, Briony. Let's concentrate on one miracle at a time."

"Cristine is going to be fine. God has big plans for her."

The words had no sooner left her mouth than a nurse hurried toward them. "The doctor says you can sit with her for a while."

Ty's eyes flickered with hope. "She's better?"

"No change. Not yet." The nurse turned, motioned to the door. "Please come."

Bri followed them to Cristine's bed, but she stopped

Ty outside the door. "Faith and trust, Ty. They open the door to God and allow Him to show the way."

He grinned halfheartedly as his fingers laced through hers. "I'm trying to see that, Bri. I've had a wonderful fifteen months with that little girl. If that's all I get, I'll try to be glad." His mouth trembled for a minute, but he regained his control. "Will you pray with me, help me ask God for the ability to accept His decision? Whatever it is."

She stood on her tiptoes and brushed his cheek with her lips. "I'd love to pray with you."

They sat by the bed praying, sometimes aloud, sometimes silently. The dark night stretched endlessly on until Bri could keep her eyes open no longer. Though nothing had changed in Cristine's condition, though the labored breathing and tortured coughs still continued, Bri's assurance never wavered.

"This is a test, Ty," she murmured as her head drooped against his shoulder, her eyes too heavy to open. "Will we trust or will we lean unto our own understanding?"

He held her close, head bent. Just before she drifted off, Bri heard him repeat a scripture she vaguely remembered. *"Before they call, I will answer."*

The answer was on the way, she just had to wait.

"Briony?" A light kiss brushed across her cheek as a muscular arm shook her gently awake. "Bri?"

"What?" She forced her lids up and peered at him.

"Someone wants to say 'good morning.'"

Bri surged forward, her eyes flying to the small body still lying in the bed. Cristine's big blue eyes were wide open and sparkling with life. Though her face was still a little warm, she exhibited none of the lethargy from the night before.

"Hello, darling," Bri whispered. "Auntie Bri is so glad to see you smile."

"Bee." Cristine's eyes fluttered for a moment, then drooped closed.

"She'll sleep a lot today, but she's definitely on the mend."

"What was it?" Ty's voice almost broke, but he kept his eyes on the doctor and his arm firmly wrapped around Briony.

The doctor shook his head. "I'm not sure if we'll ever know. We see this sometimes—a viral infection that takes over, then disappears. There's no rhyme nor reason to either the illness or the cure." He shrugged, slinging his stethoscope around his neck. "Just another little miracle from heaven, I guess."

"Uh-huh." Ty grinned down at Briony. She smiled mistily up at him.

"I'll check in later, but she's going to be fine."

"Thank you, Doctor." Ty stood, stretched, then pulled Briony to her feet and into his arms. One finger laced through the blond curls that clung to her neck and cheek. He stared into her eyes for a long time.

"And thank you. You gave me something I thought I'd lost forever, Briony."

"Your faith was there. You just needed to dig it out and dust it off."

"I don't deserve you," he whispered, face glowing with love. "God knows I don't deserve Cristine, either. But there's no way I'm letting either of you go. You're my life. You make everything good and beautiful again. I love you, Briony Green."

At last he'd said it, on his own, without prodding or fear. Briony spent several long minutes tucking that memory away in her heart. Then she wrapped her arms around him.

"I love you, Tyrel Demens."

"Enough to marry me? Enough to spend whatever time we have together, knowing you'll never have that baby you long for?" His hands cupped her face, his eyes intent as he scrutinized every detail. "Will my love be enough, Briony?"

The joy in her heart suffused her body as she smiled up at him. "Your love is far beyond anything I ever dared dreamed of," she whispered, as the first rays of dawn filled the room with a peach blush. "It's a gift so great, it could only have come from God. I'll spend every day praising Him for allowing me to behold such wonder."

He kissed her, fully and completely, his heart laid bare. "And you won't mind that we won't share a child?"

The need for reassurance could only be assuaged by her love. Briony knew that. But she knew one thing more.

"Look there, Ty. Look right into this crib and tell me if we don't already have a child, a very blessed baby just waiting for us to love." She saw the pride, relief, love and joy warm his face. "How could we possibly ask for more than Cristine?"

"We couldn't." He nodded as one tear rolled down his craggy cheek. "We couldn't possibly."

"Right." She kissed him quickly, then searched for her bag. From it she withdrew her notepad and a pencil.

"Now, we need to start making plans. I've got less than a week till I start my new job, remember? If we're going to get married, I have a couple of friends who insist on being there."

He stared at her. "I forgot about your job. What will you do?"

"I'll move in with you, of course." She grinned at his wide-eyed surprise. "After we're married."

"But—"

"They did say I'd be doing some work in Banff, Ty."

He nodded slowly, his eyes confident, assured. "And after that, we'll just have to trust God." He teased her. "I know you like everything in order and nailed down, but this is one time when your lists won't work, Briony." He grinned at her, his arms tight around her waist. "Marrying me is going to disrupt your life, Professor."

"And yours." She winked. "How do you feel about a wedding next Friday?"

Ty laughed. "I feel pretty good about it." He leaned to whisper in her ear. "I'll marry you any day you want, as long as Cristine is out of here."

"She will be." Briony pulled out her cell phone and dialed, her eyes on the baby's sweet face.

"Clarissa? It's Briony. Can you and Blair come up here? Please?"

"What's wrong?"

Bri snuggled against Ty as happiness overflowed. "I'm planning a wedding," she said. "And I need a little help to make sure this groom doesn't get away."

"Not a chance, sweetheart." Ty held her fast, his eyes shining with love. "Not a chance."

Chapter Fourteen

On the last Friday of June, Bri stood beside Ty and smiled at the dear friends gathered in a mountain glade Ty had chosen especially for their wedding.

"I don't know who to throw my bouquet to," she told Clarissa, smiling as the children raced through the wildflowers, Cristine among them. "You two are already happily married."

"And intending to stay that way, with God's help." Blair patted her swollen tummy, then shook her head at her husband's enquiring look. "Although, if this baby doesn't show up pretty soon, Gabe is going to have a heart attack."

"Gabe will do just fine. We all will. God promised." Clarissa glanced up at the sky and frowned. "I don't like the look of those clouds."

They scurried en masse toward the helicopter Gabe had hired to carry everyone to the secluded wedding.

"Don't worry, it's just a little summer shower. It'll be gone before you know it." Briony watched as Ty scooped up Cristine and strode back toward them. "I feel like I'm dreaming," she whispered. "I don't think I've ever been so happy."

Clarissa winked at Blair. "She finished the diary last night."

"You didn't tell me that." Ty helped her over the hillocks, his eyes worried. "Is everything all right?"

"Everything is perfect." She smiled her thanks when Clarissa's husband, Wade, took Cristine. "I'll tell you all about it later, Ty. But for now, just know that my sister had no qualms about giving her daughter to you. Remember Mrs. King said she saw Bridget by a house?"

He nodded.

"Bridget was watching you play with Cristine. It was the day before she set off to come home to us." Bri threw her arms around him and squeezed. "She knew, Ty, she *knew* Cristine was in the right place, right in your arms, where God wanted her."

He clutched Bri tightly against his body, whispering words of thanks to the Father who loved his children enough to test them.

"I love you, Briony Demens."

"I love you, Ty."

One year later Briony climbed up the last few feet into the glade where she'd been married. Ty lay sprawled out on the grass, softly snoring as the sun beat down on him.

She eased the backpack from her shoulders, then sat down, barely able to contain the love she felt inside.

"You're late." Ty's hands slid over her shoulder as his mouth found a sensitive spot on her neck.

"I know. I got held up in Calgary." She turned and kissed him back.

"Where's Cristine? Everything all right?" He frowned, staring into her eyes. "Bio-Tek's still standing?"

"Our daughter is with your mother and Giselle. For a few days. Bio-Tek's fine. They're moving more of my stuff out of their office to the building the park service supplied in Banff. We'll start seedlings in the greenhouse soon."

"Good." He gave her a long and satisfying kiss. "I'm so blessed, Briony. You and Cristine are all the family I'll ever need."

"I hope you don't mean that." She held her breath at the glint of pure love shining in his eyes.

"Why?" Ty frowned. "I thought you were happy."

"I am. You know that."

His face tightened; his eyes grew bleak as he fought against the doubts. "But you still wish we had a baby."

She knew the words cost him. He'd worked so hard on his faith, come so far in his trust of God's plan. But it was clear that she'd reminded him of his first wife's desperate need to have a child. Bri rushed to reassure him.

"I love you, Ty. You know that. And I love Cristine. If she's all we ever have, that's more than enough for me."

He frowned. "If?"

Bri found her courage and laid out the facts. "Remember Mrs. King?"

His face wrinkled up in distaste. "The woman from the church group who didn't approve of me or Andrea?"

"That's the one. She caught me just as I was leaving town on my way here."

Ty stared off into the distance, his eyes fixed on the trees he loved to care for. "Oh?"

For a moment Bri was content to sit quietly, surrounded by such vast beauty, content to share it with the man who joined her in her love for this place. Her eyes welled with tears. How great God was. How truly awesome His plans.

"Professor?" Ty snuggled up beside her, his arm around her waist. "What's wrong? Did Mrs. King say something?"

"Oh, yeah. She said something, Tyrel."

He sighed. "We just have to get past it, honey. We're good parents to Cristine. We love her. Eventually Mrs. King will see that."

"Apparently she already has."

"Huh?"

Bri nodded, her heart full to bursting as she gazed into his beloved face.

"Mrs. King has her niece staying with her. The girl needed a place to hide out, people to talk to. You remember the young girl who's been attending our church off and on? She's part of that support group, the one Andrea and Bridget attended."

"That's nice." His thumb brushed the tear off her cheek.

Bri nodded. "It really is, Ty, because Mrs. King says her niece intends to give her baby up for adoption as soon as it's born. Mrs. King says that after watching us with Cristine, her niece believes we'd make the best parents for the child. She wants to know if we're interested."

"*If* we're interested?" He jerked upright. He grabbed

Bri's hands, tugged her to her feet and whirled her around. "Of course we're interested. What's with the 'if'?"

Bri hid her smile as he hugged her tight. "She has just one condition," she murmured against his neck, loving the fresh woodsy smell of his clothes.

Her eyes rose to the clear blue sky as realization of the miracle of this gift from the Father welled within. Silently she sent praises winging to heaven.

Ty pressed her away until he could peer into her eyes. "What condition?" he whispered fearfully. Then his face split in a grin of pure delight. "I don't care what condition Mrs. King has, my darling. Why should I? Another child for us can only be a God thing, can't it?"

Bri laughed out loud. "Absolutely," she agreed.

"Then I'd love for us to adopt that blessed baby."

"Well, that's the thing, you see." Bri allowed herself one long minute to savor the peace and trust flooding his countenance. Then she told him.

"It's not 'a' baby."

"It's not a baby?" He frowned, scratched his head and stared. "Then what is it?" He glimpsed the look in her eyes and inhaled sharply. "Twins?" he whispered.

"Nope." Bri shook her head. "Triplets."

Ty sat down. Hard. His face paled, his hands clenched and he gulped for air. "Three babies?" His eyes begged her to explain.

Bri chuckled as she plunked down beside him and placed her hand in his. "Mrs. King just found out, too. I think she's in as much shock as you."

"No wonder!"

"Anyway, her niece is undergoing a C-section in

about three hours. The doctors feel it's time. The babie
will be early, but apparently they're healthy enough an
should do very well."

"But—the mother? Is she certain about her decision
Her aunt isn't pushing her?"

Bri's heart warmed at the thought that this big ma
could be more concerned about the needs of a pregnan
teenager than his own wants and desires.

"Apparently she decided not to have an abortion afte
Mrs. King offered her a place to stay, but she's alway
maintained that she wouldn't keep the child. They go
talking about Bridget a few months ago. Once she hear
Bridget's story, she began to watch Cristine." Bri shoo
her head at her own stupidity.

"They've been past our place a lot on their 'walks,
but I didn't realize why. Mrs. King said seeing Cristine
and the love we have for her, decided the issue." She
hugged close to his side.

"She's only seventeen, Ty, and desperately afrai
that her babies won't have a home to go to, that they'
end up in some government care, separated, unloved
She *wants* us to have them. Us!"

Ty squeezed his eyes closed. A tear rolled down hi
cheek. When he finally spoke, his hushed voic
touched her heart.

"I give up, God," he said on a broken sob. "I don'
understand You, I'm not sure if I ever will, but thank You."

Briony touched his chin, tilted it up, unable t
withhold her joy one minute longer. "Babies, Ty. He'
giving us three blessed babies to add to our family."

"Sons," he breathed, his fingers grazing her cheek

as the tears rolled down. His face changed, softened. "Or more beautiful daughters?"

"I don't know, Ty. We're supposed to go to Calgary right away. If we hurry, we might even see them born."

"Born? Oh, my!" He peered down at Bri. "I'm going to be a father again," he said in stunned surprise.

She giggled. "Yes, darling. I know."

The impact of God's tender care flooded over them as the soft afternoon air swept across the glade.

"'Before they ask, I will answer.'" Ty's whisper brushed across her hair.

"He had it all planned, Ty. He knew exactly what He was doing, every step of the way. His ways are perfect and right and just."

"I'm only just beginning to understand that." Ty hugged her close. "Don't let me forget, Bri, will you?"

"We'll remind each other," she said firmly. "And every single day we'll remind our children how blessed we are to have a Father who loves us more than we can possibly imagine. Maybe someday it will help them to trust Him."

"You are one very smart scientist, Prof." He kissed her. "I don't believe I've told you half often enough."

Bri grinned. "You can tell me now."

Ty shook his head, his eyes filled with love as he pulled her upright, then led her across the meadow.

"Not now. Maybe later."

"Why not now?" She pouted.

"Because right now we have to go welcome our kids into God's world." His mouth curved with delight. "Come on, Mama."

Bri trotted at his side, her heart full. All of this because of Bridget's blessed baby!

"You're too quiet," Ty said later as he drove down the road toward Calgary, toward the future. "What's going on?"

"I'm making up a list—"

"Uh, Professor?"

"Yes?"

"Just this once, let's forget your list. God never follows it, anyway." His eyes shone with a joy too big to be contained. "Why don't you snuggle up next to me and we'll remind each other of our blessings?"

"Okay," she whispered.

And she did.

* * * * *

Dear Reader,

Thanks so much for picking up this third book in the
IF WISHES WERE WEDDINGS series. I hope that,
with me, you began to see ways in your own life in
which God turned bad into good, made joy out of
sadness, answered before we could even form the
question.

Day after day I find new things about Him, new ways
to catch a glimpse of a God who so loves me He would
go far out of His way to work His pleasure in my life.

May you find your life blessed by the often quiet,
gentle brush of His fingers over the pages of your life
and may you hear His sweet voice in the midst of life's
biggest uncertainties.

Blessings to you,

Lois
Richer

Between his work at Weddings by Woodwards and his twin boys, widower Reese Woodward doesn't have time for love. Then he meets Olivia Hastings, a woman with troubles of her own. She's wary of closeness as well…but who can resist the twins— or their father? Soon a second chance at love begins to blossom.

Look for

Twice Upon a Time

by

Lois Richer

Available April wherever books are sold.

www.SteepleHill.com

Steep
Hill

LI87

REQUEST YOUR FREE BOOKS!

FREE INSPIRATIONAL NOVELS

LUS 2

FREE

MYSTERY GIFTS

YES! Please send me 2 FREE Love Inspired® novels and my 2 FREE
mystery gifts (gifts are worth about $10). After receiving them, if I don't wish to
receive any more books, I can return the shipping statement marked "cancel".
If I don't cancel, I will receive 4 brand-new novels every month and be billed
just $4.24 per book in the U.S. or $4.74 per book in Canada, plus 25¢ shipping
and handling per book and applicable taxes, if any*. That's a savings of over
20% off the cover price! I understand that accepting the 2 free books and gifts
places me under no obligation to buy anything. I can always return a shipment
and cancel at any time. Even if I never buy another book, the two free books
and gifts are mine to keep forever.

113 IDN ERXA   313 IDN ERWX

Name _____ (PLEASE PRINT) _____

Address _____ Apt. #

City _____ State/Prov. _____ Zip/Postal Code

Signature (if under 18, a parent or guardian must sign)

Order online at www.LoveInspiredBooks.com

Or mail to Steeple Hill Reader Service:

IN U.S.A.: P.O. Box 1867, Buffalo, NY 14240-1867
IN CANADA: P.O. Box 609, Fort Erie, Ontario L2A 5X3

Not valid to current subscribers of Love Inspired books.

Want to try two free books from another series?
Call 1-800-873-8635 or visit www.morefreebooks.com

Terms and prices subject to change without notice. N.Y. residents add applicable sales
tax. Canadian residents will be charged applicable provincial taxes and GST. Offer not valid
in Quebec. This offer is limited to one order per household. All orders subject to approval.
Credit or debit balances in a customer's account(s) may be offset by any other outstanding
balance owed by or to the customer. Please allow 4 to 6 weeks for delivery. Offer available
while quantities last.

Your Privacy: Steeple Hill Books is committed to protecting your privacy. Our Privacy
Policy is available online at www.SteepleHill.com or upon request from the Reader
Service. From time to time we make our lists of customers available to reputable
third parties who may have a product or service of interest to you. If you would
prefer we not share your name and address, please check here. ☐

LIREG08R

Love Inspired SUSPENSE
RIVETING INSPIRATIONAL ROMANCE

WITHOUT A TRACE

Without a Trace: Will a young mother's disappearance bring a bayou town together...or tear it apart?

WHAT SARAH SAW
by MARGARET DALEY
January 2009

FRAMED!
by ROBIN CAROLL
February 2009

COLD CASE MURDER
by SHIRLEE McCOY
March 2009

CLOUD OF SUSPICION
by PATRICIA DAVIDS
April 2009

DEADLY COMPETITION
by ROXANNE RUSTAND
May 2009

*Available wherever books are sold,
including most bookstores, supermarkets,
drugstores and discount stores.*

Steeple Hill®